Illustrations of the
ENGLISH STAGE
1580-1642

Illustrations of the
ENGLISH STAGE
1580-1642

R. A. FOAKES

Stanford University Press

STANFORD, CALIFORNIA

1985

Stanford University Press
Stanford, California

© R. A. Foakes, 1985

Originating Publisher: Scolar Press, London
First published in the U.S.A. by Stanford University Press, 1985
Printed in Great Britain

ISBN 0–8047–1236–0
LC 83–40517

Contents

Acknowledgements, vii
Abbreviations, ix
List of illustrations, xi
Preface, xiii

A
Maps and panoramas
1

B
Drawings, plans and vignettes
relating to the stage
43

C
Illustrations relating to the stage
in printed texts of plays
87

D
Miscellaneous illustrations connected
with the English stage
149

E
Illustrations in play-texts having
no reference to the stage
163

Index, 176

Acknowledgements

I am grateful to numerous librarians and archivists who have helped me with their prompt and courteous replies to inquiries, and have arranged to supply me with photographs. Many others have also generously assisted me by providing information and guidance, and I am indebted in particular to Thomas L. Berger, Carey Bliss, Michael Hattaway, C. Walter Hodges, Richard Hosley, Jerzy Limon, Kate McLuskie, Sir Oliver Millar, Alison Newman, Samuel Schoenbaum, W. Schrickx, F. K. Stanzel and Sir Ellis Waterhouse. My greatest debt is to John Orrell, who made available to me his ideas and discoveries relating to the theatre in the period. His important analysis of the Norden, Visscher and Hollar engravings and drawings in *The Quest for Shakespeare's Globe* (1983) appeared too late for me to take full advantage of it, but references to it have been added where appropriate.

I am grateful to the following persons and institutions for permission to reproduce material in their possession: Bodleian Library, Oxford (item 45, shelfmark Mal. 249(1); item 66, shelfmark 4 L 62 (12) Art); British Library, London (items 3, 14, 15, 20, 22a, 23a, 27, 32, 33a, 44, 46, 48, 49, 52, 59, 76, 78, by permission of the British Library Board); Devonshire Collection, Chatsworth (items 18, 19, 30d, 33b, by permission of the Chatsworth Settlement Trustees); Dulwich College (item 24); Guildhall Library (items 1, 4, 10, 11, 12a, 12b, 21, 22b); Henry E. Huntington Library, San Marino, California (items 31, 34, 35, 37, 38, 39, 40, 41, 42, 43, 45, 47, 50, 51, 53, 54, 55, 56, 57, 58, 60, 61, 62, 63, 64, 65, 67, 68, 69, 70, 71, 72, 73, 74, 75, 77, 79); Iveagh Bequest, Kenwood (item 12c, by permission of the Greater London Council); John Rylands Library, University of Manchester (item 17); Magdalene College, Cambridge (items 2, 23b, by permission of the Master and Fellows); Marquess of Bath, Longleat House (item 25); National Portrait Gallery (items 54d, 54e); Royal Geographical Society, London (item 8); Royal Library, Kungliga Biblioteket, Stockholm (items 6, 7); Royal Library, Windsor (item 9, by gracious permission of Her Majesty the Queen); Southwark Diocesan Board of Education and the Greater London Record Office (item 13); Stiftsarchiv, Rein, Austria (item 28); Trustees of the Late Earl Berkeley (item 30e); University Library, Utrecht, Bibliothek der Rijksuniversiteit te Utrecht (items 5, 26); Worcester College Library, Oxford (items 29, 30a, 30b, 30c, 36, by permission of the Provost and Fellows); Yale Center for British Art, Paul Mellon Collection (item 16).

R.A.F.

Abbreviations

(Place of publication is London unless otherwise stated.)

Adams	John Cranford Adams, *The Globe Playhouse* (2nd edition, 1961).
Bentley, *JCS*	G. E. Bentley, *The Jacobean and Caroline Stage* (7 vols, Oxford 1941–68).
Berry, *Theatre*	*The First Public Playhouse: The Theatre in Shoreditch 1576–1598* (Montreal, 1979).
Chamberlain, *Letters*	*The Letters of John Chamberlain*, edited by N. E. McLure (2 vols, Philadelphia, 1939).
Chambers, *ES*	E. K. Chambers, *The Elizabethan Stage* (4 vols, Oxford, 1923).
Chambers, *WS*	E. K. Chambers, *William Shakespeare: A Study of Facts and Problems* (2 vols, Oxford, 1930).
Foakes and Rickert, *HD*	*Henslowe's Diary*, edited by R. A. Foakes and R. T. Rickert (Cambridge, 1961).
Greg	W. W. Greg, *A Bibliography of the English Printed Drama to the Restoration* (4 vols, 1962).
Gurr	Andrew Gurr, *The Shakespearean Stage 1574–1642* (2nd edition, Cambridge, 1980).
Harris and Tait	John Harris and A. A. Tait, *Catalogue of the Drawings by Inigo Jones, John Webb and Isaac de Caus at Worcester College Oxford* (Oxford, 1979).
Hazlitt's Dodsley	*Dodsley's Old English Plays*, first issued by Robert Dodsley (1744), ed. W. C. Hazlitt (15 vols, 1874–6).
Hind	A. M. Hind, *Engraving in England in the Sixteenth & Seventeenth Centuries* (3 vols, Cambridge, 1952, 1955 and 1964).
Hodges, *Globe Restored*	C. Walter Hodges, *The Globe Restored* (1953; 2nd edition 1968).
Hodges, *Second Globe*	C. Walter Hodges, *Shakespeare's Second Globe* (1973).
Hosley	Richard Hosley, 'The Playhouses', in J. Leeds Barroll, Alexander Leggatt, Richard Hosley and Alvin Kernan, *The Revels History of Drama in English: Volume III 1576–1613* (1975), pp. 119–235.
Howgego	James Howgego, *Printed Maps of London circa 1553–1850* (second edition, Folkestone 1978, replacing the first edition by Ida Darlington and James Howgego, 1964).
King	T. J. King, *Shakespearean Staging, 1599–1642* (Cambridge, Massachusetts, 1971).
Leacroft	Richard Leacroft, *The Development of the English Playhouse* (1973).
Linthicum	M. C. Linthicum, *Costume in the Drama of Shakespeare and his Contemporaries* (1936; reissued New York, 1963).
MSR	Malone Society Reprints.
Orgel and Strong	Stephen Orgel and Roy Strong, *Inigo Jones: The Theatre of the Stuart Court* (2 vols, London and Berkeley, 1973).
Orrell	John Orrell, *The Quest for Shakespeare's Globe* (Cambridge, 1983).
Reynolds	G. F. Reynolds, *The Staging of Elizabethan Plays at the Red Bull Theater 1605–25* (New York, 1940; reprinted 1966).
Rhodes	Ernest L. Rhodes, *Henslowe's Rose, The Stage and Staging* (Lexington, Kentucky, 1976).
Roxburghe Ballads	*The Roxburghe Ballads*, edited by W. Chappell and J. W. Ebsworth (9 vols, 1869–99).
Schoenbaum	S. Schoenbaum, *William Shakespeare: A Documentary Life* (Oxford, 1975).

Scouloudi	Irene Scouloudi, *Panoramic Views of London 1600–1666* (1953).
Shakespeare's England	*Shakespeare's England: An Account of the Life & Manners of his Age* (2 vols, Oxford, 1916).
Shapiro, *SS* 1	I. A. Shapiro, 'The Bankside Theatres: Early Engravings', *Shakespeare Survey* 1 (1948), pp. 25–37.
Shapiro, *SS* 2	I. A. Shapiro, 'An Original Drawing of the Globe Theatre', *Shakespeare Survey* 2 (1949), pp. 21–3.
Smith	Irwin Smith, *Shakespeare's Globe Playhouse: A Modern Reconstruction* (New York, 1956).
Southern	R. W. Southern, *Changeable Scenery: Its Origin and Development in the British Theatre* (1952).
SS	*Shakespeare Survey* (Cambridge, 1948–).
TFT	Tudor Facsimile Texts, edited by J. S. Farmer (1907–13).
TLS	*Times Literary Supplement.*
TN	*Theatre Notebook* (London, Society for Theatre Research, 1946–).
Wickham, *EES* II	Glynne Wickham, *Early English Stages Volume Two 1576–1660*, Part I (1963); Part II (1972). These are referred to as II i and II ii.

List of illustrations

A: Maps and panoramas

1 G. Braun and F. Hogenberg, Map of London published in *Civitates Orbis Terrarum* (1572).

2 *Civitas Londinum*, Map of London attributed to Ralph Agas (drawn before 1590, published 1633).

3 William Smith, *The Particular Description of England* (1588).

4 John Norden, Map of London published in *Speculum Britanniae. The first parte* (1593).

5 *The View of the Cittye of London from the North towards the Sowth*, engraving inserted in a manuscript journal of 1629–30 (date unknown; about 1597–9).

6 John Norden, View of Southwark in the engraved panorama *Civitas Londini* (1600).

7 John Norden, Map of London inset in *Civitas Londini* (1600).

8 Jodocus Hondius, View of London, inset from the map of Great Britain in John Speed, *Theatre of the Empire of Great Britain* (1611).

9 Francis Delaram, Engraving of James I on horseback, with a view of Bankside and London (undated; probably later than 1610).

10 J. C. Visscher, Panoramic view of London, *Londinum Florentiss[i]ma Britanniæ Urbs* (1616).

11 View of London, Vignette from the title-page of Henry Holland, *Herwologia Anglica* (1620).

12 Claude de Jongh, Sketch of London Bridge from the West (1627).

13 Map of the Manor of Paris Garden (1627).

14 Cornelis Dankerts, Map of London (about 1633; revised version about 1645).

15 Matthias Merian, View of London, in J. L. Gottfried and M. Merian, *Neuwe Archontologia Cosmica* (1638).

16 Wenceslaus Hollar, Drawing of Bankside viewed from St Mary Overie (between 1636 and 1644).

17 Wenceslaus Hollar, Preparatory Sketch for the 'Long View' (1638).

18 John Webb, View of London, in a background design for William D'Avenant's *Britannia Triumphans* (1638).

19 Inigo Jones, View of London, in an alternative design for William D'Avenant's *Britannia Triumphans* (1638).

20 Vignette on the title-page of Sir Richard Baker's *A Chronicle of the Kings of England* (1643).

21 Wenceslaus Hollar, 'Long View' of London from Southwark (1647).

22 Wenceslaus Hollar, 'London and Old St Paul's from the Thames'.

B: Drawings, plans and vignettes relating to the stage

23 John Scottowe, Drawing of Richard Tarlton (?1588).

24 Drawing, possibly of a stage, in a letter from Philip Henslowe to Edward Alleyn (?1593).

25 Attributed to Henry Peacham, Drawing of a scene from William Shakespeare's *Titus Andronicus* (?1595).

26 Johannes de Witt, Sketch of the interior of the Swan Theatre, as copied by Aernout van Buchel (?1596).

27 Plan for the conversion of Christ Church Hall, Oxford, in 1605.

28 Drawing of an actor, probably John Green, in the part of Nobody (1608).

29 Inigo Jones, Drawings for a conversion to a theatre, probably relating to the Cockpit in Drury Lane (1616–18).

30 John Webb, after designs by Inigo Jones, Drawings relating to the conversion of the Royal Cockpit into a theatre (1629–30).

xi

31 Vignette of a stage from the title-page of William Alabaster's *Roxana* (1632).

32 John Webb, after Inigo Jones, Plan for conversion of a hall into a temporary theatre, probably the Paved Court, Somerset House (1632–3).

33 Inigo Jones, Drawing for the conversion of the Tudor Hall, Whitehall, into a theatre for *Florimène* (1635).

34 Vignette of a stage from the title-page of Nathanial Richards's *Messalina* (1640).

35 Mildmay Fane, Earl of Westmorland, *Candy Restored* (1641).

36 Designs for an unidentified conversion to a theatre attributed to Inigo Jones, and copied by John Webb (date uncertain).

C: Illustrations relating to the stage in printed texts of plays

37 Christopher Marlowe, *Tamburlaine*, Parts I and II (1590 and 1597).

38 Thomas Heywood, *If You Know not Me, You Know Nobody*, Parts I and II (1605–6).

39 *Nobody and Somebody* (?1606).

40 Robert Armin, *The History of the Two Maids of Moreclack* (1609).

41 Thomas Middleton and Thomas Dekker, *The Roaring Girl* (1611).

42 Samuel Rowley, *When You See Me, You Know Me* (1613).

43 John Cooke, *Greene's Tu Quoque*, or *The City Gallant* (1614).

44 Thomas Kyd, *The Spanish Tragedy* (1615).

45 Thomas Heywood, *The Four Prentices of London* (1615).

46 Christopher Marlowe, *Doctor Faustus* (1616).

47 Thomas Middleton and William Rowley, *A Fair Quarrel* (1617).

48 *Jack Drum's Entertainment* (1618).

49 Francis Beaumont and John Fletcher, *A King and No King* (1619).

50 Francis Beaumont and John Fletcher, *The Maid's Tragedy* (1619).

51 *Swetnam the Woman-Hater arraigned by Women* (1620).

52 Francis Beaumont and John Fletcher, *Philaster* (1620).

53 Thomas Middleton and William Rowley, *The World Tossed at Tennis* (1620).

54 Thomas Middleton, *A Game at Chess* (1624).

55 Robert Greene, *Friar Bacon and Friar Bungay* (1630).

56 George Ruggle, *Ignoramus* (1630).

57 Thomas Heywood, *The Fair Maid of the West* (1631).

58 Edward Forsett, *Pedantius* (1631).

59 Thomas Heywood, *The Iron Age*, Parts I and II (1632).

60 *Arden of Faversham* (1633).

61 Thomas Heywood, *A Maidenhead Well Lost* (1634).

62 William Sampson, *The Vow-Breaker* (1636).

63 [? Thomas Dekker], *The Merry Devil of Edmonton* (1655).

64 Thomas Dekker, William Rowley and John Ford, *The Witch of Edmonton* (1658).

65 Sir William Lower, *The Enchanted Lovers* (1658) and *The Amorous Fantasm* (1660).

D: Miscellaneous illustrations connected with the English stage

66 William Kemp, *Kemps Nine Daies Wonder* (1600).

67 Robert Fludd, *Microcosmi Historia* (1619).

68 Sketch, possibly of a stage, in a copy of the 1600 Quarto of William Shakespeare's *2 Henry IV*.

69 *The Stage-Players Complaint* (1641).

70 Henry Marsh, *The Wits, or, Sport upon Sport*, Part 1 (1662), and Francis Kirkman, *The Wits, or, Sport upon Sport* (1673).

E: Illustrations in play-texts having no reference to the stage

71 Robert Wilson, *The Three Lords and Three Ladies of London* (1590).

72 R.A. [? Robert Armin], *The Valiant Welshman* (1615, 1663).

73 William Haughton, *Englishmen for my Money*, or *A Woman will have her Will* (1616).

74 Robert Gomersall, *The Tragedy of Lodovick Sforza*

Duke of Milan (1628).

75 T.R., *Cornelianum Dolium* (1638).

76 *Canterbury his Change of Diet* (1641).

77 T.B., *The Rebellion of Naples* (1649).

78 S.S. [Samuel Sheppard], *The Jovial Crew*, or *The Devil Turned Ranter* (1651).

79 *Wine, Beer, Ale and Tobacco* (1658).

Preface

It is not long since models of Shakespeare's theatre based on the reconstruction proposed by John Cranford Adams in *The Globe Playhouse* (1942) were to be found in colleges and libraries – some, indeed, are still on view. His concept of an octagonal theatre, tall for its diameter, featuring a highly decorative stage area, with a large inner stage or 'study' curtained off from the main stage, and a gallery above with two bay windows overlooking the stage, was developed primarily from the Globe as depicted in the Visscher panorama of 1616.[1] In this decorative but unreliable view Adams found evidence for the three huts and cupola built over the stage in his model.[2] His book seemed to give scholarly sanction to a popular image of the Globe, and versions similar to his were widely accepted as authentic; such an image was featured, for instance, in the opening scenes of Laurence Olivier's film of *Henry V*. The Adams model included features, like the inner stage, which had been accepted as necessary by a generation of scholars working in the early twentieth century.[3] By the 1940s this concept of an Elizabethan stage was being seriously challenged, as by George F. Reynolds in his examination of the staging of plays at the Red Bull Theatre published in 1940. More recently a quite different image of the theatres of Shakespeare's age has emerged,[4] as the pictorial evidence has been more carefully analysed and evaluated, and traditions of staging have been more thoroughly investigated; as a result, the Adams design is now discredited. Recent studies of Elizabethan theatres have shown that Adams based his proposed design on unreliable visual evidence, and an indiscriminate use of verbal evidence, such as stage-directions, which he culled from sources often untrustworthy and not relevant to the Globe. Partly in reaction against such a freewheeling method, scholars have tended to become cautious, and much more scrupulous in attempting to determine the reliability of the evidence, and in their investigation of the characteristics and repertories of theatres and companies. In particular, the work of Richard Hosley and Glynne Wickham has given us a new set of images and convictions about the Elizabethan stage.

The effect has been chastening. Instead of speculating about what might have been possible, the recent tendency has been to emphasise how little was necessary for the staging of many Elizabethan plays. So the old orthodoxy characterised by the Adams version has given way to a new conventional wisdom, which strips away a good deal from once familiar images of the Elizabethan stage and offers something less flamboyant than the well-known drawings of C. Walter Hodges' *The Globe Restored* (first published in 1953). A recognition that octagonal or hexagonal images of theatre buildings derive from unauthoritative maps has led to the current belief that the Globe must have been multi-sided, with perhaps sixteen or twenty-four sides. Study of individual theatre repertories, paying attention where possible to what appear to be prompt-copy or authentic stage-directions, has led to the further realisation that many plays can be performed using only two stage doors, and without recourse to an inner stage or 'study'. So the new orthodoxy has returned to the well-known drawing by Johannes de Witt of the Swan Theatre, to find there confirmation of its assumptions. For this drawing shows a stage with two doors and no inner stage, and has altogether a spare appearance. Such a stage also provides a neat link with the usual concept of the stages used by companies performing in the private halls of great houses or colleges; these halls often had a screen near one end with two doors corresponding roughly to the appearance of the stage-façade in de Witt's drawing.[5]

I am aware that such a quick and crude outline of recent developments simplifies a complex pattern of change, but it summarises perhaps not unfairly what has happened. The new orthodoxy has proved persuasive because it is based on a much more careful and scholarly assessment of the evidence than were the old assumptions. At the same time, I think it is important to understand the new orthodoxy as a historical development, subject to its own fashions, prejudices and limitations. In the first place, it might be accused of taking caution to extremes, in asking not what stage facilities and properties the production of a particular play might have employed if all the hints in the dialogue and in the often incomplete and sparse stage-directions were followed up, but rather what minimum in the way of furniture and effects was absolutely required. Secondly, the drawing of the Swan Theatre has assumed a special importance as a basic point of reference for the design of the large public open-air theatres, and it has acquired an authoritative status it hardly seems to deserve, since it is a drawing made, so to speak, at second hand, a copy by Aernout van Buchel of a lost original. At the end of his account of the theatres of the period, Glynne Wickham refers to this copy, of a rough sketch made by a foreigner visiting London about 1596, as 'the best evidence we possess'.[6] Thirdly, the new orthodoxy has, on the whole, remained geared to the tantalising concept of a reconstruction of the Globe, as proposed recently in London and in Detroit, and hence to what we now think was possible in preference to what the evidence seems to show. So the Globe is thought of as multi-sided, having perhaps sixteen or twenty-four sides, in spite of the implications of its name, and in spite of the fact that the most authentic drawing, that of Wenceslaus Hollar, shows it to be round, because, the argument runs, 'no one working under pressure of a normal concern for costs would have taken the very considerable trouble' to shape beams into curves.[7] Furthermore, the new orthodoxy has been chiefly concerned with the shape, design and size of theatres, especially the Swan, because of the de Witt drawing, and the Globe, because the ideal of a modern reconstruction haunts Shakespearians. So controversy has focused upon certain issues – such as whether there was an inner stage or not – about which the evidence is debatable. As a result, some kinds of evidence, such as that provided by frontispieces or illustrated title-pages to plays, have been generally neglected. Books on the Elizabethan theatre tend to use a selection of illustrations designed to support the author's argument, often, as noted, in relation to some hypothesis about the appearance of one or other stage or theatre related to an attempted modern reconstruction, or a design for a reconstruction. It is thus not easy for a student of the period to gain more than a very rough sense of the range of illustrations that survive, or to appreciate the placing and significance of any one illustration in relation to the others.

All this is not intended to suggest that the new orthodoxy has got it wrong. It may well be correct in many of its claims, and I wish merely to draw attention to the extent to which its conclusions remain speculative, and are based upon a particular way of regarding the evidence, emphasising some aspects rather than others. To envisage the theatre in the period 1576 to 1640 requires an effort of imagination that is really quite difficult; as we look back we tend to foreshorten historical time, and fall into the habit of treating this long period as if it were homogeneous, as if '*the* Elizabethan theatre' persisted unchanged through it. So the de Witt drawing of the Swan has come to be treated as authoritative in relation to the whole period. It is the only drawing of the interior of a public playhouse that survives, and the temptation, not easily resisted, has been to generalise from it, as if all public theatres had the same design. Certain images, like this one, or the drawing from *Titus Andronicus*, have become so familiar that we take them, and the conclusions usually drawn from them, for granted. My concern is not to attempt to prove or disprove these conclusions, but to subject the visual evidence to a fresh scrutiny.

The aim of this book is to gather together and present in sequence within specific groupings the illustrations relating to the theatres, stages and drama of Shakespeare's age, roughly 1580 to 1640, with a few additional items drawn from later in the seventeenth century. Probably I have overlooked some evidence, and more will no doubt be discovered, but this book provides for the first time a reasonably complete presentation of the important visual evidence known to survive. Some of these items are familiar, but some are hardly known at all, and a number have been discovered very recently. Each illustration is accompanied by a commentary which attempts a cool appraisal, in order to see and describe what is there, and to suggest a possible interpretation, or interpretations, without prior commitment to any belief or viewpoint.

I suspect that many readers will be surprised by the number of illustrations that survive. They are not of equal importance, of course, and some have little or no significance; but I have included, for instance, those title-page illustrations which have no connection with the theatre, precisely to establish – not in each case apparent – why they are useless as evidence. These apart, a large number of illustrations of varying quality and relevance provide much scope for interpretation. I have tried to write a neutral commentary on each, but it is not the easiest of tasks simply to describe what is there, and the very act of description often involves an element of speculation, and inevitably of interpretation. No commentary could be complctcly objcctivc, but my design has been to provide the information necessary for the reader to make up his own mind about the value as evidence of each item. To provide further help, a list of basic references is also given; these are not intended to be exhaustive, but to guide the reader to the most significant recent appraisals of plays referred to, or of problems raised by any particular illustration.

The illustrations are of several different kinds, and although the categories overlap to some extent, they fall fairly readily into five groups, designated A, B, C, D and E. The first, group A, consists of maps, panoramas and views of London, mostly printed, but some in the form of sketches or drawings, which include theatre buildings. I have not included the numerous later maps and panoramas based upon those illustrated in Section A, for they provide no useful evidence about theatre buildings.[8] In his essay 'The Bankside Theatres: Early Engravings' in *Shakespeare Survey* 1 (1948), I. A. Shapiro surveyed the pictorial evidence then available, establishing the authenticity of Hollar's views, and the derivative nature of most of the others. Since this study was published, however, a certain amount of new material has come to light, like the view of London from the north to the south (5), the drawing of London Bridge by Claude de Jongh (12), and Hollar's drawings for the Long View (16, 17); further evidence has also emerged to confirm the importance of the Hollar views. Group B includes drawings and title-page vignettes which specifically illustrate actors, stages or plans for conversions of halls into theatres. Although some of these items are familiar, several have been recently identified or were not hitherto noticed, like the plan for converting Christ Church Hall in Oxford into a theatre in 1605 (27), the drawing of the actor John Green in the part of Nobody (28), and the drawings for the conversion of the Drury Lane Cockpit (29).

The third group, C, is drawn from printed texts of plays, and consists of those frontispieces and illustrated title-pages which appear to relate to the staging of them. I say 'appear' because sometimes it is difficult to determine the relevance or significance of a title-page block or engraving, and some that look as though they might refer to the theatre do not; hence it seemed worth including in a kind of appendix, group E, the illustrations to plays which apparently have no connection with the stage. These illustrations in printed play texts have received curiously little attention. They were reproduced in W. W. Greg's *A Bibliography of the English Printed Drama to the Restoration* (4 vols. 1962), and those relating to the better-known plays have sometimes been used to adorn modern editions, but almost invariably without comment. The fourth group, group D, contains a few miscellaneous items which do not fit in elsewhere, notably the frontispiece to *The Wits* (1662), and the symbolic theatre drawings of Robert Fludd. In each group the illustrations are presented in chronological order, with a commentary that attempts to describe what is in the illustration, and, in the case of group C, to relate it to the action of the play concerned.

The book thus constitutes a kind of descriptive survey of illustrations relating to the stage in England from the rise of professional theatres in London to their closure in the Commonwealth period; it has no argument, and therefore no conclusions are offered. It is, however, more than simply a survey, in that each illustration has been reappraised, or in some cases studied for the first time, in an attempt to understand its significance and its value as evidence. If the commentaries on each item lead to no general conclusions, they contain certain overall implications which are of importance. I would draw attention to three points in particular. One is that all the illustrations, even the simplest, need to be studied carefully, and can turn out to be puzzling or ambiguous. This is true notably of some of the most familiar examples, the significance of which tends to be taken for granted. So, for example, the well-known drawing by Henry Peacham relating to *Titus Andronicus* (25) is generally thought to depict what he saw at an actual performance (to paraphrase Dover Wilson's comments on it in *Shakespeare Survey* 1), but close examination of it shows that it does not correspond to any point in the action of the play, and is not likely therefore to have been drawn from life. A second implication, perhaps a correlative of the first, is that it is important to maintain a healthy scepticism in studying the visual evidence, and not to sink into the complacency of assuming that any of it has special authority. An example here would be the de Witt drawing of the Swan Theatre (26) which, in many accounts of the stage in Shakespeare's time, has been treated as a more or less authoritative guide to the internal appearance of public theatres; it is, in fact, an inexpert drawing, copied from the lost original, and study of it suggests that it would be rash to place much reliance upon it. The third implication concerns the title-page illustrations; if the general effect of the commentaries is to promote scepticism about the value as evidence of some familiar illustrations, or about received interpretations, at the same time they draw attention to evidence that has been neglected, in title-page illustrations to printed plays, which throws some light on stage practices, costumes and properties.

The originals of the illustrations assembled here are scattered in various libraries and archives, and some items have hitherto been reproduced only in a random and unsatisfactory way. So, for example, it proved difficult to track down the 1627 map of Paris Garden Manor

(13) for, although this had been reproduced on a small scale in the *Survey of London* in 1950, only one theatre historian, Richard Hosley, so far as I know, has published an enlargement of the Swan Theatre, a detail from this map, in the *Revels History of Drama* (1975). This gives little sense of the original – which, it turns out, is no longer where Hosley found it, but has been relocated in the Greater London Record Office, where it is now on deposit. Even now many students of the period probably know only the drawing by Philip Norman made in 1901 from a late eighteenth-century copy of the map now in the Guildhall Library in London, for part of this was reproduced by I. A. Shapiro in his important essay in *Shakespeare Survey* 1, and a sketch based on it was used by Glynne Wickham to illustrate his *Early English Stages*, Vol. II, Part i, p. 308. This story shows why a more systematic survey of the evidence is needed, and also why such a survey as is here presented may turn out to be incomplete.

In any case, further visual evidence will almost certainly be discovered from time to time. In the last few years a number of items have come to notice, like Hollar's preparatory sketch for his 'Long View' (17), first reproduced by Graham Parry in 1978, or have been identified, like the drawing for the conversion of the paved court in Somerset House into a theatre (32), which was correctly interpreted for the first time by John Orrell in 1977. Two illustrations, 27, the plan for the conversion of Christ Church Hall, also identified by John Orrell, and 28, the drawing of the actor John Green, have not been hitherto used in studies of the theatre of the period. The plan for the conversion of Christ Church Hall in 1605 is especially interesting, since the stage was set up at the opposite end from the screen and its doors. This runs counter to the theory that players were in the habit of using the screen as their stage-façade, perhaps with a curtain across it, and the screen-doors for exits and entrances. It also sets a question mark against the claim that the model for the stage-façade of playhouses like the Theatre or the Swan was the 'screens passage of the Tudor domestic hall, modified to withstand the weather' by the insertion of heavy doors in the two openings.[9] So in the nature of things this presentation cannot be exhaustive, but it should provide a basic reference guide for an understanding of the range of visual evidence that remains, and an important adjunct to histories of the drama, and studies of the theatre, which inevitably reproduce a small selection of the known materials. The book does not attempt to deal with the stage in Europe, which is a subject on its own, except for an occasional concern with English actors working overseas. It also excludes the masque, because the numerous known illustrations have already been generously reproduced, and the work of Inigo Jones in particular has been superbly covered by Stephen Orgel and Roy Strong in *Inigo Jones: The Theatre of the Stuart Court* (2 vols, 1973). Its primary concern, in any case, is with the professional theatres of Shakespeare's age, but drawings relating to special conversions of halls for royal performances, including those by Inigo Jones, are included, since these relate to the productions of plays, and to the development of indoor professional theatres, the so-called private theatres, of the period.[10]

NOTES

1. *The Globe Playhouse*, frontispiece and Pl. 20, facing p. 274.
2. See the reproduction of Visscher's view of London, and the commentary on it, item 10 below.
3. Hosley, p. 234, has remarked in relation to the 'inner stage': 'The concept, originating in the nineteenth century, was extensively developed by scholars working early in the twentieth century, Poel, Archer, Thorndike, Lawrence, Granville Barker and others. These men recognised the need to explain references in Elizabethan stage directions to "curtains" and "discoveries", yet they were, I believe, so accustomed to realistic conventions of the contemporary proscenium arch stage that they could hardly conceive of Renais-

sance production without a stage element roughly corresponding to the proscenium arch curtain.' I wonder if a different set of contemporary conventions now affects our current concepts of Elizabethan stages.

4. Notable advances were made by I. A. Shapiro in his study of 'The Bankside Theatres: Early Engravings', *SS* 1 (1948), 25–37; by Richard Hosley in 'The Origins of the Shakespearian Playhouse', *Shakespeare Quarterly*, XV (1964), 29–39, and 'The Discovery-space in Shakespeare's Globe', *SS*, 12 (1959), 35–46; and by R. W. Southern in *The Staging of Plays before Shakespeare* (1973). Their work has fed into the comprehensive reassessments by Hosley in the *Revels History of English Drama*, Vol. III (1975), and Glynne Wickham's *Early English Stages*, Vol. II (2 parts, 1963 and 1972).

5. See Hosley, p. 130, where he refers to Richard Southern, *The Staging of Plays before Shakespeare*, and uses Southern's sketches of a possible performance in a hall.

6. Wickham II ii 201.

7. Richard Hosley, 'The Theatre and the Tradition', in ed. Herbert Berry, *The First Public Playhouse: The Theatre in Shoreditch 1576–1598* (Montreal, 1979), p. 53.

8. The range of derivative views is analysed in Irene Scouloudi's splendid descriptive catalogue (1953).

9. Hosley, p. 131.

10. For a useful checklist of works relating to all aspects of staging in the period, see Michael Shapiro, 'Annotated Bibliography on Original Staging in Elizabethan Plays,' *Research Opportunities in Renaissance Drama*, XXIV (1981), 23–49.

A
Maps and panoramas

I

Map of London in *Civitates Orbis Terrarum*, published by G. Braun and F. Hogenberg (Cologne 1572), and sometimes known as the Hoefnagel map, because of its dubious ascription on the grounds of style to Georg Hoefnagel.

This large view of London, measuring 12⅜ in. × 18⅞ in. (322 mm × 480 mm), is very detailed, and is probably a copy made from a lost English original. No scale is given, and the eye is distracted by such decorative features as the elegant group of figures apparently walking in fields south of Bankside; these can be seen in the section reproduced here, extending from Paris Garden in the west to London Bridge in the east. The map represents St Paul's Cathedral (not included in this section) with the spire which was destroyed in 1561, so the original drawing may have been made before that date. Although the detail in this map is impressively minute, it is not always accurate, or consistent with other more reliable maps. It was published before the first theatres were built in London, and shows, south of the river in Southwark, two buildings, one marked 'The beare bayting', and the other, to the west of it, 'The bowll baytyng'. A German visitor to London in 1584 described a visit to a bear-baiting entertainment, where dogs fought with three bears, a horse, and a bull, after which there was dancing and fireworks; this visitor, Lupold von Wedel, described the place as a 'round building three stories high, in which are kept about a hundred large English dogs, with separate wooden kennels for each of them.' Other witnesses give similar testimony, Thomas Platter in 1599 also remarking on the circular shape of the building, with galleries containing seats for spectators, and provision behind the 'play house' for about 120 dogs in separate kennels. Bear-baiting continued to be a popular sport until well into the reign of James I. John Stow's *Survey of London* (1598) mentions 'two Beare gardens, the olde and new places, wherein be kept Beares, Buls and other beastes to be bayted. As also Mastives in severall kenels'. However, Norden's map of 1593 and its revised version of 1600 show only 'The Beare howse' or 'Bearegard[en]' (see 4 and 7 below), roughly corresponding in location to 'The bowll baytying' on the Braun and Hogenberg map, and it seems that the more easterly house had disappeared by 1593.

The constructions shown on the map appear to be no more than open circular frameworks made of posts and beams, with a waist-high wall in each opening between the posts at which spectators are sketched standing as if to watch the sport inside. Oscar Brownstein thinks these can be taken as 'relatively accurate and relatively well-drafted representations' (p. 86), although the general nature of the map does not suggest a concern for accuracy, and these primitive arenas are shown with no entrances for animals, and no means of regulating spectators or preventing anyone from seeing the sport. By the 1580s baiting houses had galleries with seats and standings in the yard for spectators. There must have been some fence or barrier to protect spectators, and prevent animals running amok or escaping, and the illustrations in the Braun and Hogenberg map could be taken as indicating an early form of such barriers. Brownstein believes there were permanent grates at the Beargarden, and assumes that, whereas in a playhouse such as the Swan 'the galleries shown in the Swan drawing seem to be raised high enough to put the heads of seated spectators above the level of the stage' (p. 89; see 26 below), the lowest of the raised levels for spectators in the regular playhouses and in the Beargarden were different, 'the latter being both lower and for standing only'. This may be correct in relation to the early baiting houses, but does not allow for the possibility that removable barriers could have been set up in the arena. Brownstein's argument also assumes that the Hope, built in 1613, was the first multi-purpose playhouse used for fencing, baiting and playing.

The visual evidence provided by this illustration is of doubtful value, but it coincides with the accounts of visitors in one important respect, showing these buildings to be round and open to the air. The actor Edward Alleyn bought the Beargarden in 1594, and in 1604 he and his father-in-law, Philip Henslowe, obtained the office of Master and Keeper of Bears, Bulls and Mastiff Dogs, which was still part of the establishment of the Royal Household. When Henslowe pulled down the Beargarden in 1613, it was in order to erect in its place the Hope Theatre, with a house for bulls, and a stable, so that it could serve as both 'plaie house' and 'game place', according to the contract, which specifically distinguishes the old Beargarden, as simply a 'game place', from the new 'plaie house or game place'. The baiting of bulls or bears was part of a show which included other forms of entertainment, and the buildings erected for this purpose anticipated in many respects the design of the public theatres built on Bankside, beginning with the Rose in 1583.

Oscar Brownstein, 'Why Didn't Burbage Lease the Beargarden?', in Berry, *Theatre*, 81–96
Chambers, *ES*, II 450–71
Foakes and Rickert, *HD*, 299, 301
Hosley, 125–6 (Fig. 2)
Howgego, 2
Shapiro, *SS* 1, 26
Smith, 17 (Pl. 1)
Wickham, *EES* II, ii 242 (Pl. IV)

2

Civitas Londinum, woodcut attributed to Ralph Agas; probably printed from blocks made between 1570 and 1590, and known only from the print published about 1633.

This large woodcut, measuring 28½ in. × 72½ in. (724 mm × 1842 mm), bears the royal arms of James I, which are probably a later insertion in a map that appears to have been based in part on the Braun and Hogenberg view (1 above), and to have been wildly out of date when the only known print of it was published about 1633. The Bankside area reproduced here seems in particular to be largely derivative, and the representation of 'The Beare bayting' and 'The bolle bayting' correspond in general location and layout so closely that there is no reason to think the 'Agas' map has any independent authority. Although it gives a sense of greater height, detail and realism to the two buildings, there is no evidence to suggest that any of

the changes are authentic, and this map repeats a curious feature of the Braun and Hogenberg map in showing a small group of spectators apparently watching the sport from outside 'The bolle bayting', as though they could see through the walls.

Hosley, 125–7 (Fig. 3)
Howgego, 8
Leacroft, 31–2 (Fig. 22)
Shapiro, *SS* 1, 25–6
Smith, 18 (Pl. 2)
Wickham, *EES* II, ii 242–3 (Pl. V)

3

William Smith, *The Particular Description of England* (1588).

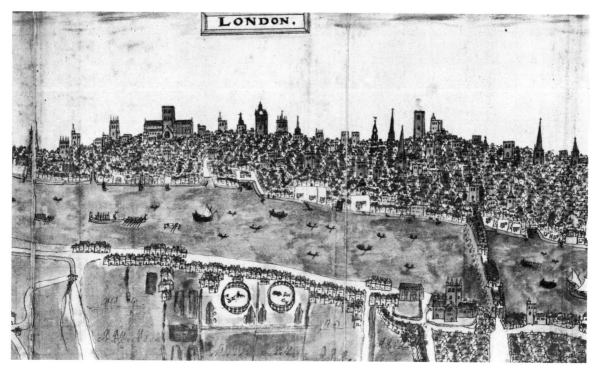

This volume in the British Library (BL Sloane MS 2596) contains a crude, coloured drawing of London measuring, when unfolded, 6⅞ in. × 17⅜ in. (175 mm × 442 mm) within the borders. It depicts London, as in the Braun and Hogenberg, and Agas, maps (1 and 2 above) from a notional aerial viewpoint south of the River Thames, and it is probably partly derived from one or other of these. Like these maps, it shows two arenas on Bankside, with animals sketched in to suggest bull-baiting and bear-baiting, with kennels for the dogs and stalls for the other animals nearby. Stewponds coloured blue are shown to the east, but the ponds between the arenas, and to the south of them between the rows of kennels, as illustrated on both previous maps, are here omitted. The arenas are coloured brown, and the kennels, like the roofs of houses, are coloured red. The whole drawing depicts London between Westminster and the Tower, and incorporates the arms of Queen Elizabeth and of the City of London. It seems intended to convey a decorative impression of the city, and has no value as evidence about Bankside. The Rose, erected in 1587, was established as a playhouse on Bankside by 1588 (see 4 below), and the drawing certainly does not represent the area as it appeared at that time.

Howgego, 13
Wickham, *EES* II, ii 54, 243 (Pl. VI, No. 6)

4

John Norden, *Speculum Britanniae. The first parte. An Historical and Chorographical Description of Middlesex.* London 1593.

This contains, between pp. 26 and 27, a bird's-eye view of London, measuring 8 in. × 6 in. (204 mm × 153 mm) within the borders, and inscribed 'Pieter Van den Keere fecit 1593. Ioannes Norden Anglus descripsit anno 1593'. The map is especially interesting for its provision of numerous references to particular buildings and places in London. John Norden was known as an expert surveyor, so that his map is likely to be authoritative evidence for the location of important buildings. The map shows the Beargarden, and 'The playhowse', or the Rose Theatre built by Philip Henslowe in 1587 off Rose Alley between the River Thames and Maiden Lane. This was the third of the so-called 'public' theatres erected in London, following Cuthbert Burbage's 'Theatre' built in north London in 1576, and a second, built south of the river in Newington Butts about 1580, about which nothing is known. Like the 'Theatre', the Rose had galleries for spectators surrounding an area exposed to the open air, in which 'groundlings' stood around a thrust stage to watch performances. The details in the map cannot be trusted. According to the deed of partnership with John Cholmley entered into by Henslowe in January 1587, the 'parcel of ground or garden plot' where they were building their theatre measured 94 feet square, had 'brigges', 'wharffs' and 'wayes' leading to it for which

6

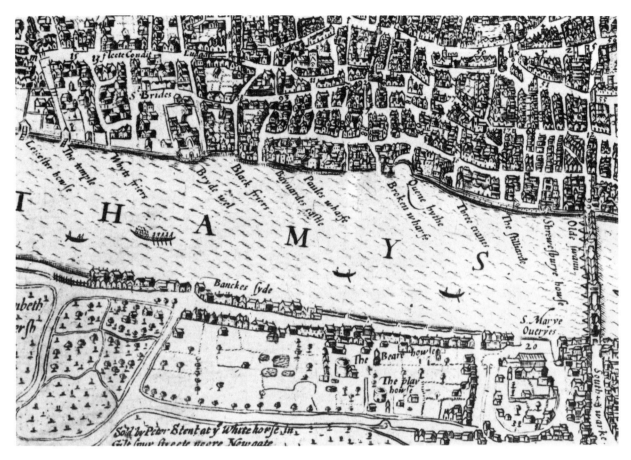

the partners were responsible, and their property included a 'small tenemente or dwellinge howse' south of the theatre, which they seem to have thought of as a kind of booth for refreshments, a place to 'keepe victualinge in'. This may be the house shown on Norden's map to the south of the Rose, and not adjoining it. The deed states that 'Rosse Alleye' led from the Thames to their ground, and that there was a 'waye leading into the saide Mayden Lane'; Norden shows the second, but not the first of these, which may have been too narrow and negligible for his purposes. It was in this theatre that the first performances of plays by Marlowe took place, and the great actor Edward Alleyn made his name there. Alleyn himself acquired the Beargarden, 'The Beare howse' as it is called on the map, in 1594. According to William Lambard's *Perambulation of Kent* (1596), visitors to the Bearhouse, or Paris Garden, the Bell Savage, or to the theatre, 'to beholde Beare baiting, Enterludes, or Fence playe' had to pay a pennie at the gate, another at the 'entrie of the Scaffolde', meaning presumably the galleries, and a further penny for a 'quiet standing'. It is not altogether certain that his description can be trusted, since the wording in 1596 (p. 233) is the same as that in the first edition (1576, pp. 187–8) except for the insertion of 'or

Theatre' in the list of places of entertainment, but this may merely indicate that charges for admission at playhouses like Burbage's Theatre and Henslowe's Rose were based on prices prevailing elsewhere. It seems that the various buildings may have been used at this time for several different kinds of entertainment. It is notable that both 'The Beare howse' and the Rose are shown as round buildings.

Chambers, *ES*, II 358–9
Foakes and Rickert, *HD*, 304–6
Hind, I 204 (Pl. 114)
Howgego, 5
Shapiro, *SS* 1, 28–30 (Pl. VI)
Smith, 18 (Pl. 3)
Wickham, *EES* II, ii 57–62, 243–4 (Pl. VII)

5

Abram Booth, from *The View of the Cittye of London from the North towards the Sowth*
c. 1597–9.

This engraving, on three sheets measuring 3¾ in. × 11¾ in. (95 mm × 298 mm) (East), 3¾ in. × 16¾ in. (95 mm × 425 mm) (Centre) and 3¾ in. × 11⅞ in. (95 mm × 302 mm) (West), is known from a copy included in the manuscript journal of Abram Booth, now MS 1198 Hist. 147 in the library of the University of Utrecht. It contains the only known representation of the theatres in Shoreditch, north of the Thames, and in the area now better known as Hackney. It is not, unfortunately, very informative. The two buildings surmounted by flags are thought to be the Theatre, built by James Burbage in 1576, and the Curtain, erected soon afterwards, probably in 1577. The exact location of the Curtain is not known, but it seems to have been to the south of the Theatre, which probably stood at or near what is now the junction of Curtain Road and New Inn Yard. Shakespeare's company, the Lord Chamberlain's Men, played at the Theatre until about 1597, when they seem to have moved to the Curtain; in 1598–9 the Theatre was pulled down, and its timbers were transported south of the Thames for use in the erection of the new Globe Theatre. There has been much debate concerning which of the buildings shown in the engraving is the Theatre and which the Curtain, and the uncertainty about this indicates how difficult

it is to interpret the detailed features shown there. If the building on the left is the Theatre, then the two projecting wings could be crude representations of external staircase towers, such as were called for in the contract for the Fortune Theatre. Two (or possibly three in the projection to the right) levels of windows are shown, with a black mark at ground level possibly indicating a doorway. There was no right of way to the Theatre from Holywell Lane, and the main entrance seems to have been from Finsbury fields, through a gate made in the brick wall marking the precinct of an old nunnery, but it is not possible to locate this on the engraving.

The shape of the building cannot easily be determined. The hatching that suggests a concave appearance may have been intended to produce the opposite effect and signify a round building. Johannes de Witt, visiting London in 1596, called all the theatres he saw (the Rose and the Swan, south of the Thames, the Theatre and the Curtain north of the river) 'Amphiteatra', which literally refers to circular or semi-circular buildings. In addition, 'Fame', speaking the epilogue in *The Travels of the Three English Brothers* by John Day, William Rowley and George Wilkins (1607), a play performed at the Curtain' addresses 'Some that fill up this round circumference'.

It would, however, be rash to claim that the engraving provides clear evidence of the shape. Richard Hosley categorically declares (p. 53) that the Theatre 'was built to a ground plan in the shape of a polygon', because he assumes that 'under pressure of a normal concern for costs' builders would not have gone to the trouble to shape wooden beams to a curve, and he reads this engraving as depicting eight sides. It could just as well be round or square, with two staircase turrets drawn massively out of scale, and the whole is so crude that any interpretation must be speculative. The building seems to be of three stories, with a construction at the rear projecting above the roof-line of the main building, and surmounted by the flag or sign of the theatre, corresponding roughly to the 'hut' shown in the de Witt drawing of the Swan Theatre (26 below). The flag appears to project from a cupola, which provides a visual link between this, the Visscher view of the first Globe (10), and the second Globe in Hollar's 'Long View' (21), although both the Utrecht drawing and the Visscher view are of dubious value as evidence. The other theatre in the engraving is marked only by the flag projecting apparently from a pitched roof which may indicate the 'hut' above the stage, but the rest of the Curtain, if this it is, is hidden behind a cluster of other buildings.

A. M. Hind, in his great study of engraving in England during the sixteenth and seventeenth centuries, at first dated this c. 1610–20, but revised his dating to 1598 or later, in the belief that only one theatre had been identified in the engraving (by Leslie

Hotson, in the *Times Literary Supplement* in 1954), so that the panorama must have been drawn after the removal of the theatre to be used in building the Globe in 1598–9.

Chambers, *ES*, II 362, 384–6, 399, 402, 482
John Day, *Works*, ed. A. H. Bullen, reprinted with an introduction by Robin Jeffs (1963), p. 404
Sidney Fisher, *The Theatre, the Curtain, & the Globe* (Montreal, 1964)
Foakes and Rickert, *HD*, 308
Hind, II 112–14 (Pl. 52–3)
Hodges, *Globe Restored*, 110–11 (Pl. 7)
Richard Hosley, 'The Theatre and the Tradition of Playhouse Design', in Berry, *Theatre*, 47–79 (Figs 1 and 2), 51, 54
Leslie Hotson, *Times Literary Supplement*, 26 March 1954, pp. 7, 14
Leslie Hotson, *Shakespeare's Wooden O* (1959), 304–13
Rosemary Linnell, *The Curtain Playhouse* (1977)
A. Merens ed., *Een Dienaer der oost-Indische Compagnie te Londen in 1629* ('S-Gravenhage, 1942)
Schoenbaum, 104–6
Wickham, *EES* II, ii 63–8, 250 (Pl. XXXII, No. 34)

6

Civitas Londini, an engraved panorama of 'the moste Famous Citty LONDON', 1600, compiled 'By the industry of Jhon Norden'.

This large panorama, measuring 49 $\frac{5}{16}$ in. × 13 $\frac{3}{4}$ in. (1252 mm × 349 mm), is known from the copy surviving in the Royal Library at Stockholm. It was engraved on four sheets, perhaps by more than one hand, for the sheet representing the area to the east of Bankside is more heavily engraved than the others. The legend in the cartouche roughly centred near the foot of the panorama states that it was 'performed' in 1600, and a smaller cartouche adds 'By the industry of Jhon Norden', which may mean that the whole was drawn or revised by Norden, and engraved later by someone else; the word 'perform' was often used to mean perfect, complete by adding what was lacking, or finish off, as well as simply make or execute. The distinction is important because the panorama differs in essential details from the inset map of London (4 above). Norden was a cartographer and surveyor, not an engraver, and there is every reason to think that he was responsible for the maps inset in the panorama, which are revisions of his maps for *Speculum Britanniae*, but the panorama may well have been drawn by someone else, for it shows the theatres (reading from east to west the Globe (recently erected in 1598–9), the Rose, the Beargarden

and the Swan) as hexagonal or octagonal buildings, whereas the maps show them as round. The panorama has been shown to be incorrect in various details, especially in its representation of the church of St Mary Overie (now Southwark Cathedral), locating it too far west of London Bridge, and giving it features it did not possess. Its representation of the theatres is also evidently wrong in scale and relationship. The Globe, furthest south, and closest to the eye of the spectator, is rendered smaller than the others, and mostly concealed by trees. The Rose, set a little further back, is shown as slightly larger, and with a row of windows high in the walls, three to each face. The Beargarden, further away still, is shown as a much taller building, and, like the Swan, the furthest away and largest, it shows two windows in each face of the outer wall, one above the other. Each theatre has a flag marking it, and the Globe and Rose show what could be the roof of the hut at the same level as the ridge roof running round the outer wall. As shown, the Swan would have been enormously larger than the Globe. However, there is no reason to trust the detail of Bankside in the panorama, which seems to have been drawn with an artist's

licence. The theatres are located roughly where they should be, and the panorama has considerable importance because it is the first view of London showing the theatres as polygonal rather than round, and because it was a source for several later views of London, like those of Visscher and Merian (10 and 15 below). There has been much debate about the shape of the theatres, and the trustworthiness of Norden's maps and panorama is an important issue. On the face of it, the map would appear to be more reliable as evidence about the theatres than the panorama, and this is confirmed by the more authoritative later maps and views, notably Hollar's 'Long View' (21 below).

Hodges, *Globe Restored,* 110 (Pl. 6)
Hosley, 137, 141 (Fig. 13), 177, 179 (Fig. 40)
Orrell, 39–40, 60–3 (Pl. 24–5)
Scouloudi, 19–22
Shapiro, *SS* 1, 29–30 (Pls IV B, VIII A)
Smith, 18–19 (Pl. 5)

7

John Norden, inset from *Civitas Londini*, 1600.

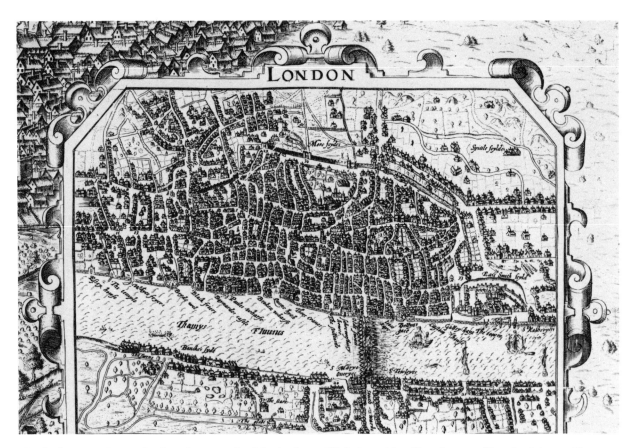

Norden's map of 1593 (4 above) was revised for inclusion as an inset in the lower right corner of the large panorama of London entitled *Civitas Londini*, and 'performed' in 1600 according to a cartouche centred near the bottom of it (see 6 above). A smaller cartouche attached to this states that it was produced 'By the industry of Jhon Norden', but there is no indication of the engraver. The revised map measures $5\frac{1}{4}$ in. $\times 7\frac{5}{8}$ in. (133 mm $\times$ 194 mm), and is slightly smaller than that of 1593. The revisions include the addition of the Swan Theatre, built probably in 1595, and the Globe, erected in 1599. The map shows the Globe to have been the furthest south of all the Bankside theatres, and the small building to the east of it may have been the 'alehouse' (according to a ballad on the burning of the Globe), or 'dwelling-house adjoyning' (according to a letter John Chamberlain wrote on 8 July 1613), which was destroyed with the Globe in the fire which consumed both in 1613. This theatre was certainly thatched, as several contemporary accounts of the fire establish that the roof was set alight by the discharge of guns during a performance, perhaps the first performance, of Shakespeare's *King Henry VIII*. The hatching in this map in the representation of the Globe and the theatre to the north-west of it may be intended to indicate a thatched roof.

This second theatre, called simply 'The playhowse' in 1593, is now labelled 'The Stare'. The name on the earlier map is explicable, for in Philip Henslowe's notes in 1592 and 1595 of repairs to it he calls it simply

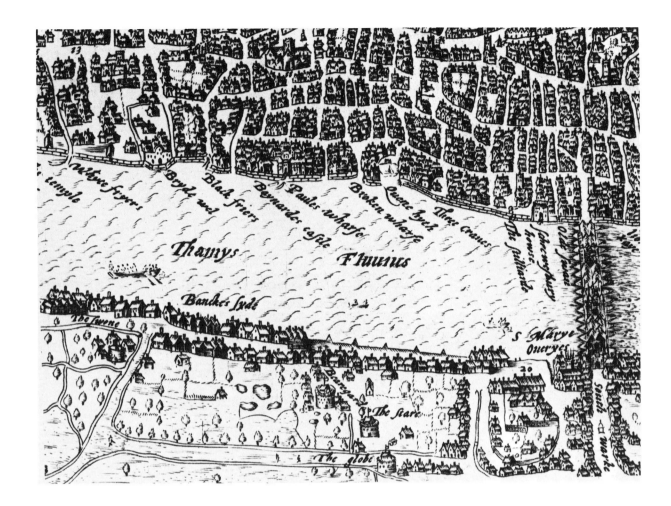

'my playhowsse', and it is not clear when it became generally known as the Rose, though there is some evidence that it was so known in 1591 or 1592. Certainly by 1597 Henslowe entered into contracts with several actors requiring them to play 'in my howsse only knowne by the name of the Rosse', so that the name 'The Stare' is strange, and so far unexplained, except as an error.

Norden's revision shows more detail than the 1593 map. The Globe, the 'Star' or Rose, and the Beargarden are all shown with elevated structures projecting above the roof-line and supporting a flagpost. Each has a row of windows well above ground-level, two rows in the case of the Beargarden, and what looks like a door on the south side. The detail of the Swan is more obscure, but it is correctly located, and, as in a plan of the area dating from 1627 (see 13 below), it is shown, like the other playhouses, as a circular building.

These theatres were all built south of the Thames so as to be outside the jurisdiction of the City of London authorities. The continuous struggle of the authorities to control plays and theatres resulting, in 1574, in an Act of Common Council imposing elaborate regula-

tions for licensing theatres and companies of actors, and for censoring plays, led to the building of playhouses in suburbs not subject to all these controls. The maps suggest that the population of Bankside was not large, and grew little between 1593 and 1603, but it was easy to cross the river by London Bridge, or by boat. The Swan was built due south of Paris Garden stairs, and the Thames watermen developed a thriving trade in ferrying customers across the river, for at one time, when the Rose was closed for some reason, they petitioned the Lord Admiral to allow playing there again, since they had 'muche helpe and reliefe for vs, oure poore wives and Children by meanes of the resorte of suche people as come vnto the said playe howse'.

Chambers, *ES*, II 406–7, 411, 415, 420–1
Foakes and Rickert, *HD*, 6, 9, 239, 283–5, 304–5
Hodges, 108 (Pl. 2)
Hosley, 137–8 (Fig. 8), 177–8 (Fig. 37)
Howgego, 5
Scouloudi, 19–22
Shapiro, *SS* 1, 28–9 (Pl VII)
Smith, 18 (Pl. 4)
Wickham, *EES* II, ii 57–62, 244 (Pl. VII, No. 9)

8

Jodocus Hondius, View of London, engraving, 1610, from the map of Great Britain engraved by Hondius for John Speed, *Theatre of the Empire of Great Britain* (1611).

This view of London, measuring $2\frac{11}{16}$ in. × $5\frac{5}{8}$ in. (68 mm × 143 mm), was engraved in 1610, probably in Amsterdam, and gives what Irene Scouloudi justly describes as a 'crude impression of the city'. Jodocus Hondius the elder lived in London between 1583 and 1593, when he returned to the Netherlands; the date when this view was drawn is not known, but it does not show the Rose Theatre, which was pulled down probably in 1606. Two theatres are depicted, one a circular building, usually identified as the Globe, the other with ten or twelve sides, closer to the river, which must be the Beargarden. The Globe is shown with a windowless lower storey of larger diameter than the two upper stories, which have rows of evenly spaced windows. There is a flagpole, but no 'hut' or roof-line projecting above the stage area. The drawing of the Beargarden is more hazy; one row of windows is shown, with a blurred roof-line that makes the building look more like a fortress than a theatre. The details of the Bridge and the buildings on the north bank are very inaccurate, and the artist has squeezed as much in as possible without much regard for scale or relationships, as can be seen by comparing his version of St Paul's Cathedral with that in Hollar's 'Long View' (21 below). There is no reason to trust the details of the buildings on the south bank either, and possibly the only points of significance are that, once again, the Globe is shown as round, and that the theatres are marked by flags.

Bentley, *JCS*, VI 247–8
Chambers, *ES*, II 377
Hind, II 67–87
Hosley, 177, 179 (Fig. 38)
Scouloudi, 22–3
Shapiro, *SS* 1, 31–2 (Pl. VIII B)
Smith, 19–20 (Pl. 7)

9

Francis Delaram, engraving of King James I on horseback, showing a view of Bankside and London; undated, but probably after 1610.

The
High and mighty
Prince, IAMES
KING of great
Britanie, Fraunce
and Ireland, &c.

This view, measuring 11 in. × 8¾ in. (280 mm × 223 mm), has some connection with the Hondius view of 1610, and may be in part derived from it; both show the Globe as a circular building with a larger diameter at the lower level than in the two upper stories. Here, however, the viewpoint has shifted much further south, so that a third theatre to the west, the Swan, now comes into the picture. The viewpoint seems also to have moved to the east, to the extent that the Globe is now shown to the west of the Beargarden, and not, as in the Hondius view, to the east. At the same time, St Paul's is shown as if seen from the west, which is quite inconsistent with the depiction of the theatres. This view probably therefore was not based upon a drawing of the scene, but upon previous views, and there is no reason to trust its details. The Globe and Beargarden are represented as in the Hondius view, the first as round with two rows of windows in the upper stories, the second as octagonal with one row of windows. The Swan is shown as virtually identical with the Beargarden, an octagonal building, with one row of windows, and a slightly lower roof-line, though this may be an accidental feature of a casual engraving. The major difference from the Hondius view is that here each theatre is drawn with a 'hut' showing above the roof-line of the galleries, a gabled structure not unlike that in the Swan drawing (see 26), with a flag projecting from it. The Hondius view showed no 'hut' at either the Globe or Beargarden, so this would seem to be a correction of the Hondius view, and could have been based on observation. However, the virtual identity of the 'huts' shown, and of the Swan and Beargarden, suggest that the artist was showing what he took to be common features rather than attempting to be accurate, and Hollar's 'Long View' (21) shows how different the roof-lines of the Globe and the later Beargarden or Hope were. The main concern of this engraving was to present a large equestrian portrait of James I, and the view of London is merely the setting and background for this, so that there was no need for the artist to be particularly concerned with accuracy.

Chambers, *ES*, II 377
Hind, II 224–5 (Pl. 127)
Shapiro, *SS* 1, 32–3 (Pl. X)
Smith, 20 (Pl. 6)

10

J. C. Visscher, *Londinum Florentiss[i]ma Britanniae Urbs* (Amsterdam 1616).

This large and highly decorative panoramic view of London was engraved on four sheets, each measuring 16½ in. × 21¼ in. (419 mm × 540 mm), and it appears to show the city as it was about 1600. It includes Bulmer's water tower, built in 1594, and Bedford House, which became Worcester House after 1600, so the incorporation of the Stuart coat of arms and the date 1616 is rather misleading. Visscher was born in 1587, and there is no proof that he ever visited London; indeed, there is little doubt that much of his panorama was derived from Norden's *Civitas Londini* (6 above), and he even repeats the spelling of 'The Gally fuste' (meaning 'foist', a light galley worked with sails and oars) and 'The Eell Schipes' against boats depicted in the water. These names must be derivative, but the boats themselves, though roughly alike, are drawn with much more elaboration and suggestion of detail in the later engraving. It looks as though Visscher allowed himself an artist's licence to embroider here what he found in the earlier panorama. It exists in two states, but the differences between them in the representation of Bankside are insignificant. In both, three theatres are shown and marked as 'The Globe', 'The Bear Gardne', and 'The Swan'. The first two are shown as octagonal, the last apparently as twelve-sided. It is very possible that, as in the case of the boats on the Thames, Visscher elaborated here with an artist's licence what he found in the panorama of *Civitas Londini*; perhaps not noticing the Globe in that, which is almost concealed by trees, he has taken from it the Rose, Beargarden and Swan, and for pictorial effect has enlarged them, and located the Globe and the Swan quite incorrectly and much too near the river. It has to be said that the boundary of the view as restricted by his plates would not have allowed the delineation of a correctly sited Globe, and Visscher used his artist's licence to locate it north even of where the Rose (probably pulled down about 1606) would have been. It looks as though he had by him also the 'Agas' and Braun and Hogenberg maps (2 and 1 above), and placed the Globe and the Swan to correspond with the Bearbaiting and Bullbaiting houses depicted on them. As on these maps,

there are spectators looking from the outside through windows into the theatres, confirming a suspicion that these are conventional figures, placed there merely to give a sense of scale. There is no reason to take them, or the windows, or any feature of the buildings, very seriously, as they are likely to have been drawn from previous maps and views, developed by the artist's imagination, and probably owe little to observation.

Visscher's engraving was made in Amsterdam, and there is no evidence to show whether preliminary drawings were made for it in London; but his panorama is clearly dependent upon previous maps and views, and he can be shown to have elaborated other details, such as the 'Gally fuste', that he found in them. The shape of the Swan, which is shown as hexagonal in the *Civitas Londini* panorama, was again probably elaborated fancifully by Visscher to make it 10- or 12-sided, and endowed with more windows than in the earlier views. There is no reason, consequently, to

18

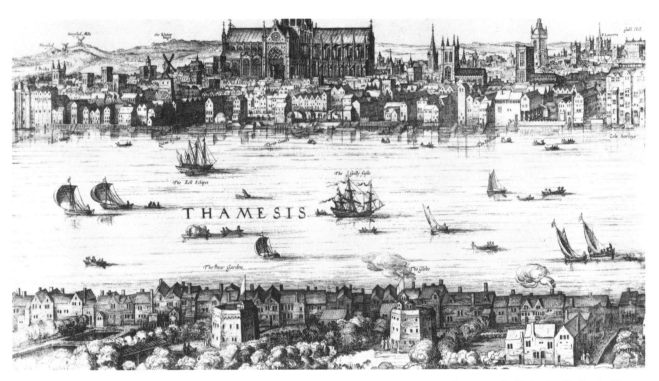

trust the details in the Visscher view. He had no concern for accuracy, as is shown by the mislocation of the Globe, which was south of Maiden Lane, as indicated on Norden's revised map of 1600 (6 above), and by his placing of the Swan apparently on the river bank; I. A. Shapiro has pointed out a number of other errors. Visscher seems above all to have been concerned to achieve as decorative an effect as possible, and in this he was successful. Yet his view has been more influential than perhaps any other in establishing a conventional image of the Globe as an octagonal building, as in the reconstruction by John Cranford Adams, which must be said, like Visscher's engraving, to have no authority. At the same time, the depiction of the Globe has an intriguing detail, the cupola on top of the 'hut', from which the flag seems to project, and which is not shown in the drawings of other theatres, or of the Beargarden. This visual detail links with the view of the theatre in the Utrecht view of London (5 above), and with the cupola shown on the second Globe in Hollar's 'Long View' (21); all three theatres were used by the Lord Chamberlain's, or King's, Men, the company to which Shakespeare belonged.

Adams, pp. 8–9, 28-30 (Pl. 8)
Chambers, *ES*, II 410
Hind, II 95–104 (Pls 50, 51)
Hodges, 107 (Pl. 1)
Hosley, 137–9 (Fig. 11), 177–8 (Fig. 40)
Orrell, 35ff (Pls 20–3)
Scouloudi, 24–9
Shapiro, *SS* 1, 30–1
Smith, 20–3 (Pls 8, 9)

11

View of London on the title-page of Henry Holland, *Herwologia Anglica* (Arnhem 1620); engraving, unsigned and artist unknown.

This crude bird's-eye view compresses a wide span of London into a cartouche measuring $2\frac{1}{4}$ in $\times 3\frac{3}{4}$ in. (57 mm $\times$ 95 mm), and includes on the west side the bend of the River Thames round to Westminster. It seems to have some connection with the Hondius view (8 above), perhaps through some lost original which served as a source for both. There is a similarity in the depiction of the Globe as a circular theatre with a larger diameter at the lower than at the upper level, no 'hut', and a large flag waving above it. The Beargarden is also shown, or more probably the Hope Theatre which replaced it in 1614 on or near the same site; the detail is hazy, but it too appears to be shown as a circular building, not unlike the Globe, and again with no 'hut' showing above the roof-line of the galleries. The Hope was to some extent modelled on the Swan Theatre, according to the contract for building it, and may have been intended largely to replace it. There is little evidence of performances at the Swan after the opening of the Hope, but the playhouse remained, and was still standing, though fallen into decay, in 1632. It is likely, then, that it was in use, at any rate from time to time, and G. E. Bentley thinks Prince Charles's Company may have worked there before moving to the Curtain in 1621, and that Princess Elizabeth's Company played there after this date. The Swan is not shown on the engraving in Holland's book, and while this could be explained as a deliberate omission because the drawing for the engraving was made at a time when the Swan was not being used as a theatre (between 1614 and 1620?), it is perhaps just as likely that it was left out through carelessness. This engraving appears to have no independent authority.

Bentley, *JCS*, VI 249–52
Chambers, *ES*, II 466–70
Hind, II 145–6 (Pl. 68)
Rhodes, 6 (Pl. 25)
Scouloudi, 41–2
Shapiro, *SS* 1, 33 (Pl. IX)
Smith, 20
Wickham, *EES* II, ii 70

12

Claude de Jongh, Sketch of London Bridge from the West (1627).

This drawing, which measures 9 in. × 39 in. (229 mm × 991 mm), was made as a preliminary sketch for the artist's oil painting, 'View of Old London Bridge' (1630), now in Kenwood House. The drawing, dated 'London the 18 of Aprill 1627', is in the Guildhall Library in London. Claude de Jongh, probably a native of Utrecht where he was a master in the painters' guild, was born about 1600, and visited London a number of times. He made another oil painting, a re-working of the scene, in 1650, including St Mary Overie (Southwark Cathedral, as it is now) on the right, where it is masked in the drawing by a large five-storied house. This house may be the large house just to the right of the Beargarden (marked 'The Globe') in Hollar's 'Long View' (21). The tower of St Olave's Church can be seen, and to the right of this two pennants which appear to mark the site of two theatres with their roof-lines just visible. These are presumably the Hope or Beargarden, nearer the river, and the Globe. The point of view from which the drawing was made is somewhere in mid-river, at the spot marked by a barrel or mooring buoy in the foreground. Thus the theatres are seen from the north-west, a direction opposite to that in Hollar's 'Long View'. The drawing is freer and fussier than Hollar's sketch for the 'Long View' (16) and, although it gives a very detailed impression of the river-frontage and the bridge, the roof-lines of the theatre buildings at the rear are more casually sketched in. They appear to be roughly the same height, but the Globe, being further away from the viewpoint, should have appeared to have a lower roof-line (see 21 below). This may be due to inaccuracy in the drawing. The roof-line of the Hope is level, with no sign of the peak shown in the 'Long View', and the Globe has a 'hut' that looks much smaller than the large superstructure depicted by Hollar, with a flag pole projecting from in front of it. The Hollar drawing does not show a flag pole at the Globe. The detail of the roofs in de Jongh's sketch is too hazy to draw any further conclusions.

Oliver Millar, *The Age of Charles I: Painting in England 1620–1649* (1972), pp. 46–7 (Item 60)

Right: detail of the de Jongh sketch of London Bridge.
Below (left and right): de Jongh's oil painting 'View of Old London Bridge'.

23

13

Map of Paris Garden Manor showing the Swan Theatre (1627).

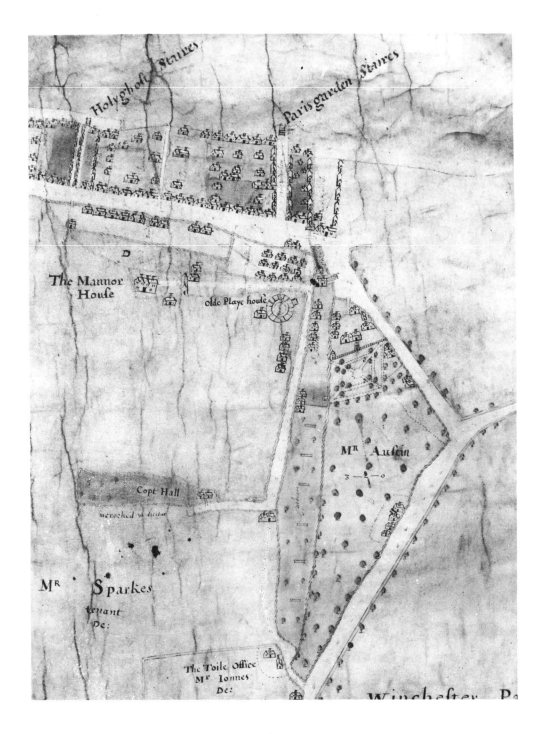

In 1618 the steward and copyholders of the manor of Paris Garden, a marshy area of not much more than a hundred acres to the west of Bankside, asked for a survey to be taken of the 'extente circuite boundes and limittes of the Copieholdes of this Manor before the next generall Courte and a plott exactly and fairely made'. A certain Thomas Aldwell was appointed to make the map, and was paid £5 for it. The map was not presented until December 1627, and the titles of the copyholders were confirmed by the Crown in 1629. The map, in ink on vellum, measures roughly $22\frac{3}{4}$ in. × 29 in. (578 mm × 737 mm) within a double frame of thick brown rules. Most of the area belonged to the Lord of the Manor, Thomas Browker, and is uncoloured, but the houses and land occupied by others are coloured in yellow, red and green, now faded. The map includes a scale showing that it is based on a measurement of 6 perches, or 33 yards, to one inch, and this may be reasonably accurate for land measurements, but buildings are represented in a stylised fashion, and not to scale.

The map shows Paris Garden stairs at the river's edge, giving on to 'Paris Garden Lane'. This leads to a wide road, the Upper Ground, and south of this, about 140 yards from the River Thames, just to the west of a lane which later became Green Walk, and then Hopton Street, is marked the 'Olde Playe house'. This was the Swan Theatre, built about 1595 by Francis Langley, who acquired Paris Garden Manor in 1589, and sold it to Hugh and Thomas Browker in 1601. The history of the Swan is narrated in relation to Johannes de Witt's famous drawing of it (see 26 below); by the time this map was made it had probably 'fallen to decay', as Nicholas Goodman reported in *Holland's Leaguer* (1632, signature F2ᵛ). On the map the Swan is represented by a double circle, with a fainter small circle within the inner ring; the outer circles are divided into sixteen segments by fifteen short lines, which may be no more than a kind of hatching to show this area was roofed. On the north-east side is a projection that might be a stair-turret, and to the south-west a house seems to abut on to the theatre. The outer ring has a diameter of $\frac{21}{32}$ in. (approximately 17 mm), which, by the scale of the map, would represent about 65 feet, and the Swan was certainly much larger than this if, as de Witt said, this was the largest ('amplissimum') of the London theatres in 1597. The representation of the Swan on the map must be regarded as schematic, and it provides no evidence of its appearance or condition; it is important as confirming the existence of the building as an old playhouse in 1627, as showing a circular building, and as providing the best evidence of its precise location. The map is on deposit in the Greater London Record Office; it

formerly belonged to the Steward of the Manor, then passed into the possession of Christ Church Parochial School, and when this was closed came into the custody of the Southwark Diocesan Board of Education. The whole map was reproduced, much reduced in size, as Plate 65 in the *Survey of London*, Vol. XXII (1950), but the only account of the theatres to include a print of the detail showing the Swan is that by Richard Hosley in *The Revels History of English Drama*. The Guildhall Library in London possesses a late copy of the map, made probably in the eighteenth century, and a drawing from it made by Philip Norman in 1901 was reproduced by I. A. Shapiro in *Shakespeare Survey* 1; both of these are very inaccurate versions of the original map.

Chambers, *ES*, II 359, 411–14, 458–61
Hosley, 137–8 (Fig. 10)
William Ingram, ' "Neere the Playe Howse": The Swan Theater and Community Blight', *Renaissance Drama* New Series IV (1971), 53–68
Philip Norman, 'The Accounts of the Overseers of the Poor of Paris Garden, Southwark, 17 May 1608 to 30 September 1671', *Surrey Archaeological Collections*, XVI (1901), 55–136 (drawing from map reproduced facing p. 55)
Shapiro, *SS* 1, 29 (Pl. IXB)
Survey of London, Vol. XXII, Bankside (1950), pp. 96–8 (map reproduced as Pl. 65, facing p. 96)
Wickham, *EES* II, i 308, ii 68–71

I4

Cornelis Dankerts, Map of 'the Cittie of London' (attributed to Augustine Ryther)
(Amsterdam c. 1633 and c. 1645).

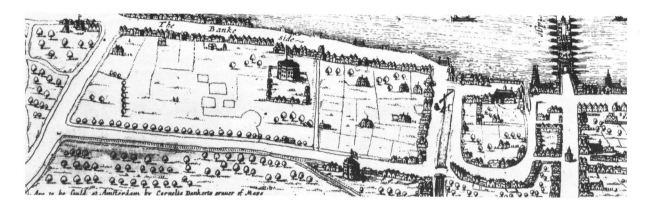

There has been some confusion about the two earlier versions of this map (further versions appeared about 1675 and again about 1710). The second version (now dated about 1645) has no imprint and omits the Globe Theatre, so that it has been taken to represent an earlier 'unfinished' state of the map, and has sometimes been assumed to be based on a drawing made as early as about 1605 (see Smith, 23; Adams, 4). In fact the first edition appears to be that containing the imprint 'Are to be sould at Amsterdam by Cornelis Dankerts grauer of Maps'. In this map, measuring 13 in. × 16⅝ in. (330 mm × 422 mm) within the borders, the Globe is shown as a polygonal building south of Maiden Lane. To the north-west of it a larger, octagonal structure shown in a square enclosure must be the Beargarden or the Hope. Dankerts seems to have drawn the basic plan of Southwark and Bankside from Norden's map in *Speculum Britanniae* (1593; 4 above), but tidied it up and made it much neater, as the four ponds sketched roughly to the left of the Beargarden in the 1593 map (and shown more clearly in the revision in *Civitas Londini*, 1600) are turned into squares, and look more like fields. However, Norden showed the Globe only in the revised version of his map in 1600, so Dankerts may have had access to this too, since he shows it in much the same location. Norden depicts the Globe as round, while Dankerts makes it hexagonal or octagonal, which suggests he may also have studied Bankside as shown in the panorama as well as the map in

Civitas Londini (see 6 and 7 above). The later version is dated at about 1645 because it does not show the Globe (demolished in 1644), but only the Hope, which stood until 1656. A copy of this later version in the British Library has a list of streets in the left-hand margin to help the user 'in his finding out of Streets, Lanes or Places in London'. In spite of this, there is nothing to suggest that Dankerts had seen Bankside, and he seems to have contented himself with a map based on much older views and maps, supplemented by some general knowledge of where major buildings stood; so he does not show the Rose, torn down by 1606, on either map, and the Globe only on the earlier one; the Swan does not figure at all, since it was just off the map to the west. The evidence therefore implies that these maps have no authority in their representation of playhouses.

Adams, pp. 4, 9 (Pl. 5)
Chambers, *ES*, II 427, 470
Howgego, 9
Shapiro, *SS* 1, 26
Smith, 23 (Pl. 11)

I5

Matthias Merian, View of London, engraving, in J. L. Gottfried and M. Merian,
Neuwe Archontologia Cosmica (Frankfurt, 1638).

This large panorama, measuring 8 3/10 in. × 27 1/2 in. (207 mm × 698 mm) has no independent authority, but is based on the earlier views represented in *Civitas Londini* (1600; 6 above) and the Visscher panorama of 1616 (10). It appears to depict the city as it was in about 1600. The key to the reference numbers against some of the buildings in the section reproduced here identifies 37 as 'The Globe', 38 as 'The Bear Gardne', and 39 as 'The Swan'. The Globe and Beargarden are copied roughly from the Visscher view, as is the Swan, all shown as polygonal. Merian seems to have taken from the *Civitas Londini* view the square building with what appear to be balconies or open galleries, shown to the south-east of the Swan Theatre. In this panorama he found four theatres, including the Rose, pulled down by 1606, and so he inserted a fourth theatre between the Beargarden and the Globe and nearer to the river. He evidently did not realise that Visscher's placing of the Globe was incorrect, and because of this the Rose is shown as north-east of the Beargarden, and not where in fact it was located, south-east of it. In other words, Merian based his view on

Visscher's 1616 panorama of London, but added from the earlier *Civitas Londini*, 1600, details not shown in Visscher, without apparently realising that he was, in incorporating the Rose Theatre, compounding errors by displaying in the wrong location a building that, in any case, had been demolished by 1606.

Among the views of London related to the Merian engraving is an oil painting attributed to Claude de Jongh in London's Tower Hamlets Central Library (formerly Stepney Public Library); this has been reproduced as the front endpaper in S. Schoenbaum's *William Shakespeare: Records and Images* (1981). The date of this painting is not known, but Irene Scouloudi guessingly assigned it to 1627, on the basis of a drawing by de Jongh in the British Museum. It appears to be based on the Merian engraving, displaying the same topographical inaccuracies and showing heads stuck on poles on the south gate of London Bridge. However, it is much coarser in detail, and is characterised by a vertical enhancement of prominent buildings like St Paul's Cathedral, making them appear to have been squashed sideways. The appearance of the theatre buildings also is distorted, showing them with walls sloping inwards, so that the Globe appears almost conical. This painting would seem therefore to be a more debased version of the Merian view than the parallel painting at Chatsworth by Thomas Wyck (1616–77), which also distorts some of the larger buildings to make their height more impressive, but is closer to Merian in its representation of theatres; this is reproduced in the catalogue of the exhibition *Treasures from Chatsworth*. Neither of these attractive oil paintings has any authority, for both are late depictions of the city as it was in about 1600, and both are derivative from the Merian and Visscher panoramas.

Hosley, 137, 140 (Fig. 12)
S. Schoenbaum, *William Shakespeare: Records and Images* (1981), front endpaper and commentary on it
Scouloudi, 42–4
Shapiro, *SS* 1, 31
Smith, 23 (Pl. 10)
Treasures from Chatsworth: The Devonshire Inheritance (International Exhibitions Foundation, London, 1979–80), p. 37 (Pl. 40)

16

Wenceslaus Hollar, Drawing of Bankside viewed from St Mary Overie, headed '[East Part of] West part o[f] Southwarke toward Westminster', made between 1636 and 1644.

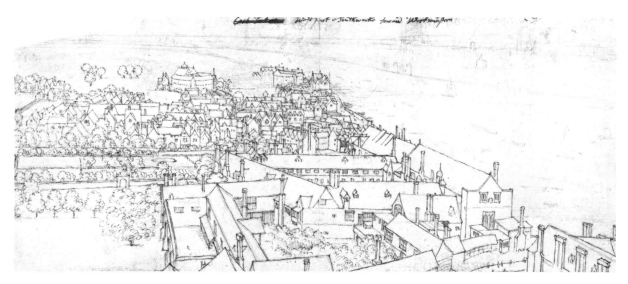

This drawing, measuring 5 in. × 12⅛ in. (127 mm × 308 mm), in pencil overdrawn in pen and ink, was presumably made when Wenceslaus Hollar was living in London between 1636 and 1644. It was used as the basis for the relevant part of his 'Long View' (see 21), but the details are fresher and less schematic, and the proportions of the two theatres shown are slightly, but significantly, different. No buildings are named in the drawing, but the theatre building near the river must be the Beargarden or Hope (built 1614), and that further south the second Globe. Both are shown as circular buildings, but they differ in detail. The contract survives for the building of the Hope Theatre, which was designed for use as playhouse and bearpit; it was to be the same shape and size, 'of such large compasse, fforme, widenes, and height as the Plaie house called the Swan', which the drawing of Johannes de Witt (26) confirms was cylindrical. The contract specifies two external staircases to serve the three stories, one of which is clearly shown in the drawing, and a removable stage set on trestles. Perhaps the tiring house was also removable, but the syntax of the contract is ambiguous: 'a fitt and convenient Tyre house and a stage to be carryed or taken awaie, and to stand vppon tressells good, substanciall, and sufficient for the carryinge

and bearinge of such a stage'. There was to be a 'Heavens all over the saide stage, to be borne or carryed without any postes or supporters to be fixed or sett vppon the saide stage', the bottom storey was to contain two boxes suitable for gentlemen, and the builders were instructed too to 'make turned collumes vppon and over the stage'. It is not clear where these columns were, but if upon the stage, then they must have been ornamental, and removable like the stage. There is no indication as to how the 'Heavens' were to be built, and it may be presumed that Hollar's drawing does not show them. In *Bartholomew Fair*, performed at this theatre in October 1614, Ben Jonson suggests that the Hope was 'as durty as *Smithfield*, and as stinking every Whit', so that it may never have been a very attractive location for companies of actors. Although an allusion in Nicholas Goodman's account of Elizabeth Holland and her brothel in *Holland's Leaguer* (1632), signature F2ᵛ, implies that it was still used by players, 'though *wild beasts* and *Gladiators* did most possesse it', surviving records all refer to it as a house for bear-baiting and other forms of gaming and entertainment. Probably then, by the time Hollar drew it, the stage had been removed altogether, and the curious peak in the roof-line may represent the

29

'Heavens', or what was left of this superstructure; for this too may have been largely dismantled if the Hope was no longer used for acting and had become altogether what it is called in the 'Long View', namely the 'Beere bayting h[ouse]'.

South and east of the Beargarden is depicted the second Globe Theatre, erected in 1614 after the first Globe was destroyed by fire in 1613, on the foundations of the old theatre. According to John Stow's *Annals or a General Chronicle of England*, continued by Edmund Howes (1618), pp. 1003–4, the second Globe was 'new builded in farre fairer manner than before'. Hollar's drawing shows a circular building with two external stair turrets, and a row of windows corresponding roughly to the middle gallery level. The most distinctive feature is the large superstructure with twin gables projecting above the roof-line, and surmounted by a small cupola, tower or lantern. The purpose of this is not known, but as a visual detail it links interestingly with the projections that might be cupolas in the Utrecht view of London showing the theatre in about 1599 (5), and with the Visscher view, showing a version perhaps of the first Globe (10); all three playhouses were used by Shakespeare's company, the Lord Chamberlain's Men, or King's Men as they became under James I. The superstructure presumably provided an extensive cover over the stage, with a 'Heavens' above, but there is no further detailing, other than a horizontal line which might indicate a large beam, to help in interpreting this. The north stair-turret appears to carry a flagstaff, though in the drawing it looks more like a chimney. Further comment on this drawing leads inevitably to a comparison with the slightly different version etched in Hollar's 'Long View', and the discussion is continued in relation to this: see 21 below.

Chambers, *ES*, II 466ff
Hodges, *Globe Restored*, 109–11 (Pl. 5)
Hodges, *Second Globe*, 34–5, 46–7
Hosley, 176–7 (Pl. 12a)
Orrell, 1–31 (Pl. 2)
Schoenbaum, 90ff, 227
Shapiro, *SS* 2, 21–3 (Pls XI, XII)
Smith, 24 (Pl. 12)
Wickham, *EES* II, ii 71–8 (Hope)
Iolo Williams, 'Hollar: A Discovery', *The Connoisseur*, XCII (1933), 318–21

17

Wenceslaus Hollar, Preparatory Sketch for the 'Long View' (1638).

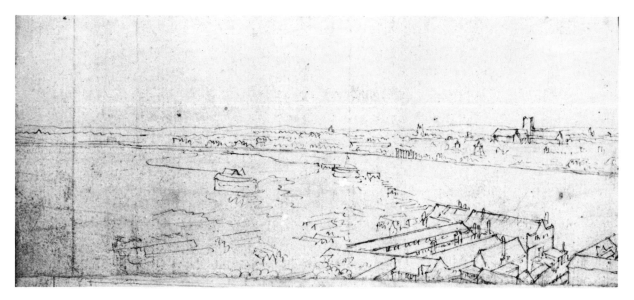

Another sketch by Hollar showing the Globe and Hope Theatres was reproduced in *Shakespeare Survey* 31 (1978). It is contained in a book of Hollar drawings compiled by the diarist John Evelyn, and is now in the John Rylands Library, Manchester (English MS 883, f. 24ᵛ). The drawing is not dated, but forms one half of a panorama of London dated 1638, the other part being in the Pepysian Library in Cambridge. It is a loose sketch, in pen and brown ink, measuring 3⅖ in. × 7⅗ in. (85 mm × 193 mm), and appears to be another preparatory drawing for the 'Long View' (21). Hollar's other preparatory sketch of Southwark (16) shows the area from Winchester House in the foreground to the Globe and Beargarden (Hope) in the middle distance carefully inked in over pencil in considerable detail, the area beyond being only vaguely indicated. The Rylands Library sketch gives as much weight to the background area north of the river as it does to the south bank, and its concern appears to be with the placing and relation of major buildings to one another in the general composition of the panorama. The angle of view is slightly different from that in the Yale sketch and the 'Long View', and the corner of the church tower of St Mary Overie (now Southwark Cathedral)

is shown to the right in the foreground, suggesting an imaginary viewpoint south of it. The Globe is shown prominently, but with little detail; the projecting double gable is again a notable feature, but there is no hint of a lantern or cupola above this. A line running along the wall of the theatre suggests that a row of windows there was clearly visible. The Globe is again drawn as a round building, with a hint of a peaked roof like that shown at the Beargarden in the Yale drawing and in the 'Long View'. No flagpole is shown, but the much more rudimentary sketch of the Beargarden shows a flag, confirming that this was a particularly noticeable feature here. Hollar gave no indication in this sketch of staircase turrets at either theatre building. The sketch probably shows the most obvious features of the theatres as they appeared to Hollar, but it offers no warrant for putting much weight on the details shown, or for drawing inferences from what is not shown.

Orrell, 1–31 (Pl. 4)
John Orrell, 'A New Hollar Panorama of London', *Burlington Magazine*, CXXIV (1982), 501–2 (Pls 25, 27)
Graham Parry, 'A New View of Bankside', *SS*, 31 (1978), 139–40 (Pl. 1A)

18

John Webb, View of London, in a background design for William D'Avenant's masque
Britannia Triumphans (1638).

This rough sketch of the city from a viewpoint east of London Bridge, measuring 8 $\frac{3}{16}$ in. $\times$ 12 $\frac{7}{16}$ in. (211 mm $\times$ 316 mm), seems to have been drawn from sight. Although many details are omitted or vaguely indicated, this sketch is unlike previous views, recording correctly the fact that the roof-line of the choir of St Mary Overie (now Southwark Cathedral) is higher than that of the nave. The theatre shown as a round building with a superstructure of 'huts' surmounted by a flagpole, opposite the west end of St Paul's Cathedral, is probably the Globe. This is how it would have appeared in relation to St Paul's from a point south and slightly east of the bridge, and it might well have largely or wholly masked the Beargarden, which, from this angle, stood directly behind it. Further to the west is another building of indeterminate shape with a flagpole rising from it. It has no superstructure, and is shown with a row of dots which may indicate windows, and a rough, irregular roof-line. This must be the Swan, and is evidence that this theatre was still stand-ing in 1637 or 1638 when John Webb made this sketch. By 1632 this playhouse was said to have 'fallen to decay, and like a dying *Swanne*, hanging downe her head, seemed to sing her own dirge' (*Holland's Leaguer*, 1632, signature F2^{r}); possibly the irregular roof-line indicates something of that 'decay'. Two other buildings are prominently shown; one, half-way between the theatres and apparently to the north of them, or closer to the river bank, has not been identified, and seems to be wrongly sited to correspond to the square building with balconies shown in the *Civitas Londini* panorama of 1600, and the Merian view of 1638 (see 6 and 15). The tower shown to the south-east of the Globe probably indicates St George's Church, Southwark.

Chambers, *ES*, II 414
Hosley, 137ff
Orgel and Strong, II 670–1 (Pl. 335)
Shapiro, *SS* 1, 33 (Pl. XIVA)
Smith, 25 (Pls 14, 15)
Wickham, *EES* II, ii 68–71

19

Inigo Jones, View of London, in an alternative design for William D'Avenant's masque *Britannia Triumphans* (1638).

This alternative sketch, measuring $10\frac{3}{4}$ in. $\times$ $14\frac{1}{4}$ in. (273 mm $\times$ 362 mm), was made from a different viewpoint, much further west, so that the west face of the transept of St Paul's Cathedral is visible, and much closer to the river. The consequent narrowing of the field of view effectively excludes all but one of the theatres, and this must be the Swan, since this was the most westerly, and stood more or less opposite St Paul's. Although more detail is shown in this sketch, the theatre is only roughly indicated as a circular building with a large flag projecting from it. It also appears to have a projection that might be a chimney on the right, but otherwise the roof-line is unbroken, and, as in the other sketch, no superstructure is seen. It appears to be lower in height than the surrounding houses; in Webb's version (18) the Swan stands in height well above the surrounding buildings, and has dots which may be intended to suggest windows. The differences between the sketches cannot be taken as having much significance, since Inigo Jones was designing a recognisable panoramic view of the city for the spectators at a masque, and had no need to do more than indicate the major landmarks. The two sketches, however, appear to establish that the Swan, a circular building, was still standing in 1637, and perhaps, if the presence of a flag is to be taken seriously, was still in use as a playhouse, even though it was said to have 'fallen to decay' in 1632 (see 18 above).

Chambers, *ES*, II 414
Hosley, 137ff (Fig. 9)
Orgel and Strong, II 668–9 (Pl. 334)
John Peacock, 'Inigo Jones's Stage Architecture and its Sources', *Art Bulletin*, LXIV (1982), 195–216, especially p. 206
Shapiro, *SS* 1, 33 (Pl. XIVB)
Smith, 25 (Pl. 15)
Wickham, *EES* II, ii 68–71

20

Sir Richard Baker, *A Chronicle of the Kings of England* (1643).

This folio has an engraved title-page which is divided into panels. In the centre is a cartouche containing the title, with a portrait of the author beneath this, and above it a portrait of Charles I. At the top on the left is a panorama of St Albans ('Verulam'), and on the right one of Lincoln; below these are figures of a Roman (on the left), and a Saxon (on the right); next come an oval panorama of London (on the left), and York (on the right), and below these are figures respectively of a Dane and a Norman. The tiny panorama of London is contained in an oval measuring $1\frac{1}{2}$ in. × 2 in. (38 mm × 51 mm). It shows two theatres, both of them round, with flags flying. The Globe, the one nearer the viewer, appears to have two stories, the lower one of a greater diameter than the upper, and both have rows of dots suggesting windows. The theatre nearer the river bank, which should be the Beargarden or Hope, is even more vaguely indicated, as a multi-sided, or possibly square building. A comparison with the Hondius engraving of 1610 (see 8 above) shows that this little panorama is derived from the Hondius view, and as a debased derivative of that it has no value whatever as pictorial evidence.

Hind, III 141
Rhodes, 6 (Pl. 27)
Scouloudi, 23–4

21

Wenceslaus Hollar, 'Long View' of London from Southwark (1647).

This fine large panorama of London extends across seven sheets of paper, each section of the view measuring 15¼ in. × 18 in. (387 mm × 457 mm). The two westernmost sections represent two theatre buildings, incorrectly labelled – the Globe, labelled 'Beere bayting h', and the Hope, or Beargarden, labelled 'The Globe'. The theatres are not named in Hollar's preparatory drawings for the 'Long View' (16 and 17 above), and the wrong identification in the etching is probably an accidental consequence of the production of the etching in Antwerp in 1647. Hollar had left England in 1644, and based his 'Long View' on drawings made in London between 1636 and 1644. It probably represents the city much as it was at the time he left it, for he incorporated the alterations to the south transept of St Paul's Cathedral completed by Inigo Jones in 1642. By this time the Swan Theatre had apparently been demolished after falling into decay (see 18 above), but the Hope, or Beargarden, remained in use until 1656, primarily as a theatre for variety shows, bear- and bull-baiting (see 16 above).

In the etching the theatres appear noticeably more squat in relation to the houses around them than in the more detailed of Hollar's two drawings (16). The appearance of the Beargarden is not notably different in other respects, except for the large flagpole projecting from inside it (see also Claude de Jongh's drawing, 12 above). The representation of the Globe, however, shows significant differences of detail. The structure surmounted by twin gables and projecting into the arena of the theatre is markedly larger in relation to the whole, and a diagrammatic projection shows that it would have extended more than half-way across the arena. Even in the drawing, which is likely to be more reliable, the gabled cover over the stage would have extended almost to the centre-line (Hodges, *Shakespeare's Second Globe*, pp. 38–9), or well over 30 ft into an arena perhaps 72 ft in diameter. The size of this cover over a stage oriented to the north-east lends support to the argument of R. B. Graves ('Shakespeare's Outdoor Stage Lighting', pp. 243–6) that such large canopies, a developing feature of the public theatres after Henslowe's modifications to the Rose in the 1590s, related to a desire on the part of the players to achieve an evenly distributed light overall. The tower, cupola or lantern surmounting this structure is right at the back of it in the etching, and more towards the centre in the drawing. The gable ends are hatched in the etching, and have a faint suggestion of vertical beams, whereas the drawing shows merely what might be a horizontal beam. In *Shakespeare's Second Globe*, pp. 55ff, Hodges speculates that the second Globe was built with no posts on stage, and that the superstructure was 'simply a great open timber

roof, the front of which was covered across with a screen-wall to keep out wind and weather', but there is no evidence for this apart from Hollar's drawing. The analogy he draws with the Hope, where the Heavens were 'to be borne or carried without any posts or supporters to be fixed or set upon the said stage', is suspect because the Hope was designed to serve both as a playhouse and a bull- and bear-baiting house, and it had a removable stage. In the drawing the theatre has what looks like a flagpole, which is missing from the etching. Finally, the relation of the Globe to the houses around it is different in the etching, in which a house masks most of the easterly stair-turret, and obscures the windows between this and the northerly turret, which is clearly depicted in the drawing, but only vaguely suggested in the etching.

The etching was worked up later from drawings made in London, and it has now been established that Hollar drew his view from the tower of St Saviour's Church in Southwark (formerly known generally as St Mary Overie, and now Southwark Cathedral), on which is marked a *statio prospectiva* in the panorama of London headed 'CIVITAS LONDINI' (1600; see 6 above). Hollar seems to have used a perspective glass or drawing frame which enabled him to achieve a remarkable accuracy in representing buildings and their relation to one another. From known measurements and orientations it has proved possible to establish the approximate size and height of the Globe and Hope Theatres; John Orrell calculates that the Globe was about 102 ft wide, and 31 ft high to the eaves, and the Hope also had a diameter of about 100 ft, and was roughly 32 ft high to the eaves. (In his searching review of *Shakespeare's Second Globe* in 1975, Richard Hosley argued that the playhouse frame, like that of the Fortune Theatre, was likely to be 34 ft high, and that Hollar was inaccurate in representing it.) The Hope looks smaller in the drawing, but stood some distance further north and west from the viewing-point. An interesting feature of both buildings is that the stages appear to have faced north-east, perhaps to shield the actors on the stage, and the highest-paying spectators, from the heat and glare of the westering sun during afternoon performances in spring, summer and autumn; this is the best explanation yet offered for the orientation of these stages, but it might be argued that an arrangement ensuring that they were shaded in summer would also make them too dark in the depths of winter, when daily performances took place, according to Henslowe's Diary. R. B. Graves, however, in the fullest study yet made of the implications of stage-orientation in the public theatres, suggests that these provided 'a well shaded stage with neither artificial light for general illumination nor the extreme contrasts of light and dark due to direct sunlight' ('Shakespeare's Outdoor Stage Lighting', p. 247), and the actors sought an even, natural, subdued light in which to perform, far different from the glare and spotlights of modern theatres.

Bentley, *JCS*, VI 212–14, 251–2

Chambers, *ES*, II 466ff

R. B. Graves, 'Orientation of the Elizabethan Stage', *TN*, XXXIV (1980), 126–7

R. B. Graves, 'Shakespeare's Outdoor Stage Lighting', *Shakespeare Studies*, XIII (1980), 235–50

Gurr, 126 (Pl. 22)

Hodges, *Globe Restored*, 109 (Pl. 4)

Hodges, *Second Globe*, 11–35, 46–7

Hosley, 176–7 (Pl. 12b)

Richard Hosley, 'The Second Globe', *TN*, XXIX (1975), 140–5

Leslie Hotson, *Shakespeare's Wooden O* (1960), pp. 258–79, 304–9

Leacroft, 38–9, 44, 47 (Fig. 26)

Orrell, 1–31, 152–7 (Pls 6–12)

John Orrell, *Shakespeare Newsletter*, XXIX (May 1979), 20

Graham Parry, *Hollar's England: a mid-seventeenth-century view* (Salisbury, 1980), Pl. 60

Schoenbaum, 90–5, 227

Scouloudi, *Panoramic Views of London* (1953), 60–3

Shapiro, *SS* 1, 34–5; *SS* 2, 21–3

Wickham, *EES* II, i 304–5, ii 71–8, 248 (Pl. XXVI)

Iolo Williams, 'Hollar: A Discovery', *The Connoisseur*, XCII (1933), 320

Alan B. Young, 'Elizabethan Stage: "That Glory to the Sober West" ', *TN*, XXXIII (1979), 80–5

22

Wenceslaus Hollar, 'London and Old St Paul's from the Thames'.

This drawing (British Museum Print Room 1882–8–12489) affords a glimpse of the Blackfriars Theatre, used by the King's Men after 1608. The size of this theatre, 66 × 46 feet, and its rough location are known, since it was converted from part of the parliament chamber in the upper frater of what had been the monastery of Blackfriars. The large chamber, 'created in the first instance to house great assemblies' (Smith, p. 100), measured about 100 × 46 feet internally, according to a survey of 1548; parliament met there under Henry VIII in 1523, and the divorce proceedings against Katherine of Aragon took place there in 1529. Our knowledge of what happened to the buildings in the next century depends upon verbal accounts in deeds and indentures, notably Sir William More's deed whereby he sold the property to James Burbage in 1596. These verbal descriptions are open to varying interpretations, and have led to different reconstructions of the plans and internal arrangements of the rooms by Chambers, Smith, Hosley and Wickham. Indeed, at this point speculation takes over, because in the absence of diagrams it is not possible to interpret what information survives about subdivisions and alterations known to have been made, while modifications, demolitions, and new constructions may have been effected of which no record is left. In 1596 Burbage acquired 'seven great upper rooms as they are now divided ... sometimes being one great and entire room' (Bentley, *JCS*, VI.5); at the north end was a little buttery, with two upper rooms occupied by Charles Bradshaw, and two rooms or lofts in the possession of Edward Merry, 'the one of them lying and being above or over the said two upper rooms or chambers' which Bradshaw had, and also a further 'room or garret' above the rooms or lofts kept by Merry. In addition, there were various lodgings with a kitchen known as the middle rooms, 'more or less lying and being directly under part of' the seven great upper rooms (Malone Society *Collections*, II.1.61). This suggests a maze of vertical subdivisions, in addition to the horizontal division of the great chamber into seven rooms. A lawsuit of 1612 also refers to 'a certain room called the Schoolhouse, and a certain chamber over the same', devised by Richard Burbage, and separate from the great hall (Wickham, II.ii.133).

It would seem that James Burbage converted two thirds of the parliament chamber on the upper floor, not the paved hall underneath, into a theatre, since there is evidence that the audience had to descend stairs to reach the street (Bentley, *JCS*, VI.5–6). The height of the theatre is not known, but the outer walls were of stone, and it had a vaulted roof. Beyond this, in effect there is little evidence about the way in which Burbage adapted the building. The parliament chamber appears to have been wider than the old buttery to the north of it, perhaps by as much as sixteen feet, and Hosley assumed that these buildings must have had different roof heights (*Revels*, p. 201, and cf. Wickham, p. 134), but there is no reliable external evidence, apart from that provided by Hollar's drawings. Hosley followed Hodges, p. 109, in supposing that the long roofline visible in Hollar's 'Long View' to the west of Baynard's Castle, and close to the river, represents Blackfriars. They were misled by the name 'Blackfreyars' in Hollar's print, which is placed too far to the west, against Bridewell dock at the mouth of the Fleet ditch; Blackfriars stairs and lane led north from the Thames some distance east of the Fleet ditch. In other words, the building they identified as Blackfriars is too far west, the wrong side of the Fleet ditch, and too close to the river to be the parliament chamber, and it must be the roof of Bridewell. John Orrell has shown this by drawing attention to a sketch by Wenceslaus Hollar known as 'London and Old Saint Paul's from the Thames'.

This drawing, in pen and brown ink, presents a view down river from Durham House, and is of uncertain date. In Orrell's view, Hollar was deliberately fixing the location of each spire or tower, and was 'tied to the facts of the landscape before him' (p. 17). Perhaps so, but the sketch has the appearance of being casual and impressionistic in much of its drawing, and indeed, its size, roughly $3\frac{1}{2}$ in. × $11\frac{1}{2}$ in. (88 × 294 mm), would hardly permit any fine rendering of particulars. Hollar seems to have gone twice over some outlines to make them bolder, and his sketch shows two buildings with long rooflines below the nave and crossing of St Paul's Cathedral. The lower of these, the one closer to the river, must be Bridewell, and the higher one, further from the river bank, corresponds in location roughly to the upper frater of Blackfriars, the site of the playhouse. This shows as a long unbroken roofline running north to south, with a gable visible at the south end. The walls of the west face are blank towards the south end of the building, except for dots and a line of uncertain meaning, but Hollar picked out a feature at the north end that caught his eye. Here are shown four bays, each marked by a window surmounted by a shallow arch, and with vertical dividers between the bays. These appear to represent an extension to the west of the building, for they terminate about a third of the distance along the roofline in a tall, blank gable, which seems intended to mark the end of the extension. Is this where Bradshaw lived? Or might it be Burbage's schoolhouse? Verbal records unfortunately do not help, so that such questions cannot be answered.

This identification of Blackfriars from the west would suggest that it was prominent enough to be seen from the east in Hollar's 'Long View' of London as viewed from the tower of St Saviour's church. If so, it would lie behind and slightly to the north of Baynard's Castle, and to the east of St Bride's church, the tower of which, with its four pinnacles at the corners, stands high above surrounding properties in Hollar's perspective. There indeed can be seen a substantial gabled roof with two projections from the centre-line of the gabled roof which could be chimneys or lanterns. Part of the gable at the south end can also be seen. If this is the east side of the building outlined from the west in the sketch, then the relation between the two faces is not easy to determine, but the 'Long View', as a finished drawing, provides a much fuller record than the sketch, and presumably renders in better detail what Hollar actually saw. At the same time, caution is necessary about claiming too much for Hollar's accuracy either in locating buildings or the rendering of details. What can be said is that the Blackfriars theatre occupied part of a large and prominent building, with a lofty roofline, and was located in the southern part of Blackfriars precinct. The large building shown in Hollar's 'Long View' fits best what is known about it, and lies roughly in the right situation, as viewed from St Saviour's, between St Bride's tower to the west, and the low tower of St Ann's, Blackfriars, to the north. The visual evidence provided by these two drawings does not greatly extend our knowledge, but the verbal accounts of the Blackfriars complex need to be reassessed in the light of them, and conjectural reconstructions like those of Wickham (p. 134) and Hosley ('A Reconstruction', p. 79) cannot easily be squared with what the drawings show.

Bentley, *JCS*, VI 4–7
Chambers, *ES*, II 475–515
Collections Vol. II Part 1 (Malone Society Reprints, 1914 for 1913)
Hodges, *Globe Restored*, 109
Hosley, 197–226
Richard Hosley, 'A Reconstruction of the Second Blackfriars', *Elizabethan Theatre*, ed. David Galloway (1969), 74–88
Orrell, 16–19
Irwin Smith, *Shakespeare's Blackfriars Playhouse* (New York, 1964)
Wickham, *EES* II, ii 123–38

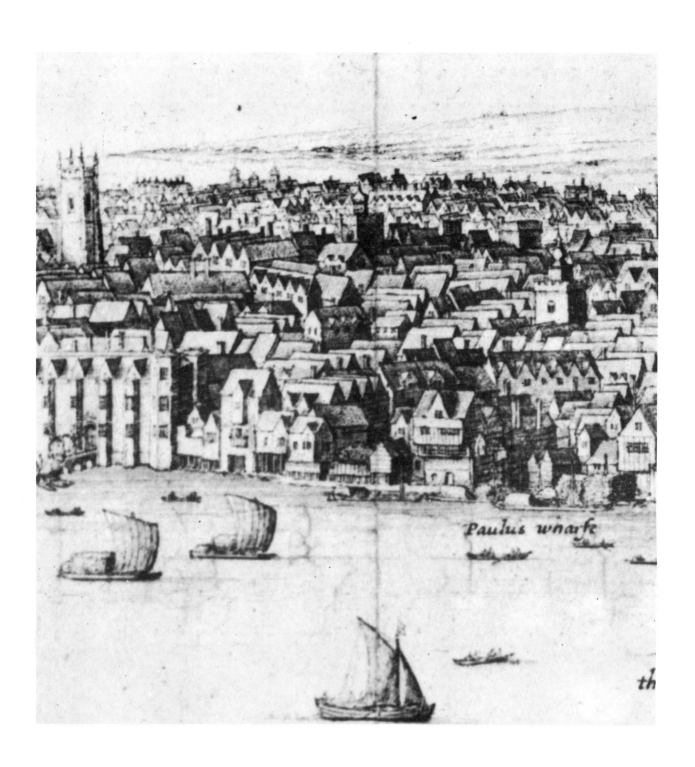

Paulus wharfe

th

B
Drawings, plans and vignettes
relating to the stage

23

John Scottowe, Drawing of Richard Tarlton (?1588).

The picture here set down
within this letter. T:
A right doth shew the formea
of Tharlton vnto the shap

When hee in pleasaunt wise,
the Counterfet expreste
of Clowne in cote of russet ·
and sturtups in ý reste. hew.

Whoe merry many made,
when he appeard in sight.
The graue and wise as well as
at him did take delight. rude,

The partie nowe is gone,
and closlie clad in claye,
Of all the Jesters in the lande
he bare the praise awaie.

Now hath he plaid his pte,
and sure he is of this.
If he in Christe did dieto liue
with him in lasting blis.

Harleian MS 3885, f. 19, in the British Library, contains an elegy on the death of the famous clown Richard Tarlton, who was the leading comedian of the Queen's Company from its founding in 1583 until his death in 1588. He had great celebrity in his time and was long remembered, as, for example, in the Induction to Ben Jonson's *Bartholomew Fair* (1614). He wrote plays, one of which, *The Seven Deadly Sins*, was described by Gabiel Harvey in 1592 as 'famous', and composed jigs, but was known affectionately by his facility as a jester, for which he found favour with Queen Elizabeth. He seems to have been known by his appearance, and may have dressed as a jester not only to perform at court, but for his performances in jigs and perhaps in plays. So the volume of tales published after his death as *Tarlton's News out of Purgatory* (1590) describes him as 'attired in russet, with a buttond cap on his head, a great bag by his side, and a strong bat in his hand'. A little later, in 1592, Henry Chettle recalled him in *Kind-Heart's Dream* 'by his sute of russet, his buttond cap, his taber, his standing on the toe and other tricks'. *Tarlton's Jests* (transferred from one publisher to another in the Stationer's Register in 1609, but known only from an edition of 1638) further describes him as having a squint and a flat nose. This has a woodcut on the title-page based upon the drawing in Harleian MS 3885, which shows him with a flat nose, playing on a tabor and pipe, wearing a cap, and with a large bag at his side. He is clothed in a 'suit of russet', and is shown as short, broad-faced, sturdy, and with curly hair, wearing a moustache and short pointed beard. The drawing is done in ink within an elaborate scroll formed from the upright of the letter 'T', which is larger than the five stanzas of verse accompanying it. These claim that the drawing shows him as he was

> When he in pleasant wise
> the Counterfet expreste
> of Clowne with cote of russet hewe
> and sturtups with the reste.

The last line refers to the 'startups' Tarlton wears in the drawing, rough leather shoes reaching to the ankles or above, and worn by rustics or clowns.

Scottowe's drawing is related to a similar but larger drawing stuck in an album called *Heads in Taille-Douce* in the Pepys Library, Magdalene College, Cambridge, catalogue reference PL 2980/311b. This simplifies the figure in some details, showing, for example, no pin through the top of the purse at Tarlton's girdle, and no sign of a garment underneath his jerkin, and it appears to be derivative from the Scottowe drawing.

C. R. Baskervill, *The Elizabethan Jig* (1929, reprinted New York, 1965), pp. 95–105

Chambers, *ES*, II 342–5; III 496–7; IV 243

Gurr, 84–7 (Pl. 12)

Alexander Leggatt, *The Revels History of Drama in English Volume III 1576–1613* (1975), pp. 99–101 (Pl. 7)

Linthicum, 258–9

45

24

Drawing, possibly of a stage, in a letter from Philip Henslowe to Edward Alleyn (?1593).

In September 1593, when Edward Alleyn was touring in the provinces with Lord Strange's Men, Philip Henslowe wrote to him from London, supplying him with news of his family and the city. One of these letters, dated 28 September 1593, consists of a sheet folded once to make four pages. The first two pages are occupied by the letter; the last page bears the address, and also sketches of four heads, all imitated from one another, and a full-length figure of an old man leaning on a staff and holding out his hand. The third page is blank except for the sketch reproduced here, which measures $3\frac{1}{2}$ in. $\times 5\frac{3}{4}$ in. (89 mm $\times$ 146 mm), and the phrase 'A Imbroydered carpett' written in Henslowe's hand, and in a darker ink, to the left of it. It is not possible to determine who made the sketch, or when it was made. Alleyn must have brought the letter back to London with him when he returned there after the abatement of the plague. Henslowe's note about the carpet may relate to some alterations in Alleyn's rooms referred to in the letter. It seems likely that this note, and the drawing, were made soon after their reunion, perhaps in 1593 or 1594, and that the sketch was drawn by one of them – probably Henslowe, who scrawled phrases and made a sketch of a head on another surviving letter to Alleyn written in 1598.

The drawing reproduced may simply be a doodle, and if it does relate to the theatre, it is not at all clear what it is intended to represent. The two pillars might suggest the pillars supporting a canopy over the stage, such as the Swan and Fortune Theatres possessed (see 26). The lines joining the tops of the columns vaguely suggest a roof there, although the crudeness of the sketch makes the columns appear to be free-standing. The long rectangle at the bottom could be a flat or vertical surface. Above this are two tiers of steps or seats turning in to flank steps leading back from the centre. These end in a row of faint vertical lines, and some still fainter horizontal lines through and above these seem intended to close off the perspective with a hint of a solid background. Three heavy lines superimposed across the bottom of the central steps, and ending in tiny circles or open dots, suggest a barrier of some kind. If the sketch relates to the stage, the point of view remains ambiguous; it could suggest a view of the stage from the auditorium, or a view of the theatre from the stage.

In an ingenious attempt to make better sense of this sketch, Neil Carson argues that it is an illustration of an entrance to the galleries from the yard of a public theatre, perhaps the Globe, since this was used as a model for the Fortune, built for Henslowe and Alleyn in 1600. The columns would then be main posts supporting the gallery and running from the foundation of the theatre to the floor of the second gallery, while the central stairs would give access to seats, and also provide extra seating at crowded performances. The whole argument is, of course, speculative, and further depends upon dating the drawing at a time when Henslowe and Alleyn were planning for the Fortune Theatre.

Neil Carson, 'The Staircases of the Frame: New Light on the Structure of the Globe?', *SS*, 29 (1976), 127–32
R. A. Foakes and R. T. Rickert, 'An Elizabethan Stage Drawing?', *SS*, 13 (1960), 111–12
Foakes and Rickert, *HD*, 281–2
R. A. Foakes, ed., *The Henslowe Papers* (2 vols, 1977), II 14 (reproduces the whole document, with all the drawings on it, in facsimile)
W. W. Greg, *Henslowe Papers* (1907), p. 47
Gurr, 127 (Pl. 21)
Rhodes, 181–2 (Pl. 28)

25

Henry Peacham (?), Drawing of a scene from William Shakespeare's *Titus Andronicus*
(?1595).

This drawing is on the second page of a sheet of paper folded once to give four pages, which is now among the manuscripts in the library of the Marquess of Bath at Longleat House, Wiltshire (Harley Papers, Vol. I, f. 159ᵛ). The drawing runs across the top of the page, and a line underneath separates it from a passage of forty lines from *Titus Andronicus*, written out very neatly in a hand that mixes secretary and italic forms. These lines are drawn partly from Act I, Scene i, partly from Act V, Scene i (Aaron's speech), and end with a speech-heading for a character who does not speak in the play. In the lower left-hand margin is the signature 'Henricus Peacham', in an italic hand, and beneath it a date which is difficult to interpret, 'Anno mᵒ qᵒ g qᵗᵒ'. This begins easily enough as the year one thousand (millesimo), five hundred (quingentesimo), and ends with five (quinto), but the third letter, which looks like 'g', has not been explained. E. K. Chambers read it as '9', and the date as '1595', but he was probably influenced by the endorsement which is written on the opposite page, 'Henrye Peachams Hande *1595*'. This is in a different hand altogether, and is probably to be discounted as a forgery by John Payne Collier made in the nineteenth century.

There are thus four separate elements to consider: the drawing, the passage of text drawn from the play, the signature and date which may be in the same hand as the text, and the endorsement, which is certainly in a different hand. *Titus Andronicus* was published in 1594; this first Quarto was followed by others in 1600 (Q2) and 1611 (Q3), and it was subsequently included in the First Folio of Shakespeare's plays in 1623 (F). The passage of text written beneath the drawing includes the line, 'Set fire on barnes and haystackes in the night' (V.i.133); Q1 has 'haystalkes', which was changed to 'haystakes' in Q2 and Q3, and 'haystackes' in F. This, and other variants, led Dover Wilson to think that this passage could have been taken from the Folio rather than Q1, but we cannot be certain about this. The fact that the scribe took speeches from Act I and Act V and cobbled them together suggests further that he was trying, not very successfully, to discover what part of

the action of the play the drawing illustrates. In fact, he got it wrong. The passage begins at I.i.104, with the addition of an invented stage direction, 'Enter Tamora pleadinge for her sonnes going to execution'; here Tamora is on stage with her three sons (Alarbus, Demetrius and Chiron) as prisoners of Titus, who has four of his sons on stage. Titus hands over Tamora's eldest son Alarbus to be 'sacrificed', and Tamora pleads for his life in the first speech. After this, in the play, the four sons of Titus march Alarbus off stage to kill him, and the drawing may be intended to illustrate the text at this point (I.i.129). Here Titus has with him the two men who brought on a coffin in the scene, or two soldiers, while Tamora is now accompanied by Aaron the Moor and two sons who, like her, are kneeling to plead for Alarbus's life. This is the scene in the drawing, but the scribe seems to have wanted to provide some speech to characterise Aaron, and altered Titus's response to Tamora's pleading so as to forge a link with Aaron's speech at V.i.125, where Aaron is prisoner of Lucius, and is speaking from a ladder, which he has been forced to climb.

The scribe may have been puzzled by the stance of Aaron, who holds a drawn sword in his left hand, for this is not appropriate to either scene, since Aaron as a servant of Tamora, his 'imperial mistress' (II.i.13), is presumably included with her among the prisoners of Titus in I.i, while in V.i, as noted, he is again a prisoner, this time taken captive by Lucius. Whatever the explanation for his choice of speeches to set down, it looks as though the text has no direct relation to the drawing, and could have been added later, and by another hand. If the date below the signature is 1595, then it can hardly relate to the passage of text; its position, however, establishes a spatial relation, which casts doubt on the interpretation of the curious notation of the year. In any case, there is no necessary connection between the text with the signature and date, on the one hand, and the drawing on the other. Henry Peacham graduated from Cambridge in 1595 and is thought to have been born about 1576; he published a treatise on art, *Graphice*, in 1606, and is best

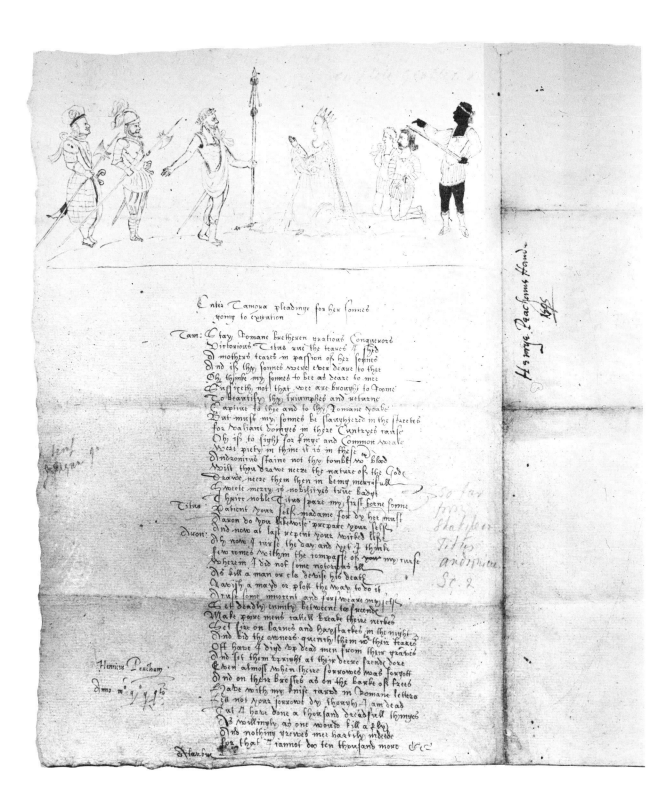

Enter Tamora pleadinge for her sonnes
goinge to execution

Tam: Stay Romane bretheren gratious Conquerors
Victorious Titus rue the teares I shed
A mothers teares in passion of her sonne
And if thy sonnes were ever deare to thee
Oh thinke my sonnes to bee as deare to mee
Sufficeth not that wee are brought to Roome
To beautify thy triumphes and returne
Captive to thee and to thy Romane yoake
But must my sonnes be slaughtered in the streetes
For valiant doynges in there Cuntryes cause
Oh if to fight for kinge and Common weale
Weare piety in thine it is in these
Andronicus staine not thy tombe w. blood
Wilt thou drawe neere the nature of the Gods
Drawe neere them then in being mercifull
Sweete mercy is nobilityes true badge

Titus   Thrice noble Titus spare my first borne sonne
Patient your selfe madame for dy hee must
Aron do you likewise prepare your selfe

Aron   And now at last repent your wicked life

Oh now I curse the day and yet I thinke
Few comes withinn the compasse of my curse
Wherein I did not some notorious ill
As kill a man or els devise his death
Ravish a mayd or plott the way to do it
Accuse some innocent and forsweare my selfe
Set deadly enmity betweene too freends
Make poore mens cattell breake theire neckes
Set fire on barnes and haystackes in the night
And bid the owners quench them w. their teares
Oft have I digd vp dead men from their graves
And set them vprighte at their deere frends doore
Even almost when theire sorrowes was forgott
And on their breastes as on the barke of trees
Have with my knife carved in Romane letters
Lett not your sorrowe dy though I am dead
Tut I have done a thousand dreadfull thinges
As willingly as one would kill a fly
And nothing greves mee hartily indeede
But that I cannot doo ten thousand more &c.

Alarbus

Henricus Peacham

so far
this
Statfiler
Titus
Andronicu
Sc. 2

Henrye Peachams Hand

known as the author of *The Compleat Gentleman* (1622), in which he describes himself as addicted from childhood to drawing the faces of people. He could well, therefore, be the artist who made the drawing, but various puzzling questions about it, and its connections with the writing on the manuscript, remain insoluble.

It remains to consider the drawing. Beginning on the left there are first represented two soldiers, each trailing a halberd, one with the blade pointing down, and one with the blade pointing up. They are in different costumes; the one on the left wears long baggy trousers caught at the ankles, a large hat with a feather at the side, and carries a scimitar, or curved sword, slung in a baldrick worn over the right shoulder. The general effect may have been designed to suggest an eastern costume, Turkish or Persian perhaps. The second soldier appears to be further away than the one on the extreme left but trails a halberd in front of this one, so that the perspective is unclear. He wears breeches, what may be a helmet with plumes at the side, a breastplate and shoulder armour, and a sword hung perhaps on a belt. This suggests a more conventional Elizabethan costume. In front of him stands Titus, 'bound with laurel boughs' (I.i.74), wearing a tunic, toga and sandals, and also with a sword at his side. In his left hand he holds a ceremonial staff or spear, perhaps to mark Titus's command as general, or perhaps anticipating his line, 'Give me a staff of honour for mine age' (I.i.198). His right arm is swept back, as if pointing off stage, where perhaps Titus's two sons have taken off Alarbus (I.i.129). Confronting him is the kneeling figure of Tamora, wearing a crown as Queen of the Goths, a loose robe with elaborately decorated sleeves, and what may be a train or cape falling from her shoulders.

Behind her kneel two young men, one fair, one dark-haired and bearded: they both wear tunics, and one has a sash or baldrick across the right shoulder. The dark-haired one has his wrists tied in front, and the other may be presumed to have his hands tied behind his back. They carry no arms, their heads are bare, and they are evidently prisoners and supplicants. On the extreme right, and nearer the spectator, stands a black-skinned figure also dressed in tunic and sandals, and wearing a band tied round his forehead. His right arm is outstretched, with a finger pointing ambiguously, but probably at the kneeling youths; in his left hand he carries a drawn sword, and appears to be indicating that he is ready to use it on them. Nothing is shown apart from the seven figures, and a vague suggestion of a surface on which they kneel or stand.

It has been claimed that the artist 'depicts, without doubt, what he actually saw at a performance of the play' (J. Dover Wilson, *Shakespeare Survey* 1, p. 20), but this is to overlook certain puzzling features of the drawing. It appears to represent the tableau at I.i.130, with Tamora pleading for Alarbus, who has just been taken off stage, but this is a crowd scene, and the stage direction at I.i.69 requires 'as many as can be' to be present on stage. In addition, the central feature of this scene is the 'coffin covered with black' borne in by two men; this is supposed to contain the bodies of dead sons of Titus slain by the Goths, and it is in retribution for them that Alarbus is to be killed. Later in the scene, after the execution of Alarbus, the coffin is ceremoniously placed in 'the tomb' (lowered through a trap?) containing other dead sons of Titus. Neither the crowd on stage, nor the men who carry in the black-draped coffin, nor the coffin itself, the centrepiece of the scene, are shown in the drawing. Moreover, the black figure on the right does not have the bearing of a prisoner, but looks more like an executioner.

Perhaps all this helps to explain the scribe's choice of speeches set down as a gloss on the drawing; he could have searched the play in vain looking for a scene which fits the drawing exactly, and perhaps picked on Aaron's speech from Act V to illustrate the cruel Moor suggested by the figure brandishing a sword in the drawing. There is, in fact, no reason to suppose this drawing was made at a staging of the play; it is more likely that it was drawn from recollection afterwards, possibly bringing together into a group separate sketches of individual actors made when watching a performance. The tableau at I.i.129 is a striking moment in the opening scene, but Aaron is a prisoner here, and has no speaking part, so it is inconceivable that he could have appeared as he does in the drawing. Tamora is pleading, as in the speech the scribe chose (I.i.104), but the absence of Alarbus and two of Titus's sons points to the moment at I.i.130 where Tamora is no longer pleading but crying, 'O cruel, irreligious piety', to which her son Demetrius adds, 'madam, stand resolv'd'. In other words, the drawing does not fit any point in the action, and probably was not drawn from the life.

At the same time, it may well relate to an actual performance, and if it belongs to 1595, then it refers to an early staging of *Titus Andronicus*, though, as John Munro suggests (*TLS*, 1949), it needs to be understood in relation to a tradition of multiple representation: in its combination of episodes from Act I and Act V, and sketching of all the figures in profile, the drawing conforms to the same convention as the woodcuts illustrating the title-pages of such plays as *The Spanish Tragedy* (1615), *A Maidenhead Well Lost* (1634), and *The Witch of Edmonton* (1658), nos. 44, 61 and 64 below. The most striking aspect of the group shown is the variety of costume, Goths dressed like Romans, Titus as an ancient Roman, but his two sons or followers in variations of contemporary costume of the Tudor period, and carrying halberds, a Tudor weapon first used in the reign of Henry VII. Tamora wears a loose gown with elaborate puffed and embroidered sleeves, which again belongs to the sixteenth century rather than to ancient Rome. This medley of costumes suggests a casual attitude towards both historical accuracy and consistency. Dover Wilson thought the drawing shows that 'the lower classes' were costumed in contemporary dress, and an attempt was made 'to attain accuracy in the attire worn by patricians'. There is no reason to accept such an interpretation; the two soldiers on the left may be Titus's sons and 'patricians'. In any case, Casca's reference to Caesar's 'doublet' in *Julius Caesar* shows that Shakespeare did not think historically in relation to costume. The ballad on *Titus Andronicus* entered in the Stationers Register on the same day as the play, 6 February 1594, is illustrated by a woodcut showing a procession of horsemen dressed in Elizabethan costume, and a guard holding a halberd. One other feature is the representation of Aaron as black, which may show what was usually supposed to be the colour of a Moor, and hence have a bearing on Othello, and the presentation of other such figures in the drama of the period.

Chambers, *WS*, I 313
E. K. Chambers, 'The First Illustration to Shakespeare', *The Library*, 4th Series, V (1925), 327–9
Gurr, 182–3 (Pl. 32)
Hodges, *Globe Restored*, 130–1 (Pl. 45)
Eldred Jones, *Othello's Countrymen* (1965), pp. 123–4 (Pl. 3)
Leacroft, 30–1 (Fig. 21)
John Munro, *TLS*, 10 June 1949 and 1 July 1949; and J. Dover Wilson, 24 June 1949
Rhodes, 182 (Pl. 29)
Schoenbaum, 122–3
Shakespeare's England, II 527, 531
Smith, 145 (Pl. 24)
Gustav Ungerer, 'An Unrecorded Elizabethan Performance of *Titus Andronicus*', *SS*, 14 (1961), 102–9
ed. Eugene M. Waith (Oxford Shakespeare, 1984), pp. 20–7
J. Dover Wilson, ' "Titus Andronicus" on the Stage in 1595', *SS* 1, (1948), 17–22 (Pl. 1)

26

Johannes de Witt, Sketch of the interior of the Swan Theatre, made about 1596, as copied by Aernout van Buchel.

This most famous of drawings associated with the theatre of Shakespeare's age has been frequently reproduced, and has often been taken as providing an accurate image of the interior of the Swan. It is important to note that Johannes de Witt was a Dutchman, one of a number of European travellers who visited London during the period and recorded their impressions. The manuscript of de Witt's *Observationes Londinenses* has vanished, but his friend and former fellow student at Leyden, Aernout van Buchel of Utrecht, copied out some of de Witt's notes on London, and also copied the sketch he had made of the Swan. The drawing is thus a copy of a lost original, and it is not known how good an artist de Witt was, or how accurately van Buchel copied what he saw. The sketch shows a circular arena inside a circular theatre with three tiers of galleries for spectators. A large rectangular stage (*proscænium*) projects into the arena, supported on what look like two massive short columns. These seem to be unrelated to the two decorated columns with Corinthian capitals supporting a canopy extending over part of the stage. At the rear of the stage is a tiring-house (*mimorum aedes*) where the actors kept properties and costumes; they entered and left the stage through two round-arched double doors. Above these the second storey of the stage façade shows a row of six windows, or possibly boxes, with a number of what may be spectators watching the three figures acting out a scene on the stage; no other spectators are shown in the theatre, so that these might be musicians. Above all of this is a superstructure projecting higher than the roof (*tectum*) of the galleries, with two windows, and a doorway where a musician blows a wind instrument with a flag on it, presumably a signal to announce the beginning of a play. This 'hut' could have housed machinery to create various kinds of special stage effects, notably descents from the 'Heavens'. A flag bearing the sign of the Swan flies above the highest roof-line.

The drawing takes as its notional point of view a spot roughly at roof-level opposite the centre of the stage and tiring-house, from where the side wall of the 'hut' would not have been visible. The distortion of perspective which allowed van Buchel to include this and the musician standing there probably affects much of the drawing. So the two entrances (*ingressus*) may well be in the wrong place, again in order to include them; in any case, they are difficult to interpret, as they seem to be unrelated to the continuous beams, rows of seats, and pilasters above them. They may indicate entries into the yard from outside the playhouse, or steps from the yard to the galleries, in which case the level of the arena was below that of the lowest gallery. This bottom gallery is labelled '*orchestra*' where it is nearest the stage; this was where the senators sat in the theatre in ancient Rome, and may indicate expensive seats. The middle gallery is labelled '*sedilia*', or benches, and the upper one '*porticus*', which means colonnade or gallery. The most prominent feature of these galleries is the large number of columns shown; if the hatching can be trusted, it may indicate three rows of seats in the lower galleries, and two in the top one.

It may well be that some general features of the interior of the Swan are here recorded, but it is difficult to judge how much reliance can be placed upon them. At the same time, note should be taken of the evidence produced by John Gleason that de Witt and van Buchel were much interested in drawing and painting; that de Witt's drawings were good enough to interest engravers, and twenty-one of van Buchel's drawings illustrating his travels were reproduced. It seems likely, as Gleason claims, that in his sketch de Witt was aiming to illustrate the way the Swan worked, and that such a drawing uses 'pictorial conventions' of the period, and needs to be 'read against iconographic traditions of the time' (p. 338). It is also significant that de Witt took the term '*amphiteatra*', which he used to describe the four theatres he saw in London, from the treatise *De Amphiteatro* (1584) by Justus Lipsius. This treatise on reconstructing the Colosseum in Rome includes a plate showing it in vertical half-section, with gladiators performing, but no spectators other than the solitary figure of the emperor, and with the parts labelled for identification, as in the sketch of the Swan. This helps to explain the conventions de Witt may have been

tectum

porticus

sedilia

orchestra

mimorum
ædes

ingressus

proscænium.

planties sive arena

quintum sed apparu et structura, bestiarum comestati
oni destinatum, in quo multi ursi tauri, et stupenda
magnitudinis canes, distinctis cauetis et septis aluntur, qui
ad

53

following, but many difficulties of interpretation remain.

The stage appears to be deeper than it is wide (the stage at the Fortune was 43 ft wide, according to the contract, and 27½ ft deep). The relationship between the façade and gallery at the rear of the stage and the 'hut' above is impossible to determine, since the relationships between the various planes, and between them and the galleries, is unclear. Furthermore the various heights, of the stage, the gallery or boxes over the stage, the canopy, and the other features of the theatre, appear to be out of scale. The two pillars under the stage have usually been interpreted as trestles, but look more like supporters for the columns rising from the stage itself. It has also been suggested (Gurr, p. 125) that they could represent not supports, 'but gaps in hangings draped around the stage to conceal the understage area'.

The Swan was a new theatre when de Witt visited it, having been opened probably in 1595. In 1597 the presentation of 'lewd-matters' at the Swan in Thomas Nashe's play, now lost, *The Isle of Dogs*, stirred the Privy Council to impose a restraint on performances of plays on 28 July 1597, and to order the destruction of theatres in and about London. This order was never carried out, and the whole affair had a very temporary effect on other theatres; the effect at the Swan itself was more serious, for many of the company of actors playing there seem to have left when the owner, Francis Langley, was unable to obtain a new licence to perform plays after the restraint on playing ended in November 1597. It seems doubtful whether it was ever regularly used by an established company of actors thereafter. One consequence of this is that hardly any extant plays are known to have been acted there. On 6 November 1602 Richard Venner played an elaborated practical joke by announcing the performance there of a show called *England's Joy*, a spectacular entertainment on the reign of Queen Elizabeth. The bill announcing this survives, and promises a conclusion in which Queen Elizabeth 'is taken up into Heauen, when presently appeares, a Throne of blessed Soules, and beneath vnder the Stage set forth with strange fireworkes, diuers blacke and damned Soules, wonderfully discribed in their severall torments.' Since the affair appears to have been a hoax, and Venner absconded with most of the takings leaving the audience to revenge 'themselves upon the hangings, curtains, chairs, stooles, walles, and whatsoever came in their way, very outragiously', the bill cannot be taken as establishing the use of the 'Heavens', or of the area 'beneath under the Stage'.

The only extant play which can be positively linked with the Swan is Thomas Middleton's *A Chaste Maid in Cheapside*, written about 1611, and first printed in 1630,

'As it hath beene often acted at the Swan on the Bankeside.' The stage directions for this play require two doors ('Enter at one Dore . . . At the other Dore . . .', V.iv), mention the 'Musicke-Roome', where a sad song is sung (also V.iv), and call initially in I.i for a shop to be 'discovered', though this seems to be merely an indication of location and social setting. The play's action is straightforward, and makes no use of an upper stage or of trapdoors. In other words, nothing in it is inconsistent with what the de Witt sketch shows. At the same time, the evidence of one play-text is not much to go on, and the latest editor of the play, R. B. Parker, concludes that the stage-directions may have no reference to the de Witt drawing, or the Swan Theatre. De Witt's sketch seems to show spectators in the 'boxes' above the stage, and the 'music-room' could have been obscured from his view by the canopy or 'shadow' extending to the two large columns. If there were spectators or 'groundlings' in the arena when he attended he may not have been able to see exactly how the stage was mounted, and his drawing provides no sense of the 'hangings, curtains, chairs, stooles' damaged by the disgruntled audience who came to see *England's Joy* in 1602.

Doubt must remain, then, about the accuracy of de Witt's rough sketch. It may be correct in the major features shown (a circular theatre, with three tiers of galleries, thrust stage, canopy supported on two columns, two doors to the stage, no inner stage, and a set of rooms or boxes for spectators above the stage), but if so, then these are features of the Swan, and not necessarily of other theatres of the period. When Philip Henslowe reconstructed the Beargarden as the Hope in 1613, he stipulated in the contract that it was to be built to the same specifications of 'fforme, widenes and height' as the Swan, and with two external staircases as at the Swan; the instructions in the contract continue:

And shall also build the Heavens all over the saide stage, to be borne or carryed without any postes or supporters to be fixed or sett vppon the saide stage, and all gutters of leade need full for the carryage of all such Raine water as shall fall vppon the same; And shall also make Two Boxes in the lowermost Storie fitt and decent for gentlemen to sitt in; And shall make the particions betwne the Rommes as they are at the saide Plaie house called the Swan; And to make turned collumes vppon and over the stage . . .

The partitions between the 'rooms' may be the five partitions shown in the de Witt sketch above the stage, or partitions between 'rooms' in all the galleries. If there were 'two Boxes' at the Swan, de Witt does not show them. It has been assumed that the Hope differed from the Swan in the requirement that the 'Heavens' should be carried without posts on the stage, supporting it, but the 'Heavens' in the de Witt drawing do not appear to have 'supporters' on the stage, and this too may be a link between the two theatres. The contract goes on to call for 'turned columns' on the stage and over it; those *on* the stage may have been like the ones shown at the Swan, and those *over* the stage perhaps marked the front of the divisions between the rooms or boxes there, as again is suggested in the de Witt sketch. The reason for building the Hope to the pattern of the Swan may have been that the Swan, like the Hope, was conceived as a multi-purpose theatre, with a removable stage and canopy, allowing for 'feats of activity', such as were performed at the Swan, and the bear- and bull-baiting for which the Hope was designed. (But see 1 above.) The only other representation of the Swan showing the 'Heavens' as a superstructure rising above the roof-line of the galleries occurs in the Delaram engraving (9 above), which is of dubious authority. It is more often depicted without any 'hut' projecting above the galleries, which may mean that the 'Heavens' were removable, and were taken away when the Swan ceased to be used regularly as a playhouse, some time after 1597.

'A Note on the Swan Theatre Drawing', *SS*, 1 (1948), 23–4 (Pls II, III, IVA)
Chambers, *ES*, II 411–14, 466–7, 521; III 454, 500–3
John B. Gleason, 'The De Witt Drawing of the Swan Theatre', *Shakespeare Quarterly* 32 (1981), 324–38
W. W. Greg, *Dramatic Documents from the Elizabethan Playhouses* (2 vols, Oxford 1931, reprinted 1969), VIII
Gurr, 122–6 (Pl. 20)
Hodges, *Globe Restored*, 13ff, 108 (Pl. 3)
Hosley, 136–74 (Pl. 11)
William Ingram, ' "Neere the Playe House": The Swan Theater and Community Blight' *Renaissance Drama* n.s. IV (1971), 53–68
Leacroft, 30–6 (Fig. 21)
Thomas Middleton, *A Chaste Maid in Cheapside*, ed. R. B. Parker (Revels Plays, 1969), pp. lix–lxvi
D. F. Rowan, 'The "Swan" Revisited', *Research Opportunities in Renaissance Drama*, X (1967), 33–48
Schoenbaum, 108–10
Smith, 47–8 (Pl. 17)
Wickham, *EES* II, i 301–9 (Pl. 8); II ii 9ff, 68–73

27

Plan for the conversion of Christ Church Hall, Oxford, into a theatre for a royal visit, August 1605.

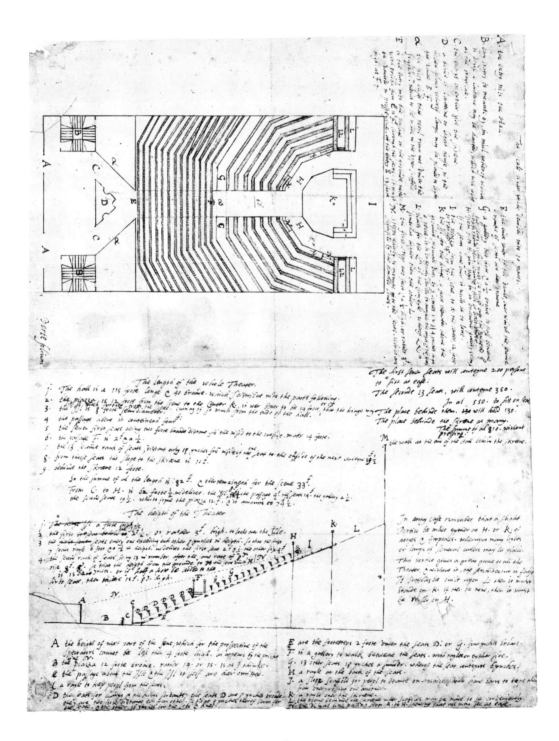

This drawing with elaborate notes relating to the conversion of a hall into a theatre for a royal performance was noticed by John Orrell among a collection of miscellaneous drawings and manuscripts of German origin in a large folio now catalogued as British Library MS Additional 15505, f. 21. It consists of a sheet of paper measuring about 11¾ in. × 15 in. (298 mm × 381 mm), which has been laid down, and is formed of two smaller sheets stuck together; probably they were once the two halves of a single sheet folded once, which would explain the note 'verte folium' at the foot of what might, for convenience, be called page 1. On this is the plan in ink of the greater part of a hall, showing seating arrangements for the conversion of the hall into an auditorium. Measurements of a central gangway (6 ft wide), and of the passage behind the halpace, or raised platform on which a throne could be erected (4 ft wide), are marked on the drawing. Other features are marked by letters, and a key to these is provided above the drawing, together with a note of the scale, 1/10 in. representing 1 ft. According to the scale the area shown in the drawing measures 40 ft × 80 ft. The other part of the sheet contains further notes in the same hand, a clear italic script, written along the length of the sheet, or sideways-on to page 1. This begins with a list of details of measurements under the heading 'The length of the whole Theater', which is followed by notes on 'The heigth of the Theater'. These notes incorporate a diagram showing the edge of the stage, and the rake of the seating up to the rear of the hall. To the right of this is a further note on the erection of a 'portico' for lighting the auditorium.

The notes on the length of the theatre include the statement that the hall is 115 ft long and 40 ft broad, which corresponds to the hall of Christ Church Oxford. Plays were performed there before James I in 1605, and before Charles I in 1636. On this later occasion Anthony à Wood reported that William Strode's *The Royal Slave* was 'acted on a goodly stage, reaching from the upper end of the Hall almost to the hearth place', and the stage fittings included 'three or four openings on each side thereof, and partitions between them', or side-wings, with back-shutters, and the effects included various changes of perspective scenery, all designed by Inigo Jones in the full maturity of his powers. The details given on the manuscript tally much better with what is known of the presentation of four plays, three in Latin and one in English, during a royal visit to Oxford in 1605. On this occasion, Philip Stringer reported that two of 'his Majestie's Master Carpenters' were employed to contrive the stage, seats and scaffolds, and 'they had the advice of the Comptroller of his Works'. Inigo Jones was hired to 'further them much, and furnish them with rare devices, but performed very little, to that which was expected. He had for his pains, as I heard it constantly reported, £50' (Nichols, I.558). According to the same source, 'The stage was built close to the upper end of the Hall, as it seemed at the first sight. But indeed it was but a false wall painted and adorned with stately pillars, which pillars would turn about, by reason whereof, with the help of other painted clothes, their stage did vary three times in the acting of one Tragedy'.

In 1605 Inigo Jones was beginning his career as a stage designer, and, as far as is known, he first devised the staging of a masque for Ben Jonson's *Masque of Blackness* in January 1605. His use of a false wall, incorporating *periaktoi* which could be turned to provide three changes of scene in one play, was appropriate for the pastoral *Alba*, the tragedy *Ajax Flagellifer*, and the comedy *Vertumnus*, a setting in classical style for three Latin plays. The changes of scene amazed everyone, according to the account of Isaac Wake in *Rex Platonicus* (1607), who wrote: '*Peripetasmata* [i.e. *periaktoi*] and mansions were skilfully provided with machinery to represent a variety of places and things, so that not only for the spectacles on different days, but also within a single play, new façades for the whole stage were made to appear with diversity and speed, to the amazement of everyone. In the middle of the hall the royal throne was erected, surrounded by a railing, for the King and Queen, with places provided for the nobility on both sides, and the remaining space, between the throne and the stage, a little lower . . .'; but though these were remarkable at the time, they were much less ambitious than those Jones was to create later on. Philip Stringer also noted that 'Behinde the foresaid false wall there was reserved five or six paces of the upper end of the hall, which served them to good uses for their howses and receipt of the actors, &c.' The sketch of a section through the seating on the manuscript shows the end of the stage as raised not less than 4 ft above floor level, and also indicates the beginning of a rake, a feature that struck Isaac Wake, who described the stage as 'gently sloping (which greatly added to the dignity of the actors as they entered, as if descending from a hill) and ending on a level' (p. 46; as translated in Orgel and Strong, II 823). This is the earliest known raked stage in England, and the first to be illustrated. The manuscript provides no other information about staging.

The plan shows the auditorium extending from the front of the stage at the top to the hall screen marked 'C' on the plan. The notes attached to it are uncertain about the depth of the 'piazza' (I), the space between the halpace (K) and the front of the stage; the plan is scaled at 12 ft, but the notes recommended 'it were better to bee 14 foote, or 15 that the kinge may sit so much further from the scene'. The measurements given assume the 'piazza' to be 14 ft deep. This allowed 33 ft for the depth of the stage, but a false wall was built 'five or six paces from the upper end of the hall', so if this was between 12 and 14 ft from the end wall, the effective stage depth for the actors would have been about 18 to 20 ft, allowing for the thickness of the false wall. The stage presumably extended across the width, 40 ft, of the hall.

The seating in the hall shows two rather spacious rows of seats for the Lords of the Council on either side of the royal box or 'isle', and parallel to the steps leading up to this. Behind this are seven rows of benches, stepped so that each row is 8 in. higher than the one in front, and the front bench raised 1½ ft or 2 ft above the level of the 'isle', which in turn stood 1 ft above floor level. The idea was that those sitting behind the 'isle' would be able to see over it, which may explain the curious use of this term, rather than state, throne, or box; in effect, it seems to have been simply a kind of platform. The seven forward rows of seats, 'for Ladys & the Kings servants', were 8 in. wide and allowed a space of 16 in. for 'legs & knees'. Behind these a passage is shown, and then thirteen further rows of seats, even more cramped, and allowing only 18 in. for each row; these benches were 6 in. wide (see note G, p.61 below), providing a gap of 12 in. between rows. A passage under the centre of these seats led to a point E, giving on to two stair-wells at the rear, marked B. Two areas marked α on the plan provided standing room, and required bars to prevent spectators 'from overpressing one another'. In the centre at the rear was a structure with 'hollows' in it, marked D, where lamps could be placed to light the 'vault' of the entrance passage, E to F, under the benches. The rake of the seating was designed to provide good sightlines for the audience, with seating for 550, standing for 130, and another 130 placed on scaffolds behind the screen, a total of 810. The aim seems to have been to squeeze in as many as possible, and the seating arrangements appear to have been very compressed; if the benches in the public theatres were placed at such narrow intervals, it would readily account for the records indicating that audiences could exceed 3000 in number, as, for example, at the Globe, when Middleton's *A Game at Chess* was performed in 1624, and 'there were more than 3000 there on the day that the audience was smallest' (Bentley, *JCS*, IV.871; see also 54 below).

The various small ifs and alternatives in the notes show that the plan could be modified, and the reminder at the end to construct a 'portico', meaning what would now be called a pergola, a frame supported on posts, in which to place lamps of various colours, is particularly interesting, as a feature to which the

Comptroller of the Works, or whoever drew up the document, attached great importance. This was to give 'a great grace to all the Theater', perhaps because nearly all the spectators would pass by it as they made their way to the seating. In the event the plan was altered. The representatives of the court who went ahead to oversee the arrangement for the royal visit to Oxford were displeased, and 'utterly disliked the stage at Christ Church, and above all, the places appointed for the chair of state, because it was no higher, and the King so placed that the auditory could see but his cheek only'. The Vice-Chancellor and the workmen involved defended what had been done, maintaining 'that by the art perspective the King should behold all better than if he sat higher' (Nichols, I.538), but it was more important for the King to be seen than for him to see. Philip Stringer, reporting this, went on to say that finally the King's 'isle' was moved to a distance of 28 ft from the stage. Since the 'isle' as shown on the plan was to have been 14 ft from the stage, it must have been moved back a further 14 ft, so that the front steps of the 'isle' were level with the point marked N on the plan, where the front rows of seats meet the central gangway. This would have necessitated rearranging the seating of the front seven rows, and probably making them run parallel with the sides of the hall, as in Inigo Jones's later conversions of halls for royal performances (see 32 and 33 below). The aim, perhaps not understood by the Comptroller or Jones at this early stage, was to ensure that the principal members of the audience could see the King, not that they could witness the play.

With reference to the performances before the King and Queen at Oxford in 1605, Stephen Orgel has commented (Orgel and Strong, I.7):

The special nature of such stages is worth emphasising. They were employed only at court or when royalty was present; they were not used in the public or private playhouses. The implications of this deserve more attention than they have received. Jones's stage subtly changed the character of both plays and masques by transforming *audiences* into *spectators*, fixing the viewer, and directing the theatrical experience toward the single point in the hall from which the perspective achieved its fullest effect, the royal throne ... Through the use of perspective the monarch, always the ethical centre of court productions, became in a physical and emblematic way the centre as well. Jones's theatre transformed its audience into a living and visible emblem of the aristocratic hierarchy; the closer one sat to the King, the 'better' one's place was, and only the King's seat was perfect. It is no accident that perspective stages flourished at court and only at court, and that their appearance there coincided with the reappearance in England of the Divine Right of Kings as a serious political philosophy.

This is important as a recognition of the special nature of such occasions; the next royal visit involving plays in Oxford did not take place until 1636. At the same

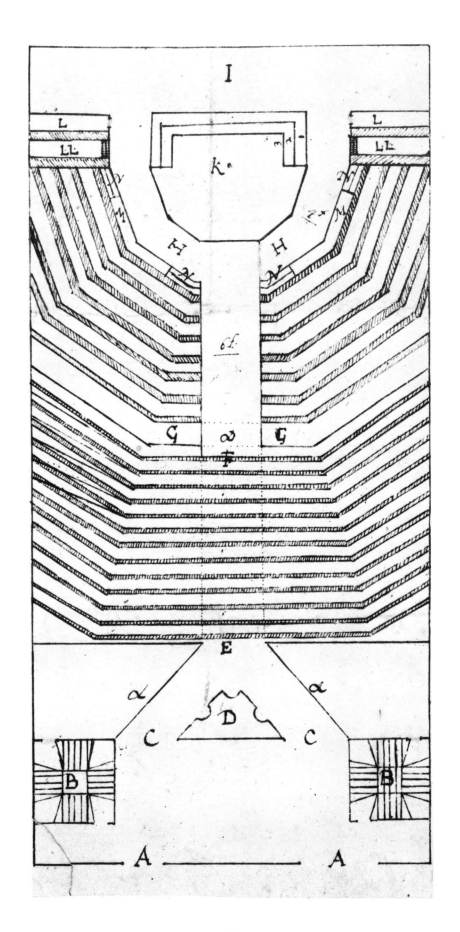

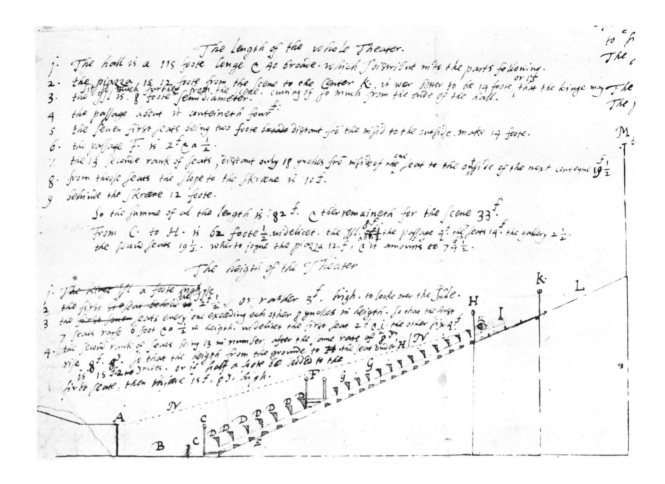

time, certain qualifications need to be made. For the 1605 performances in Christ Church, it was not Inigo Jones but court officials who insisted on placing the King where many of the audience could see him, in the centre of the hall; and he was so far from the stage as not at all to have the best seat, if Philip Stringer can be trusted, who said, 'there were many long speeches delivered which neither the King nor any near him could well hear or understand' (Nichols, I.538). The aim of the Vice-Chancellor and others at Oxford was no doubt to provide a lavish entertainment for the royal party, and they overdid it. Contemporary witnesses give conflicting reports but the first play, *Alba*, included almost naked men, which gave offence, and many songs and dances, which proved tedious, and on the third night the King, understandably weary, fell asleep. On the fourth day Samuel Daniel's *Arcadia Reformed* (*The Queen's Arcadia*), a play in English, was performed apparently on the morning of the day of their departure before the Queen, Prince and courtiers; the King did not attend it (Nichols, I.553). This seems

to have pleased the Queen after the tedium of *Alba* and *Ajax*. The plays on this occasion were not such as the professional players would perform in their theatres.

At the same time, the manuscript contains information of relevance to the regular London theatres, notably in the measurements and spacing of benches. The 'portico' containing lights is interesting in relation to the lighting of auditoria in the private theatres. No information is given about stage lighting, other than that for *Vertumnus* a palm tree was represented in the centre with twelve branches, each bearing a light. Although Stephen Orgel is surely correct in his general argument that royal performances were designed to embody 'the age's most profound assumptions about the monarchy' (*The Illusion of Power*, p. 8), and that elaborate perspective settings were a feature of court, not of public productions, we simply do not know whether what was being done at the new private theatres of the Paul's boys and children of the Chapel Royal after 1599 had any influence on the way halls were converted into theatres for special occasions, and the evidence is too scanty to establish exactly what changes and developments took place in staging in the professional theatres over the long period from 1605 to 1640. However, it seems likely that the private theatres catering for better-class audiences learnt a lot from the court spectacles, as is suggested by the drawings of Inigo Jones for the conversion of the Drury Lane Cockpit in 1616–18: see 29 below.

Bentley, *JCS*, III 134–41
Chambers, *ES*, I 130–1, 233–4; III 276, 332
J. Nichols, *The Progresses, Processions, and Magnificent Festivities of King James the First* (4 vols, 1828), I 530–62
Orgel and Strong, I 6–8; II 823–6
Stephen Orgel, *The Illusion of Power: Political Theatre in the English Renaissance* (Berkeley, 1975)
Orrell, 128–35, 168–70 (Pl. 33)

A transcription of the notes on the manuscript:

the scale is an ynch deuided into 10 parts.
A. the entry into the Hall.
B. easy stayrs to mounte by, in midl wherof which is voyde a lanterne may be hanged, which will light al the stayrcase.
C. the entrys on eyther side the skreene.
D. a kinde of lanterne or light house, in the hollow places wherof lamps may be placed to light the vaute E.F.
a. the sides closed that peopl runn not vnder the scaffolde, needles to bee made in the vpper scaffold.
E. is the entry into the passage on the grounde noted with pricks from E to F. through the seats. It must be vaulted in prospectiue, at the entry E 13 foote high at F.7.
F. the ende [wher] of the vault, ouer which the seconde ranke of seats are heer drawne.
G. a gallery two foote & a $\frac{1}{2}$ broade to pass betweene the seats, which must be raysed over the passage α, 8^y to pass rounde about, leauing 7 foote at least vnder.
H. from F. to H. you pass in an vncouered gallery because if the seats came ouer it would bee to lowe.
I. the piazza from the scene, to K. the center, 12 foote. or rather 14′ or 15′.
K. the Isl for the kinge, a foote eleuated aboue the grounde, mounted vnto by 3 degrees 1.2.3/ 4 ynches high a peece. it is vnequally deuided to aunswer the angls of the seats.
L. places for the L:^{ds} of the Counseyle wherof L.L. is somewhat higher then the other L.
M. the first stepp two foote & a $\frac{1}{2}$ high. or rather 3^t:
N. stepps wherby to mounte into the seats. which are signified by the hached Lines.

The length of the whole Theater.
j. The hall is a 115 foote longe & 40 broade. which I distribut into the parts following.
2. the piazza is 12 foote from the scene to the Center K. it wer better to bee 14 foote, or 15 that the kinge may sit so much further from the scene. cutting of so much from the ende of the hall.
3. the Isl is 8 foote in semi diameter.
4. the passage about it conteineth four^t:
5. the seuen first seats being two foote [broade] distant frō the insid to the outside. make 14 foote.
6. the passage F. is 2^t & a $\frac{1}{2}$.
7. the 13 seconde rank of seats, distant only 18 ynches frō inside of [the] one seat to the outside of the next conteyne 19$^t\frac{1}{2}$.

8. from thoose seats the slope to the skreene is 10 f.
9. behinde the skreene 12 foote.
So the summe of al the length is. 82^t· & ther remaineth for the scene 33^t.
From C. to H. is 62 foote $\frac{1}{2}$. uidelicet. the Isl 8^t. the passage 4^t. the 7 seats 14^t. the gallery 2$\frac{1}{2}$. the second seats 19$\frac{1}{2}$. wherto joyne the piazza 12f, & it amounts to 74$^t\frac{1}{2}$.

The heigth of the Theater
j. [The Kings Isl a foote high]
2. the first [st] seat behind [it] the Isle 2$^t\frac{1}{2}$. or rather 3^t. high. to looke ouer the Isle.
3. the [first seuen] seats euery one exceeding ech other 8 ynches in heigth. so that the first 7 seats rayse 6 foot & a $\frac{1}{2}$ in heigth. uidelicet. the first seat 2 f & $\frac{1}{2}$. the other six. 4^t.
4. the second rank of seats being 13 in number, after the same rate of 8^{yn}, rise 8^t· 8^y· so that the heigth from the grounde to [H.] the seat vnder H is 15f. [10] 2 ynches. or if half a foote be added to the first seate, then they are 15 f. 8^y· high.
[Sketch of section through seating.]
A. the height of next part of the scene; which for the prospectiue of the spectators cannot bee less than 4 foote high. as appears by the prickt line N.
B. the piazza 12 foote broade. rather 14. or 15. 15 as I thinke.
[C] the passage about the Isle and the Isl it self are heer omitted.
C. a rayle to keep peopl from the seats.
D. the seats for Ladys & the Kings seruants; the seats D are 8 ynches broade. they are two foote distante ech from other. so that 8 ynches therof serues for the seate, & the other 16 ynches for the legs & knees.
E. are the footesteps 2 foote vnder the seats D. or G. four ynches broade.
F. is a gallery to walk betweene the seats. with rayles on eyther side.
G. 13 other seats 18 ynches a sunder. wherof the seat conteyns 6 ynches.
H. a rayle at the back of the seats.
J. a slope scaffold for peopl to stande on. which should haue barrs to keepe them from ouerpressing one another.
K. a rayle ouer the skreene.
L. the roome behinde the skreene wher scaffolds may be made to see conueniently.
N. the visual line passing from A. to H. shewing that all may see at ease.
The first seuen seats will conteyne 200 persons to sitt at ease.
The seconde 13 seats, will conteyne 350.
In al 550. to sit on seats
The place behinde them. [130] will hold 130.
The place behinde the skreene as many.
The summe of al 810. without pressing.
M. the wall at the end of the Hall behind the skreene.
In anny case remember that a slight Portico bee made eyther at H. or K. of hoopes & firrpooles. wherupon many lights or lamps of seueral coulers may bee placed. This portico giues a great grace to all the Theater, & without it, the Architectur is false. If scaffolds bee built upon L. then it must stande on K. if ther bee none, then it must be reysed on H.

28

Drawing of an actor, probably John Green, in the part of Nobody (1608).

John Green is first mentioned as an actor in Robert Browne's company touring in Germany in 1606. Browne appears to have returned to England in 1607, but Green stayed on, and late in that year the company went to Austria to perform at the court of Archduke Ferdinand at Graz, where they staged a number of plays in November 1607, and again from February 1608. The Archduke was away at the time, but a charming letter to him from his sister, the Archduchess Maria Magdalena, dated 20–22 February 1608, lists the plays staged by Green's company at the Shrovetide festivities, showing that they acted a different play every night for eight nights in succession, and then three more after a day's break. Among the plays acted was *Nobody and Somebody*, which she found most entertaining ('gewaltig artlich'). The plays were probably performed in German, and a manuscript rendering into German of this play survives in the Stiftsarchiv, Rein, in Austria, where it is catalogued as MS 128. This has a dedication by 'Joannes Grün Nob. Anglus' (i.e. Nobilis Anglus, celebrated Englishman) to the Archduke Maximilian, Ferdinand's brother, and presumably dates from 1608. The manuscript is illustrated by a full-length watercolour portrait of a red-haired actor costumed in the role of Nobody, measuring $12\frac{1}{4}$ in. $\times 7\frac{7}{8}$ in. (311 mm $\times$ 200 mm). This is headed 'NEMO', and against the figure is written 'Neminis Virtus ubiq[ue] laudabilis', 'The virtue of nobody is everywhere praiseworthy'. The sketch probably portrays the actor Green himself in the main role of the play, dressed in the traditional costume, all breeches and no body (see 39 below). Underneath this special pair of blue breeches that come up to his neck, he wears a garment with green sleeves, and a ruff round his neck. He also has on green stockings, black boots laced up round his ankles, and a blue hat with three feathers in it. This hat is not unlike that worn by Thomas Greene in *Greene's Tu Quoque* (1614; see 43 below), which appears to have made him look a fool, and would have been appropriate to the character of Nobody, whose companion is a clown, and who is regarded as responsible for everything that goes wrong, until the end of the play when Somebody is exposed as the true culprit. Nobody holds a book (a bible or missal?) in one hand, and a rosary with a cross attached to it in the other; these were presumably added for the benefit of the Catholic audience in Graz, and the woodcut on the title-page of the English version of the play, printed about 1606 (see 39 below), shows Nobody holding a scroll in one hand, his other hand in his pocket. In the manuscript the figure seems to be depicted in his role as unmasker of Somebody and revealer of the truth at the end of the play, when the virtue of Nobody becomes apparent. The rather solemn-faced actor has a red moustache and short red beard. There is no reason to identify him, as Chambers does (*ES*, II.282 and note) with an English actor with long red hair who is on record as killing a Frenchman at the end of the company's visit to Graz. The costumes in the drawing and woodcut differ in detail but are basically similar, and show what a striking feature of a performance these must have been. The drawing has been reproduced in Willi Flemming, *Das Schauspiel der Wanderbühne* (Potsdam, 1931), and more recently in black and white in the volume containing drama in a three-volume anthology, *Dichtung aus Österreich*, ed. Heinz Kindermann and Margaret Dietrich (Vienna and Munich, 1966).

Chambers, *ES*, II 281–4, 320; IV 37

Irene Morris, 'A Hapsburg Letter', *Modern Language Review*, 69 (1974), 12–22

Orlene Murad, *The English Comedians at the Habsburg Court in Graz 1607–1608* (Salzburg Studies in English Literature, 81, 1978), especially pp. 52–5

Willem Schrickx, 'English Actors at the Courts of Wolfenbüttel, Brussels and Graz during the Lifetime of Shakespeare', *SS*, 33 (1980), 166–7; also *SS*, 36 (1983), 142–3

29

Inigo Jones, Drawings for a conversion to a theatre, probably relating to the Cockpit in Drury Lane (or the Phoenix), 1616–18.

Among the architectural drawings by Inigo Jones and John Webb assembled in a volume at Worcester College, Oxford, are four, on two numbered sheets, 7B and 7C, measuring $12\frac{3}{4}$ in. $\times$ $16\frac{7}{8}$ in. (324 mm $\times$ 429 mm), which provide in some detail an exterior elevation, a plan, and two interior elevations of a theatre. Attention was drawn to these by D. F. Rowan, who cautiously identified the plan and exterior elevation as showing the Anatomy Theatre of the Barber-Surgeons designed by Inigo Jones in 1635–6; he explained the interior elevations as an 'imaginative theatre project from the teeming mind of Inigo Jones, never executed by the

Company' (*Shakespeare Survey*, 23, p. 126). The identification of the plan and exterior elevation as showing a design for the theatre of the Barber-Surgeons, commissioned in 1636, was made by a cataloguer in 1919, and represents his conjectures. Glynne Wickham, who pointed this out (*EES* II, ii 238, n. 71), went on to note similarities with the elevation and plan of the Cockpit-in-Court, designed by Inigo Jones and drawn by John Webb in 1629–30 (see 30), and supposed that the two sets of drawings belong to the same period; he therefore suggested that the interior elevations numbered 7B and 7C might relate to another commission received by

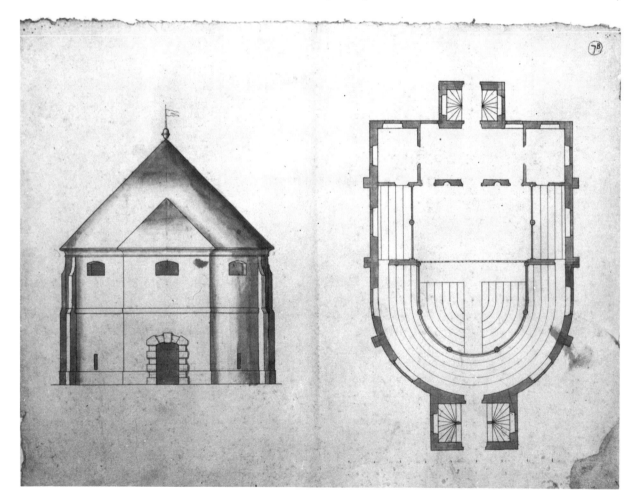

Jones in 1629, the Salisbury Court Theatre. More recently John Orrell has proposed that they relate to the conversion of the Cockpit in Drury Lane to a theatre in 1616, the theatre subsequently named the Phoenix. Although there is no direct evidence to link the drawings with any specific theatre, this last identification is the most convincing.

In support of his case Orrell showed that an expert on the drawings of Inigo Jones, John Harris, had assigned this group on stylistic grounds to the period roughly between 1616 and 1618. Furthermore, the shell of the building, as shown in the exterior elevation, with its buttressed walls and absence of classical detail, 'might have come from almost any mason's hand' (*Shakespeare Survey*, 30, p. 158), and suggests, as does the relationship of the parts in the design of the interior, that 'the width of the theatre was a datum from which Jones began' (p. 160), and that the drawings relate to the conversion of an already existing building. The shape of John Best's cockpit which Christopher Beeston arranged to make into a theatre in 1616 is not recorded, but there is evidence to show that cockpits were normally polygonal, like the Royal Cockpit (30), or round. The Drury Lane cockpit may well have been round, for its builder, John Best, who erected it about 1609, also built in the same period a cockpit which is known to have been round at Royston. The most probable explanation of the drawings, then, is that they show designs for the conversion of a round cockpit into a U-shaped theatre.

The exterior elevation shows a building with a conical roof, which was extended in a ridge above the new stage area, as shown in the interior elevations. A projecting porch with its entrance door contained a double stairwell, as the plan shows, with side windows illuminating the lower stairs, and another window above the entrance. The small windows, marked like slits, on the lower level, seem to have provided light for a passageway running inside the wall of the auditorium below the lower tiers of seats, to which at some point they must have given access. High above a string-course is a row of rather larger windows, but still small in relation to the building, which lit the upper galleries and the interior of the theatre, as the interior elevations show. The plan makes clear that the semi-circular end of the building was filled with seating, which extended on

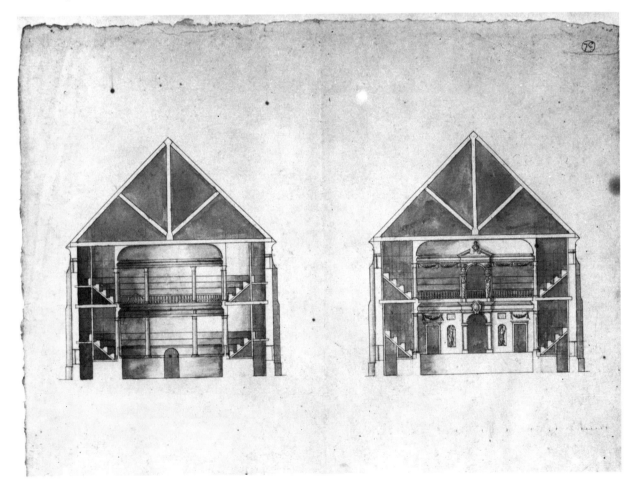

65

both sides of a rectangular stage area. Behind this is a stage façade with three entrances, and at the back of this an area corresponding to the tiring-house of the public theatres, with a room on either side. Another porch and stairwell at this end of the building gave access to the gallery at the rear of the stage.

The interior elevations (drawing 7C) illustrate further details. The stage façade is less ornamented than that Jones designed in 1630 for the Royal Cockpit (30), and seems to have been constructed to present an elegant, simple classical frontage. A central door with a round arch is surmounted by a cartouche; on either side is a niche containing a sculpted figure, and a plain, smaller, square-headed door with a decorative moulding above. The emphatic horizontals of the cornice above the three stage doors effectively cut off the lower façade from the gallery above, except in the centre, where the cartouche links the central entrance with a more elaborate arched doorway above, surmounted by a pediment. A railing runs across the front of the gallery, and is continued across this central arch, which perhaps served as an upper playing area, a window, or a music-room. The posts of this doorway are ornamented with figures bearing bowls of flowers, linking with the decorative mouldings carried on either side across the façade. The broken pediment above the central door is surmounted by a bust.

The interior elevations show that there were two tiers of seats, and that the railing was carried along the front of the gallery all round the theatre. At the opposite end from the stage can be seen the columns supporting the galleries and the roof, which are also indicated on the plan. The entrance at the rear of the auditorium is at ground level, and the elevations do not show seating in the area in front of the lower gallery, whereas the plan indicates an arrangement of benches on either side of a central gangway. The first tier of seating in the lower gallery was on a level with the raised stage. The indications of scale given by Inigo Jones have provided a basis on which John Orrell has worked out the probable measurements of this theatre. It was 40 ft wide and 55 ft long, excluding the porches or stair-turrets at each end. The stage was about 23 ft wide and 15 ft deep. The central stage doorway measured 6 ft across, and, as shown in the interior elevations, the tiers of benches for spectators were only 18 in. apart, providing little leg-room (but see 27, above).

The building was a substantial one, made of brick with a tiled roof. It would seem that Jones adapted it in such a way as to effect a compromise between his interest in designs based on Vitruvius or Palladio and the usual style of a Jacobean theatre. Jones probably visited Italy between 1598 and 1603, in the service of Francis Manners, brother of the Earl of Rutland, and

he spent some time there in the train of the Earl of Arundel between 1613 and 1615. He acquired, studied and annotated copies of Vitruvius, *De Architectura*, Andrea Palladio, *I Quattro Libri dell'Architettura*, and Sebastiano Serlio, *Tutte l'Opere d'Architettura, e Prospettiua*; he also made extensive use of other Renaissance theorists. On this tour he visited Vicenza, where he saw Palladio's famous Teatro Olimpico, built in 1580, and modelled on the ancient Roman theatre; in this the arrangement of seating left a semi-elliptical space, the orchestra, in front of the stage, which provided a rectangular playing area with a stage façade or *frons scenae* containing five doors through which every member of the audience would have a perspective view of street scenes. The stage façade Jones designed for the Drury Lane conversion borrows the round-arched central opening, the square-headed flanking doors, and the niches with figures in them, from Palladio's conception; but in filling the semi-circular space in front of the stage with seating, as shown in the plan, in continuing the seating on either side of the stage, and in providing a gallery above, he was conforming to the more usual arrangements of Jacobean theatres. There is no hint of scenic vistas behind the openings in the stage-façade, which provide three entrances for actors, as against the drawing of the earlier Swan Theatre (26), which shows only two stage doors.

Among the drawings by John Webb at Worcester College are copies from the original design by Palladio for the Teatro Olimpico, and, on the same sheets, a plan of a theatre, with the elevation of a stage façade, in the manner of Palladio, but modified in various ways, most notably in the single large archway at the centre of the *frons scenae*, giving on to a vista of a Serlian street scene. For this theatre and façade, thought to be derived from designs by Inigo Jones, Webb provided measurements and annotations which differ from the dimensions as indicated by the scale of the drawings. The central arch is $1\frac{1}{2}$ squares high as drawn, but a memorandum note refers to it as two squares high; the width of the stage is 50 ft 6 in. as drawn, but a note on it reads '52: fo: $\frac{1}{2}$ to make ye Arch two squares high'; the stage is 13 ft deep as drawn, but the measurement noted on it is 14 ft 9 in.; and the height of the elevation is 38 ft by scale, but 43 ft according to the annotations. It is not known whether Webb was in this way annotating and revising a design for adapting an existing building, setting down and correcting information about a theatre he had perhaps seen in Italy, or simply projecting a possible design which was never carried out. No connection has been established between the drawings and an actual building, but they show the interest Webb and Jones had in Palladio's theatre, and the arrangement of the auditorium, the semi-circular seating plan, the orchestra, and the stage with its side-doors, are all borrowed from the design of the Teatro Olimpico. Jones probably thought of providing a large central opening and vista because the stage in his plan is much less wide than that of Palladio's theatre. These drawings may throw light on the way in which Jones adapted the ideas he obtained from his study of Palladio in his conversions of the Drury Lane Cockpit and of the Royal Cockpit. (For further comment, see 36 below.)

Bentley, *JCS*, VI 47–77

R. B. Graves, 'Daylight in the Elizabethan Private Theatres', *Shakespeare Quarterly*, 33 (1982), 80–92

Gurr, 147–50 (Pl. 25)

Harris and Tait, 14–15 (Pls 11–12), 17, 92–3 (Pl. 126)

John Harris, Stephen Orgel and Roy Strong, *The King's Arcadia: Inigo Jones and the Stuart Court* (1973), 55–6, 63–5, 108–9 (Pls 194, 195)

Leacroft, 65–73 (Figs 46, 47)

John Orrell, 'Inigo Jones at the Cockpit', *SS*, 30 (1977), 157–68 (Pls II–V)

D. F. Rowan, 'A Neglected Jones/Webb Theatre Project: Barber-Surgeons' Hall Writ Large', *SS*, 23 (1970), 125–9 (Pls I and II) (This is a shorter version of an article with the same title published in *New Theatre Magazine*, IX (Summer, 1969), 6–15

D. F. Rowan, 'A Neglected Jones/Webb Theatre Project, Part II: A Theatrical Missing Link', *The Elizabethan Theatre*, II, ed. David Galloway (Toronto 1970), pp. 60–73

D. F. Rowan, 'The English Playhouse: 1595–1630', *Renaissance Drama*, n.s. IV (1971), 37–51

Wickham, *EES* II, ii 118–19, 140–4 (Pls. XXIV, XXV)

30

John Webb, after designs by Inigo Jones, Drawings relating to the conversion of the Royal Cockpit into a theatre, the Cockpit-in-Court, 1629–30.

These drawings, made by John Webb after the 'Designes and Draughts given by the Surveyor', Inigo Jones, for the conversion of the Cockpit-in-Court in 1629–30, are appropriate here even if, as John Harris believes, they compose a text-book study made possible after the restoration of Charles II. The three drawings, together measuring 14 in. × 17$\frac{5}{16}$ in. (356 mm × 457 mm), represent (a) the ground-plan, (b) the elevation of the *frons scenae* or stage-façade, and (c) a larger scale plan of the stage and *frons scenae*. The accounts of the Office of Works relating to the reconstruction in 1629–30, and to repairs made in 1632, do not refer to chimneys or to stage-rails. Bricklayers were paid in 1662 for cutting two chimneys at the playhouse, and these are shown in a painting by Cornelis Danckerts of 1674. The plans show only one fireplace, probably also added in 1662. In 1660 workmen were paid for 'setting vp a rayle ballisters upon the stage making two other seats for ye gentlemen Vshers' (Boswell, 14), which may indicate partitioning off a small area for ushers, and it is not clear when the rails, shown as marking off the front of the stage on drawing (c), were added. So far as is known, no major alterations were made to the theatre between 1630 and 1660.

The stage plan and elevation has a scale marked in ink, and the overall plan a pricked-out scale; on the basis of these, the dimensions have been calculated as showing an octagon with a maximum width of 36 ft, inside a square with sides 58 ft long. These measurements make sense, and relate well to what is known about Cockpits, but must be regarded as a rough guide. The ground-plan shows the curved stage-façade at the rear of a stage area that has a rectangular projection into the auditorium. In front of this is a pit with seating, and at the rear a small rectangle marking the position of the halpace (or raised platform on which a throne could be placed).

On either side are other rows of seats for spectators, so arranged that none had their backs to the King when he was present, but all had a good view of the stage. The auditorium makes use of the original octagonal shape of the cockpit, but the stage area has been redesigned.

The stage-façade has five doors, and behind it is the tiring-house, or rather its lower floor, showing a fireplace on the left, two windows in the rear wall, and staircases in each corner. Behind the royal box is another staircase which provided private access for the King into the theatre. The stage would have been about 34 ft wide, and 16 ft deep to the centre door of the façade. The larger-scale plane of the stage-façade shows the shape of the pillars, with projecting columns, and the stage, which has stage-rails marking its rectangular boundary.

The elevation of the stage-façade shows the view of it from the centre, as the King would have seen it from the royal box. The large, round-arched double doors in the centre are flanked by Corinthian columns, and the other four smaller doors are also set between columns. The level above has a large central aperture or window. On either side are two busts set between carved wreaths, on the left Thespis, the father of Greek tragedy, and on the right Epicharmus, the corresponding figure in relation to comedy. Between the window on the upper floor and the central stage doorway is a larger cartouche containing the inscription 'Prodesse & Delectare' (to profit and to please), a reference to Horace, *Ars Poetica* l. 333. The blank walls above the other four doors are ornamented with empty recesses.

The accounts of the Office of Works throw further light on these drawings, and on the theatre. They show that the stage-façade was painted, and the capitals of the ten Corinthian columns on each level were gilt. Behind the façade the lower room, with its windows and fireplace, served as a dressing-room, and the room above it was used as a wardrobe for costumes, and as a musicians' gallery. A false ceiling of blue cloth stuck all over with stars made of silver foil was designed to 'cover all the roome over head' in the Cockpit, with provision for 'hanging the Throne and Chaire' in such a way that they could be lowered through the false ceiling 'to come downe from the Clouds to the Stage'. The Cockpit thus had a 'heavens' and a painted stage-façade, as did the Elizabethan public theatres. The

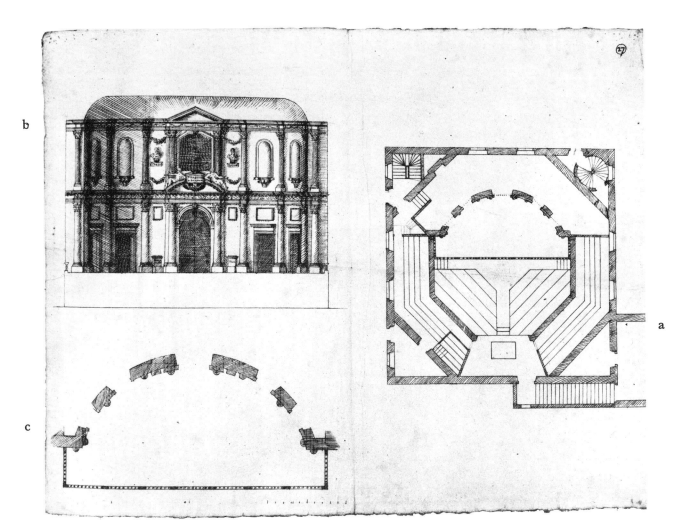

b

c

a

accounts also show that there were two levels of galleries with seats for spectators, and a room under the stage. The two main staircases in the corners of the building behind the stage and tiring house presumably enabled the audience, and the actors and theatre personnel, to move between the various levels of the building. Other smaller staircases shown in the ground-plan give access from floor level to the stage or first level of galleries, or from the pit to the galleries. No mention is made of a trap-door on the stage, but the existence of a room underneath it suggests that there must have been one. The acting area was lit by candelabra. The walls and galleries were decorated with paintings by Palma (this could have been either Palma Vecchio or his grand-nephew Palma Giovane) and Titian.

Thus, in spite of the small size of this theatre, designed under royal patronage, with its small raised stage, and curved neo-classical stage-façade, it possessed many of the characteristics of the earlier public playhouses. A list of what were probably the first plays performed there in 1630 survives (Folger Shakespeare Library MS 2068.8), and this shows that the King's Men put on 16 plays, nearly all old ones, including *Volpone* (1606), 'Olde Castle', which may be *Henry IV* (1597), *The Maid's Tragedy* (1610), and *Every Man in his Humour* (1598). The favourite dramatists were Beaumont and Fletcher, represented by seven plays, one (*Rollo Duke of Normandy*, or *The Bloody Brother* (1619)) performed twice. In relation to this, it is notable that the drawings show no sign of an 'inner stage', although some of the plays put on there required effects like a bed (used in *Volpone* and in *The Maid's Tragedy*), masques, dumb-shows and discoveries (as in *The Maid's Tragedy* and *The Duchess of Malfi*), and a banquet with a table and seats for about ten characters (*Rollo*). It is not known how all these were managed. If the stage was 34 ft wide, then the centre door on the stage would have been about 4 ft wide, and the other doors roughly 2½ ft wide, as they are shown on the plan and elevation drawn by John Webb. It seems that it would have been difficult to manoeuvre large properties on and off the stage, and there would hardly have been room for the 'large four-poster bed' Wickham

d

envisages as being used (*Shakespeare's Dramatic Heritage*, p. 158).

Among the drawings of Inigo Jones in the great collection of the Duke of Devonshire at Chatsworth is one (d) showing a proscenium with a round arch and a perspective setting. At the top of the sheet is written 'for yᵉ cockpitt for my lo Chamberlain 1639'. The arch of the proscenium crosses the lower part of the drawing of a head and shoulders of a young woman in the top left corner. The sketch is a rough one, rapidly drawn on a sheet already used, and may have been a preliminary idea for the setting of William Habington's *The Queen of Aragon*, presented by the Earl of Pembroke, Lord Chamberlain, in honour of the King and Queen, on 9 April 1640. This play was in fact staged at the hall in Whitehall, so that if this sketch was a first idea for it, the intention must initially have been to stage it at the Cockpit. However, the play for which the setting was

sketched cannot certainly be identified. In the sketch there are three wings on each side of the stage representing tents, a back-cloth depicting a sky with 'clouds', and in the centre at the rear a 'citti of releve', a flat partly cut away so as to make the 'city' stand out against a cloth behind it. The round arch with a cartouche in the centre is mounted on twin columns on either side. This shows how Jones might have transformed the Cockpit for special occasions by erecting a temporary proscenium to create an illusionistic setting in perspective. In this way ideas derived from Serlio and Palladio could transform for special purposes what was basically a modified form of Elizabethan theatre (see the commentary above on 29).

The Cockpit-in-Court was used as a theatre after the restoration of Charles II, and some Wardrobe Accounts relating to it survive from 1662. There is also extant a painting (e) inscribed 'WHITEHALL & ST. JAME'S

e

PARK, TIME OF CHARLES 2nd BY DANCKERT'
now in Berkeley Castle, which shows two sides of the
exterior of the Cockpit at this period. The painting
depicts a panorama of the buildings in Whitehall as
viewed from St James's Park, and the Cockpit is the
square building behind the pond and statue on the
right. There are no windows on the ground floor, but
the side facing the pond in the picture has two doors,
one at each corner, with windows in the walls above
these. This appears to correspond to the wall marked
A in the Webb ground-plan; the door on the left gave
admittance to a stairwell and the stage; the door on the
right afforded entrance into the galleries. Confirmation that this is the wall facing the viewer is provided
by the location of the chimney above the fireplace in
the tiring-house, which is shown on the left side of
the roof. The picture shows two windows lighting the
tiring-house, and two windows lighting the galleries,
as in the ground-plan. It also shows that the upper
galleries and the room above the tiring-house were also
lit by two windows pierced in each wall. The walls are
castellated above the roof-line, and the steeply pitched
roof rises to a central lantern. The basic features thus
correspond well with the ground-plan shown in the
drawing by John Webb, and add some further details
about the exterior of the building.

John H. Astington, 'Inigo Jones and the Whitehall Cockpit',
The Elizabethan Theatre, VII, ed. G. R. Hibbard (Toronto, 1980),
pp. 46–64
Bentley, *JCS*, VI 267–84
Eleanore Boswell, *The Restoration Court Stage* (1932), pp. 10–14
Gurr, 153–5 (Pl. 27)
Harris and Tait, 11–12 (Pl. 5)
Hodges, *Globe Restored*, 133–5 (Pl. 55)
Leacroft, 73–7 (Fig. 51)
Orgel and Strong, I 26–7; II 786–8 (Pls 26, 443)
Orrell, 142–6 (Pl. 36)
Wickham, *EES* II, ii 78–89, 246–7 (Pls XVIII–XXI)

3 1

Vignette of a stage from the title-page of William Alabaster's *Roxana* (1632).

Probably while he was a student at Cambridge, in about 1590, William Alabaster (1567–1640) made a Latin version of an Italian play, Luigi Grato's *La Dalida* (1567), for performance in Trinity College. The play was first printed in 1632 as acted, a long time previously, in this college, and with a claim on the title-page that it was carefully edited. This was soon followed by another edition, with a title-page presenting the tragedy of *Roxana* as restored from plagiarisms, amplified and acknowledged by the author. The title-page is illustrated by a border of small engraved panels, one of which shows a vignette of a stage; two depict full-length female figures in 'classical' costumes, and one a man with his arm round a woman. Alabaster's play was an old academic work, never performed in a regular theatre, and there is nothing to connect the vignette with any particular stage. It shows a group of spectators standing around the three sides of a stage which has low railings, as if to mark it off from the groundlings in the arena. Three actors are shown on the stage, and occupy so much of it that, if any attempt at accuracy could be supposed, the stage must have been quite small (see below for further comment on this point). One is dressed as a woman wearing a robe with a high standing collar; a bearded man wearing a sort of cloak is making suit to her, while on the left stands a figure in a tunic wielding a curved scimitar. Behind these are curtains or drapes, one pulled back as if to suggest a space behind. Two boxes or divisions of a gallery above, separated by a sturdy pillar, contain four other figures, apparently spectators watching the action.

The most striking feature of the sketch is the shape of the stage, which is not rectangular like those at the Globe, Fortune and Swan, but could be a segment of an octagon, or half a hexagon. This was a stage-shape familiar by 1632, as developed from the octagonal arenas of Cockpits. The Royal Cockpit in Whitehall had been used occasionally for performances of plays from 1607–8, and the Cockpit in Drury Lane was converted into the Phoenix Theatre in 1617. In 1629–30 the Royal Cockpit, or Cockpit-in-Court, was

adapted by Inigo Jones into a theatre, and the basic plan of this building was an octagon within a square (see 30 above). The *Roxana* vignette may then be based upon a form of stage that had become well-known by 1632. For the Cockpit-in-Court Inigo Jones designed an elaborate stage façade (*frons scenae*) with five doors, and it seems more likely therefore that the vignette, with its curtains or hangings, reflects a simpler adaptation of a former cockpit, such as Christopher Beeston may have used in the Phoenix when converting it for use by an adult Company as a public theatre. The curtains are particularly interesting because current opinion, relying heavily on the Swan drawing (26), has tended to dismiss the notion of an 'inner stage' in the Elizabethan theatre, and claims instead that a discovery-space was provided when necessary by a curtain or hanging fitted up in front of one of the stage doors. However, there are numerous references in a variety of plays to the use of curtains or hangings (Chambers lists many in *ES*, III.80–2), and a poem attributed to Sir Walter Raleigh, published in 1612, has the couplet:

> Our graves that hide us from the searching sun
> Are like drawn curtains when the play is done.

The *Roxana* vignette shows curtains that are drawn across the full width of the stage.

If the identification of the drawings described in 29 above as relating to the Phoenix, or Cockpit in Drury Lane, is correct, then the *Roxana* vignette does not show the stage-façade of that theatre, which has a round-arched opening in the centre, flanked by two other doors. It may represent a generalised impression of a theatre of this kind. If the stage was about 34 ft wide at its base, as at the Cockpit-in-Court (30 above), then the sides of the stage shown in the vignette would not have been more than about 15 ft long. One other feature of the vignette that deserves attention is the presence of stage-rails. These are referred to in Thomas Middleton's *Black Book* (?1604), and perhaps in Shakespeare's *Henry VIII*, V.iv; there is, however, no mention of them in the extant contracts for building

theatres, and none are shown in the de Witt drawing of the Swan (26 above). Stage-rails are shown in the *Messalina* frontispiece (1640; 34 below), so that it seems safe to conclude that they were a familiar sight by the 1630s (a stage-direction 'Sit on the Railes' occurs in *The Hector of Germany*, printed in 1615).

Adams, 93–5, 136, 299

Chambers, *ES*, III 80–2, 207–8

E. K. Chambers, ed. *Oxford Book of Sixteenth-Century Verse*, p. 499

Gurr, 138–9 (Pl. 24)

Hodges, *Globe Restored*, 26–7, 132 (Pl. 50)

Leacroft, 28–9 (Fig. 20(a))

Reynolds, 30–1, 88

D. F. Rowan, *The Elizabethan Theatre*, I, 89–102 (on the Cockpit-in-Court)

J. W. Saunders, 'Vaulting the Rails', *SS*, 7 (1954), 69–71, 73

Smith, 48–9 (Pl. 18)

Wickham, *EES* II, ii 46–7, 82, 87ff, 232–5

John Webb, after Inigo Jones, Plan for conversion of a hall into a temporary theatre, probably the Paved or Lower court at Somerset House in 1632–3.

This drawing in ink on linen, measuring 15½ in. × 11¾ in. (394 mm × 298 mm), is on the inner pages of a sheet folded once to give four pages, now ff. 9 and 10 in British Library MS Lansdowne 1171, a collection of early drawings relating to theatrical activities. On the outer pages is written the name 'Inigo Jones' (f. 9ʳ), apparently in a later hand, but the plan, drawn by John Webb, appears to relate to Jones's task, as Surveyor of the Works, in setting up a theatre in the winter of 1632–3 for 'a Pastorall and Maske to be performed by the Queene and her Ladies'. The masque has not been identified, but the pastoral was Walter Montagu's *The Shepherd's Paradise*, staged in January 1633, with the Queen playing the leading role. It has recently been shown by John Orrell that the plan of the hall in the drawing corresponds to the lower or paved court at Somerset (also known as Denmark) House. A warrant of 3 November 1632 to Inigo Jones orders the 'Timber worke of yᵉ Sceane wᵗʰ ye Stage & degrees' to be properly carried out, and accounts relating to the setting up of this temporary theatre also survive. These specify payments for 'framing and razing a greate house of fir timber and Dealeborde in the paved Courte', for 'putting up Degrees', putting a 'Cloth in the Ceeling', erecting a 'State', and also for taking down the degrees at the lower end of the hall and altering them for the masque. The accounts also indicate that there were 'railes round aboute the Stadge at the foote of the Degrees'.

The plan in the drawing shows a T-shaped room, with the stage set up at the wide end. Using the scale which accompanies the plan, Orrell has calculated the length of the room as 76 ft, and the width as about 50 ft at the wider end, and 35 ft at the narrower end. The plan is a rough one, but it indicates a raised stage with central steps leading up to it, and behind are four pairs of flat wings, grooves for the back shutters, and three pairs of posts, put there to support the layers of relieve scenes in front of the backcloth. The area behind this is inscribed 'passage behind the backcloth', and at the front, to the right of the stage (left in the drawing) a roughly square area with degrees in it

is marked 'musick house'. The body of the hall was filled with seating raised in degrees to create a U-shaped auditorium with the 'State' in the centre. The accounts include payments to a carpenter for making 'two outletts at the end where the Sceane was', apparently referring not to exits but to the spaces on either side of the stage providing the extra width. The structure made by the carpenter was 25 ft high, which presumably refers to the proscenium arch he built; a setting for the play showing how the proscenium may have looked survives, and is reproduced as 30(d). If the short lines on either side at the front of the stage represent the pilasters for the proscenium arch, then these were about 2 ft 6 in. wide, and the stage width between the pilasters was about 30 ft. The depth of the stage to the backcloth was approximately 20 ft. The 'State' set up centrally for the King is marked '7f ½', which indicates its width, corresponding to the scale, of 7 ft 6 in., and is also inscribed '3 fo. 8', or 3 ft 8 in, the measure of its depth; the step leading up to it has the measure '1f', or 1 ft.

The accounts relate to a period of four months, and probably cover the erection and dismantling of this temporary theatre. *The Shepherd's Paradise*, a long, neo-platonic pastoral, was written by a man who had spent a good deal of time in France on royal service, and had been involved in the negotiations leading to the marriage of Charles I to Henrietta Maria of France. Montagu deliberately adopted the spirit of French *préciosité* in a play which is reported as lasting seven or eight hours, and in which the Queen 'excelled really all others both in acting and singing' (letters of 10 and 13 January 1633; *JCS*, IV.918). The performances in which the Queen took part stimulated much interest among court and diplomatic circles, and provided an excuse for the prosecution of William Prynne, whose *Histriomastix*, viciously attacking women actors as whores, was published, by an unfortunate coincidence, just after the play was first staged. The play was eventually printed in 1659 as 'Privately Acted before the Late King *Charls* by the Queen's Majesty, and Ladies of Honour'. The plan made by Jones for the alterations

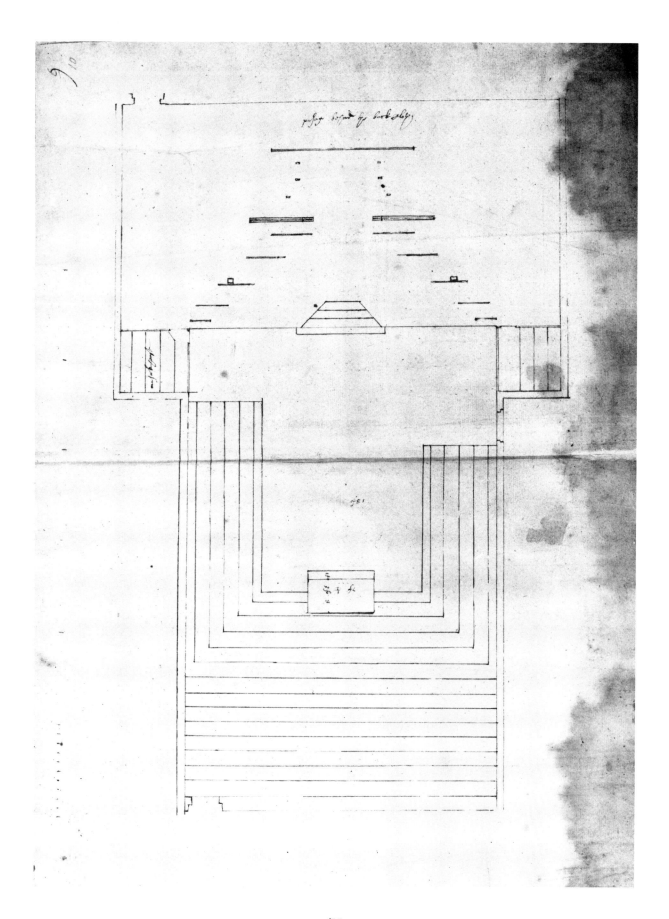

in the lower court gives no sense of the lavish spectacle
with numerous changes of scene which this expensive
production involved; these included, for example,
a proscenium and standing scene similar to that reproduced on p. 79. (It is perhaps worth noting that at
least two other drawings for a proscenium arch with a
standing scene survive, one for a French pastoral performed by the Queen and her ladies in Somerset House
in 1626, and the other possibly for a tragedy, also in
Somerset House, in 1629–30; Orgel and Strong, II.
383–5, Pl. 135 and II.397, Pl. 141.) A rectangular
opening was framed by richly ornamented columns
supporting a cross-beam with a cartouche bearing the
name of the play at its centre. The raised stage had a
double set of steps leading up to it from the floor of the
hall, and the perspective scene created the effect of a
pastoral landscape with buildings and a hill in the
distance. Other sketches of scenes and costumes for this
play are reproduced in Orgel and Strong.

Bentley, *JCS*, IV 916–21
Harris and Tait, 17, 92–3 (Pl. 126)
Leacroft, 60–3 (Fig. 40)
Orgel and Strong, II 504–36
John Orrell, 'The Paved Court Theatre at Somerset House',
British Library Journal, 3 (1977), 13–19
Southern, 46–7 (Pl. 7)
Wickham, *EES* II, ii 154–6, 223–4 (Appendix D)

33

Inigo Jones, Drawing for the conversion of the Tudor Hall, Whitehall, into a theatre for the presentation of *Florimène* (December 1635).

Inigo Jones was commissioned in October 1635 to prepare the hall at Whitehall as a theatre for the staging of the lost pastoral *Florimène* in December. The 'argument' of the play was published, showing that it had five acts, a number of scene-changes, special effects like the descent of Diana in a chariot, and four '*intermedii*' between the acts, with scene-changes and dances to represent the four seasons. The argument was printed presumably because the play was performed in French. The performance was followed by antimasques in English written by Aurelian Townshend. An extensive series of designs by Inigo Jones for this production survives, and these have been thoroughly documented and splendidly reproduced in Orgel and Strong. The elaborate conversion of a hall over two months to provide scaffolds, degrees for seating, angled side-wings on the stage, a back-shutter, private boxes for various people, and a state for the King and Queen, all for the production of a single spectacular court entertainment, is a far cry from the activities of the London theatres putting on performances for a paying public. The plan of the stage and auditorium, however, is reproduced here as (a), showing how Inigo Jones arranged the stage and seating for a royal performance. The measurements marked on the plan show that a stage was built from the screens at one end of the hall, extending about 34 ft into the hall. The two screen doors, clearly shown, gave access to a space 3 ft 4 in. deep behind a backcloth. In front of this at 18-in. intervals are three 'works of Relevo to Remove', or removable flats partly cut away to provide a three-dimensional effect (see 30 above). In front of this, at an interval of 2 ft 4 in. is the rear of the shutter, shown open, with a gap of 13 ft. On each side in front of this are four angled side-wings, for a perspective scene behind a proscenium. The depth of the stage from shutter to proscenium appears to have been 16 ft, and the stage extended a further 7 ft beyond the proscenium. The stage occupied the entire width of the hall, 40 ft, and was 4 ft 6 in. high, with a slender rake raising it to 5 ft at the rear. The proscenium (b) shows that the centre of the stage was cut back at the front, where two

flights of steps were built on the right and the left leading down to the central space in the auditorium.

Degrees of seating were arranged around three sides of the auditorium, with certain areas designated as 'M^r S^{r}vayours box', 'Sir thomas Edmonds his box', 'The Cowntesse of Arundelles box', 'The ladie marquis her box'. In each corner at the rear of the auditorium stairs are shown, and a slip pasted on the lower corner is inscribed, 'this stayrs are but flatt staued laders'. In the centre stands a halpace or state for the King and Queen, 11 ft wide, and separated from the seating around by a passage 2 ft 2 in. wide; it would appear to have been about 7 ft deep, including the two steps leading up into it. The measurements for the space in front of the royal state or box are not given, but it would appear to have been 15 ft 4 in. wide, opening out to 20 ft, by 21 ft deep. Here dancers, or actors for that matter, could come down off the stage to perform directly in front of the King and Queen. The plan shows the outer walls of the hall, and eight tiers of steps or degrees arranged around the walls for the rest of the audience. These occupied about 12 ft 6 in., and presumably provided four rows of narrow benches for seating, with equally narrow gangways between. On either side of the stage in front of the proscenium are shown three steps or degrees, which may have been reserved for the musicians who played music for the various songs and dances included in *Florimène*. The whole plan is drawn in ink on a large linen sheet formed by pasting two small sheets together and adding a strip along the bottom. The plan measures 13¼ in. × 26½ in. (337 mm × 674 mm), and is inscribed at one end, 'the ground platt of the hall as it was made Redie for a pastorall in the hall at whitthall wch was ackted by the ffrench on St Thomas day the 23rd of decemb^r 1635'.

The basic arrangement of the hall is similar to that designed for the conversion at Somerset House in 1632 (see 32 above). Both plans in turn may be related to Inigo Jones's drawings for the conversion of the Royal Cockpit in 1629–30 (30), which appear to show how Jones adapted his style of converting halls for special

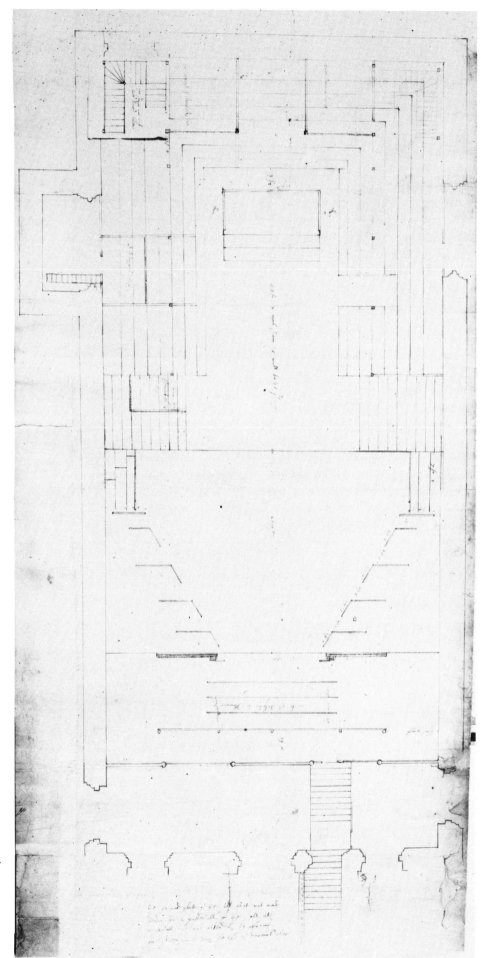

a

b

one-off court performances in modifying the Cockpit, so that it could be used by professional companies like the King's Men, who presented sixteen plays there before a court audience in 1630. This in turn relates back to Jones's designs for converting the Cockpit in Drury Lane, probably in 1616–18 (29 above). These were private or indoor theatres, very different in their size and arrangements from what is known of the public theatres, but from the time when they took over Blackfriars as a winter house, the King's Men must have learned to adapt to playing in a theatre with an auditorium measuring 46 ft × 66 ft (Bentley, *JCS*, VI. 11). The Cockpit in Drury Lane (later the Phoenix) was 40 ft × 55 ft, and the Cockpit-in-Court was designed in an octagon within a building 55 ft square. The Salisbury Court Theatre, opened in 1630, was noted for its small size (Bentley, *JCS*, VI.92–3). It would be interesting to know what influence the

development of private theatre design had upon the appearance, design and practices of the public theatres, but no visual evidence remains.

Bentley, *JCS*, V 1333–5
Leacroft, 56–61 (Fig. 36)
Orgel and Strong, II 630–59 (Pls 321–4, 326)
Richard Southern, *Changeable Scenery* (1952)

34

Vignette of a stage from the title-page of Nathanial Richards's *Messalina* (1640).

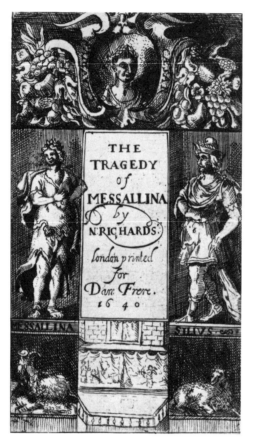

This tragedy, written about 1634–6, is the only play extant by Nathanial Richards, and it was performed by the adult company, the King's Revels, probably at the Salisbury Court Theatre. The only early edition of the play was published in 1640 with an engraved title-page which includes a vignette of a stage, representations of the head of the emperor Claudius, and full-length figures of Messalina, his wife, and Caius Silius, her lover, put to death for adultery with her. The costumes of these two figures seem intended to represent an idea of Roman styles, though Silius wears a modern hat with his tunic and sandals; the costume of Messalina resembles the 'classical' costumes of the two standing female figures shown on the *Roxana* title-page (31 above). It is impossible to determine whether there is any link between these figures and the way the performers were costumed. At the foot of the title-page is a representation of three sides of a stage similar to that in the *Roxana* vignette. It shows what is probably half of an octagon, again with low stage railings. At the rear are curtains drawn across the whole width visible. The one to the left has a standing figure and what look like trees on it, that to the right shows the winged figure of Cupid about to shoot an arrow in front of a vaguely indicated landscape. The general suggestion is of curtains or hangings painted or embroidered with scenes.

Above this is a wall made of brick, or painted to look like brick, with a central window, which also has curtains drawn across it. The stage curtains hang from a narrow projection or canopy running along the wall just below the level of the window. The wall and canopy are both carried round a corner on each side of the vignette, paralleling the shape of the stage, though the stage-curtains extend across almost the full width of the stage. In other words, the stage-façade or *frons scenae* has three sides like the stage, but whereas the three sides of the stage are of about equal length, the front of the stage-façade appears to be much wider than the sides.

The Salisbury Court Theatre was the last theatre built in London before the civil disruptions which began in 1642. It was opened in 1630, and the site has been identified, but nothing is known for certain about its design. However, if it is to be related, as Glynne Wickham thinks (*EES* II.ii.144–7), to designs by Inigo Jones (see 29 above) now in Worcester College, Oxford, these show a building with a semi-circular auditorium facing a rectangular stage area. The *Messalina* vignette seems to represent a different kind of stage, based upon an octagonal plan, like that of the Royal Cockpit (see 30 above). The drawn curtains on the stage and at the window or gallery, and the empty stage, apparently represent a stage before or after a performance. The lines in front of the curtains may be intended merely to suggest the stage-surface there; the broken markings in front of these, slightly to the right of centre-stage, have been taken to signify a trap-door (Wickham, *EES* II.ii.88), but it is not clear that they have any such significance. On the matter of the curtains and stage-rails, see 31 above.

Adams, pp. 93–9 (Pl. 24)
Bentley, *JCS*, V 1002–4
G. E. Bentley, 'The Salisbury Court Theater and its Boy Players',
Huntington Library Quarterly, 40 (1977), 129–49
Hodges, *Globe Restored*, 26–7, 132 (Pl. 49)
Leacroft, 28–9 (Fig. 20(b))
Reynolds, 30–1
J. W. Saunders, 'Vaulting the Rails', *SS*, 7 (1954), 69–71, 73
Smith, 48–9 (Pl. 19)
Wickham, *EES* II, ii 88–9, 144–8

35

Mildmay Fane, Earl of Westmorland, *Candy Restored* (1641).

This amateur work, written by an aristocrat for private performance by members of his family and household at his seat, Apthorpe, survives in two manuscript versions, one in the British Library (MS Add. 34221), and the other in the Huntington Library (MS HM 771). The second of these includes two drawings of scenic arrangements for a rectangular stage with a recess at the rear. One drawing shows a plan of the stage, with three pairs of flat wings at each side, and curtains at the rear, which presumably opened to reveal a relieve or a painted scene. The side-wings are shown standing at a peculiar angle in relation to possible spectators, but this may be intentional with reference to the second drawing, which provides a side-view to show how each of the wings was mounted on a central pivot, and could be turned by pulling on a rope leading to the rear of the stage. The wings could thus be used to depict two different scenes, and the plan is perhaps intended merely to show them schematically as revolving wings. The play itself deals with recent political events, but oddly tries to combine realism with allegory. The author seems to have known some later plays of Ben Jonson, but had no great talent himself as a dramatist. The drawings, however, show that he had a sophisticated grasp of advanced contemporary techniques of staging. The arrangement shown in the drawings suggests a development beyond the fixed wings used for *Florimène* in 1635 (33 above), or the setting of three pairs of fixed flat wings drawn for the Cockpit Theatre in 1639 (see 30 above); it also uses a different principle from the side shutters moving in grooves as shown in John Webb's drawings for the elaborate masque *Salmacida Spolia* in 1640 (Orgel and Strong, II.736–41).

The pages of the manuscript have ornamental ink lines providing margins and a frame within which the text of the play could be written. The text, written in ink, occupies thirty-two pages, and is followed by two leaves blank except for the ink lines. The stage drawings are on what, if numbered, would be pages 34 and 35. It looks as though the draughtsman simply used the ink lines to frame his drawings, which may not be to scale. If the proportions of the larger drawing are roughly correct, the stage would have been about twice as wide as it was deep, with a space behind the curtain equivalent to $\frac{2}{9}$ths of the depth of the stage. The title-page of the manuscript shows that a perspective scene was used, and describes it as follows:

The Scene

A picture of Diana with a Cressant under which in a scroule written in greate

CANDY RESTORED

vnder which in perspective a goodly fabrick or Cittie the Emblem of Concord Vnitie and peace. Vnder which A landskipp representing the springe for the fresh greennesse of itt and those innocent, and vsefull delights of hunting both y^t Iland hath been famous for, and that season fitted the temperature of the ayer too, wch wth out a settled recovery of peace and tranquillity the greene had withered, and the pleasure been dead or layd a sleepe./

On either side the stage a treble entry ouer which Heroes men of armes in armes and Battles Painted to paint out the horrid shape of discord which without a miletary word turne silently faces about at the chang in states fortune and ar backt wth nothing but fresh greenes & faire garden Landskips wch consent in vniformity wth ye scene it selfe ye trauerse being drawne.

The background included a picture of Diana with a crescent, a city and a landscape, and on each side were the 'treble' entries made possible by the three flat revolving wings on each side of the stage, as shown in the drawings; the curtains at the rear were drawn only at the play's climax to reveal Diana and the scenic devices behind it.

Bentley, *JCS*, III 293–5

Clifford Leech, ed., *Mildmay Fane's Raguaillo D'Oceano, 1640 and Candy Restored, 1641* (Bang's Materials for the Study of Old English Drama, Louvain, 1938)

Allardyce Nicoll, *Stuart Masques and the Renaissance Stage* (1938, reprinted New York 1963), pp. 151–3

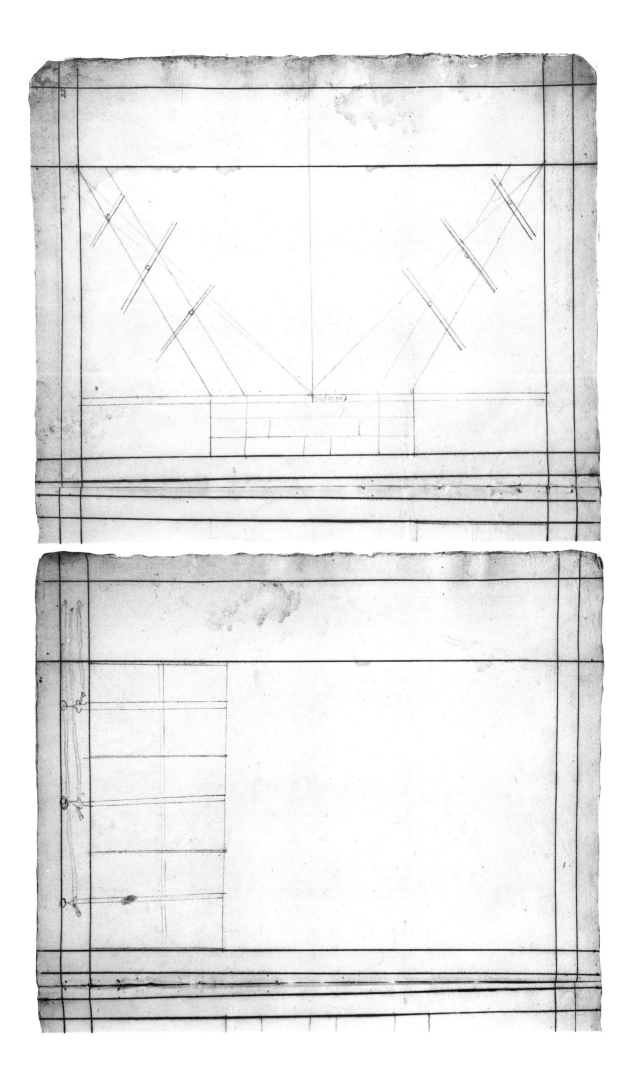

36

Designs for an unidentified conversion to a theatre attributed to Inigo Jones, and copied by John Webb (date uncertain).

Perhaps two drawings in Worcester College, Oxford, attributed to Inigo Jones, should be included here. They are in pen and ink, on the left half of a sheet measuring $15\frac{1}{4}$ in. $\times 11\frac{3}{4}$ in. (390 mm $\times$ 300 mm), the other half containing drawings by John Webb of sections of the Teatro Olimpico at Vicenza. These designs may relate to a temporary conversion in Somerset House, where Jones was commissioned on a number of occasions from 1625 onwards to stage performances. The plan shows semi-circular tiers of seats arranged, without any provision for the entrance or exit of spectators, on the model of the plan of a theatre in Sebastiano Serlio's *Second Book of Architecture* (1545, translated into English 1611). The measurements given on the plan show that the design was for an area 52 ft wide by about 69 ft deep, and this could have been located in the lower court at Somerset House, where a performance was staged in 1633. Other measurements give the 'bredth of ye Orchestra' as 43 ft, which was also the depth of the auditorium from the front of the stage. The stage façade was designed to stand 14 ft 9 ins back from the front of the stage, with the arch opening on to a perspective scene, 14 ft wide. The plan indicates angled side wings, and the scene, as shown through the arch in the elevation of the *frons scenae*, is not unlike the tragic scene Orgel and Strong think may have been associated with a 'Stage and Scene to bee made at Somerset House' which Inigo Jones was commissioned to design in 1629. The measurements at the side of the elevation show that it would have stood 39 ft high; the stage is shown as rising 4 ft above the floor, the lower range of columns, measuring $12\frac{1}{2}$ ft high, stood on a base 4 ft above the stage, and the higher row of columns measured $9\frac{1}{2}$ ft, with the frieze and entablature standing 4 ft above the architrave. At the side John Webb wrote, 'And in ye designe this Arch is in heigns most two squares: whereby ye length of ye stage comes to bee lesse then is heere drawne'. This relates to the further inscription on the stage-plan, '52: fo: $\frac{1}{2}$ to make ye Arch two squares high'. This suggests that the drawings are not to scale; if the arch were 'two squares' high, it would presumably rise to 28 ft, twice the opening of 14 ft. As shown on the elevation, the arch would need to be about 18 ft or 19 ft wide to correspond with the given measurements for height, and a scaling down of height and width would mean reducing the width of the stage by 8 ft or more. Presumably these are preliminary designs, and there is no evidence to show either when Inigo Jones made them, or whether they were ever carried out. (For further comment, see 29 above.)

Chambers, *ES*, IV 353–65
Documents of Serlio, Sabbattini and Furttenbach, translated by Allardyce Nicoll, John H. McDowell and George R. Kernodle, edited by Barnard Hewitt (Coral Gables, 1958), pp. 21–33
Harris and Tait, Item 15 (Pl. 126), and Item 249
Orgel and Strong, I 397 (Pl. 141)

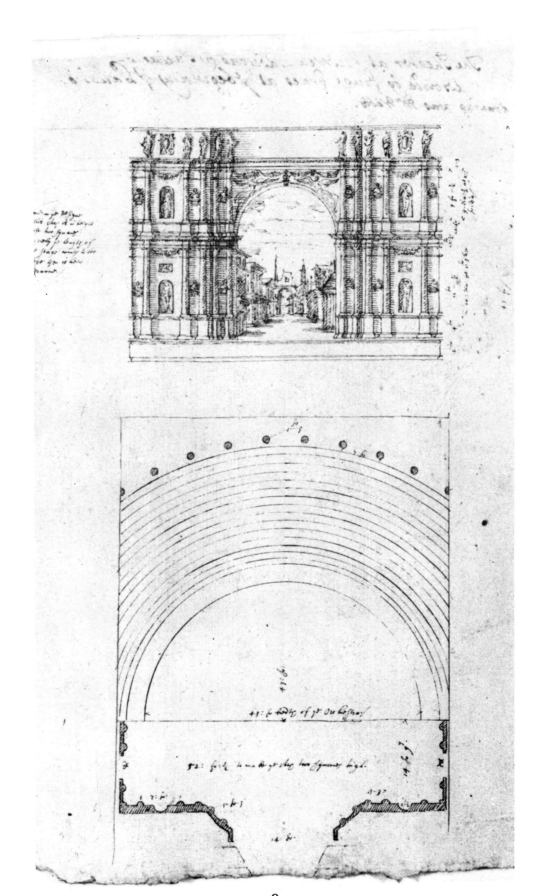

C
Illustrations relating to the stage
in printed texts of plays

37

Christopher Marlowe, *Tamburlaine*, Parts I and II (1590 and 1597).

When Marlowe's famous two-part play *Tamburlaine* was published in 1590, the text was accompanied by a woodcut illustrating the hero. It shows the upper half of a figure in full body-armour, with a baldrick slung across the left shoulder. The head is bare, the face bearded. The part was played for the Admiral's Men by Edward Alleyn (1566–1626), who was a young man when the play was staged, probably in 1588. A portrait of Alleyn, bearded, and wearing a large black hat, hangs in Dulwich College; it is by an unknown painter, and probably shows him when he was much older, at about the time when Dulwich College was completed in 1616. It is tempting to connect the woodcut with this, but there are only superficial resemblances, and it seems more likely that the woodcut represents a typical military figure, and has no immediate connection with the play. As a 'thrice renowned man-at-arms' (Part I, II.v. 6), Tamburlaine no doubt wore some kind of armour in battle-scenes, and his army is described at one point as including 'Three hundred thousand men in armour clad' (Part I, IV.i.21); but in spite of much reference to arms and fighting in the dialogue, the clues to costuming relate mainly to pomp and colour, as when Tamburlaine changes from white to scarlet (Part I, IV.iv), and then to black (Part I, V.i.63) at the siege of Damascus. The inventories of costumes relating to the stock of the Admiral's Men in 1598 include for Tamburlaine a coat with copper lace and crimson velvet breeches, but no mention of armour. In the third edition of the play in 1597 another woodcut was added illustrating Zenocrate. Like the first cut, it shows the upper half of a figure, and the top corners are again hatched to provide a framing curve above the head. It shows a female head wearing what may be a coronet, from which falls to her shoulders either her hair or a head-dress. She wears ornamented necklaces, and a gown with puffed and scalloped sleeves. The play provides no evidence about the costuming of Zenocrate, and it is not possible to say whether this woodcut relates to it. It seems more probable that it is a conventional representation of a richly-dressed woman, and, like the woodcut of Tamburlaine, has no immediate bearing on the play.

Another possible representation of Alleyn as Tamburlaine has been identified in an illustration in Richard Knolles, *The Generall Historie of the Turks* (1603). This book includes a number of portraits of Islamic potentates in the form of medallion heads framed in square ornamental borders, incorporating the initials 'L I', or Lawrence Johnson, and usually, but not always, containing the date 1603. The book, a substantial folio, presents a full and detailed history, in contrast to Jean Jaques Boissard's much smaller *Vitae et Icones Sultanorum Turcicorum* (1596). This contains a series of brief lives, in Latin, of a great range of sultans, each one illustrated by a portrait head, and includes too accounts of one or two Eastern European Christian rulers, who are shown in their portraits as bareheaded, in contrast to the sultans, who all wear turbans of some sort. To illustrate Richard Knolles's book, Lawrence Johnson copied a number of the heads from Boissard's lives, designing his own less elaborate borders for them. All those he copied are shown in turbans, and the one exception, the portrait of Tamburlaine, has no counterpart in Boissard's book, in which he is barely mentioned and not illustrated. Lawrence Johnson must have based this portrait, on p. 236 of *The Generall Historie of the Turks*, on some other source. The portrait is unlike any of the others, in showing a waist-length figure in an oval within an oblong frame; the area around the oval within the frame is covered with hatching, except for the artist's name, 'LAWRANCE IOHNSONN. SCVLP', in the bottom left corner. The portrait shows a bareheaded, bearded figure, with his hands on the belt he is wearing; he is shown in contemporary European dress, although the inscription beneath includes the date of his death as 1402. Martin Holmes describes the figure as wearing a doublet, a jerkin with short sleeves, 'buttoning down the front to waist-level and apparently fitted with pleated skirts or bases, and over that again a long garment of brocade or damask, clasped at the throat only and fitted with slashed shoulder-rolls and scalloped, tasselled fringes, the outline of which is represented in the falling-band at the neck' (Holmes, p. 12). The

89

account of Tamburlaine given by Richard Knolles states that he 'was for the most part bareheaded' (p. 235), and that the portrait presents 'his lively counterfeit' (p. 236). Holmes believes that the robe with scalloped fringes belongs to an 'accepted convention for fantastic, outlandish or "period" costume on the stage' (p. 12), that the figure is shown wearing a wig, and that it is, in effect, a portrait of Alleyn in the role in Marlowe's play, wearing his 'cotte with coper lace' listed in *Henslowe's Diary*. It is pleasant to wonder if Alleyn had made Tamburlaine so famous that Lawrence Johnson would incorporate a portrait of him in a large general history of the Turks, and certainly the portrait is an oddity in the volume; but it has to be said that the costume may be conventional, in the style of illustrations of historical figures in chronicles, rather than theatrical, and an association with Alleyn and the stage remains speculative.

W. A. Armstrong, 'Shakespeare and the Acting of Edward Alleyn', *SS*, 7 (1954), 82–9
Chambers, *ES*, III 421–2 and II 296–8
ed. J. S. Cunningham (Revels Plays, 1981)
Foakes and Rickert, *HD*, 321, 322
Martin Holmes, 'An Unrecorded Portrait of Edward Alleyn', *TN*, V (1950–1), 11–13
G. L. Hosking, *The Life and Times of Edward Alleyn* (1952)
J. D. Jump, ed. (Regents Renaissance Drama Series, 1967)
Richard Knolles, *The Generall Historie of the Turks* (1603)

38

Thomas Heywood, *If You Know not Me, You Know Nobody*, or *The Troubles of Queen Elizabeth*, Parts I and II (1605, 1606).

The first part of this two-part play ends with the death of Mary Tudor and the ceremonial presentation to the new Queen Elizabeth of her crown, as various characters bring on other properties of royalty:

> . . . Howard *the sceptre*, Constable *with the cap of maintenance*, Chandos *with the Sword*, Thamo *with the Collar and a George, four Gentlemen bearing the Canopy over the* Queen, *two Gentlewomen bearing up her train, six gentlemen* Pensioners, *the* Queen *takes state*.

It is appropriate that the title-page should bear a woodcut of Queen Elizabeth in state, holding an orb and sceptre, crowned, and sitting in a canopied chair of state bearing the royal initials 'ER'. However, the play concerns her youth, and her attainment of the throne, so that it ends when Elizabeth was twenty-five. The illustration on the title-page (a) seems based upon an engraving made late in her reign, c. 1595–1600, by William Rogers, or upon the well-known engraving derived from that by Rogers, and made after the Queen's death, perhaps in 1603, by Crispin van de Passe (Strong, E30, Post. 3 and 4; pp. 114, 152 and Plate XVI). Both of these engravings show the Queen standing, but the wide farthingale she is wearing needed only slight adjustment in the drawing to convert her in the woodcut to a seated figure. The woodcut (b) shows less detail than the engravings but represents the Queen as wearing the same gown, with its diamond pattern, the same crown, necklaces and jewel on her forehead, and carrying the same orb and sceptre. The only noticeable differences are that in the woodcut she lacks the long fourfold chain of pearls hanging to her waist in the engravings, and also the wide rebatoes spreading fanwise from her shoulders.

The same block was used for the title-pages of the next four editions of the play, published in 1606, 1608, 1610 and 1613. When it was reprinted by a different printer in 1623, a cruder woodcut of Queen Elizabeth was used to adorn the title-page (c), showing her as a standing figure, with orb and sceptre, wearing a crown, and with the high standing collar or rebato sprouting from her shoulders. The florid ornamentation of the gown is different, but again this appears to be derived from the Rogers or de Passe engravings. The seventh

a

b

edition (1632) was printed from the sixth, but the eighth edition, issued in 1639, contains a prologue and epilogue not in the earlier editions, stating that the author has corrected the imperfections of the text (Heywood lived until 1641). The title-page of this edition (d) has a much smaller woodcut, which seems to be based on earlier portraits of the Queen wearing a headdress with a long veil or train and a pleated ruff. A number of portraits and engravings show her in this style of costume, and all date from about 1580–90 (Strong, P52–5, W15, 17; pp. 70–2, 124). The Queen is almost invariably shown with the sceptre in her right hand, and the orb in her left; perhaps the artist forgot that his drawing would be reversed in the process of printing. This may have been a deliberate attempt to suggest a younger Elizabeth, but the cut is too crude to be more than a gesture in this direction.

Part II ends with the defeat of the Spanish Armada, and the Queen greeting Sir Francis Drake and Frobisher. It was printed in 1606, and then reissued with a cancel title-page which bears a fine woodcut of Queen Elizabeth, copied with great care from an engraving which had been used as a frontispiece to two books published in 1588, and which circulated in separate impressions (Strong, W17, p. 124). This may have been deliberately chosen as a representation of Elizabeth in the Armada year. It was used again in the second edition of 1609. The third and fourth editions, published in 1623 and 1632, both use as a title-page illustration the woodcut that appears in the 1623 edition of Part I. All these illustrations are derived from portraits of Queen Elizabeth, and have no connection with the stage. Presumably an audience in 1605 or 1606, or for that matter at later revivals of what were evidently popular plays, would have been familiar with the image of Queen Elizabeth as numerous engravings, cuts, coins and medals portrayed her. It seems likely that the boy-actor playing this role in Heywood's narratives of events in her career up to 1588 would have been costumed to look like her, and it is especially interesting to find a portrait of her made in the Armada year used for Part II.

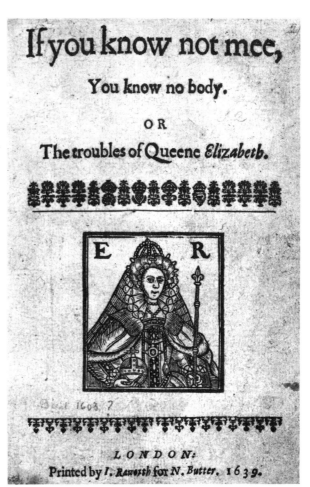

c   d

Chambers, *ES*, III 342–3

A. M. Clark, *Thomas Heywood* (1958), 31–4, 107–8

Greg, 215, 224 (a II)

Linthicum, 167–8

MSR, 1934 (1935)

ed. R. H. Shepherd, *Dramatic Works* (1874, reprinted 1964),
I 189–350

Roy Strong, *Portraits of Queen Elizabeth I* (Oxford, 1963)

93

39

No-Body and Some-Body (?1606).

NO-BODY,
AND
SOME-BODY.

With the true Chronicle Hiftorie of Elydure,
*who was fortunately three feuerall times
crowned King of England.*

*The true Coppy thereof, as it hath beene acted by the
Queens Maiefties Seruants.*

Printed for Iohn Trundle and are to be fold at his fhop in
Barbican, at the figne of No-body.

This 'true Chronicle Historie of Elydure' concerns the final displacement of the flinty King Archigallo by his tender-hearted brother Elidurus, and may be the same as the play 'albere galles', for which Henslowe paid Thomas Heywood and Wentworth Smith in September 1602. The play is of a kind popular in the 1580s and early 1590s, when histories of mythical English kings seem to have been in vogue; the *Three Lords and Three Ladies of London* (see 71 below) is a play in this mode. The text as it stands contains allusions to the reign of James I, and if Heywood and Smith revised an old play in 1602, as seems likely, it must have been updated again before its publication, probably in 1606, since it was entered in the Stationers' Register in March of that year. The play has a title-page illustration of the character of Nobody, and a woodcut at the end depicting Somebody. These two figures relate to the morality tradition, and the comic subplot in which Nobody is held responsible for the misdeeds of Somebody throughout the land, until in the end the true villain is revealed and executed, revamps material and ideas that had long been familiar. It seems to have retained an appeal for audiences in the early seventeenth century, and a part of their pleasure no doubt was derived from the way the actors playing Nobody and Somebody were costumed. When Nobody first appears, his companion the Clown asks him 'why do you go thus out of fashion? you are even a very hoddy doddy, all breech' (ll. 375–6). A 'hoddy doddy' was a short dumpy person, the term being related to the idea of a snail. So the text confirms that his costume was all breeches, 'And no body', as Nobody replies. Later on the Clown confronts Somebody and says, 'I'll tickle your long waist for this' (l. 1511), drawing attention to his costume, which, by contrast, had to be all body and no breeches. Several other comments and jokes in the text refer to the peculiar costuming of these characters (as at l. 804, and ll. 1199–1207), and the illustrations may well show how the Queen's Men dressed their actors. Nobody holds what I take to be a crudely represented roll of papers in his hand, suggesting the bonds, leases and petitions pulled out of his pockets at the end of the play.

Here are, my liege, bonds, forfeit by poor men,
Which he releas'd out of the usurers' hands,
And cancell'd. Leases, likewise forfeited,
By him repurchas'd. These petitions
Of many poor men, to prefer their suits
Unto your highness.

(lines 1937–42)

Somebody wears a sword, and wields a stave, as he
continually seeks a fight with Nobody, and is notorious
for the outrages he commits; when he is exposed in the
last scene, Nobody says,

Somebody swaggered with the watch last night,
Was carried to the counter; *Somebody*
Once pick'd a pocket in this Play-house yard,
Was hoisted on the stage and sham'd about it.

(lines 1892–5)

Somebody's sword and stave in the woodcut are
appropriate to his role as swaggerer.

The play was evidently popular because of the figures of Nobody and Somebody, and it was included in
the repertory of the company of English players who
travelled in Germany and Austria in 1607–8. It was
performed before the Archduke Maximilian in Graz in
1608, and this led to the preparation of a German
translation of the play; the manuscript has a dedication
by John Green, a leading member of the company, and
is illustrated with a sketch of him in the part of Nobody
(see 28 above). The play was also included in a volume
of *Engelische Comedien und Tragedien* published in Ham-
burg in 1620. Further testimony to the popularity of
Nobody as a comic figure in the play, when it was
revived in London in 1602, may be found in Ben
Jonson's *Entertainment at Althorp* (June 1603), in which
he introduced a character 'in the person of No-body
... attired in a pair of breeches which were made to
come up to his neck, with his arms out at his pockets,
and a cap drowning his face.' The speech intended for
him seems on the occasion to have gone unheard, but
Jonson expected his appearance to 'move' the 'laugh-
ter' of the audience. Either the play was well known,
or the costume of Nobody was traditional and familiar,
for Jonson assumed that his aristocratic audience,
which included the Queen and Prince Henry, a Duke,
Earls and Countesses, would be amused by Nobody.

SOME·BODY

Chambers, *ES*, II 281–3, 285; IV 37
A. M. Clark, *Thomas Heywood*, 26–8
Greg, 229
R. Simpson, ed., *The School of Shakespeare* (1878), Vol. I
TFT (1907)

40

Robert Armin, *The History of the Two Maids of Moreclack* (1609).

THE
Hiſtory of the two Maids of More-clacke,
VVith the life and ſimple maner of Iohn
in the Hoſpitall.

Played by the Children of the Kings
Maieſties Reuels.

VVritten by Robert Armin, ſeruant to the Kings
moſt excellent Maieſtie.

LONDON,
Printed by N.O. for Thomas Archer, and is to be ſold at his
ſhop in Popes-head Pallace, 1 6 0 9.

Armin was a member of the Lord Chamberlain's Company by 1599, and seems to have succeeded William Kemp as their leading player of fools and clowns when Kemp left the company in that year. Armin gained some reputation also as a writer, and showed an interest in the concept of the fool, and the potentialities of the role, in his *Fool upon Fool* (1600), revised as *A Nest of Ninnies* (1608). The one play he certainly wrote, *The Two Maids of Moreclack*, seems to have been first acted in the reign of Queen Elizabeth, and topical allusions in it suggest it was composed probably between 1597 and 1599. It was published in 1609, apparently much revised, and as performed by the Children of the King's Revels. In a preface addressed 'To the friendly peruser', Armin refers to a time when he acted the part of 'John of the Hospital', a simpleton or natural fool. His part in the play is limited to occasional appearances with his 'nurse' in attendance as an entertainer, and he has no function in the plot. Possibly this part was cut in revision, and that of Tutch, a domestic fool, added or expanded; at one point (H3ᵛ) they come in together on stage, Sir William Vergir addresses John by name, and, according to the speech-headings, Tutch replies. The part of John was presumably more important originally, for the title-page is headed 'THE History of the two Maids of More-clacke, / With the life and simple maner of IOHN / in the Hospitall'. The character is based, it seems, upon a figure from life, who is described in Armin's *Fool upon Fool* thus (F1ʳ):

> *John* was a very fool that all man knows;
> Flat cap, blue coat, and Inkhorn by his side;
> A nurse to tend him, to put on his clothes,
> Yet was a man of old years when he died.
> Two staring eyes, a black beard, and his head
> Lay on his shoulder still, as sick and sad;
> And till the very time that he was dead,
> He halted with the dearest friend he had.

The blue coat was the dress of serving-men and of charity children, and later became especially associated with the boys of Christ's Hospital; according to Armin's prose account which follows (F1ᵛ), John was

placed by the City of London as a 'Fostered fatherless
child' in Christ's Hospital. The woodcut on the title-
page of *The Two Maids of Moreclack* shows Armin
dressed for the part, with beard, hand on one side, flat
cap, long blue coat, and inkhorn at his side.

Chambers, *ES*, III 210.
ed. J. P. Feather, *Collected Works of Robert Armin* (1972)
Greg, 285
Shakespeare's England, II 262–3
Enid Welsford, *The Fool* (1935), pp. 162–4

4 1

Thomas Middleton and Thomas Dekker, *The Roaring Girl* (1611).

The character of Moll, the 'roaring girl' in this play, was based on Mary Frith (?1589–1662), who had become well known by the time Middleton and Dekker collaborated on it. According to a biography of her published as a pamphlet after her death in 1662, Mary Frith grew up as a tomboy, took to wearing men's clothes, became skilful with the sword and other weapons, and 'vindicated for her sex the right of smoking'. She gained a popular fame for breaking with convention and challenging men in their own activities, and later became notorious as a bawd and cutpurse. She had attended a play at the Fortune Theatre, where *The Roaring Girl* was later acted, in 1604 or 1605, dressed as a man, and had made 'immodest and lascivious speeches' there, besides sitting on the stage to play on the lute and sing a song. Her exploits drew the attention of writers, and an account of her 'mad pranks' by John Day was entered in the Stationers' Register in 1610. No copy of this is known, but she was introduced by Nathan Field into his play *Amends for Ladies* (1612) as a tough bawd attempting to seduce the virtuous heroine. This was no doubt prompted by *The Roaring Girl*, in which Moll is presented as virtuous, overcoming by the sword her would-be seducer, and crying:

> I scorn to prostitute myself to a man,
> I that can prostitute a man to me.
>
> (III.i.109)

Later in the play (V.i.291) she refers to her 'younger days' when she had been 'apt to stray', implying that she has at some stage reformed. Middleton and Dekker turn her into a popular heroine, challenging a comparison with the 'roaring boys', a phrase in use from about 1590 until well into the eighteenth century to describe young hooligans who were given to quarrelsome and riotous behaviour in order to show off their virility. Although the best-known allusions to them are in comic terms, as in Ben Jonson's portrait of a would-be 'angry boy' in Kastril in *The Alchemist* (1610), and in the scenes of a school for quarrellers in Middleton and Rowley's *A Fair Quarrel* (1617), they could be regarded as a serious menace, as John Davies of Hereford suggested in *The Scourge of Folly* (1611), in saying 'The Devil is ne'er dear . . . while roaring boys do live'.

Moll Cut-Purse, then, was based on a living woman, and the costume shown in the woodcut may well also be largely taken from the life, and represent what the boy-actor who played Moll wore. In II.ii Moll insists on ordering wide breeches, 'the great Dutch slop' (II.ii.80) shown in the frontispiece, and above this she has 'a French doublet' (II.ii.89), and a standing collar (III.iii.26). The text implies that she has a prominent codpiece, but this is masked by a cloak in the woodcut. Moll is shown as smoking a pipe, and carries a sword in her left hand (was she, or the actor who played the part, left-handed?). She wears a hat adorned with ribbons and what looks like a flower, her slops are tied in huge bows at the knee, and she has on fashionable shoes with rosettes on them. The whole effect was no doubt designed to mix fashions and be rather outrageous. Probably this illustration shows us more or less how Moll appeared on stage. The sentence printed down the side of the woodcut is not from the text of the play, but perhaps relates to the opening of Act II when Moll first appears in a petticoat, and then changes her costume (or 'case') to dress as a man.

Chambers, *ES*, III 296–7
E. K. Chambers, 'Elizabethan Stage Gleanings', *RES*, I (1925), 77–8
ed. Andor Gomme (New Mermaid Series, 1976)
Greg, 298

42

Samuel Rowley, *When You See Me, You Know Me* (1613).

WHEN YOV SEE ME,
You know me.
Or the famous Chronicle Hiſtorie of king
Henrie the Eight, with the birth and vertuous life
of EDVVARD Prince of Wales.

As it was playd by the high and mightie Prince of Wales
his ſervants.

By SAMVELL ROVVLY, ſervant
to the Prince.

AT LONDON,
Printed for *Nathaniell Butter*, and are to be ſold at his ſhop in Paules
Church-yard neare S. *Auſtines* gate. 1613.

This play was first published in 1605, with a printer's ornament on the title-page. The second edition in 1613 seems to have been printed by the same printer, Thomas Purfoot, as *If You Know not Me You Know Nobody* (see 38 above). These plays are related in title, and Rowley's chronicle of the reign of Henry VIII seems to have prompted Heywood to write his narrative drama on the career of Queen Elizabeth. Purfoot illustrated Heywood's play with cuts of Queen Elizabeth, and the 1613 edition of *When You See Me, You Know Me* is illustrated with a large woodcut showing Henry VIII standing, feet apart, with a collar and chain round his neck, gloves in one hand, and the other loosely holding the cord supporting his dagger. This portrait is based on Holbein's famous fresco painted in 1537 for the Privy Chamber in Whitehall Palace, which was destroyed by fire in 1698. His cartoon for it survives, and shows Henry in the same posture, though viewed from an angle, rather than from directly in front, and with a different background; in the fresco Henry was portrayed standing in front of his father Henry VII. The woodcut thins out the details of Holbein's portrait, but the general correspondence, even to the double cord round Henry's waist, and large codpiece, is striking. The only notable difference is that the woodcut reverses Henry's hat; in Holbein's cartoon the feather hangs over his right shoulder. The background in the woodcut differs also from that in early copies of Holbein's portrait, such as that in the Walker Gallery in Liverpool, and simply provides a frame for the majestic figure of the King. This image of Henry seems to have been well known, and its use with the title of this play suggests that Rowley indeed exploited a recognisable portrait; the character of Henry in the play is given to expletives and to crying 'Ha!', suggesting the forceful authority traditionally associated with the mature Henry VIII, and the play ends with a meeting in state between Henry and the Emperor Charles V, for which a regal appearance would have been necessary. It is likely that the actor playing the King was costumed in the manner shown in the woodcut.

Chambers, *ES*, III 472
Greg, 212(b)
MSR (1952)
Roy Strong, *Holbein and Henry VIII* (1967)
E. K. Waterhouse, *Painting in Britain 1530–1730* (1953), pp. 8–9,
(Pls 4 and 5)

43

John Cooke, *Greene's Tu Quoque*, or *The City Gallant* (1614).

Greenes Tu quoque,
OR,
The Cittie Gallant.

As it hath beene diuers times acted by the Queenes Maiesties Seruants,

Written by Io. Cooke Gent.

Printed at London for *Iohn Tryndle*. 1614.

The title *Greene's Tu Quoque* marks the celebrity of the actor Thomas Greene in the part of Bubble, the servant who suddenly inherits wealth and tries to become a city gallant. Greene, who died in August 1612, was a sharer in Queen Anne's Men, and a prefatory note by Thomas Heywood records his affection for a notable actor, of whom he says there were none 'of better ability in performance of what he undertook, more applauded by the audience, of greater grace at the court, or of more general love in the city'. The play seems to have been written about 1611, and was performed at the Red Bull, as a joke in the text confirms:

Geraldine. Why, then, we'll go to the Red Bull: they say Green's a good clown.
Bubble. Green! Green's an ass.
Scattergood. Wherefore do you say so?
Bubble. Indeed, I ha' no reason; for they say he is as like me as ever he can look.

Greene's catchphrase in the part of Bubble as city gallant is 'Tu quoque', because 'a gentleman should speak Latin sometimes'. The woodcut on the title-page shows a figure with the phrase 'Tu quoque. To you Sir' ballooning from the mouth; although 'Tu quoque' is Bubble's common retort when saluted by others, or when he is at a loss for words, he never uses these exact words. It is impossible to say whether the figure represents Greene, but he was a well-known and popular actor, whose memory remained alive for years, as is shown by the publication of four epigrams on him in Richard Braithwaite's *Remains after Death* (1618). It seems likely that an effort was made to portray him in the cut. On becoming a gallant, his first thought is to clothe himself properly, and he orders quantities of 'horse-flesh-coloured taffeta, nine yards of yellow satin, and eight yards of orange-tawny velvet'. The slashed doublet worn by the figure in the woodcut, and the paned round hose, were old-fashioned by 1614; these, giving a parti-coloured effect where the slashes or panes revealed a contrasting colour in the lining, like the girdle and purse at the waist and the hat with two feathers standing up like cuckold's horns, would suggest that when Bubble dressed as a gallant, he only

succeeded in looking like a fool. At one point in the
action Bubble is cheated out of his cloak, and learns to
wear what he thinks is Italian fashion, which makes
him the laughing-stock of other characters. He is
evidently wearing an incongruous felt hat when he discovers that his clothes are not in the Italian fashion
after all, but 'the fool's fashion'. It is possible therefore
that the woodcut shows Greene in his costume as the
clownish city gallant.

Chambers, *ES*, III 269–70
Greg, 323
ed. Hazlitt's Dodsley (1875), XI 173–289
Reynolds, *passim*
TFT (1913)

44

Thomas Kyd, *The Spanish Tragedy* (1615).

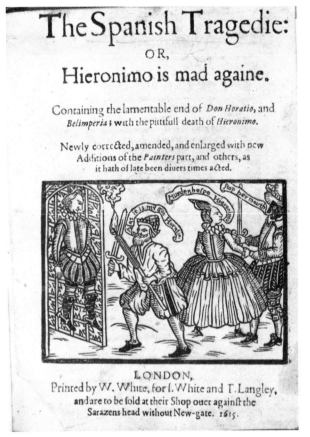

The well-known illustration of the murder of Horatio in this play first appeared on the title-page of the edition of the play published in 1615. The first known edition dates from 1592, and the further editions that appeared in 1594, 1599, 1602, 1603, 1610–11 and 1615, together with the numerous allusions to *The Spanish Tragedy* or to Hieronimo, suggest that the play remained alive on the stage, although no specific references to performances are known after 1599, other than such statements as that on the 1615 title-page that the play 'hath of late been divers times acted'. The illustration conflates three moments in II iv and II v. One is the hanging of Horatio in 'the arbour' (II iv 53); the illustration shows his body hanging by a rope tied round his neck in a kind of trellis-work arch, stuck all over with leaves or flowers. There must have been such a stage-property, with a seat or bench within it on which Horatio could sit with Belimperia, to whom he says,

> The more thou sit'st within these leavy bowers,
> The more will Flora deck it with her flowers.
> (II.iv.24–5)

In the illustration Horatio is shown as hanging from the front arch of the arbour, and no seat is visible. Horatio is shown as wearing doublet and hose, a ruff, and, somewhat oddly, boots and spurs. A second moment illustrated is that when Balthazar and Lorenzo, having carried out the murder, drag Belimperia away with them; the text runs:

Belimperia: Murder! murder! Help, Hieronimo, help!
Lorenzo: Come stop her mouth, away with her.
(II.iv.62–3)

At this point the murderers are disguised, and in the illustration Lorenzo has on a kind of black mask. His costume is similar to that of Horatio, except that he wears a large hat, has a collar instead of a ruff, and wears shoes with the rosettes that were especially fashionable in the early years of the seventeenth century. Belimperia is dressed in a gown with rolls or epaulettes at the shoulders, and her hair is drawn back from the forehead in what looks like a form of head-

dress. The third moment is Hieronimo's discovery of the body of his son:

> Alas, it is Horatio my sweet son!
> (II.v.14)

Hieronimo in fact speaks this line after the stage-direction 'He cuts him down', but the illustration shows him approaching the arbour, with sword in one hand and a torch or link in the other. He has on his shirt, in accordance with the stage-direction at the beginning of II.v, 'Enter Hieronimo in his shirt, &c.', with his breeches or hose roughly pulled up over it, and is wearing what looks like a night-cap and slippers. The costumes are generally appropriate to the period between 1590 and 1615, except perhaps for the 'roses' or rosettes ornamenting Lorenzo's shoes, which seem to have become fashionable around 1600. The illustration as a whole may have no direct connection with stage performances, and certainly no attempt has been made in it to suggest a stage, but it is not unreasonable to assume that the 'arbour' used in staging the plays and the costumes, were something like those represented on the 1615 title-page. According to the *Diary* of Philip Henslowe, Ben Jonson was paid for additions to the play in 1601 and in 1602, which suggests it was in the repertory of the Admiral's Men at this time. The inventory of the company's properties taken in March 1598 disappointingly does not include an 'arbour', and the only properties listed which might

have served are a wooden canopy and a bay-tree. At least one other play in the company's repertory called for an arbour (*A Looking Glass for London and England*), so that it seems they must have had such a property, even though Hieronimo later says he found his son 'hanging on a tree' (IV.iv.111). The author of the Fourth Addition (1602) also thought of Horatio as being hung on a tree, and says at one point (l. 63):

> This was the tree, I set it of a kernel . . .
> Till at the length
> It grew a gallows and did bear our son.
> It bore thy fruit and mine: wicked, wicked plant.

There is perhaps no real contradiction here; in the text of II.iv and II.v, the place where Horatio sits with Belimperia, and is killed, is three times called a 'bower' (II.iv.4, 24; II.v.11), and in the stage-direction at II.iv.53 an 'arbour', which could mean a bower of which the sides and roof are formed by the branches of trees, or a lattice-work frame covered by the leaves and branches of climbing shrubs or trees. The illustration shows a lattice-work frame, which would be appropriate for a stage-property, but it would be perfectly understandable for characters to refer to it as a tree. A similar block was used to illustrate a ballad based on the play, and also called 'The Spanish Tragedy'. It is undated, and survives in two copies, of different editions, both dating probably from 1625 or later, since it is not included in the list of ballads made for Henry Gosson, the printer, and his partners, and entered in the Court of the Stationers' Company in December 1624. Other earlier editions may be lost, but in any case the woodcut illustrating it appears to be derived from that used in the 1615 edition of the play.

Chambers, *ES*, III 395–7
ed. P. W. Edwards (Revels Plays, 1959)
Foakes and Rickert, *HD*, 182, 203, 321–2
Arthur Freeman, *Thomas Kyd: Facts and Problems* (Oxford, 1967), 135–6
Greg, 110(g)
Reynolds, 73–5
Roxburghe Ballads, II 450
Shakespeare's England, II 531–2

45

Thomas Heywood, *The Four Prentices of London* (1615).

In his preface to the first edition of this play in 1615, Heywood apologises for it as 'written many years since, in my Infancy of Judgment in this kind of Poetry, and my first practice', and also says it had been a fashionable kind of play 'some fifteen or sixteen' years earlier. He may have been thinking of the popular heroics of plays like Shakespeare's *Henry V*, for his play is possibly to be identified with the *Jerusalem* performed by Lord Strange's Men in March and April 1592, or with the second part of *Godfrey of Boulogne*, first played in July 1594. Since the latter play is a second part, it is more likely that the *Four Prentices* is Heywood's first play, and was written by 1592, when Heywood was about twenty-two. The play is set vaguely in the reign of William the Conqueror, and Godfrey, Earl of Boulogne, banished to London, has apprenticed his four sons to a mercer, a goldsmith, a haberdasher, and a grocer. They all go off to fight in the crusades, and the play ends with them each killing a pagan king and assisting at the conquest of Jerusalem. The four apprentices straddle history, and are no doubt intended as heroic projections of those in the audience at the Rose Theatre. They are especially skilled in the use of pikes, the standard weapon of the infantry, and at one point in the play they give a demonstration in the art of using them, marked by the stage-direction, 'They toss their pikes'. This incident evidently made its mark, for in *The Knight of the Burning Pestle* (?1607), Francis Beaumont, mocking the absurdities of heroic romances like Heywood's play, has his apprentice Ralph pretend to be a Knight of a 'holy order' at the insistence of the grocer his master, who rejects the boy's objection that 'it will show ill-favouredly to have a grocer's prentice to court a King's daughter' with the retort, 'Read the play of *The Four Prentices of London*, where they toss their pikes so' (IV, ll. 45–50). Beaumont was satirising the whole genre of such plays, but this specific reference shows that he had Heywood's play very much in mind, and, if it is to be taken literally, that the play was in print. The play *Jerusalem* was entered in the Stationers' Register in June 1594, but if it was printed then, no copy survives.

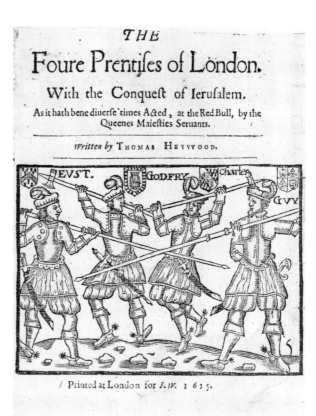

The woodcut on the title-page of the 1615 quarto was evidently made for the play, but could just as well belong to 1594. It shows the four prentices in process of tossing their pikes. To be more accurate, the two nearest the viewer, Eustace to the left, and Guy to the right, hold pikes, which had pointed blades of steel at the head, and the other two have halberds, which combined the spear and battleaxe. They are crudely depicted as wearing body-armour to the waist, and armour on the shoulders and arms. They also wear wide breeches or slops, boots and spurs, and their flat caps show they are apprentices. Three of them have curved swords or scimitars, and one a straight sword. Armour for the shoulders and arms was no longer in common use by the end of the sixteenth century, and the style in which the prentices are represented may be intended to suggest a former age, just as the scimitars may link them with the Crusades and wars with the Soldan of Babylon and the Sophy of Persia. The rest of their costume belongs to Heywood's time, and the woodcut seems to reflect the play's casual assimilation of past into present, and freedom with anachronisms (at one point Charles and Godfrey enter with pistols). The woodcut also shows the shields of the prentices, which are much in evidence in the battle-scenes towards the end of the play. One stage-direction describes Godfrey's shield as 'having a Maidenhead with a Crown in it', and later Godfrey says 'A Virgin crown'd it is the Mercers' Arms'. Charles carries a shield bearing the Haberdashers' Arms, quartered with a 'red lion' he once killed. Eustace says he bears the 'Grocers' arms' upon his shield, and Guy's shield likewise carries the arms of the Goldsmith's company. These are all depicted in the woodcut. The prentices are shown on a vaguely indicated landscape with no background, and this has nothing to do with the theatre; the costumes, shields, and exercise with the pikes, all relate well to the text of the play.

Chambers, *ES*, III 340–1
A. M. Clark, *Thomas Heywood* (1958), pp. 24–6, 210–12
Foakes and Rickert, *HD*, 17, 22
Greg, 333(a)
Linthicum, 209–10, 218
Reynolds, *passim*
Rhodes, 183, 196–7 (Pl. 33)
ed. R. H. Shepherd, *Dramatic Works* (1874, reprinted 1964), II 159–254

46

Christopher Marlowe, *Doctor Faustus* (1616).

The first quarto (A) of *Doctor Faustus*, issued in 1604, and reissued in 1609 and 1611, has a printer's device on the title-page; the second quarto (B), printed in 1616, and five later reprints (1619, 1620, 1624, 1628 and 1631), all include the same woodcut on the title-page, showing Doctor Faustus conjuring up a devil. The only copy of the Quarto of 1616, which is in the British Library, has a damaged title-page, and the woodcut is reproduced here from a later quarto. It shows Doctor Faustus standing within a circle (more of an oval as the woodcut represents it) with the signs of the zodiac, a book in one hand and a staff in the other. The setting the artist had in mind was 'Faustus in his study', where the opening stage-direction of the text places him in the first Quarto. In Scene I Faustus proposes to conjure in a 'grove' (ll. 150, 152), as he does in Marlowe's source for this episode; the stage-entries for Scenes I and V locate Faustus in his study, but the entry for Scene III is unlocalised, and towards the end of it Faustus instructs Mephistopholis:

> Go and return to mighty Lucifer,
> And meet me in my study at midnight,
> And then resolve me of thy master's mind.
> (100–2)

It looks as though Marlowe had the 'grove' vaguely in mind, but nothing in the text of Scene III requires a specific location, and it would have been economical for the actors to present the sequence of early scenes involving Doctor Faustus with his 'study' as the setting. The illustration in the woodcut very possibly relates to Scene III as it was staged, with Faustus conjuring in a circle:

> Within this circle is Jehovah's name
> Forward and backward anagrammatiz'd
> The breviated names of holy saints,
> Figures of every adjunct to the heavens,
> And characters of signs and erring stars,
> By which the spirits are enforc'd to rise . . .
> (III.8–13)

Faustus tries 'the uttermost magic can perform' with a Latin spell, recited presumably from one of the 'neo-cromantic books' (I.49) he opened in Scene I. The

effect of his conjuring is marked by the direction 'Enter a Devil', so hideous that Faustus cries:

> I charge thee to return and change thy shape;
> Thou art too ugly to attend on me.
>
> (III.25–6)

The woodcut represents this moment in the action. The artist did not attempt to represent all the signs and names Faustus says were in his 'circle', but the general image is appropriate. The 'study' is suggested by a floor marked in rectangles and a rear wall with a window in the centre. An armillary sphere hangs on the wall to the left, a skeleton celestial globe made of metal rings, as used by Ptolemy, and by later astronomers and astrologers. This is fitting, for Cornelius tells Faustus that a good grounding in astrology provides 'the principles magic doth require' (I.139), and later Faustus debates with Mephistopholis about 'divine astrology' (VI.34). To the right hangs a crucifix, and above this is a crudely indicated shelf with three clasped books on it, and a circular object which may be on the shelf or hanging on the wall. The significance of this is uncertain; it may be another cross within a circle, another reminder that Faustus was a noted divine and theologian. Faustus is shown in what is probably meant to be a surplice, with his doctor's gown over it, and wearing his doctor's hat. He wears a ruff, a cord or belt at his waist, and the V-shape on his breast suggests a chain or ribbon round his neck. The depiction accords with Faustus as 'grac'd with doctor's name' (Prologue,

l. 17), and, if the crudeness of the woodcut conceals the ornament hanging on his breast, the figure may be intended to suggest the image of Faustus as created by the famous actor Edward Alleyn, whose performance of the role in the 1590s remained sufficiently alive in memory for Samuel Rowlands to refer to it in *The Knave of Clubs* (1609):

> The Gull gets on a surplice
> With a cross upon the breast
> Like *Allen* playing *Faustus*
> In that manner he was dressed.

The 'devil' in the woodcut has a human face and hair, and is shown with one reptilian arm ending in a claw, wings, horns, and a tail. The ugly devil that appears to Faustus in Scene III enters at line 25, and goes off at line 28 without speaking, returning as Mephistopholis at line 36. The woodcut may have no relation to stage practice in its representation of this devil, but if it does, it suggests the use of a trapdoor, with the 'devil' appearing from below; did an actor enter, or was some monstrous shape seen half-emerging from the stage?

In the B quarto (1616), a much changed and expanded version of the A-text, the word 'Dragon' appears in the middle of the Latin invocation used by Faustus to summon this devil. This has been converted into the stage-direction 'Dragon appears briefly above' in some modern editions, like that edited by J. D. Jump for the Revels Plays. The use of a dragon is confirmed by the item 'j dragon in fostes' included in the 1598 list of properties belonging to the Admiral's Men, and the added stage-direction is, in effect, taken from the source-book, *The History of the Damned Life, and Deserved Death of John Faustus*; according to this, Faustus conjured in a wood, and suddenly a dragon appeared hovering in the air, which changed into a globe, and then into a fiery man, and then into a friar. However, in the text of the play, Faustus calls on Mephistopholis to rise ('surgat Mephistopholis!', III.19–20), and the intrusion of the word 'Dragon' here could just as well be an anticipatory stage-direction for the appearance of the 'Devil' a few lines later. It is at least possible that the woodcut illustrates something of the way this devil 'entered', as a dragon thrust forth from under the stage. The B-text adds a direction at the beginning of this scene calling for the entry of Lucifer and four devils (above? or where?) to witness Faustus conjuring. The woodcut contains no reference to these, and indeed the dialogue of the scene assumes Lucifer to be elsewhere, in hell, where Faustus sends Mephistopholis to negotiate terms. This stage-direction appears to be an addition to Marlowe's scene, a pointless one, merely providing another opportunity for the 'devils' who appear later (for example, at V.82) as the servants of Mephistopholis to display their antics. These are remembered in accounts like that in *The Black Book* (1604) of someone as possessing 'a head of hair like one of my Devils in Dr. Faustus when the old Theatre crackt and frighted the audience', or that in John Melton's *The Astrologaster* (1620):

Another will fore-tell of Lightning, and Thunder that shall happen such a day, when there are no Inflammations seen, except men go to the *Fortune* in Golding-Lane to see the Tragedy of *Doctor Faustus*. There indeed a man may behold shag-haired Devils run roaring over the Stage with Squibs in their mouths, while Drummers make Thunder in the Tyring-House, and the twelvepenny Hirelings make artificial Lightning in their Heavens.

These references both point to actors dressed as hairy devils roaring about the stage, which fits the devils Banio and Belcher summoned by Wagner in the comic Scene IV, or the devils who chase away the Knights in Scene XIII. The ugly 'Devil' seen by Faustus when he first conjures is not likely to have been presented as one of the 'shag-haired' figures who later serve Mephistopholis, and the appearance of a 'dragon', or a figure like that in the woodcut, rising through a trap-door, would have been far more appropriate at this point. The woodcut, then, may tell us something about the staging of Scene III.

John Bakeless, *The Tragicall History of Christopher Marlowe* (2 vols., Cambridge, Mass., 1942), I 297–300
ed. Fredson Bowers, *The Complete Works of Christopher Marlowe* (2 vols., Cambridge, 1973), pp. 123–271
Chambers, *ES*, III 422–4
T. W. Craik, 'The Reconstruction of Stage Action from Early Dramatic Texts', *The Elizabethan Theatre*, V, ed. G. R. Hibbard (Toronto, 1975), 81–2
Foakes and Rickert, *HD*, 320
Greg, 205(d)–(i)
Anthony Harris, *Night's Black Agents: Witchcraft and Magic in Seventeenth-Century Drama* (Manchester, 1980), pp. 152–4 (Pl. 13)
ed. J. D. Jump (Revels Plays, 1962)
facsimile of 1604 and 1616 texts, Scolar Press, Menston, 1970
John Melton, *Astrologaster* (1620), p. 31
Reynolds, 134, 156
Rhodes, 184 (Pl. 34)
Shakespeare's England, I 457

47

Thomas Middleton and William Rowley, *A Fair Quarrel* (1617).

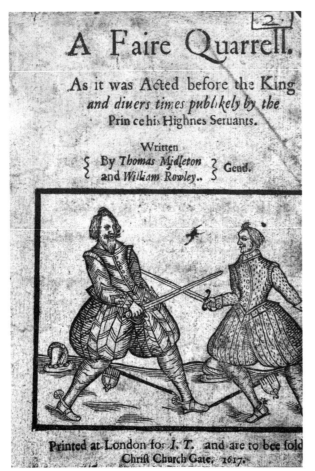

The first quarto of this play, written not long before it was published in 1617, has a rather crude woodcut on the title page showing two men fighting with drawn swords. The men wear short, pointed doublets and long, full hose or slops reaching below the knee, a fashion in vogue at the time the play was written; they also, rather oddly, wear spurs. They are shown in a vaguely indicated landscape, with their hats and scabbards removed and lying on the ground. The figures are distinguished from one another, possibly with some care, and in relation to an incident concerning two of the principal characters in the opening scene. The taller one on the left has a full beard, and may be intended to suggest the Colonel, who has 'a beard' (I.i.84), while the shorter figure may indicate Captain Ager, who is called 'a boy' by the Colonel (I.i.84), a few lines before they draw swords on one another. The woodcut may then have some relation to the main 'quarrel' in the play, which comes to a climax in III.i, when the two characters fight in earnest and the Colonel falls wounded, though not, as it turns out, mortally. At the same time, as the play's latest editor points out, contemporary manuals relating to fencing and duelling are illustrated with woodcuts of this kind, and the postures of the two men, intended to show perhaps the technique of the 'low ward' in defence, may have been copied from such a work.

Bentley, *JCS*, IV 867–70
Greg, 352(a1)
ed. R. V. Holdsworth (New Mermaids Series, 1974)
Shakespeare's England, II 395–407
A. L. Soens, 'Two Rapier Points: Analysing Elizabethan Fighting Methods', *Notes and Queries*, New Series, 15 (1968), 127–8

48

Jack Drum's Entertainment (1618).

This play, probably written by John Marston about 1600, was first published in 1601, with a numbered list at the end of the twelve male and four female parts. It was printed again in 1616, and in 1618, and this third edition has a woodcut on the title-page. 'Jack Drum's entertainment' was a phrase in common use meaning a rough reception, or turning an unwelcome guest out of doors, as in Shakespeare's *All's Well that Ends Well*, III.vi.35. There the phrase is connected with the braggart Parolles, and there may be a link of this kind in *Jack Drum's Entertainment*. The title refers primarily to the witty servant Jack Drum, who is foiled in his attempt to seduce Winifred, but it is also probably intended to relate to the cuckolding of Brabant Senior by the flamboyantly comic Frenchman, Monsieur John fo de King. The woodcut shows a figure wearing a slashed doublet, with wide sleeves, paned like the full slops or breeches, and sporting an elaborate codpiece. A huge feathered hat is partly cut off where the block has been trimmed. He wears too a dagger, and in his left hand holds a short pike or halberd. The huge moustaches add to the general impression of flamboyance, and the illustration may have been intended to suggest Monsieur in the play. However, there is nothing in the text to indicate his appearance, and the woodcut may have no direct reference to the play. It was used to adorn several ballads, all later than the play, such as the second part of 'An Excellent New Medley', which ends blessing the King and Queen, and so belongs to the reign of James I or Charles I.

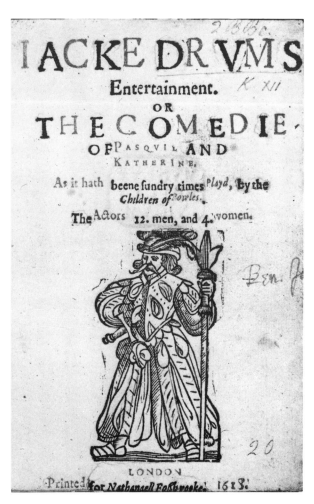

Chambers, *ES*, IV 21
Greg, 177(bII)
Linthicum, 209–10
Roxburghe Ballads, I 54, 70; II 167
ed. Harvey Wood, *Plays of John Marston*, 3 vols. (1939–9), III 175–241

49

Francis Beaumont and John Fletcher, *A King and No King* (1619).

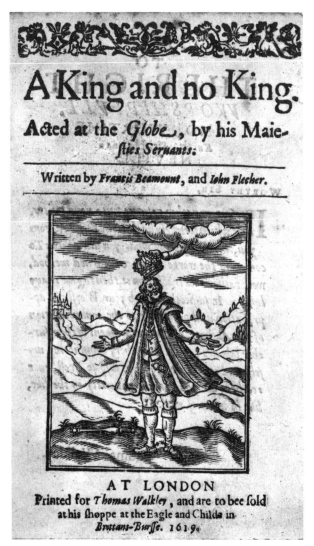

A King and No King, written about 1611, was first published in 1619 in a quarto which has a woodcut illustration on the title-page. This shows a figure rather elaborately dressed, wearing a cloak, a sword, booted and spurred, and set in a fanciful hilly landscape. A sceptre lies on the ground, while an arm emerging from a cloud is either removing a crown from his head, or placing one on it. The image is appropriately ambiguous in relation to the play, and provides a fitting emblem for it. It suggests the *deus ex machina* device by which Arbaces, King of Iberia, discovers in Act V that he is really the son of the old counsellor Gobrius, and has no title to the throne, but at the same time is made free to marry the Princess Panthea, now no longer his sister, and thus become King again. The outspread arms of the figure in the woodcut cannot be related to any specific moment in the play's action, and the outdoor costume has no special relevance; so although the woodcut neatly emblematizes the play's central issue, it probably has no relation to the play in performance.

Chambers, *ES*, III 225
Greg, 360(a)
ed. R. K. Turner, Jr. (Regents Renaissance Drama Series, 1964)
ed. G. W. Williams, *The Dramatic Works in the Beaumont and Fletcher Canon* (General Editor Fredson Bowers; Vol. II, Cambridge, 1970), pp. 167–314

50

Francis Beaumont and John Fletcher, *The Maid's Tragedy* (1619).

This play was written before *The Second Maiden's Tragedy*, which was licensed for performance on 31 October 1611, but it was not published until 1619, when it appeared with two different imprints on the title-page, as printed for Richard Higgenbotham, and as printed for Francis Constable. All title-pages incorporate a woodcut, which must have been made for the play. It relates to V.iii, the scene in which Aspatia is wounded by Amintor. Aspatia had expected to marry him, but, at the King's behest, Amintor took Evadne as his wife, not realising that she had been the King's mistress. Late in the play, in the climactic scene, Aspatia, 'in man's apparel', pretending to be her brother, confronts Amintor, and picks a quarrel with him. Amintor is reluctant to fight, but, after being struck and kicked by the disguised Aspatia, he draws his sword, and in the ensuing fight, the wronged Aspatia receives the wound (V.iii.100) from which she subsequently dies (V.iii.226). The play is vaguely located in Rhodes, but most of the scenes may be supposed to take place in a palace or at any rate indoors; so this scene begins with Aspatia encountering a servant who goes off to seek Amintor and returns with him a few lines later. The landscape in the woodcut thus appears to be fanciful, and to have no connection with the play, which, according to the title page, had been performed in the private indoor theatre at Blackfriars. The costumes the characters are shown wearing may well, on the other hand, relate to the way the play was presented, and were in fashion about 1619. Both wear short-skirted doublets with rolls or wings at the shoulders, full breeches or upper hose reaching almost to the knees, and ribbon or silk garters tied in bows below the knees. The two figures have ruffs and hats with feathers, and wear shoes with roses. Amintor is shown in the act of wounding Aspatia in the breast, and blood spurts from her doublet. Amintor's hat is on the ground, and this may show the result of the stage-direction 'She strikes him', just as the blood needs to be seen to accord with Amintor's conceit,

> Behold,
> Here lies a youth whose wounds bleed in my breast . . .
> (V.iii.144–5)

The Maides Tragedy.

AS IT HATH BEENE
diuers times Acted at the *Blacke-friers* by
the KINGS Maiesties Seruants.

ASPATIA.   AMINTOR.

LONDON
Printed for *Richard Higgenbotham* and
are to be sold at the Angell in PAVLS
Church-yard, 1619.

and to match the blood-stained figure of Evadne, who is also on stage at this point.

Chambers, *ES*, III 224–5
Greg, 357(a)
ed. A. Gurr (Fountainwell Drama Series, 1969)
Linthicum, 206, 243–4
ed. H. B. Norland (Regents Renaissance Drama Series, 1968)
ed. Robert K. Turner, Jr., in *The Dramatic Works in the Beaumont and Fletcher Canon* (General Editor Fredson Bowers; Vol. II, Cambridge, 1970), pp. 3–166

51

Swetnam the Woman-Hater arraigned by Women (1620).

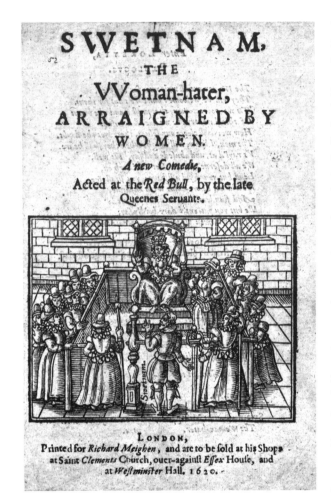

SWETNAM,
THE
VVoman-hater,
ARRAIGNED BY
WOMEN.

A new Comedie,
Acted at the *Red Bull*, by the late
Queenes Seruants.

LONDON,
Printed for *Richard Meighen*, and are to be sold at his Shops
at Saint *Clements* Church, ouer-against *Essex* House, and
at *Westminster* Hall. 1 6 2 0.

The main action of this play, drawn from a Spanish romance also used by Fletcher for *Women Pleased*, concerns the wooing of Princess Leonida by the young Prince of Naples, Lisandro, who disguises himself as a friar to gain access to her. They are betrayed by her waiting-maid Loretta, seized by her other suitor, the old nobleman Nicanor, and brought to trial. Leonida is sentenced to death after being tried, and Lisandro apparently kills himself, but it turns out that Nicanor has a change of heart, the lovers are not dead after all, and the play ends happily. In spite of the vaguely Italian setting, with its references to Naples and Sicily, the central episodes in the play involve the figure of Misogynos, who successfully pleads against Leonida, and then, in Act IV, is tried himself by women. Misogynos is another name for Joseph Swetnam, and the play was provoked by his attack on women in *The Arraignment of Lewd, Idle, Froward and Unconstant Women* (1615). At least four pamphlets were published in reply to this, one in 1616, and three in 1617, but the most notable retort was the play, published in 1620 as a 'new Comedie'. Swetnam's attack on women was reprinted four times before 1620, and the play was probably written after the publication of his book of instruction in sword-play, *The School of the Noble and Worthy Science of Defence* (1617), since the play has a number of references to Swetnam as a fencer.

The woodcut on the title-page relates to the 'trial' of Swetnam in Act IV. This begins with the stage-direction, 'Enter all the Women' (I2ᵛ), where Aurelia, Queen of Sicily, an Old Woman, a Scold, Atlanta (really Lorenzo disguised as an Amazon), a Boy, and several other women (the list of actors on the verso of the title-page calls for 'Three or four other Women') are on stage, perhaps eight or nine in all. The women torment Swetnam by having him bound to 'this Post' (I3ʳ), and by pricking or scratching him; then 'Enter two Old Women and Swash', Swash being Swetnam's male servant. At this point the trial begins:

> *Atlanta*: He hath arraign'd us for inconstancy:
> But now we'll arraign him, and judge him too,
> This is woman's counsel: Madame, we make you

116

Lady Chief Justice of this Female Court,
Mistress Recorder, I. *Loretta*, you
Sit for the Notary: *Crier*, she:
The rest shall bear inferior offices,
As Keepers, Serjiants, Executioners.

(sig. I4ʳ)

Aurelia, the Queen, acts as Chief Justice, and the central figure in the woodcut wears a crown. Atalanta sends off an old woman to 'call a Jury Full', and realises a bar is needed for the prisoner; she says

We want a Bar. O these two foils shall serve:
One stuck i' the Earth, and cross it from this Tree.
Now take your places, bring him to the Bar . . .

(I4ʳ)

After the trial she bids the 'jury' to give their verdict, and 'two Old Women' enter to cry 'Guilty', and produce a copy of Swetnam's book on the arraignment of women. He is sentenced to wear a muzzle, to be led in the streets, and bound to posts to be baited by women, while his books are to be burned. The illustration shows the 'post', which doubled as a 'tree', and the foils (used earlier in the scene when Atalanta overcame Swetnam in a fencing match) are there, used as described in the text to form a 'bar'. The woodcut evidently was made to illustrate this scene. On the right of the judge (Aurelia) is a seated figure, perhaps Loretta as notary. The figures standing on the right may be the other officers of the court as mentioned in Atalanta's speech cited above, including the 'Recorder', which may mean chief witness or, in effect, prosecutor, the 'Sergeants', lawyers who assisted the Recorder, the 'Crier', who kept order, and the two 'Keepers' who

guard Swetnam. On the left is a group of about a dozen representing the jury. Aurelia sits on a throne mounted on steps, and all the figures but one stand at a barrier forming three sides of a square. All the numerous women wear apparently identical costumes, with ruffs, farthingales and tall-crowned hats. The scene begins with eight or nine 'women' on stage, calls for two more to enter, and then a 'jury full', so that the text would seem to demand the presence of more than twenty actors dressed as women, and possibly for this occasion adult as well as boy-actors were pressed into service for so many non-speaking parts – this might explain the stage-directions calling specifically for 'Old Women'. There is no indication within the scene of barriers being set up, and indeed it begins with a 'banquet' in an 'orchard' (I1ʳ), the post doubling in service as a tree. The woodcut may give a general impression of the staging of the scene, but the floor marked out in rectangles, and the rear wall, apparently of brick, and with two windows in it, has features in common with other woodcuts illustrating scenes with doors, and may be no more than a conventional way of representing interiors (see, for instance, 46, 55 and 60).

Bentley, *JCS*, IV 14, 6–8
Greg, 362
ed. A. B. Grosart (Manchester, 1880)
Reynolds, 44–6
TFT (1914)

52

Francis Beaumont and John Fletcher, *Philaster* (1620).

Philaster was written probably in 1609, and was first printed in 1620 as acted 'at the Globe'. A second quarto followed in 1622, 'corrected and amended', and presented the play 'As it hath beene diverse times Acted, at the Globe, and Black-Friers'. Modern editions are usually based on this second quarto, which was indeed corrected, but incorporated also some small but significant changes, one of which bears upon the woodcut illustration which appeared on the title-page of the first quarto. This relates to the most sensational moment in the action, when Philaster stabs and wounds 'in the breast' (IV.v. 85) the Princess Arethusa, who has followed him into a 'forest' (IV.v.75) out of devotion to him. A 'Country Gallant' (Q1) or 'Country Fellow' (Q2) intervenes, and in an ensuing fight Philaster is in turn wounded and goes off. In the following scene Philaster stumbles across Bellario, who, he believes, has been 'taken with' Arethusa (III.i.100) in lust, and he wounds Bellario too. Philaster falls, faint for loss of blood, and Bellario urges him to 'Hide, hide' (Q1) or 'Fly, fly' (Q2), which he does by creeping into a bush. The illustration shows Arethusa lying on a bank with what seems intended as a gash in her completely exposed and very feminine bosom. By her sits 'A Cuntrie Gentellman', booted and spurred, wearing gloves, a hat with a large feather in it, and an elaborate ruff, and resting his sword on his right shoulder. Further to the right Philaster, also with drawn sword, seems to be in the process of hiding in the bushes. The illustration perhaps, then, conflates two incidents from IV.v and IV.vi. The landscape shown in the woodcut seems unrelated to stage performance, and elaborates on Arethusa's lines at the beginning of IV.v:

> I'll follow you boldly about these woods,
> O'er mountains, through brambles, pits, and floods . . .

There must have been some stage effects, perhaps painted hangings and property trees, to suggest a 'forest', and to enable Philaster to creep 'out of a bush' (IV.vi. 85 S.D.), but the illustration throws no light on how the actors staged these scenes. The full exposure of the breasts was a feature of fashionable women's

dress between about 1600 and 1620, but there is no
evidence to show how boy-actors playing women's roles
were costumed at this time. In other words, the illustration may well tell us nothing specific about the staging
of the play, and yet it is based on the text of the first
quarto in showing the 'country gentleman' dressed, like
Philaster himself, as a courtier; in Q1 this character
is called a 'gallant', but in Q2 he dwindles into a
'Country Fellow', whose rusticity is evidently intended
to emphasize a contrast between country and court.
The illustration thus shows this character as he may
have been costumed originally; in a performance of the
revised version printed in Q2 this character must have
been dressed in a way that marked him off from the
courtiers.

Chambers, *ES*, III 222–4
Greg, 363(a)
ed. Andrew Gurr (Revels Plays, 1969)
Shakespeare's England, II 94
ed. Robert K. Turner, Jr., in *The Dramatic Works in the Beaumont
and Fletcher Canon* (General Editor Fredson Bowers; Vol. I,
Cambridge 1966), pp. 369–540

53

Thomas Middleton and William Rowley, *The World Tossed at Tennis* (1620).

This curious piece is called a 'masque' or 'device' on the title-page, and the prologue, written for presentation on a public stage, indicates that it was 'intended for a royal night'. It begins with an induction 'prepared for his Majesty's Entertainment at Denmark House', but it seems that it was not presented there as intended in late 1619 or early 1620. Instead it passed into the repertory of Prince Charles's Men. It appears from the statement in the address to the reader that it was 'born on the bank-side of Helicon', or acted in a theatre on Bankside; in 1639 it was still in the repertory of the King and Queen's Young Company, or Beeston's Boys, at the Phoenix Theatre. The masque as printed does not have the usual form of a court masque, and was probably altered and expanded from its original form in order to make it more suitable for presentation on the public stage. In the course of the piece, which consists of about 900 lines of dialogue and song, and includes several pageants and dances, Jupiter 'descends' to sit on a throne, and then 'leaves his state, and to show the strange removes of the world, places the orb whose figure it bears in the midst of the stage'. The orb passes through the hands of various characters in the dialogue following this, until the final dance, in which all the 'removes come close together'; here the Devil and Deceit try to seize the world or orb, but the Lawyer who has it resigns it to the king, and it passes again from 'Majesty to Valour, Valour to Law again, Law to Religion, Religion to Sovereignty, where it firmly and fairly settles, the Law confounding Deceit, and the Church the Devil'. A few lines later, 'They all deliver the orb up to the King'.

The title-page illustration relates to this part of the masque. The Devil and Deceit are thrust aside, and the orb, labelled 'The World', is being passed among six characters. The figure in the centre of the group on the left is probably the King (or Majesty), the large feathered hat and general appearance perhaps being designed to suggest King James I, for whom the masque was originally composed as a compliment. On his left is a figure in a tall hat and gown, probably representing Law, who is opposite Religion (or Flamen),

The Diuell. Deceit. The World.

who wears the flat cap and surplice appropriate to a priest. The figures at the front I take to be the Sea-Captain on the left, as suggested by his hat, and Simplicity, a part developed probably by Rowley, whose costume, with belt, bag and codpiece, indicates the fool (cf. the title-page illustration of *Greene's Tu Quoque*, 43 above). The figure in the centre of the group on the right must then be Valour. These are all shown in costumes fitting the respective part in the masque, and the orb in a stand, which would have permitted Jupiter earlier to place it in the centre of the stage, probably shows what the property 'World' looked like. According to the stage-directions, Deceit is here 'confounded' by Law, and the Devil by the Church or Religion, and the illustration schematically suggests this by showing them as figures on a smaller scale holding up hands (or talons) as if unable to break into the group who are in possession of the World. Deceit is here costumed as 'a pettifogger', or sharp-practising petty attorney. The Devil has a splendid costume, complete with long tail, horns, talons, cloven feet, breasts, and an enormous phallus. The scale and appearance suggest an actor in a special 'devil's' costume (see also 46 above, the famous woodcut illustrating *Doctor Faustus*). Although the figures are shown as it were in space, with no hint of a background, the illustration relates very closely to the action of the play, and a notable feature of it is the indication above them of what looks like the bottom of a stage-curtain. The play/masque makes

use of the upper stage, where at one point the Nine Worthies are 'discovered' with the Nine Muses, all of whom then descend to the stage, entering 'at the three several doors', so that a curtain would have been required on the upper level.

Bentley, *JCS*, IV 907–11
ed. A. H. Bullen, *Works of Middleton* (8 vols, 1885–6, reprinted 1964), VII 137–93
Greg, 365(A†)

54

Thomas Middleton, *A Game at Chess* (1624).

a

According to the title-page (a) of the undated first Quarto of this play, published probably in 1625, it was 'Acted nine days together at the Globe'. This indicates what a success the play made when it was first presented in August 1624, for what evidence there is suggests that it was customary in public theatres of the Elizabethan period to perform a different play every day or two, and this practice may well have continued through the reign of James I; at any rate, *A Game at Chess* is the first play known to have had a long run on the stage. Its success was due to its topical political allegory, and the transparent satirical presentation in it of the Spanish ambassador until 1622, Count Gondomar. The play could have had a longer run, but its obvious allusion to the attempts being made to arrange a Spanish marriage for Prince Charles, and its ridicule of Spain, drew the attention of the government, and the Globe was closed, and the King's Men forbidden to act, on 18 August 1624. It is probable that the three quartos of the play, all undated but usually assigned to 1625, were all printed surreptitiously. They have engraved title-pages of some interest. The title page of Q1 is divided into three sections. The top one contains the title, and two small boxes on either side labelled 'The Black-House' and 'The White-House'. These show how entrances were used, for in the Induction the two sides in the game are called in a stage-direction to enter separately 'in order of Game', and the opening scene begins with two pawns entering, the Black Queen's pawn from the 'Black-House', and the White Queen's pawn from the 'White-House'. The second section of the engraving shows eight figures seated at a square table with a chess-board on it; the eight figures are among the principal opponents in the play; the White King, Queen, Duke (or Rook) and Bishop face their black counterparts, or the English are set against the Spanish. In the play the action is related to a chess-game, with moves, or entries, by Queen's pawns at the beginning, followed by Knights and Bishops; at one point all the 'pieces' apparently come on stage (II.ii.85), where 'Both the sides fill', and a stage-direction reads, 'Enter both Houses'. In the Induction and at this point

A letter from his Holynes

Keepe y' distance

Check mate by discovery

b

the White and Black 'pieces' were drawn up in opposition, but there is nothing in the play to show that they sat at a table.

The bottom section of the engraving (b) shows the leading characters in the main plot, the Fat Bishop (Marco Antonio de Dominis), the Black Knight (Count Gondomar), and the White Knight (Prince Charles). They are shown as in action, and the streamers from their mouths contain words that establish references, first to III.i.25, where the Black Knight brings a letter from 'Cardinal Paulus' to the Fat Bishop, and secondly to V.iii.160, where the White Knight, by pretending to be a hypocrite, draws the Black Knight to reveal his own duplicity, and cries 'we give thee checkmate by Discovery'. The figures are lifelike, and that of Count Gondomar is closely related to the portrait of him in the Royal Collections at Hampton Court, painted in 1622, before Gondomar left England in May, and attributed to Abraham van Blyenberch (e); this in turn seems to be the basis of the portrait engraved by Simon van der Passe in the same year. Another portrait, now in the Ministry of Foreign Affairs at Madrid (f), is connected with a different engraving by Willem van der Passe, also dated 1622. The engravers of the title-pages of the quartos, and that of *Vox Populi*, may well have known both of the 1622 engravings. A contemporary witness, John Chamberlain, wrote that the actors

'counterfeited his person to the life, with all his graces and faces, and had gotten (they say) a cast suit of his apparel for the purpose, and his litter', and much of the play's point would have been lost unless the political figures concerned were imitated as closely as possible; thus the engraving almost certainly shows them as they were costumed on the stage.

At the rear of this section is a bag with several figures in it. There must have been a property 'bag' of this kind, for various 'pieces', when captured, are put 'into the bag' according to stage-directions, and towards the end, at V.iii.178, there is a direction reading 'The bag opens, the Black side in it'. The bag may have been different from that shown in the engraving, but presumably had some visual link with the bags in which chess-pieces had traditionally been kept, and which often figure in the common imagery drawn from the game, as in the lines in *Jack Drum's Entertainment* (printed 1601), a play probably written by John Marston (48 above):

> And after death like chessmen having stood
> In play for Bishops some for Knights and Pawns,
> We all together shall be tumbled up
> Into one bag.

In the presentation of Middleton's play the 'bag' could be opened and closed, and characters could speak from

123

c

d

within it. At one point the bag opening is compared to Hell's mouth:

> And there behold the bag's mouth, like hell, opens
> To take her due, and the lost sons appear
> Greedily gaping for increase of fellowship . . .
>
> (V.iii.179)

The Spanish ambassador who replaced Count Gondomar in 1622, Don Carlos Coloma, sent an indignant report on the affair of the staging of *A Game at Chess* to Madrid; it is inaccurate in several details, and is based upon what Don Carlos had heard from others, for he does not appear to have seen a performance himself. He reported that he did not know the matter of the third act (he thought the play was written, like Spanish plays, in three acts) in detail, but it ended when 'he who acted the Prince of Wales heartily beat and kicked the "Count of Gondomar" into Hell, which consisted of a great hole and hideous figures; and the white king [drove] the black king and even his queen [into Hell] almost as offensively'. It has been assumed that the 'bag' which 'opens' at V.iii.179 looked like a traditional

property – Hell's mouth, such as was listed among the properties of the Admiral's Men in 1598, and perhaps for the final putting of all the black pieces in the 'bag' some special effect was achieved of 'hideous figures' to suggest hell. There would, however, have been no point in the connection with Hell earlier in the play, as at III.i.308, where the Black Knight puts the White King's Pawn into 'the empty bag'. It looks as though the play required in performance three basic stage areas, possibly something like the 'mansions' or 'houses' of medieval drama, a form of staging which, as Glynne Wickham has argued, seems to have survived in the public theatres until 1642. In *A Game at Chess* there must have been locations representing the White and Black 'Houses' from which the 'pieces' enter, and the 'bag', which probably, by some special effect, was made to symbolise Hell's mouth in the final scene. It is not certain how big this 'bag' needed to be; the action does not require the presence of sixteen 'pieces' on each side, but only seven or eight; in the final scene seven black 'pieces' are put into the 'bag'.

e

f

The title-page of the third Quarto (c) has a different illustration showing enlarged figures of the Fat Bishop and the Black Knight standing with one foot resting on a chess-board. Their costumes are similar to those shown on the title-page of the first Quarto, except that the Black Knight holds a stick in his left hand, and the chain round his neck is more prominent. Behind them is a bag, with a cord to close the neck, containing representations of the same two figures making different gestures. Count Gondomar is represented on the title-page of one of the contemporary pamphlets Middleton used in writing his play, *The Second Part of Vox Populi* (1624) by Thomas Scott, and the resemblance to the figures on the title-pages of the quartos is apparent. This title-page (d) also illustrates the litter Count Gondomar used, and his 'chair of ease', necessitated by a fistula to which reference is made frequently in the play. According to the letters of John Chamberlain, the King's Men actually got hold of Gondomar's litter, and used it to bring him on stage in V.i, where Middleton's direction calls for the Black Knight to enter 'in his litter'. The despatch of Don Carlos Coloma confirms that 'the players brought Gondomar on to the stage in his little litter almost to the life, and seated on his chair with a hole in it'. The chair is shown on the title-page of *The Second Part of Vox Populi*, and the players either obtained this or copied it; so at IV.ii.3 the Black Knight

says to his Pawn, 'Reach me my chair of ease'. The various illustrations of Count Gondomar, based as they may be on the engravings made in 1622 by Simon and Willem van der Passe, show him more or less to the life, and this is how the King's Men portrayed him in Middleton's play.

ed. R. C. Bald (1929)
Bentley, *JCS*, IV 870–9
Chamberlain, *Letters*, II 578
Greg, 412(a), (b1) and (c)
ed. J. W. Harper (New Mermaid Series, 1966)
Margot Heinemann, *Puritanism and Theatre* (Cambridge, 1980), pp. 151–65
Hind, II 257, 289 (Pls 153, 177)
Oliver Millar, *The Tudor, Stuart and Early Georgian Pictures in the Collection of Her Majesty the Queen* (2 vols, 1963), p. 83 (Pl. 46)
H. J. R. Murray, *A History of Chess* (1913)
Wickham, *EES* II, i 8–9, 218–19, 314–15
E. M. Wilson and Olga Turner, 'The Spanish Protest against "A Game at Chesse" ', *Modern Language Review*, XLIV (1949), 476–82

55

Robert Greene, *Friar Bacon and Friar Bungay* (1630).

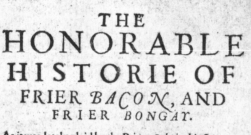

THE
HONORABLE
HISTORIE OF
FRIER *BACON*, AND
FRIER *BONGAY*.

As it was lately plaid by the Prince *Palatine* his Seruants.

Made by *Robert Greene*, Master of Arts.

LONDON,
Printed by ELIZABETH ALLDE dwelling
neere Chrift-Church. 1630.

This play was first published in 1594, when it was already an old play, performed at the Rose Theatre in February 1592, and written perhaps a year or two earlier. It seems to have remained in the possession of the same company through various changes of patron, and to have remained a popular stage-piece. A second quarto was printed in 1630, and this has a woodcut on the title-page illustrating Scene XI of the play. In this, Friar Bacon, 'drawing the curtains with a white stick', has a book in his hand and a lighted lamp by him, as he instructs Miles, his 'poor scholar', who has 'weapons by him', to watch the 'brazen-head'. Calling on Miles to 'Draw close the curtains' (l. 39), Friar Bacon falls asleep, and a little later, after Miles has taken in his hand his 'brown-bill' or halberd (l. 57), the Head speaks: 'Time is', then 'Time was', then 'Time is past'. The last phrase is accompanied by the stage-direction 'Here the Head speaks and a lightning flasheth forth, and a hand appears that breaketh down the Head with a hammer'. The woodcut shows Friar Bacon sitting in a chair speaking, and also fallen with his head on a table, asleep. The Brazen Head, apparently mounted on a wall above a shelf of books, has three loops drawn from its mouth containing the three utterances it makes. On the left is a figure with tabor and pipe, not armed like Miles in the play. According to the text, Miles sits down 'by a post' (l. 51), nods off, and wakes himself by knocking his head against the post. The woodcut does not show this, but simply a floor marked in rectangles, and a rear wall with part of a window showing to the left. A bell hangs to the right, and also an armillary sphere, an astrologer's tool. On the table is a book containing magic signs. The woodcut does not in fact represent the action in the play, but was made for a chapbook based on it, *The Famous History of Friar Bacon*, published in 1627. The printer of the 1630 quarto of the play, Elizabeth Allde, printed an edition of the chapbook in 1629, and gained in this way possession of the woodcut, which she then used on the title-page of *Friar Bacon and Friar Bungay*. The woodcut cannot then be used as evidence relating to the staging of the play. It has some interest nevertheless. Friar Bacon

126

conjures in his 'study' (stage-direction, Scene VI), and Greene's creation of this English sorcerer was probably prompted by Marlowe's success in establishing a German magician in *Doctor Faustus*; the woodcut illustration to the chapbook and play on Friar Bacon may owe something to the depiction of Doctor Faustus in his 'study' on the title-page of Marlowe's play (1616 edition). This also has a floor marked in rectangles, a rear wall with a window, a shelf of books, and an armillary sphere, and, like the *Friar Bacon* woodcut, gives no indication of side-walls (see 46 above).

Chambers, *ES*, III 328–9
Greg, 121(b)
Anthony Harris, *Night's Black Agents* (Manchester, 1980), pp. 119–23 (Pl. 11)
ed. J. A. Lavin (New Mermaids Series, 1969)
MSR (1926)
Reynolds, 134, 156–7
Rhodes, 184 (Pl. 35)
ed. Daniel Seltzer (Regents Renaissance Drama Series, 1963)

56

George Ruggle, *Ignoramus* (1630).

The author, a Fellow of Clare Hall, apparently wrote this Latin play for performance before King James I when the king visited Cambridge in March 1615. The central part, the lawyer Ignoramus, satirised the Recorder of Cambridge, Francis Brakin, and the play's treatment of lawyers, according to John Chamberlain, so angered them that they were 'almost out of all patience'; this led to something of a battle in broadsides and ballads attacking and defending the play. King James returned to Cambridge to see it again in May, and, after being published and reprinted in 1630, the play was reissued seven times between 1658 and 1737, and was translated into English by R. Codrington in 1662. The Latin text was published in a small duodecimo measuring about $4\frac{1}{2}$ in. × $2\frac{1}{2}$ in., with an engraved frontispiece showing the figure of Ignoramus in the costume of a lawyer. He wears a gown, a hat, has a broad collar or falling-band covering the shoulders, a doublet with a belt from which hangs his pen-box and inkhorn, and breeches tied with a wide band above the knee. The style of the falling-band, which in the early seventeenth century replaced the Elizabethan starched and pleated ruff, would not have been inappropriate in 1630, but may have looked old-fashioned then. The figure has a scroll extending from his mouth bearing the words 'Currat Lex', 'The law takes care'. In his right hand he bears a scroll with his name on it, and another, rolled up, in his left hand. Above and behind him is a shelf laden with books, some inscribed with titles, 'At: Academy', 'Wt: Presidents', 'Lawy: Light', 'Proclamations', and 'Statutes'. On the right of the shelf is depicted a bundle of scrolls, one partly unwound and hanging down, which has written on it 'Prowde Buzzard contra Peake: goose'. This refers to a suit which enters into account in the play on B3ᵛ, I.iii, 'Proud Buzzard Plaintife, adversus Peakegoose defendant'. The engraving thus has some relation to the play, and may indicate an appropriate costume for the central figure. Apart from the reference to the lawsuit, the engraving does not have any special connection with the action, in which Ignoramus woos but fails to win Rosabella, who marries her choice Antonio, and is doubly discomfited by being tied to a chair while his barbarous lawyer's Latinisms are exorcised, and finally having a fox's tail pinned to his back. To deliver the Epilogue he appears booted and spurred, ready to set off for London. There is no evidence of further performances of the play between 1615 and 1630, so the engraving, which appears to have been made for publication, may represent merely the figure as imagined by the unknown artist. The title-page of Codrington's translation in 1662 describes the play as 'A Comedy As it was several times Acted with extraordinary Applause, before the Majesty of King James . . .', and makes no mention of later performances.

Bentley, *JCS*, V 1027
Chamberlain, *Letters*, I 597–8
Chambers, *ES*, III 475–6
tr. Robert Codrington (1662)
Greg, L8

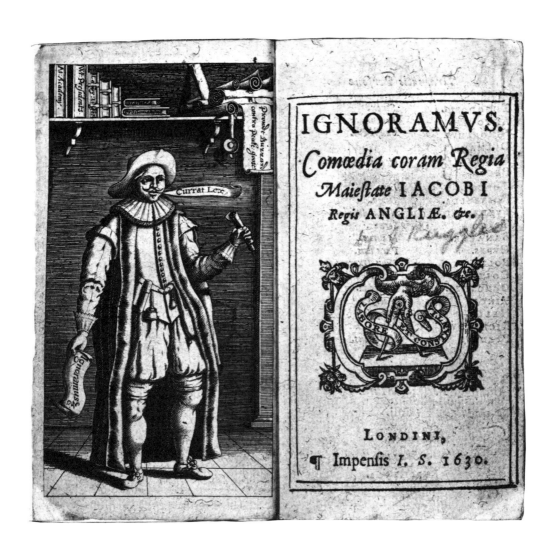

57

Thomas Heywood, *The Fair Maid of the West* (1631).

THE
FAIR MAID
OF THE WEST.
OR,
A Girle worth gold.
The first part.

As it was lately acted before the King and
Queen, with approved liking.

By the Queens Majesties Comedians.

Written by T. Heywood.

LONDON,
Printed for *Richard Royston*, and are to be sold
as his Shop in Ivie Lane. 1 6 3 1.

The first part of this two-part play is thought to have
been written by 1604, and possibly some years earlier.
The action begins in Plymouth with specific references
to the preparation of a fleet for the expedition to the
Azores under the command of the Earl of Essex in 1597.
The date of the second part is uncertain, but it may
have been composed not long before it was published
in 1631. The two parts were published together, with
identical title pages, except that 'The first part' was
changed to 'The second part'. Both quartos contain a
list of *dramatis personae*, identifying the actors who
played many of the parts. These actors all belonged to
Queen Henrietta's Men, confirming the claim on the
title-pages that the play had recently been acted by 'the
Queens Majesties Comedians'. This company was
formed about 1625. The title-pages also state that the
play had been performed before the King and Queen,
which is confirmed by the special prologue for a court
performance attached to Part I, and by Heywood's
own dedicatory letter prefixed to Part II, in which he
wrote that the plays had 'not only pass'd the censure of
the plebs and gentry, but of the patricians and praetex-
tatae [i.e. wearers of togas], as also of our royal Augustus
and Livia'. Queen Henrietta's Men were managed by
Christopher Beeston, who owned the Cockpit Theatre
in Drury Lane, also known as the Phoenix. He also had
interests in the more popular, old-fashioned inn-yard
playhouse, the Red Bull, but the Queen's Men were
associated with the Phoenix, where 'gentry' and
'patricians' were more likely to be among the audience.
Part I is a narrative play of adventure, with a straightforward sense of morality and patriotism; Part II
belongs to a later period in its much greater moral
ambiguity, and its concern with such themes as the
clash of love and honour links it with the dramatic
world of Beaumont and Fletcher. At the same time, the
action of the plays begins from the fixed point of 1597,
and they may have appealed at the Phoenix as something like 'costume' dramas, set in the reign of Queen
Elizabeth. The woodcut on the title pages is presumably intended to suggest Bess Bridges, the 'fair maid' of
the title, and central figure in the two plays. The part

was acted by Hugh Clark, who is first heard of as playing the female lead in James Shirley's *The Wedding* (published in 1629); he was probably older and a more experienced actor than many boys when he acted Bess in Heywood's play, for he seems to have married in 1627, and went on to play male roles by 1635. The illustration shows a figure dressed in a costume appropriate to the last years of Elizabeth's reign, with a large ruff, a close-fitting, stiff, pointed bodice, and a wide skirt, suggesting the support of a farthingale underneath. She wears a chain round her neck, a short cloak, and has hair or a wig elaborately ornamented. Bess begins as a tavern-keeper, and is disguised in Part I as a page and a sea-captain, but at the end of both parts must be costumed as a fine lady; her servant Clem sees her towards the end of Part II in the company of the Duke of Florence and cries, 'My mistress turn'd gallant ... I have gold and anon will be as gallant as the proudest of them' (V.iii.14). The costume in the illustration may point to a visual linking of Bess with Queen Elizabeth, for Part II ends with the Duke of Florence praising her as

> the mirror of your sex and nation,
> Fair English Elizabeth, as well for virtue
> As admired beauty ...
> (V.iv.191)

At the same time, the printer probably used an old block, for it is similar to one used for 'The World's Sweet-heart' (i.e. Mistress Money or Lady Pecunia), a ballad that is related to Richard Barnfield's *Lady Pecunia* (1598, 1605); this block appears also in two broadsheets of the 1630s, and it is possible that all ballad uses of it post-date the publication of Heywood's play.

Bentley, *JCS*, IV 568–71
Greg, 445, 446
Roxburghe Ballads, III 81, 119, 240
Shakespeare's England, II 94–6
ed. R. K. Turner, Jr. (Regents Renaissance Drama Series, 1968)
Wickham, *EES* II, ii 106–9, 117–22

58

Edward Forsett, *Pedantius* (1631).

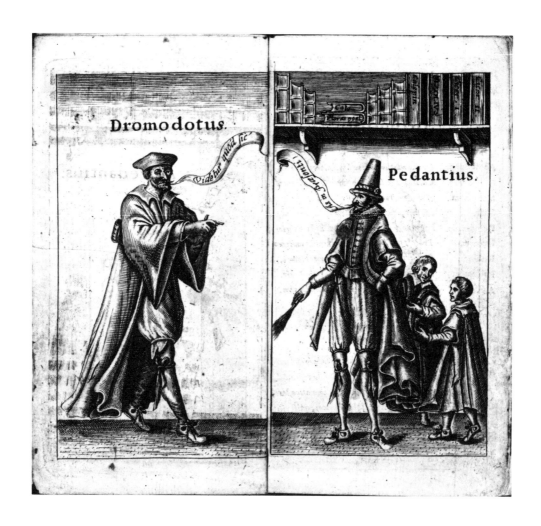

The publication of this academic Latin play in 1631 was prompted by the printing of *Ignoramus* (56). Although brought out by a different printer and bookseller, it was issued in the same duodecimo format, illustrated by similar engraved frontispieces, and prefaced by some verses headed 'Pedantius de Se', which compare the two plays and claim Lydia in *Pedantius* is prettier than Rosabella in *Ignoramus*. The play probably dates from 1581, and made something of a mark at the time. Sir John Harington refers to it three times, twice in his translation of *Orlando Furioso* (1591), and once in *The Metamorphosis of Ajax* (1596); he appears to have seen it in the company of the Earl of Essex at Trinity College when he was a student at Cambridge, and applauds it as a comedy 'full of harmless mirth'. Thomas Nashe also refers to it a number of times in various of his writings as an exquisite comedy in which Gabriel Harvey was satirised as the pedant, 'as namely the concise and firking finicaldo fine school-master, he was full drawn and delineated from the sole of his foot to the crown of his head'. In the same pamphlet, *Have with you to Saffron Walden* (1596), Nashe hints that the actors borrowed Harvey's gown 'to play the Part in, the more to flout him'. The play was performed when Harvey was hoping to be elected Public Orator of the University, and the man who defeated him, Anthony Wingfield, a Fellow of Trinity, probably had a hand in the satire, although another Fellow of this college, Edward Forsett, seems to have been mainly responsible for the play.

The play is a Plautine comedy satirising especially the two figures who are represented in the frontispieces, Pedantius, the schoolmaster who looks back to the authority of Cicero, but at the same time would like to present himself as a 'courtier and man of affairs' (G. C. Moore Smith, p. xxxi), and Dromodotus, equally pedantic, but typifying scholasticism in his constant reference to Aristotle. The first engraving, on the verso of the title-page, shows Dromodotus wearing a doctor's gown and cap, with a scroll rising from his mouth bearing the legend 'Videtur quod sic' a catch-phrase of scholastic disputation which is used in the dialogue of the play, as at ll. 1001 and 2836. The second engraving on the facing page displays Pedantius with two pupils. He is shown as a very thin man wearing a gown over a doublet, breeches tapering above the knee, with garters of ribbon tied below the knee, and pumps on his feet. He also has on a tall steeple-hat of a kind popular in the 1580s, and described by Philip Stubbs in the *Anatomy of Abuses* (1583) as 'sharp on the crown peaking up like a spear, or shaft of a steeple standing a quarter of a yard above the crown of their heads'. Behind and above Pedantius is a shelf laden with books, some labelled with titles as follows, reading from left to right: 'Cato',

'Floras poet', 'Calepin', 'Nizolius', 'Cicer. 1' and 'Cicer. II'. All of these are referred to in the text. The scroll attached to his mouth has on it the words 'As in Praesenti', which are quoted from the widely-used Latin grammar by William Lily.

These illustrations to the play are like that to *Ignoramus*, and the editor, G. C. Moore Smith, thought that 'all three portraits are no doubt equally imaginary' (p. 102). This may well be so if they were made for old plays in 1630 or 1631. At the same time, the thin figure of Pedantius in his old-fashioned costume may have some reference to Harvey, who, according to Nashe, was 'lean and meagre', habitually wore long breeches called Venetians, liked to sport 'pumps and pantofles', and was known to show off his fine leg and dainty foot in the streets of Cambridge (*Have with you to Saffron Walden*). Nashe also said the actors imitated Harvey to the life: 'not the carrying up of his gown, his nice gait or his pantofles, or the affected accent of his speech, but they personated'. The illustration of a tall thin figure shows Pedantius apparently 'carrying up' his gown in his left hand. Whoever was responsible for the illustration of Pedantius knew the play, as the labelling of the books shows, and the costume of the figure may be intended to suggest someone like Harvey, though there is no reason to suppose any attempt was made to portray him. In other words, the costume would be appropriate for performance of the role.

Bentley, *JCS*, V 1397–8
Chambers, *ES*, IV 376–7
Greg, L9
ed. R. B. McKerrow, *The Works of Thomas Nashe* (5 vols, 904–10; reprinted with corrections and supplementary notes edited by F. P. Wilson, Oxford, 1958), III 38, 68, 80
ed. G. C. Moore Smith, *Bangs Materialen zur Kunde des älteren Englischen Dramas* (Louvain, 1905)

59

Thomas Heywood, *The Iron Age*, Parts I and II (1632).

When *The Golden Age* came 'accidentally to the Press' in 1611, Heywood managed to oversee its publication and add a note to the reader describing it as 'the eldest brother of three Ages, that have adventured the Stage'. *The Silver Age* and *The Brazen Age* were published in 1613, the prefatory note in the former announcing Heywood's 'purpose by God's grace, to end with *Iron*'. This series of plays based on classical legends, and developed from his own long poem *Troia Britannica* (1609), culminated in *The Iron Age*, on the Trojan war and the destruction of the city by the Greeks, which he probably wrote in about 1613. The popularity of the subject on the stage may have led him to expand his material into a two-part play, and may also account for the delay in the publication of *The Iron Age* until 1632. In his address 'To the Reader' prefixed to *The Iron Age*, Part I, Heywood reviewed his work with some complacency, concluding with the statement 'these were the Plays often (and not with the least applause), Publicly Acted by two Companies, upon one Stage at once, and [they] have at sundry times thronged three several Theatres, with numerous and mighty Auditories'. The prefatory note to Part II is less confident, and expresses some concern that plays 'long since Writ' may not be well received in an age devoted to satire and comedy. The three theatres at which Heywood claimed his *Ages* plays were performed have not been certainly identified, but were probably the Red Bull, the Curtain and the Globe. Heywood was himself an actor with Queen Anne's Men, a company which broke up in 1619, and his name disappears from actor lists after May of that year; his comments in the prefatory note to Part II imply that his heroic plays had not been staged for some time, and there is no evidence of performance between Heywood's retirement from acting and the year of publication, 1632.

Each play has an elaborate woodcut on its title-page. That illustrating Part I shows a scene from Act II in which (as in Shakespeare's *Troilus and Cressida*) Hector issues a challenge to the Greeks, and the Greeks draw lots to determine who shall fight him, the chance falling to Ajax. In this scene a group of Trojans enters 'above

upon the walls' to watch the combat, and the heroes then 'appear betwixt the two Armies'. Ajax makes a speech which indicates how he is armed:

> behold my warlike target
> Of ponderous brass, quilted with seven oxhides,
> Impenetrable, and so full of weight,
> That scarce a *Grecian* (save myself) can lift it:
> Yet can I use it like a summer's fan,
> Made of the stately train of *Juno's* bird:
> My sword will bite the hardest adamant.
> I'll with my javelin cleave a rock of marble.

Their fight is marked by the stage-direction, 'in this combat both having lost their swords and Shields. *Hector* takes up a great piece of rock and casts at *Ajax*; who tears a young Tree up by the roots, and assails *Hector*, at which they are parted by both arm[i]es'. The woodcut represents this scene, with the walls of Troy in the background on the left, and the tents of the Greeks in the background on the right. The swords and shields of the two warriors lie on the ground. They are shown as wearing body armour and helmets. Each also seems to be wearing a tunic (Hector's ornamental skirt perhaps indicating Trojan garb, as distinguished from Ajax's plain skirt), hose and boots. Between them can be seen several figures, also helmeted, presumably including Paris and Agamemnon, who part the combatants. The woodcut is evidently based upon the text.

The illustration to Part II conflates two moments in the action. In Act II the 'Horse is discovered', the 'huge Engine' from which, some lines later, 'Pyrrhus, Diomed, and the rest, leap' out. To the right of the woodcut Pyrrhus is shown, apparently wearing armour rather like Hector and Ajax in the woodcut to Part I, and holding a spear. He has leapt from the Trojan horse, and 'the rest', also holding spears so large the horse could hardly have contained them, look down on him. His curious posture, arms extended, and facing away from the city, may be intended to suggest the emergence of the Greeks here 'as if groping in the dark', as Heywood's direction puts it. The fire, which they set going a little later, is already blazing in the city as shown to the left of the woodcut. In the foreground a

The Iron Age:

ontayning the Rape of *Hellen*: The fiege of *Troy*:
the Combate betwixt *Hector* and *Aiax* : *Hector* and *Troilus*
flayne by *Achilles* : *Achilles* flaine by *Paris* : *Aiax* and *Vliffes*
contend for the Armour of *Achilles* : The Death
of *Aiax*, *&c.*

written by T H O M A S H E Y W O O D.

Aut prodeffe folent audi Delectare.

Printed at *London* by *Nicholas Okes*. 1632.

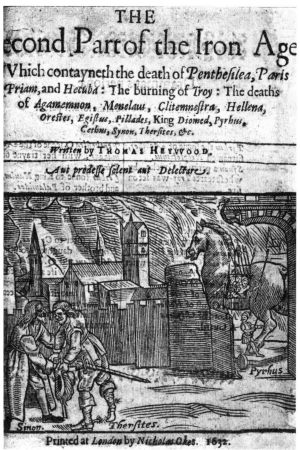

THE
cond Part of the Iron Age
Which contayneth the death of *Penthefilea*, *Paris*
Priam, and *Hecuba* : The burning of *Troy* : The deaths
of *Agamemnon*, *Menelaus*, *Clitemneftra*, *Hellena*,
Oreftes, *Egiftus*, *Pillades*, King *Diomed*, *Pyrhus*,
Cethus, *Synon*, *Therfites*, *&c.*

written by T H O M A S H E Y W O O D.

Aut prodeffe folent aut Delectare.

Printed at *London* by *Nicholas Okes*. 1632.

later episode from IV.i is illustrated, where Thersites and Sinon meet to congratulate each other on being 'conquerors in our basest cowardice': when so many heroes have perished, they survive. They are shown shaking hands, and wearing costumes appropriate to the period when the play was published; Sinon has a long gown with a cord at the waist, and wears shoes, while Thersites, who carries a wide-brimmed hat with a feather in it in his left hand, wears a jerkin, breeches, boots and spurs, and has a sword.

There is nothing that connects these woodcuts with the stage, and they may simply reflect an artist's licence. Although Heywood was an actor, he saw these plays through the press, and may have deliberately provided 'literary' stage-directions for his readers. There must have been a property Trojan horse, but the burning city could have been represented on a painted cloth. There must also have been a property rock and tree for the fight between Hector and Ajax, and a good deal of play with weapons. The performances Heywood mentions by two companies of players combining forces would have made possible a decent shot at showing the two armies making ready for battle, or watching Hector and Ajax fight. At the same time, Heywood's stage-directions sometimes refer explicitly to the

theatre, as when the Trojans enter 'at one door', and the Greeks 'at the other'. What hints there are for costuming, as in Ajax's sevenfold shield or Diomedes losing his helmet, might suggest that Heywood was imagining them costumed to suggest the ancient world; on the other hand, the use of a curtained bed in Part II shows him thinking in terms of his own age. The incongruity of Sinon and Thersites, costumed as seventeenth-century figures in the woodcut to Part II, may reflect Heywood's own casual attitude to anachronisms, especially if, as is possible, he supervised the designing of the blocks, as well as the printing of the plays.

Bentley, *JCS*, I 165, IV 556
Chambers, III 345
A. M. Clark, *Thomas Heywood* (1958), pp. 63–7
Greg, 467(AII), 468
Reynolds, 113–14
ed. R. H. Shepherd, *Dramatic Works* (6 vols, 1874, reprinted New York, 1964), III 257–431

60

Arden of Faversham (1633).

This anonymous play was first printed in 1592; the second Quarto, published in 1599, was based on the first, and the third, issued in 1633, seems to have been printed from a copy of the second. The 'Lamentable and True Tragedy of M. Arden' was based upon an actual event, the murder of Thomas Arden at the instigation of his wife in his house in Faversham in 1551. The particularly horrific character of the crime induced Raphael Holinshed to include a lengthy account of it in his *Chronicles* (1577 and 1587); it was referred to also in John Stow's *Annals of England* (1592 and 1631), and in Thomas Heywood's *Troia Britannica* (1609). In 1633 a ballad called the 'Complaint and lamentation of Mistresse *Arden* of [*Fev*]*ersham* in *Kent*' was published, so that the story remained alive in chronicles and in popular remembrance, and no doubt other references to it have been lost, since John Taylor, the Water Poet, classified this murder with other famous ones, like that of Humphry, Duke of Gloucester, as 'fresh in memory', and said, 'the fearful ends of their wives and their aiders in those bloody actions will never be forgotten' (*The Unnatural Father*, 1621). The woodcut printed on the verso of the title-page was also used under the heading of the ballad printed as a broadsheet in the same year as the play; the ballad appears to be based on the play, and the woodcut relates better to the play than to the ballad. It depicts the murder of Arden, in Scene XIV, when Black Will, acting upon the watchword given by Mosby, pulls Arden down from the seat where he is playing backgammon with Mosby, and Arden is stabbed successively by Mosby, Shakebag and Alice. The woodcut is crude, and possibly attempts to show more than one moment in the action. To the right Mosby sits opposite Arden at a table where they are playing backgammon, with a candle to show it is night ('supper time', l. 94). Arden sits on a stool, and Black Will is pulling him backwards with a towel, according to Will's plan:

> Mark my device:
> Place Mosby, being a stranger, in a chair,
> And let your husband sit upon a stool,
> That I may come behind him cunningly
> And with a towel pull him to the ground . . .
> (117–21)

In the play Mosby is the first to stab Arden, but the woodcut seems to show, in the two male figures, one holding a sword and stabbing Arden, and the other entering from a door and brandishing a weapon, the figures of Shakebag and Michael. There are also two female figures, each holding a dagger, though only Alice is present in this part of the scene, and she takes a weapon from Shakebag – the text, indeed, suggests that Will, Shakebag and Alice all use the same dagger. The second female figure may be Susan, Alice's maid and Mosby's sister, who is implicated in the crime, but enters after the deed is done. If the costumes of the two female figures, and those of Mosby and the man standing and plunging a sword into Arden, were not so different, it would be tempting to suppose the woodcut represented Mosby twice, sitting at the table and stabbing Arden, and Alice also in two places. The more probable explanation, however, is that the woodcut is simply inaccurate. In the ballad, Black Will and Shakebag simply hide, and emerge from a 'corner' (l. 158); in the play they are locked 'within the countinghouse' (Scene XIV, l. 101), and Arden's servant Michael, Alice's accomplice, who is not mentioned in the ballad, stands 'before the countinghouse door'. As in the woodcut, Arden is seated with his back to this door, and it seems that Will creeps between Michael's legs on entering, to ensure Arden will not see him (l. 229). When Will pulls him down, Arden exclaims 'Mosby! Michael! Alice! What will you do?' (l. 233), which suggests these three are by him, and Shakebag is behind (the figure in the doorway?). The woodcut represents a floor, a rear wall with two windows, and a door to one side. This seems to be a conventional representation of a room, and may be compared with that on the title-page of *A Maidenhead Well Lost* (61), or *Friar Bacon and Friar Bungay* (55). Such woodcuts, it has been said by T. S. R. Boase, are typical of illustrations to broadsides; this one, however, shows, roughly and inaccurately, the murder as it was carried out in the play, not in the ballad. The text of the play in this scene several times refers to doors; the countinghouse door conceals the murderers, who enter eventually through it; Arden enters through another door, which perhaps served as a general entrance and

exit to the rest of Arden's house, if Michael fetched the backgammon, and later wine (l. 199), and Susan and the guests also came and went through this door. Later in the scene, the body of Arden is brought out of the countinghouse (l. 332), and then carried out into the fields (l. 350); Mosby and Greene return, then leave (l. 354) a few lines before the Mayor and Watch arrive knocking on a door. It would be possible to play the scene using two stage-doors, but much easier if there were three, a house-door, through which the properties used in the scene could be brought, and which could serve as a back way out for getting rid of Arden's body, a 'street' door at which the guests, and the Mayor, knock, and the countinghouse door, so that some practical entrance into an area like that of Dr Faustus's or Friar Bacon's 'study' (see 46 and 55) would suit this play well. At the same time, the woodcut cannot be used as evidence for this, even if it may suggest something of the general disposition of the scene, and possibly appropriate costumes.

T. S. R. Boase, 'Illustrations of Shakespeare's Plays in the Seventeenth and Eighteenth Centuries', *Journal of the Warburg Institute*, X (1947), 83–108

ed. C. F. Tucker Brooke, *Shakespeare Apocrypha* (Oxford, 1908), pp. 1–35

Chambers, *ES*, IV 3–4

Greg, 107(c)

Anita Holt, 'Arden of Faversham' (*Faversham Papers*, No. 7, 1970)

Reynolds, 115–21

Shakespeare's England, III 531

ed. M. L. Wine (Revels Plays, 1973)

61

Thomas Heywood, *A Maidenhead Well Lost* (1634).

This play, unusual among Heywood's in being set in Italy, has received little attention since it was published in 1634, probably within a year or two of being written. It is a well-made piece, but has gathered a somewhat unsavoury reputation because of Heywood's curious use of a bed-trick, a variant of the dramatic device Shakespeare made familiar in *Measure for Measure* and *All's Well that Ends Well*. In Heywood's play, the Prince of Parma is led to think his betrothed Julia, daughter of the Duke of Milan, is unfaithful to him, although they are

> man and wife
> Saving the Church's outward ceremony.
> (Act II, C4^r)

He abandons her when she is with child by him, and she is duly delivered of a son. Meanwhile, the Prince of Florence falls in love with Lauretta, the daughter of a dead Milanese general, who lives in exile in the woods near Florence. When the Duke of Milan, publicly claiming Julia is a maid, arranges through the Duke of Florence a marriage between her and the Prince of Florence, they are faced with the problem of providing a virgin for the prince on his wedding-night. They employ a villain Stroza in an attempt to corrupt Lauretta with a bribe, but she offers herself anyway, out of love for the Prince of Florence, and she sneaks away during the night, Julia then taking her place. However, the Prince had given Lauretta a ring and a charter while in bed with her, and these provide crucial evidence in what follows. In the next scene the Dukes of Milan and Florence enter 'with *Julia, Stroza* and attendants' (H2^v), and sit at table, for the Prince then comes in to say of Julia:

> For the foul wrong I did her, questioning
> Her Virtue, I'll confirm her dower, and that
> Before I eat.
> (H3^v)

He then demands the ring and charter, knowing she does not have them. Stroza delays the revelation of his guilt by saying he sent them to Milan, but at this point comes the stage-direction 'Enter a Serving-man with a child in a covered Dish' (H4^r). The child is sent by the

138

Prince of Parma, whose love for Julia has revived, and he later enters to acknowledge the child his own. The play ends with a happy exchange of Julia for Lauretta, and Heywood allows no comment on the morality of the action, as the Prince of Florence returns Julia back to the Prince of Parma, and says to Lauretta,

> My Mistress first, and next my bed-fellow,
> And now my Bride, most welcome . . .
>
> (I2ᵛ)

The title-page has a large woodcut, which was used again on H3ʳ in the scene it illustrates. It represents a group at table, presumably the Duke of Milan, the Duke of Florence and the Prince of Florence in the centre, and perhaps Stroza on the left. It also shows the child in a 'covered dish', though this appears more like a small cabinet, opened to give the spectators rather than the characters a view of the interior. However, it is not an accurate rendering of the scene, for Julia and Mounsieur (the Prince of Florence's tutor) are also on stage at this point. The woodcut does not show any moment in the action, but is composite. This is especially notable in the short figure standing to the right of the table; he holds a paper in his hand suggesting the moment when a paper is found on the breast of the baby by the Prince, but he is dressed as a clown in a long guarded coat, and a fool's hat crowned by a coxcomb. The Clown in the play, who is a servant to Lauretta and her mother, is not present at this point, and comes on only at the end of the scene. In a separate compartment to the right are two figures embracing, who could represent the Prince of Florence and Lauretta, or the Prince of Parma and Julia. The figure of the Clown is of some interest, since it suggests that a form of the traditional fool's costume was still in use in the 1630s; but the other male figures are indistinguishable, and their costume, as roughly indicated in the woodcut, is consistent with the date of the play, as are the pointed beards three of them wear, a fashion familiar from portraits of Charles I. The main part of the woodcut shows a table set out on a floor, laid with a cloth, a goblet, and plates. A rear wall is indicated by two windows, as in the woodcut illustrating *Swetnam the Woman-Hater* (51 above). Four of the figures are seated at the table, and the fifth, the standing clown, appears to be very small in comparison with the rest. This may be due to a failure of scale in the drawing; the actor who played clown's roles for Queen Henrietta's Men was William Robbins, whose best-known part was Antonio, the title role in Middleton's *The Changeling*, and there is no evidence to suggest that he was dwarfish.

Bentley, *JCS*, II 547–9, IV 582–3
A. M. Clark, *Thomas Heywood* (1958), pp. 128–9, 267–8
Greg, 493
E. W. Ives, 'Tom Skelton – A Seventeenth-Century Jester', *SS*, 13 (1960), 99
ed. R. H. Shepherd, *Dramatic Works* (6 vols, 1874, reprinted 1964), IV 97–165

62

William Sampson, *The Vow Breaker* or *The Fair Maid of Clifton* (1636).

This play may have been written some years before it was published, for the only other plays associated with William Sampson are *The Widow's Prize* (1624–5), now lost, and *Herod and Antipater*, written jointly with Gervase Markham before 1621–2. The first of these was performed by Prince Charles's Company shortly before it broke up in 1625, and the other by the King's Revels Company at the Red Bull. *The Vow Breaker* may not have been presented in London, and is vaguely located on the title-page 'In Notinghamshire as it hath beene divers times Acted by several Companies with great applause'. The play is dedicated to Anne Willoughby, daughter of Sir Henry Willoughby of Risley in Derbyshire, and the action concerns events relating to the Nottingham area. There are two plots, one concerning the involvement of Nottinghamshire troops in the Anglo-Scottish wars of 1560, and the other presenting the tragic story of the 'Fair Maid' Anne. The first is derived from Holinshed, and the second from a ballad entitled 'A Godly Warning for all Maidens', or 'A Warning for Maidens', or 'Young Bateman', which was entered in the Stationers' Register first in 1603, and again in 1624. The play was printed with a woodcut illustration showing four incidents in the action involving Anne and her lover, and on the facing page were printed some verses, headed 'The Illustration', as follows:

> This faithless woman, by her friends consent
> Plighted her troth to *Bateman*! streight not content
> With his revenue! Coveting for more
> She marries *German* for his wealthy store
> There Parents iarr'd, and never could agree
> Till both of them were dround in misery.
> Young *Bateman* hangs himselfe for love of her;
> Shee drownds her selfe (guilt plaies the murtherer)
> His Ghost afrights her, sad thoughts doe her annoy
> (Alive or dead: tis shee he must enioy)
> The Morrall is Maides should beware in choise
> And where they cannot love, divert their voice.
> Parents must not be rash, nor too unkind,
> And not for wealth to thwart, their Childrens minde.
> All is not gained, that's got (ill purchasde wealth),
> Never brought comfort, tranquill, peace, and health.)
> This president, this principle doth allow
> Weddings are made in Heaven, though seald below.

The Prologue asserts that the story is true, and that the events happened 'ninety years since', although the war episodes can, as noted, be dated at 1560, which makes them rather more recent than this. The love story is loosely linked to the other plot early in the play, when Boot, Anne's uncle, who is anxious for her to marry the wealthy German, schemes to separate her from her betrothed by having young Bateman go off to fight in the wars. He returns six months later to find Anne married to his rich rival.

Although the plot involving the lovers is completed in Act IV, and Act V is devoted to the outcome of the wars, bringing Sir Gervase Clifton of Nottinghamshire, Lord Grey of Wilton, and finally Queen Elizabeth herself on stage (to grant a petition, quite irrelevant to the play, that the River Trent be made navigable), the title and illustration indicate that the story of Anne and Bateman holds the play's main interest. The woodcut shows four incidents, beginning with Bateman at the top left with a halter round his neck. This refers to the return of Bateman in Act II, on the day Anne marries German, when he says:

> Alive or dead thy promise thou shall keep
> I must, and will enjoy thee.
> (II.ii.128)

In II.iv Bateman enters 'in his shirt' with a halter round his neck, finds a 'tree' at her door, and hangs himself. The woodcut shows him in II.iv, but quoting lines from II.ii; and he is almost naked, apart from what looks almost like a belt, but may be intended to suggest a rumpled undergarment, a 'shirt' being what was worn next to the skin. Bateman points to a bracelet, containing his part of a piece of gold he and Anne split between them as token of their love.

The scene in the upper right corner of the woodcut relates to the ghost of Bateman visiting Anne in Act III. Bateman's father has his son's portrait painted (as shown in the bottom left corner of the woodcut), and enters with it in III.iv, when Anne 'Stands between the Picture, & Ghost', according to a stage-direction, and sees, as it were, two pictures, one being the Ghost,

> his Alablaster finger pointing
> To the bracelet, whereon the piece of gold
> We broke between us hangs.
>
> (III.iv.89)

In IV.ii Anne gives birth to a child, and then goes off-stage to drown herself; hence the figure by the river at the bottom right of the cut. At this point her uncle, Boot, comes on, and old Bateman with his son's picture, and they speak in turn:

Boot: How happy had I been if she had liv'd.
Bateman: How happy had I been if he had liv'd.

The woodcut shows the two men kneeling to speak these lines. The woodcut then is based closely on the action of the play, and cites lines of dialogue from it. The settings in the cut are largely fanciful, but the costumes, the bed and the picture of young Bateman may have some relevance to the staging of the play. The connection, incidentally, that Kathleen Tillotson suggested between this play and the lost *Black Batman of the North*, a two-part play written for the Admiral's Men in 1598, seems merely speculative.

Bentley, *JCS*, IV 734–5, V 1043–5
Foakes and Rickert, *HD*, 89, 92
Greg, 510
Kathleen Tillotson, 'William Sampson's "Vow-Breaker" (1636) and the Lost Henslowe Play "Black Batman of the North"', *Modern Language Review*, XXXV (1940), 377–8
ed. H. Wallrath, *Bangs Materialen zur Kunde des älteren Englischen Dramas* (Louvain, 1914)

63

[?Thomas Dekker], *The Merry Devil of Edmonton* (1655).

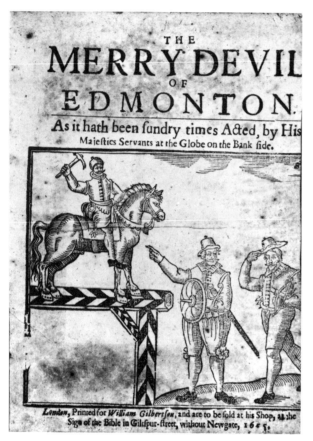

This edition has a large woodcut on the title-page, showing an enormous inn-sign of a horse and rider, and two male figures. This could easily be taken to represent the moment in V.i when Sir Arthur Clare and Sir Ralph Jerningham discover they have not been sleeping, as they thought, at the George Inn, but next door to it. The play as it stands allows the reader to think the Host of the George, Blague, has moved his inn-sign to deceive them, in order that Clare's daughter could marry her lover, Raymond Mounchensey, and use his inn for their wedding-night. However, at V.ii.11, Blague seems as surprised as anyone to find his inn-sign moved. It turns out that the woodcut had been used earlier to illustrate a prose pamphlet, *The Life and Death of the Merry Devil of Edmonton*, entered in the Stationers' Register in 1608, the year in which the play was published; the earliest known edition of this pamphlet is dated 1631. The woodcut in the pamphlet has an inscription within the bracket identifying the figure on horseback as Smug the smith, who has 'Got upon the white horse' to escape being caught by the keepers pursuing him for stealing venison. The two other figures are also identified as 'Mine Host of the George' and 'Sir Iohn', who appears as a priest in the play.

The text of the play as printed is short and corrupt, and may have been cut for performance by a company touring in the provinces. It would seem that in its original shape, as performed at the Globe, there were two large property inn-signs, one representing the George, or Saint George, and the other the White Horse. Although the text that has come down to us is confused on this matter, there are residual indications within it of these signs. So V.i takes place at an unidentified inn opposite the George, for the 'Chamberlain' of this inn says he 'will send one over' to see if Blague, the Host of the George, is stirring (V.i.121), and later Sir Arthur Clare asks 'Is not this the George?' and the Chamberlain replies 'Sfoote, our signs remov'd' (V.i.133–5). It appears from these lines, and others in V.ii, that the inn-signs have been switched. The play ends with Smug saying 'I will be Saint George again' and Sir Ralph asking, 'Did we not last night find two

S. Georges here?', to which Fabel, the magician or 'merry devil', replies 'Yes, Knights, this martialist was one of them' (V.ii.176–9). The action to which this refers is missing from the text of the play. That the play did originally provide a sensational effect in having Smug twice get upon the sign of the White Horse and impersonate St George, once in the action of the play, and a second time to round off the play, is suggested by a reference to it in Thomas Middleton's *A Mad World my Masters* (c. 1606; printed 1608), V.ii.96–8, where Follywit says, 'Why, sirrah, do you use to bring gentlemen before us for riding away? What, will you have 'em stand still when they're up, like Smug upo' th' white horse yonder?'

The references remaining in the text of the play to episodes involving the switching of inn-signs, and Smug mounting one of them, are too confused to make possible a reconstruction of the original action. The prose pamphlet may indicate what has been lost: this names the second inn as the White Horse, and includes an episode in which keepers chasing Smug at night think they see two Saint Georges, and that they are at Hoddesdon, when in fact they are outside Blague's inn in Waltham, Smug having climbed on to the White Horse to escape them. It is this very striking effect that is illustrated in the woodcut; when this was re-used for the 1655 edition of the play, the text within it was removed, leaving its significance unclear. The printer must have realised that the incident it referred to had been cut from the text he was printing. It has been suggested by W. A. Abrams that the use of elaborate properties such as large practical signs on a strong frame, which could be mounted by an actor, and also switched in the course of the play, would have been unsuitable for a touring company, and this could explain the omissions. It is hard otherwise to account for the loss of an exciting stage effect.

Although the woodcut, as far as we know, was first issued to accompany the prose tract, it has a bearing on the original action of *The Merry Devil of Edmonton*. It is even possible that the frame with the sign of a very lifelike horse **on** it is something in the style of what was introduced on the stage at the Globe when the play was performed. What the woodcut, the pamphlet, and certain otherwise puzzling lines remaining in the text of the play establish when brought together is that prominent effects in the early productions of *The Merry Devil of Edmonton* were the presence of two large inn-signs, the switching of them in the course of the play, and Smug's impersonation of Saint George twice by climbing on the white horse, and brandishing his hammer as if it were a weapon, as depicted in the woodcut. The costumes of the figures in the cut are appropriate to the early years of the seventeenth century; the short doublet, worn with rolls at the shoulders, the full hose or slops extending below the knee, as shown on the central figure, and the Spanish breeches worn by the figure on the right, all fit the period 1600–15. If, as seems likely, the prose pamphlet was produced to capitalise on the success of the play, then the woodcut may also reflect an especially successful stage-effect, but this is no more than a conjecture.

ed. W. A. Abrams (Durham, North Carolina, 1942)
ed. C. F. Tucker Brooke, *Shakespeare Apocrypha* (Oxford, 1908,) pp. 263–84
Chambers, *ES*, IV 30–1
Greg, 264(f)
The Life and Death of the Merry Devil of Edmonton (1631)
Thomas Middleton, *A Mad World my Masters*, ed. Standish Henning (Regents Renaissance Drama Series, 1965)

64

Thomas Dekker, William Rowley and John Ford, *The Witch of Edmonton* (1658).

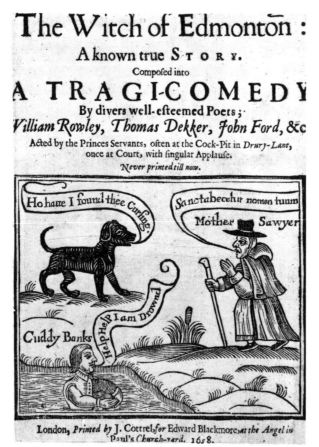

This play was performed at Court in December 1621, and dates from that year, since material in it was drawn from a pamphlet, *The Wonderful Discovery of Elizabeth Sawyer, a Witch, late of Edmonton*, published earlier in 1621. It was not printed until 1658, when it was issued with the statement 'Acted by the Princes Servants, often at the Cock-pit in *Drury-Lane*' on the title-page; this refers to the period 1621–2 when Prince Charles's Company played at the Phoenix, or Cockpit. However, the Quarto has a Prologue as spoken by '*Mr.* Bird' referring to a revival of the play, and an epilogue spoken by '*PHEN*', or Ezekiel Fenn, in the character of the maid Winifred. These were actors in Queen Henrietta's Company in the 1630s, and G. E. Bentley takes the printing of their names as pointing to a revival about 1635. The manuscript from which the play was printed in 1658 thus had connections with the Caroline stage, but there is no reason to think the woodcut made for the title-page has any reference to the theatre. It illustrates three moments in the action. One is the first entry of the Devil in the form of a Dog, in response to the imprecations of Elizabeth Sawyer, with the line:

Ho! have I found thee cursing? now thou art mine own.
(II.i.116)

The second reference is to her encounters with the Clown, Cuddy Banks, later in this scene, when he addresses her as 'Mother Sawyer', and she mumbles the spell the Dog has taught her to use in order to bring ill on those she hates, 'To death pursue 'em, Et sanc tabecetur nomen tuum' (II.i.179–82). The third reference is to Act III, where Cuddy is lured by a spirit in the shape of the maid Katherine to go after her, and his cry off-stage, 'Oh help, help, I am drown'd, I am drown'd' (III.i.90), is followed by a stage-direction calling for him to enter 'wet'.

The company must have had two dog-costumes, for the actor who played the Dog (or Devil) changes his black appearance to white in V.i. The woodcut merely shows a rather stiff representation of a black dog in a vague landscape. A small actor could presumably play a large speaking dog in the tradition of the 'hell-hound'

144

image that goes back to Cerberus, the guardian of Hades in Greek mythology. (The more usual familiar of the village wise women associated with witchcraft was a black cat.) Cuddy Banks is shown up to his waist in water, and Mother Sawyer walks on a bank. It was natural for the maker of the woodcut to present his figures in a landscape, since the play refers to particular places (Edmonton, West Ham, Enfield, Barking, Gravesend, and others), Cuddy is to meet Katherine at the end of her father's 'Pease-Field' (II.i.248), and Mother Sawyer makes her first entry in this scene 'gathering sticks'.

Bentley, *JCS*, III 269–72
ed. F. T. Bowers, *Dramatic Works of Thomas Dekker* (1958), III 482–568
Chambers, *ES*, III 298–9
Greg, 785
Anthony Harris, *Night's Black Agents* (Manchester, 1980), pp. 90–108 (Pl. 8)
ed. R. G. Lawrence, *Jacobean and Caroline Comedies* (1973)
Shakespeare's England, II 542–3

65

Sir William Lower, *The Enchanted Lovers* (1658) and *The Amorous Fantasm* (1660).

These two plays were bound together in a small duo-decimo volume, with a page measuring roughly 4¾ in. ×2½ in. (120 mm×63 mm), issued in London in 1661, and entitled *Three New Plays*, the third being a rendering from the French called *The Noble Ingratitude*. Two of the plays have engraved frontispieces. The first of these, *The Enchanted Lovers*, was printed at The Hague in 1658. The engraving, which incorporates the title twice, shows the climactic scene in Act V. The play is a pastoral, with a cast consisting mainly of cavaliers disguised as shepherds, and young ladies disguised as shepherdesses. Two of them, Thersander and Diana, are in love, but

> by th' effects of fortune and inchantment
> Thersander and Diana dye by turns,
> And live again to wail their miseries.
>   (V.ii)

V.iv begins with 'Thersander *by* Diana's *body*', according to the stage-direction, bewailing her death, and later calls for 'Diana *upon* Thersander's body', lamenting his demise. But the goddess Diana descends after thunder and lightning in the last scene to restore the lovers to life, marriage, and true love. The top and bottom sections of the frontispiece illustrate the lovers mourning in turn for one another, in pastoral landscapes. The middle section depicts a group of shepherds and shepherdesses, and is primarily decorative, in general reference to a play which has one genuine shepherd in the cast, but three cavaliers and four ladies all disguised as shepherds or shepherdesses.

The Amorous Phantasm was printed in London in 1661 and is dedicated to the Princess Royal. The play, which has a Prologue addressed 'To the Court', is a rendering from the French of Philippe Quinault. The action concerns a Duke of Ferrara, whose jealousy of Fabritio, a young man beloved by the Duke's mistress Climene, leads him to seek his death. By the end of Act I the Duke thinks he has killed Fabritio, who has in fact escaped death, and who returns as a 'phantasm'. Eventually the Duke surrenders his interest in Climene, and all ends harmoniously. There has to be available a

146

dead body at times for display, as in II.v. The frontispiece seems to illustrate three aspects of the play; in the upper left section is shown the 'dead' Fabritio, in the upper right section the Duke wooing Climene, and at the bottom Climene with Fabritio and behind her his sister Isabella. The illustration is decorative, has no clear relation to any scenes in the play, and appears to have no connection with the stage.

Sir William Lower died in 1662. He had been an officer in the King's army in the civil wars, rose to become a Lieutenant-Colonel, and was knighted in 1645. He probably spent much of the next fifteen years abroad, and may have been attached to the court in exile. During this period he made a number of translations of works in French, including six plays. His first play, *The Phoenix in her Flames*, was published in 1639, but there is no evidence that this, his later translations, or his own *The Enchanted Lovers*, were ever staged, though he seems to have written with the thought of performance in mind, to judge by the stage-directions. *The Enchanted Lovers* made some impact, for scenes were altered from it for incorporation into an untitled manuscript play now in the Folger Library.

Bentley, *JCS*, IV 725–6
ed. W. B. Gates, *The Dramatic Works and Translations of Sir William Lower* (Philadelphia, 1932)
Greg, 790(AIII), 814(AI)
Alfred Harbage, *Cavalier Drama* (1936, reprinted New York, 1964), pp. 135–7

D
Miscellaneous illustrations connected with the English stage

66

William Kemp, *Kemps Nine Daies Wonder* (1600).

Kemps nine daies vvonder.

Performed in a daunce from
London to Norwich.

Containing the pleasure, paines and kinde entertainment
of *William Kemp* betweene *London* and that Citty
in his late Morrice.

Wherein is somewhat set downe worth note; to reprooue
the slaunders spred of him: many things merry,
nothing hurtfull.

Written by himselfe to satisfie his friends.

LONDON
Printed by *E. A.* for *Nicholas Ling*, and are to be
solde at his shop at the west doore of Saint
Paules Church. 1600.

William Kemp was famous as a clown by 1590, when Thomas Nashe dedicated *An Almond for a Parrot* to him, and was equally noted during the 1590s for his dancing. The intrusion of his name in a stage-direction in the 1600 Quarto shows that he played Dogberry in *Much Ado about Nothing*. He was a sharer in the Lord Chamberlain's Men, but sold his share in 1599, and appears to have left the company. In 1602 he was acting with the Earl of Worcester's Men at the Fortune Theatre, and probably died soon after this period. On the first Monday in Lent 1600 he began his famous dance for a wager from London to Norwich, accompanied by Thomas Sly his taborer, and these two are depicted in an illustration on the title-page of his own account, *Kemps Nine Daies Wonder*. Kemp is shown in his morris dance, wearing bells on his ankles and long ribbons or scarves streaming from his shoulders. Perhaps the shirt ornamented with foliage is also part of his costume for the occasion, but the hat and breeches are representative of the ordinary dress of the period.

Chambers, *ES*, II 325–6
Foakes and Rickert, *HD*, 213–15
ed. G. B. Harrison (Bodley Head Quartos, 1923)
Shakespeare's England, 259–60, 438–40
Alexander Leggatt, 'The Companies and Actors', in *The Revels History of English Drama Volume III 1576–1613*, pp. 106–7 (Pl. 8a)

67

Robert Fludd, *Microcosmi Historia* (1619).

Volume 2 of a huge encyclopaedic work, *Microcosmi Historia*, by Robert Fludd, concerning the universe and all the works and arts of men, was published in Oppenheim in 1619, with the title *Tomus Secundus de Supernaturali, Naturali, Praeternaturali et Contranaturali Microcosmi historia, in Tractatus tres distributa*. A section of this volume is devoted to the mind of man, and, like the whole work, is illustrated with numerous diagrams or drawings, usually of an emblematic or symbolic kind. Within the section in Volume 2 on the science of the human mind is a subsection on memory, 'De animae memorativae scientia, quae vulgo ars memoriae vocatur'. Chapter X of this section offers descriptions of the theatres of the east and of the west. In this, Fludd, a mystical scientist and hermetic philosopher, was developing in his own way the idea of using a theatre as a mnemonic aid in the cultivation of the art of memory. This idea had been formulated by Giulio Camillo in his *Idea del Teatro* (1550), which associated the rising semi-circular tiers of seats with the 'universe expanding from First Causes through the stages of creation' (Frances Yates, *The Art of Memory*, p. 145). His theatre rose in seven gradations, was divided by seven gangways, and had seven columns, the seven pillars of wisdom; he does not mention the stage, but focuses his schematisation on the auditorium.

Fludd changed this scheme, and invited his reader to imagine two kinds of theatre, one of the east and daylight, and one of the west and night. He also proposed that for the art of memory the imagination works in two ways, through a 'round art' (*ars rotunda*), dealing with spiritual images, forms separated from corporeal objects, and a 'square art' (*ars quadrata*), which uses images of corporeal objects, men and animals. Although Fludd goes on to say that for the 'square art' it is important to use real buildings as places for the memory, he also regards the 'round art' as superior because it deals with spiritual entities, such as angels and demons, and uses 'natural' images, or images conceived in the imagination, whereas the 'square art' is concerned with 'artificial', or made up images. He goes on to locate the 'round art' in the etherial part of the

world in Chapter IX, and provides a diagram placing it in the eighth sphere. This sphere is shown with the signs of the zodiac, and encloses the seven spheres of the planets. This represents an order of place and sequence ('ratione loci & ordinis'), and an order of time ('ratione temporis') in relation to the motion of the spheres and the passing of the hours of the day. On either side of the sign of Aries in the eighth sphere is represented a minute schematic theatre, and these seem to relate to the further division of the order of time into two 'places', one of the east, the other of the west, the first imagined as a white theatre, the second as a black one. These are presumably represented in the sign of Aries, which begins the zodiacal year, with the 'white' theatre on the left below 'Oriens', and the 'black' theatre on the right, or the side nearer the 'Occidens'.

Fludd goes on in Chapter X to describe these 'eastern' and 'western' theatres, and this chapter is illustrated with a representation of a theatre inscribed 'THEATRUM ORBI', or theatre of the zodiac. The text invites the reader to imagine two sorts of theatre, one etherial, located in the east, white, filled with the likenesses of spiritual powers and belonging to the day, the other set in the west, black, and associated with the night. These imaginary theatres are each to have five doors equidistant from one another, opposite five columns to which they are related, and the doors and columns, the bases of which are shown in the engraving, are to serve as 'places' for the memory in Fludd's occult system. A few pages later (p. 58) is another illustration of a theatre marked 'Forma theatri', and a third illustration on p. 64 has the heading 'Sequitur figura vera theatri', or 'Here follows the true form of a theatre'. The late Frances Yates called these 'secondary' or 'subsidiary theatres' (*The Art of Memory*, pp. 321–2), but the text does not so describe them; rather they seem to be reductions from the first illustration to a more essential image of what is to be imagined; the last one has five doors on one level, and a similar pattern of five bases for columns as the firm illustration, but lacks its other detailing, apart frost the battlements now carried along the three walls. In

151

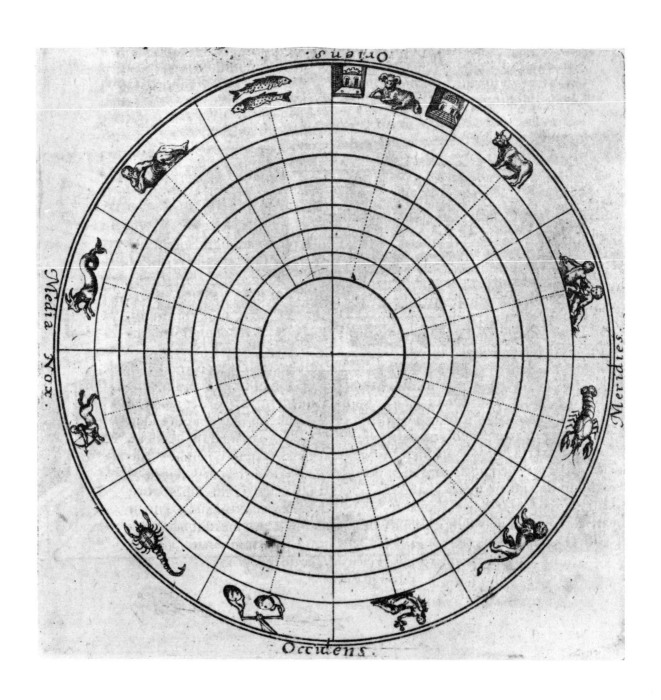

other words, the last illustration is more schematic, reduces the image of the theatre to all it is necessary to imagine for the art of memory, and can properly be labelled 'figura vera theatri'.

There remains the problem of the first illustration. The text of Chapter X begins as follows:

> I call that a theatre in which all actions of words, sentences, of parts of a speech or of subjects are shown as it were ('tanquam') in a public theatre, where comedies and tragedies are performed. Of this sort of theatres, one is to be imagined as located at an eastern point, and this must not be thought of as real or bodily, but as if it were an etherial vapour . . .

The first sentence has been taken to mean that Fludd was thinking of a real theatre, and on the basis of this, the first illustration has been identified as representing the Globe (by Frances Yates), or alternatively, the Blackfriars Theatre (by I. A. Shapiro). Frances Yates has reiterated her claim that this illustration shows 'the tiring house wall at the Globe, not the whole of it but only the two lower levels; the ground level with the three entrances; the second level with the terrace and the chamber' (*The Art of Memory*, p. 334); she thinks the five entrances correspond to entrances at the Globe, and that the balcony there had a bay window. Her argument is bound up with her belief that the builders of London's early theatres knew

the work of Vitruvius or Alberti, and that the development of the public theatres must be connected with a revival of interest in ancient theatres.

All this is speculative, and requires a considerable imaginative leap from what Fludd says, and from his illustrations, published, and presumably designed, in Germany. He is concerned with imaginary theatres, and inevitably imaginary theatres will be based on real ones. But there is in fact nothing to connect the first illustration with any specific theatre. It has some links with what we know of the London theatres, with three doors in the façade, as at the Drury Lane Cockpit (29 above), and a balcony with a projecting bay and window, as in the vignette on the title-page of *Messalina* (34 above), and the general idea of the lower and upper levels is not too remote from what is shown in the Swan drawing (26 above). At the same time, the drawing is evidently schematic, for there is no stage, and indeed it is not clear whether we are looking at a stage, or at an auditorium from the stage (as in Camillo's memory theatre). There are galleries on either side on the bottom level, but the walls otherwise are blank except for the narrow doors and windows on the gallery level at the rear. The narrow round-arched doors, and galleries with plain, square columns, might just as well relate to a German fencing-house or play-

153

house, like that at Nuremberg, built in 1628, and depicted in an engraving of 1651 (see Wickham, *EES* II.ii, Plates X and XI).

Fludd's illustration remains tantalising; it has features that are unnecessary for his memory system with its imaginary theatres; at the same time, it appears to be a symbolic, not a real theatre. It may incorporate elements from London theatres Fludd knew, but it also appears to draw on German decorative details (Richard Bernheimer, 'Another Globe Theatre', p. 25), and perhaps on aspects of German playhouses. I can see no reason for thinking that it can be used, except in the most general supportive way in relation to firmer information, as evidence about any of the London theatres of the period. Even the Latin inscription, 'THEATRUM ORBI', has been misleadingly interpreted as meaning 'Theatre of the Globe', thus providing an association with Shakespeare's theatre; it is likely, however, that Fludd had in mind the circle of the zodiac, as depicted in his diagram of the spheres on the facing page, and was occupied not with real theatres, but with theatres of the mind appropriate for his mnemonic system.

Sequitur figura vera theatri.

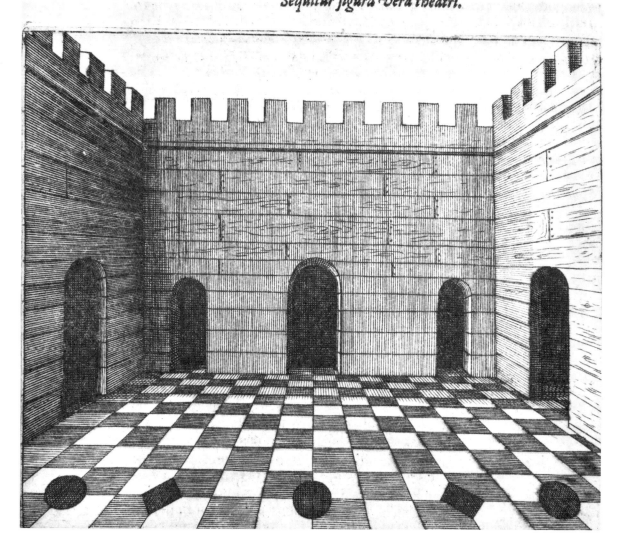

Bentley, *JCS*, VI 186n

Richard Bernheimer, 'Another Globe Theatre', *Shakespeare Quarterly*, IX (1958), 19–29

Robert Fludd, *Microcosmi Historia*, Vol. II (Oppenheim, 1619; this is the completion of *Utriusque Cosmi Maioris Scilicet et Minoris, Metaphysica, Physica atque Technica Historia*; Vol. I appeared in two parts in 1617 and 1618)

Gurr, 105–6 (Fig. 3)

Hodges, 118–20 (Pl. 18)

I. A. Shapiro, 'Robert Fludd's Stage-Illustration', *Shakespeare Studies*, II (1966), 192–209

Frances Yates, 'The Stage in Robert Fludd's Memory System', *Shakespeare Studies*, III (1967), 138–66

Frances Yates, *The Art of Memory* (1966; reissued 1969), pp. 310–54 (Pls 16–19)

Frances Yates, *Theatre of the World* (1969), pp. 92–161

68

Sketch, possibly of a stage, in a copy of the 1600 Quarto of William Shakespeare's
2 Henry IV.

On signature B2^r of a copy of this quarto now in the Huntington Library (catalogue no. 69317) is a small sketch, apparently of a stage, with three dots on it that seem to indicate the placing of characters. The sketch is drawn in a convenient space in the middle of a long sequence of prose dialogue, just after the entry of the Lord Chief Justice at I.ii.54. The sketch is apparently contemporary with, and in the same ink as, some of the annotations made in secretary hand in the quarto. This contains thirty-one annotations in two hands, both of which appear to belong to the seventeenth century (though Charles Shattuck, in *The Shakespeare Promptbooks*, refers to one as an eighteenth-century hand). One, Hand A, is marked by a darker ink, and contributed the sketch, together with a few additions or corrections, like the three commas inserted on D3^r, all in signatures B to D. The remaining annotations, in a mixed secretary and italic script, may have been added later; these begin with the addition of 'etc' to a stage-direction on B2^r, but most are on signatures F to L. These annotations expand or add to the inadequate entrances and exits in the printed text, supplying most, if not quite all, of the forty missing directions. There were similar additions and expansions of stage-directions for entrances and exits in a lost copy of the 1619 quarto of Beaumont and Fletcher's *A King and No King* (49 above), for the 1625 quarto was printed from it, and incorporates forty-two additions not in the 1619 text. These have been used to support the view that the 1625 quarto represents a prompt-book, and a similar hypothesis has been proposed by Alfred Emmet to explain the additions in the quarto of *2 Henry IV*. It would seem natural to link these additional directions with preparation for stage performances, but it is curious that the annotators confined themselves in both cases to entrances and exits, providing no anticipatory directions, and ignoring properties and other necessary effects; also, the annotator of *2 Henry IV* failed to add a few essential directions which are not indicated within the text. So the exact relation of the annotated quarto to the theatre remains uncertain. If the additions relate to preparation for a stage performance, they may date from the winter of 1612–13, when the King's Men performed a number of plays at court, among them, 'Sir John ffalstaffe', which E. K. Chambers interpreted as *2 Henry IV*, since it is included in a list of fourteen plays for which payment was made on 20 May 1613, and a supplementary list of payments made on the same day mentions payment for 'the Hotspur' (*ES*, IV.180). Possible confirmation is provided by a list of plays apparently being considered for performance at court about 1620 which includes a mutilated reference to *2 Henry IV*, convincingly interpreted as 'not plaid theis 7. yeres' (Bentley, *JCS*, I.128).

2 Henry IV was not printed again before its inclusion in the First Folio of Shakespeare's plays in 1623, and was not a popular play. On the evidence available, it seems plausible to associate the annotations in the quarto with preparations for the court performance of 1612–13. David George argued that the diagram in the quarto could represent the Globe stage, shown with a tapering thrust, and the tiring-house wall at the bottom; the two rectangular areas on either side he supposes might then be locations for spectators to sit on stage. More recently, Alfred Emmet has suggested that the stage is drawn the right way up, with the tiring-house wall, or back of the stage, at the top. Such an arrangement corresponds pretty well with hall-adaptations for court-performances (see 32 and 33 above), and is related to the Cockpit-in-Court, as converted by Inigo Jones in 1629–30 (30), but which had been used for performance of plays for many years. It seems more probable, then, that the diagram has no connection with the Globe, and that the bottom line represents the front of the stage.

If the three dots represent three characters, they may be Falstaff and his Page (stage right), and the Lord Chief Justice (stage left). A fourth character with a speaking part, a Servant, must enter with the Lord Chief Justice, as is indicated in this copy of the quarto by the addition of 'etc' in Hand B (not, as David George incorrectly states, in Hand A). Both George and Alfred Emmet assume that the Servant is omitted from the diagram because his position would be obvious as he 'would follow the Lord Chief Justice'. In fact the action here involves the Lord Chief Justice sending his servant to call back Falstaff, who appears to be slinking off stage, while Falstaff responds to the call through his Page, 'Boy, tell him I am deafe'. In any case, if 'etc' was written in later than the sketch, it is at least possible that whoever drew this diagram had not noticed the presence of the Servant.

So it is by no means certain that the sketch has to do with the staging of the scene. If it does, then the diagram possibly represents the grouping at the entry, downstage left, of the Lord Chief Justice, as Falstaff is trying to steal away unobserved stage right, but it is not apparent from the sketch why this moment in the play should have been worth recording; if there was some special comic business at this point, the diagram does not enable us to reconstruct it. The various additions to entrances and exits could indicate preparation for a performance, but a diagram suggests a later stage, blocking in rehearsal. If this is its origin, then the puzzling question, why there are no other blocking diagrams in this or any other text, remains.

Bentley, *JCS*, I 128, VI 268–9

Chambers, *ES*, II 217, IV 180

Alfred Emmet, 'Another Elizabethan Stage', *TN*, XXXIII (1979), 39–41

David George, 'Another Elizabethan Stage', *TN*, XXXII (1978), 63–8

David George, 'Another Elizabethan Stage: Further Comment', *TN*, XXXV (1981), 10–12

Charles Shattuck, *The Shakespeare Promptbooks: A Descriptive Catalogue* (Urbana, 1965), p. 141

Berta Sturman, 'The Second Quarto of *A King and No King*, 1625', *Studies in Bibliography*, IV (1951–2), 166–70

69

The Stage-Players Complaint. In A pleasant Dialogue betweene CANE of the *Fortune*, and REED of the *Friers* (1641).

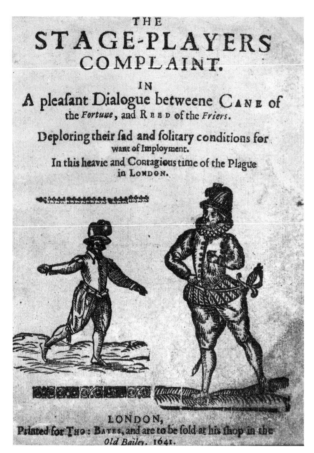

THE
STAGE-PLAYERS
COMPLAINT.

IN

A pleasant Dialogue betweene CANE of the *Fortune*, and REED of the *Friers*.

Deploring their fad and folitary conditions for want of Imployment.

In this heavie and Contagious time of the Plague in LONDON.

LONDON,
Printed for THO: BATES, and are to be fold at his fhop in the *Old Bailey.* 1641.

In this anonymous six-page pamphlet of 1641, two actors are presented in a dialogue lamenting their 'want of Imployment' due to the closing of the theatres because of plague, which was rife in London in the summer and autumn of this year. One of the actors, Andrew Cane or Keyne, was first mentioned as a player in 1622, and gained fame as a clown with the second Prince Charles's company, becoming noted for his wit; the other, Timothy Reed or Read, was another popular comedian, who acted with the King's Revels company and Queen Henrietta's Men, and was famous for his dancing. Their names were juxtaposed in a punning line in a poem prefixed to Thomas Heywood's *Pleasant Dialogues and Dramas* (1637), which refers to 'the fiery-cane, the weakest Reed', and the pamphlet a few years later evidently relied for its appeal on the fame of two well-established actors. In the text Cane is represented as eloquent and possessing a 'facundious tongue', and Reed as nimble-footed, looking back to 'the times, when my heeles have capoured over the Stage as light as a *Finches* Feather'. They are characterised no further, and on the first page are re-named 'Quick' and 'Light'. Nothing is known about the appearance of these actors, and it is not possible to say whether the woodcuts of two figures on the title-page bear any resemblance to them. The dancing figure on the left is much smaller than the one on the right, who stands with hand on hip and holding what may be a snuff-box. It is likely that the printer dug them out from stock as two vaguely appropriate blocks to decorate his title-page and attract readers. A smaller version of the block at the right was used to illustrate a ballad, 'The two Lester-sheire Lovers'.

G. E. Bentley, 'The Troubles of a Caroline Acting Troupe: Prince Charles's Company', *Huntington Library Quarterly*, 41 (1978), 217–49, especially 218–20
Bentley, *JCS*, II 398–400, 540–1, 666–7
Facsimile in *Commonwealth Tracts 1625–1650*, preface by Arthur Freeman (New York, 1974)
Roxburghe Ballads, II 598

70

Henry Marsh, *The Wits, or, Sport upon Sport*, Part 1 (1662); Francis Kirkman, *The Wits, or, Sport upon Sport* (1673).

This collection of twenty-six drolls was first published by Henry Marsh as 'Part 1' in 1662, and an expanded second edition of this, with a supplement of six additional drolls, separately paginated, was issued in 1672–3 by Francis Kirkman. Most of the drolls consist of comic episodes from popular plays, 'digested into scenes by way of dialogue', as the 1661 title-page puts it. In the preface he added in 1673, Francis Kirkman boasted that these were written by 'such Penmen as were known to be the ablest Artists that ever this Nation produced, by Name, *Shake-spear*, *Fletcher*, *Johnson*, *Shirley*, and others'. He went on to explain how the drolls were staged:

When the publique Theatres were shut up, and the Actors forbidden to present us with any of their Tragedies, because we had enough of that in earnest; and Comedies, because the Vices of the Age were too lively and smartly represented; then all that we could divert our selves with were these humours and pieces of Plays, which . . . were only allowed us, and that but by stealth too, and under pretence of Rope-dancing, or the like; and these being all that was permitted us, great was the confluence of the Auditors . . . I have seen the *Red Bull* Play-House, which was a large one, so full, that as many went back for want of room as had entred; and as meanly as you may now think of these Drols, they were then Acted by the best Comedians then and now in being; and I may say, by some that then exceeded all now Living, by Name, the incomparable *Robert Cox*, who was not only the principal Actor, but also the Contriver and Author of most of these Farces.

Ten plays or adaptations probably or certainly by Robert Cox had been published in 1653, and five of the twenty-six drolls in the 1662 collection relate to these; the expanded 1673 edition contains another seven pieces which can be attributed to Cox, who may also have been responsible for many of the drolls drawn from plays by other authors. He was a member of a 'young Company' (*JCS*, II.415) at the Cockpit Theatre in 1639, but seems to have made his name as a comedian during the Commonwealth period. Kirkman's account of the performance of drolls is borne out by a newspaper report in 1653, when rope-dancers hired Cox to present *John Swabber*, drawn from his pastoral *Actaeon and Diana*, at the Red Bull, and the

performance was presented by soldiers, who fined 'the Gentry' present 5 shillings each. Robert Cox died in 1655, and by 1673 Kirkman's readers may well have thought 'meanly' of mere entertainments like drolls.

Kirkman provided an elaborate title-page for his edition, presenting a 'Curious Collection of Several Drols and Farces', as acted in public and private, in London and in the country, 'At Charing Cross, Lincolns-Inn-Fields, and other places', by strolling players, fools, fiddlers, and 'Mountebancks Zanies'. No theatre is mentioned, and the emphasis is perhaps on the curious nature of the collection. He also included as a frontispiece the engraving first used in the 1662 edition of *The Wits*, which has a very different title-page, offering 'Variety of Humors of several Nations, fitted for the pleasure and content of all Persons, either in Court, City, Countrey, or Camp'. This frontispiece shows a rectangular stage, projecting from a rear wall, which has an entrance screened by curtains. The stage is deeper than it is wide, and has spectators on three sides. Above the stage is a gallery divided into sections by pilasters, with more members of the audience sitting on either side of the central part, above the stage entrance which is screened by another pair of curtains. These are open sufficiently to reveal a railing supported by turned columns behind, and may indicate a music room. On either side, the lower part of the balcony is masked by a frieze of paintings (painted cloth, or painted wood or plaster?) representing battle scenes (there was a frieze over the stage at the Cockpit-in-Court, as the accounts for 1631–2 record payments for renewing it; *JCS*, VI.273). The stage is lit by two candelabra hanging from above (payments were made for painting fifteen branched candelabra in the Cockpit-in-Court in 1631–2; *JCS*, VI.273), and by a row of six double lights at the front. These, too, appear to be candles in twin holders, and are not so much ancestors of the footlights with reflectors designed to illuminate the actors and first introduced in the 1830s, as general lighting of the auditorium. This is in accordance with evidence that from the beginning of the seventeenth century the private or indoor theatres were

lit by candlelight (Chambers, *ES*, II.556, IV.372; Bentley, *JCS*, II.694). The lighting, in other words, indicates an indoor theatre, but the stage, the front edge of which can be seen, appears to be made of boards mounted on trestles. It is small, and of a shape that corresponds with no known stage.

Seven figures are depicted on the stage, and are identified by their names, or the title of the play or droll to which they belong, except for the character emerging from between the curtains at the rear of the stage. This figure has a scroll extending from the mouth bearing the words 'Tue quoque', and represents Bartholomew Bubble in a droll adapted from John Cooke's *Greene's Tu Quoque* (1614; see 43 above). The title-page of this shows Bubble, as the servant-turned-master, dressed somewhat absurdly as a gallant, but in the frontispiece to *The Wits* he appears more as a fool, wearing a hat with a cockscomb. In front of him are figures marked 'Changling' and 'Simpleton'. The first presumably represents Antonio from *The Changeling* (1622) by Thomas Middleton and William Rowley, who dis-

guises himself as an idiot to gain access to Isabella, wife of the old Alibius who runs a madhouse. The droll of *Simpleton the Smith* was among those by Robert Cox published in 1653, and *The Humour of Simpleton* was included in *The Wits*. The second figure represents him entering 'with a great piece of Bread and Butter'. The droll concerns the trick by which the whore he marries, Doll, prevents him from catching her gentlemen with her. The leather apron and hammer stuck in his girdle mark his trade as a blacksmith. According to Kirkman, Robert Cox was celebrated for his appearance in this droll eating bread and butter: 'I have frequently Known several of the Female Spectators and Auditors to long for some of it'. Further downstage is the 'French Dancing M$^{r.}$', a character in 'The Humours of Monsieur Galliard', where the fun is derived from his capers and broken English. This droll was adapted from *The Variety*, a comedy by William Cavendish, acted about 1640, and published in 1649. At the front of the stage are shown on one side Falstaff and the Hostess, and on the other 'Clause'. The first two appear in 'The

Bouncing Knight or, The Robbers Rob'd', derived from Shakespeare's *1 Henry IV*, and drawn from several scenes, including the Gadshill robbery, part of II.iv, where Falstaff plays the King, and Falstaff's speech on honour and pretended death. The last figure represents Clause, who becomes King of the beggars in 'The Lame Common-wealth', drawn from John Fletcher's *The Beggar's Bush*, acted before 1622, and published in 1647.

In his edition of *The Wits*, J. J. Elson included an appendix on the frontispiece (pp. 424–7), in which he noted that *The Humour of Simpleton* is the only one of the six drolls represented which Robert Cox is known to have written and performed; he went on to say, 'Why did not the engraver show us Swabber, Simpkin, and Hobbinal, characters who are much more likely to have been seen in the Puritan days? That he did not do so is a strong hint that he was mainly depending on his imagination' (p. 426). *The Wits* contains no droll based on *The Changeling*, and possibly one was omitted for some reason. However, an alternative answer to Elson's question might simply be that Henry Marsh was anxious to advertise his ware to the best advantage, and so incorporated in his frontispiece well-known characters from five plays, plus the Simpleton from Cox's most famous droll. Elson thought the engraving provided no reliable evidence for an interior of a seventeenth-century theatre, and it certainly looks as though the artist has filled most of his drawing with an elongated stage in order to accommodate figures from six different pieces. On the other hand, the curtains at the rear and the spectators on the balcony are reminiscent of the *Roxana* vignette (see 31 above), and the arrangement of lighting by candles is an especially interesting feature; it is the earliest theatre illustration to depict chandeliers and stage lights. Glynne Wickham takes the curtains at the centre rear to be a unique depiction of an external booth (*EES* II, ii.201, 247), but they may merely conceal a discovery space, or doors, and appear to hang flush against the rear wall. There is a good deal of evidence for the use of curtains on stage, in stage-directions in public and private theatre plays (see P. W. Edwards, note in his edition, Revels Plays, 1959, p. 114, on the stage-direction in *The Spanish Tragedy*, IV.iii, where Hieronimo 'Knocks up the curtain'; and Chambers, *ES*, III.78–81), but the example most relevant here is perhaps the passage in the Praeludium to Thomas Goffe's *The Careless Shepherdess* (as revised about 1638, published 1656), where a citizen comments:

Timothy Read was a well-known comedian, who played at the Phoenix and Salisbury Court Theatres (see also 69 above). It is possible that the frontispiece to *The Wits* has a closer relation to private theatres than Elson thought. Recently both Richard Hosley and T. J. King have argued that the frontispiece depicts a practicable playhouse, either a hall-theatre, or an actual theatre, such as the Phoenix or the Salisbury Court theatre, converted from a barn in 1630 (Bentley, *JCS*, VI.90), both of which continued in use after 1642 (Bentley, *JCS*, VI.76–7, 112–14). King adduces in support of this interpretation the disparity between the costume of Falstaff as shown in the frontispiece, a fashion in vogue before the Civil War, and the dress of the spectators, who wear clothing in a style popular about 1649; Falstaff's costume, he believes, was appropriate to suggest an earlier period for an interregnum audience.

Bentley, *JCS*, II 414–15, 541; III 151; IV 501–5; V 273.
Chambers, *ES*, II 519–20
ed. J. J. Elson, *The Wits, or, Sport upon Sport* (Ithaca, 1932)
Greg, III 1243–6 (Pl. CXXIII)
Alfred Harbage, revised by S. Schoenbaum, *Annals of English Drama 975–1700* (1964), 148, 158, 170
Richard Hosley, 'Three Renaissance Indoor Playhouses', *English Literary Renaissance*, 3 (1973), 166–82, especially 179–82
Leslie Hotson, *The Commonwealth and Restoration Stage* (1928, reprinted New York, 1962), 48–9
T. J. King, 'The First Known Picture of Falstaff (1662). A Suggested Date for his Costume', *Theatre Research International*, 3 (1977–8), 20–3
Francis Kirkman, *The Wits, or, Sport upon Sport. Being a Curious Collection of Several Drols and Farces* (1673)
Henry Marsh, *The Wits, or, Sport upon Sport, in Select Pieces of Drollery* (1662)
Smith, 49–50 (Pl. 20)
Wickham, *EES* II, ii 201, 247 (Pl. XXIII, No. 24)

I never saw *Rheade* peeping through the Curtain,
But ravishing joy enter'd into my heart.

E
Illustrations in play-texts having no reference to the stage

71

Robert Wilson, *The Three Lords and Three Ladies of London* (1590).

At first sight the woodcut on the title-page of this play, written not earlier than 1588, might suggest some performance of an interlude in a hall or court. In fact, the cut was taken from a work by Stephen Batman (or Bateman), *The Travelled Pilgrim, bringing News from all Parts of the World* (1569), and it has been shown to derive from a much earlier illustration of the fifteenth century. It therefore has no reference to Wilson's play.

Chambers, *ES*, III 515 and II 520
Greg, 93
ed. Hazlitt's Dodsley (1874)

72

R. A. [?Robert Armin], *The Valiant Welshman* (1615, 1663).

This play was first published in 1615, and its echoes of Ben Jonson's *The Alchemist* seem to establish that it was not written before 1610. The author's initials on the title-page are those of Robert Armin, and although there is no other external evidence specifically to connect him with the play, internal evidence is not inconsistent with the supposition that he wrote it. The play was performed by the Prince of Wales's Men, or Prince Henry's Men, enlarged from the former Admiral's Men, a company that played at the Fortune Theatre. J. P. Feather follows Chambers in assigning the play to the second Prince of Wales's Company, patronised by Prince Charles who, however, became Prince of Wales in 1616, the year after *The Valiant Welshman* was published (Prince Henry, who died in 1612, had been created Prince of Wales in 1610). The play purports to be a chronicle history of Caradoc, and it has a comic subplot appropriate for a public theatre play. Caradoc lived in the first century A.D., and in the play is depicted as a violent soldier who overcomes his opponents in numerous fights, is crowned King of Wales, and eventually is taken prisoner and then freed by the Romans. The woodcut facing the title-page in the 1615 quarto seems to have no connection with the play, and to be merely ornamental. It shows a heavily armed Knight, wearing a helmet with extravagant plumes, and carrying a lance (or truncheon?) in his left hand; he sits astride a horse which is elaborately caparisoned and armoured, with enormous plumes at the head and tail. It could just as well be an illustration for a work on armour, but the whole effect is fanciful, and appears to have no reference whatever to the stage. This is confirmed by the reprint of the play issued in 1663 with a different woodcut, again showing a heavily armed soldier on horseback. This could have been searched out from a printer's stock of such cuts to replace the lost earlier block, and it has no connection with the staging of the play.

Bentley, *JCS*, I 198
Chambers, *ES*, II 186–90, IV 51
ed. J. P. Feather, *Collected Works of Robert Armin* (2 vols, 1972)
Greg, 327(a), 327(b)
ed. V. Kreb, *Münchener Beiträge zur romanischen und Englischen Philologie Heft 23* (Erlangen and Leipzig, 1902)
TFT (1913)

73

William Haughton, *Englishmen for my Money*, or *A Woman will have her Will* (1616).

According to Philip Henslowe's *Diary*, William Haughton was paid for writing a comedy called *A Woman will have her Will* in February and May 1598. The play was entered in the Stationers' Register in 1601, but no edition is known before that of 1616, when it appeared anonymously, under the alternative title *Englishmen for my Money*. The action of the play concerns the three daughters of a Portuguese settler in London who foil their father's design, which is to marry them off to a Frenchman, an Italian, and a Dutchman, and achieve their own desires by marrying the three Englishmen they love. In the development of the intrigues which lead to this conclusion, one of the English suitors, Ned Walgrave, is disguised as a woman. The woodcut on the title-page of the 1616 quarto could refer to this incident, or to any of the three daughters, but seems to have no specific connection with the play, apart from the general reference to the title *A Woman will have her Will*. It shows a woman in Elizabethan costume, wearing a large ruff, a long, stiff pointed bodice, and a wide farthingale. The bodice and skirt are ornamented with large flowers. She wears a chain round her neck, and her hair is taken back from the forehead and dressed over a pad, in a style fashionable in the later part of the reign of Queen Elizabeth. In her right hand she carries a large fan probably made of feathers, as was common, though the woodcut might be taken as representing leaves. The figure is costumed appropriately for 1598, but by 1616 the fashion for large farthingales had almost passed. This may signify no more than that the printer was using an old block; it is akin to, but more elaborate than, a woodcut used to illustrate various ballads, such as 'A Warning to all Lewd Livers', Part 2, (*Roxburghe Ballads*, III.26).

ed. A. C. Baugh (1917)
Bentley, *JCS*, II 451
Chambers, *ES*, I 334–5 and II 320
Foakes and Rickert, *HD*, 87–9
Greg, 336(a)
Linthicum, 181–2, 205
MSR, 1912 (1913)

Rhodes, 218
Roxburghe Ballads, I 21, 105; III 26, 52, 63, 98, 243, 290
Shakespeare's England, II 94–8

74

Robert Gomersall, *The Tragedy of Lodovick Sforza Duke of Milan* (1628).

Robert Gomersall wrote this play while he was at Oxford, mingling with others interested in poetry and drama. He was a high-minded young man, born in 1602, who took holy orders, became a noted preacher in the University, according to Anthony à Wood, and in 1628 left Oxford to become Vicar of Thorncombe in Devon (now in Dorset). There is no evidence that his full-length, five-act play in blank verse on the rise and fall of Lodovic Sforza was ever acted. It was published in 1628 with an allegorical frontispiece, which was used again to preface Gomersall's *Poems* (1633) which included a second edition of *Lodovick Sforza*. In his Epistle Dedicatory, addressed to Francis Hide, Proctor of Oxford, Gomersall compares his play with a sermon: 'Sermons had been fitter far for my setting forth, and to preach more proper than to write. But is not this to preach? . . . If I make the ambitious see that he climbes but to a fall, the usurper to acknowledge, that blood is but a slippery foundation of power, all men in generall to confesse that the most glorious is not the most safe place: is not this to cry downe Ambition and Usurpation?' The action concerns Lodovick's rise to become Duke of Milan by murdering his nephew, his misgovernment leading to riots and war, and his eventual defeat and capture by the French. The frontispiece shows a wolf sitting in a chair of state holding a sceptre, while in front another version of the wolf mauls sheep. On the left is a city, and behind the chair a lion, holding a standard bearing the French fleur-de-lys in one paw, removes a crown from the wolf's head with another paw. The whole is in an oval with the title 'SFORZA by Rob Gomersall' at the foot, inscribed in a rectangle measuring $5\frac{1}{2}$ in. $\times$ 3 in. (140 mm $\times$ 78 mm). Gomersall supplied an 'Explanation', which is perhaps hardly necessary, but further illustrates how far his thoughts were from the stage in composing a play for which he wrote in his Epistle Dedicatory, 'I can expect but a few Readers':

The Explanation of the Frontispiece
It was when Industry did sleepe
The Wolfe was Tutor to the Sheep
And to amaze a plainer man,
The thiefe was made the guardian.

But can a Wolfe forget to pray?
Can Night be lightned into Day?
Without respect of lawes or blood,
His charge he makes to be his food.
With that triumphant he sits downe,
Opprest, not honour'd with a Crowne,
And on the lesser beasts does try
A most Authenticke Tyranny:
This the French Lyon heares, and when
He's thought fast sleeping in his denne,
Vengeance and He at once doe wake,
And on the Wolfe their fury slake
Bad acts may bloome sometimes, but ne're grow high,
Nor doe they live so sure, as they shall dye.

Bentley, *JCS*, IV 512–14
Greg, 418
ed. B. R. Pearn, *Bang's Materials for the Study of the Old English Drama*, VIII (Louvain, 1933)

75

T.R., *Cornelianum Dolium* (1638).

This Latin play was published in duodecimo in 1638, with an engraved frontispiece which incorporates the title on a scroll at the top. The play, set in Genoa, concerns the visit of Cornelius to Naples, where his experience with prostitutes gives him the pox and costs him dear in medical expenses. The preface implies that the play had been acted, but if so, the date and place are not known. The authorship too remains a mystery, as there does not seem sufficient evidence to associate it firmly with Thomas Randolph. The frontispiece shows Cornelius in a sweating tub, used to cure syphilis, with three prostitutes watching him; the gloss on this on signatures A5ᵛ–A6ʳ reads: 'Qui norunt lascivienté in Prostibulo, nunc me videant dolentem in *Dolio*', i.e., 'those who knew me frolicking in the brothel now may see me suffering in the tub'. Behind the women is an open door, on the right a table with medical instruments on it, and above this a large shelf on which stand two sizeable jars. The tub is inscribed 'Sedeo in Veneris Solio, In Dolio Doleo' ('I sit on the throne of love, I suffer in the tub'), and a streamer issuing from the mouth of the half-naked Cornelius bears the phrase 'Valete o Veneris Cupidinesque' ('Farewell O sexual pleasures and lusts'). Samuel Pepys bought this play in 1660 and read it 'with great pleasure', so it seems to have hung on the bookstalls. The frontispiece has no apparent connection with the theatre, although a sweating-tub such as is shown could have been an effective and amusing property.

Bentley, *JCS*, V 962–4
Greg, 416

169

76

Canterbury his Change of Diet (1641).

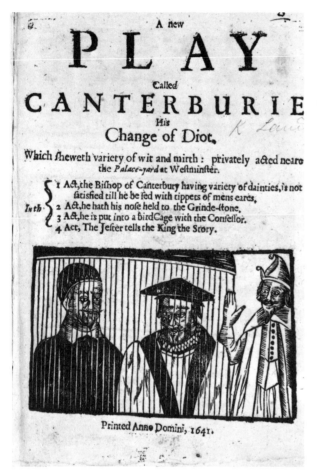

The title-page wittily states that this 'play' was 'privately acted' at Westminster, but in fact it is a pamphlet of eight pages containing an attack on William Laud, Archbishop of Canterbury, representing him as rejecting divines of his own church, and consorting with Jesuits. It is illustrated with three woodcuts, that on the title-page being repeated on p. 6, where, for 'The Third Act', the stage-direction reads, 'Enter the Bishop of Canterbury, and the Jesuit [in] a great Bird Cage together, and a foole standing by, and laughing at them, Ha, ha, ha, ha, who is the foole now?' The second woodcut, on p. 3, illustrates the first 'Act', in which a Doctor of Physic, a lawyer, and a divine bring a variety of dishes to the Archbishop's table, all of which displease him; he punishes them by cutting off their ears. The third woodcut relates to the second 'Act', in which the Archbishop comes to a carpenter's yard by the Thames to take a boat, and seeing a grindstone, takes out his knife to sharpen it. The carpenter seizes him and, according to the stage-direction, 'He tyes his nose to the Grindle-stone', as shown in the crude woodcut, which also depicts the carpenter's boy turning the stone. The 'play' has four 'acts', and a jig for an afterpiece, so that it is presented with the trappings of a full-length drama, but is simply a polemical tract in dramatic form, and could not be staged. The woodcuts crudely portray Archbishop Laud, who was impeached in December 1640, and who is depicted in similar fashion in other tracts of the times, as in *An exact Copy of a Letter sent to William Laud late Arch-bishop of Canterbury, now Prisoner in the Tower* (1641). This tract in the guise of a playlet has been convincingly attributed on stylistic grounds to Richard Overton, a vigorous Puritan satirist, and author of more than twenty pamphlets in the period 1641–2.

Bentley, *JCS*, V 1299–1300
Greg, 603
Margot Heinemann, *Puritanism and Theatre*, pp. 245–7
Don M. Wolfe, 'Unsigned Pamphlets of Richard Overton: 1641–1649', *Huntington Library Quarterly*, 21 (1957–8), 167–201

THE FIRST ACT.

Enter the Bishop of Canterbury, and with him a Doctor of Physicke, a Lawyer, and a Divine; who being set downe, they bring him variety of Dishes to his Table,

Canterbury, is here all the dishes, that are provided?
  Doct. My Lord, there is all : and 'tis enough, wert for a Princes table, Ther's 24. severall dainty dishes, and all rare.
  B. Cant. Are these rare : no, no, they please me not,
Give me a Carbinadoed cheeke, or a tippet of a Cocks combe :
None of all this, here is meate for my Pallet.
  Lawyer. My Lord, here is both Cocke and Phesant,
Quaile and Partridge, and the best varieties the shambles yeeld.

A 2   *Cant.*

The second Act.

Enter the Bishop of Canterbury into a Carpenters yard by the water side, where he is going to take water, and seeing a Grindle-stone, draweth his knife, and goeth thither to whet it, and the Carpenter followes him.
  Carpenter. What mkes your Grace here, my Lord.
  Cant. My knife is something dull friend :
Therefore *I* make bold to sharpen it here,
Because an opportunity is here so ready.
  Carp. Excuse me, Sir, you shall not doe it :
What reason have you to sharpen your knife on my stone :
youl serve me, as you did the other three : No, stay !
Ile make you free of the Grinde-stone, before you goe away.

He tyes his nose to th: Grindlo-stone

  Cant. Oh man what doe you meane.
  Carpen. Hold downe your head, it will blood you bravely ;
By the brushing of your nostrils, you shall know what the paring of an eare
is,   *Turne Boy.*   *The* Carpenters *boy turnes*
  Cant. O hold, hold, hold.   *the stone, and grinds his nose.*
Turne, qd. *I,* here is turning indeed, such turning will soon deform my face :
O *I* bleed, *I* bleed, and am extreamly sore.
  Carp. But who regarded hold before, remember the cruelty you have used
to others, whose bloud cryes out for vengeance.
Were not their eares to them, as pretious as your nostrils can be to you :
If such dishes must be your fare, let me be your Cooke,
Ile invent you rare sippets.

Iesus:

77

T.B., *The Rebellion of Naples* or *The Tragedy of Massenello* (1649).

The initials 'T.B.' also appear on the title-page of a play called *The Country Girl*, published in 1647 but written probably about 1633, which, according to the title-page, had been 'often Acted with much applause'. *The Rebellion of Naples*, 'Written by a Gentleman who was an eye-witness where this was really Acted upon that bloudy Stage, the streets of NAPLES' in 1647 may well be by a different T.B., and there is no indication that this full-length, five-act play in prose was ever acted. It was printed in a small octavo, measuring about $5\frac{1}{2}$ in. $\times 3\frac{1}{4}$ in. (140 mm $\times$ 82 mm). There are a prologue and an epilogue, neither of which refers to the play being acted. The play begins with Massenello at the head of a rabble taking over Naples, but failing to capture the Viceroy who survives to return later. In the action, Massenello's wife and daughter are poisoned, he runs mad, and is executed by the people who once supported him. The stage-direction at this point in V.iv reads 'He thrusts out his head, and they cut off a false head made of a bladder fill'd with bloud. *Exeunt* with his body'. This suggests an author who had some sense of theatre. The play is dedicated to a kinsman, John Caesar of Hyde Hall, Hertfordshire. The Epilogue presents the moral of the play:

> Let Kings beware how they provoke
> Their Subjects with too hard a Yoke,
> For when all's done, it will not doe,
> You see they breake the yoke in two:
> Let Subjects no rebellion move
> On such pretences least it prove
> As sad a thing (which God forbid)
> And fatall as to us it did.

In relation to all this, the fold-out plate spreading to the width of two pages, giving an illustration about $6\frac{1}{2}$ in. $\times 5\frac{1}{2}$ in. (165 mm $\times$ 140 mm) facing the-title page, is rather strange. It shows the General, Tomaso di Malfa, or Massenello as he was known, standing on a net, wielding a marshal's staff, with a streamer from his mouth displaying the words 'Acchiappato il pesce via la rete', or 'the fish is suddenly trapped in the net'; this streamer links him with a net being pulled by diminutive figures around the city of Naples. Behind him is an army and, behind Naples, a navy. An arm protruding from clouds directs two shafts of lightning, one against the ships, one against the city. In the bottom left corner, a scroll contains some rhyming verses in praise of Massenello. These refer to the 'silly Fish', presumably the citizens, a group of whom march out with gifts to greet him, while others kneel to him, as welcoming their destruction:

> Neither doe they dread
> The *Divine Vengeance* that is o're their head.
> And ne're will think themselves meet Fish to fry,
> Till great TOMASO, draws, the CYTY dry.

This emblematic aggrandisement of Massenello seems at odds with the play, even if the net he stands on is meant to suggest he will in turn be trapped himself. The illustration would appear to have no connection with the stage, but is unusual in its elaboration, and the 'M' who designed it evidently had his own ideas about Massenello, and knew a little Italian besides.

Bentley, *JCS*, III 8–9
Greg, 689
Alfred Harbage, *Cavalier Drama* (1936, reprinted New York, 1964), 224–5

The Fish is caught, the Net is under foot;
Whil'st Fool's cry Shall I Shall I those goe to't.
The silly Fish, whil'st left but the least
And can see through the Net the least
But Sacrifice to'th' Net the least
Burne Incense to'th' Net...
All the...

Acchiappato il pesce vha...

78

S.S. [Samuel Sheppard], *The Jovial Crew, or The Devil Turned Ranter* (1651).

The Prologue.

Bedlam broke loose? yes, Hell is open'd too:
Mad-men, & Fiends, & Harpies to your view
We do present: but who shall cure the Tumor?
All the world now is in the Ranting Humor.

This playlet in five acts is only fifteen pages long in the Quarto of 1651, and is essentially a polemical tract in dramatic form. It offers, according to the gloss on the title, 'a Character of *the roaring*, Ranters of *these Times*. Represented in a Comedie'. The word 'ranter' is first recorded in *OED* in 1649, and was applied to ranting preachers especially, including some who believed themselves incapable of sin, being in receipt of God's grace. Such figures were the targets for attack by those opposed to religious toleration, and the word 'ranter' rapidly took on the alternative meaning of a 'noisy, riotous, dissipated fellow; a rake' (*OED sb* f.2). *The Jovial Crew*, a piece not to be confused with Richard Brome's play with the same title published in 1652, presents a group of 'Joviall Ranters', men and women, drinking, singing, dancing drunkenly, and generally engaged in debauchery. It has a rudimentary plot, involving a Constable and his Watch, who bear off the drunken ranters to Finsbury gaol, where they are stripped to their shirts, which shows they are whores, and whipped off by a Beadle. The characters include 'Lucifer', and 'Pandorsus' his agent, who appear only in the first 'Act', in which the Ranters are shown in the service of the Devil. At the end of this 'Act', a stage-direction calls for Lucifer to 'Vanish in Thunder', and he never reappears. The frontispiece to the play has a four-line prologue beneath a woodcut which portrays Lucifer, with horns and a flaming head-dress, carrying a torch, and seated in a pageant-wagon like those used in masques, drawn by two dragons. Three small devils walk by the wagon, and above is a map of Great Britain, with a house, and two seated figures with crooks, presumably shepherds or pastors, apparently waving to Lucifer. This cut has no reference to the action of the playlet, except in so far as it portrays Lucifer, and, since there is no evidence of any performance, it can have no bearing on the stage. The copy in the British Library (Thomason Tracts) is dated 'Jan: 6 1650'.

Bentley, *JCS*, V 1054
Greg, 697
Orgel and Strong, I 284–5, II 811 (Nos. 91 and 466)

174

79

Wine, Beer, Ale and Tobacco (1658).

This short entertainment probably dates from about 1625. It takes the form of a dialogue or dispute between characters representing Wine, Beer, etc., and belongs to a tradition of such works, which seem to have been much liked in Cambridge; it was there that *Lingua, or the Combat of the Tongue and Five Senses for Superiority*, was written (published 1607), and later *Work for Cutlers*, a dialogue between Sword, Rapier and Dagger, and *Exchange Ware*, a dialogue between Band, Cuff and Ruff, were acted (both published 1615). *Wine, Beer and Ale, Together by the Ears* was first published in 1629, and enlarged in 1630 into *Wine, Beer, Ale, and Tobacco. Contending for Superiority. A Dialogue*, when the number of characters grew to eight, including Sugar, Nutmeg, Toast, and Water. They are distinguished in type, as Wine is a gentleman, Beer a citizen, Ale a countryman, and Water a parson, and the dialogue, embodying a quarrel between Wine, Ale and Beer, and swaggering behaviour by Tobacco, has some dramatic power. It appears to have been designed for representation, and its allusions in the text to London, and its lively setting as if in a tavern, suggest that it may have been revised for the London stage. It was reprinted in a new edition in 1658, with a large woodcut and an elaborate printer's ornament facing the title page. This shows the interior of an inn, with three women and a man casting dice, a man looking in through a window, and a large shelf with bottles on it. It clearly has nothing to do with the text of the dialogue, and was presumably added by the printer to suggest a tavern atmosphere. It seems to relate most closely to the ballad by Martin Parker, 'A good Throw for Three Maidenheads, or Three Maidenheads lost at Dice', printed with the woodcut adorning it about 1635. It was used again in other ballads, such as 'The Batchelor's Triumph' (date unknown), and 'A Song in Praise of the Leather Bottle' (about 1662). There are no female figures in *Wine, Beer, Ale and Tobacco*, and no dice are thrown. The woodcut could have been taken to represent a stage as a tavern, and perhaps this made the printer think of using it.

Bentley, *JCS*, V 1442–4
Greg, 426(c)
ed. J. H. Hanford, *SP*, XII (1915), 1–54
Roxburghe Ballads, II 31, III 427, VIII 641

Index

This index includes proper names, theatres and topics relating to the stage, and titles of plays and other early works referred to in the text.

Abrams, W. A., 143
Actaeon and Diana, 159
Acting Companies, *see* Companies of actors
Adams, John Cranford, 19, 26, 73, 81
Admiral's Men, *see under* Companies of actors
Agas, Ralph, *Civitas Londinum*, 4, 5, 19
Ajax Flagellifer, 57, 60
Alabaster, William, 72–3, 80, 161
Alba, 57, 60
Alchemist, 98, 165
Aldwell, Thomas, 25
Allde, Elizabeth, 126
Alleyn, Edward, 3, 7, 46–7, 88–9, 110
All's Well that Ends Well, 107, 113
Almond for a Parrot, 150
Amends for Ladies, 98
Amorous Fantasm, 146–7
Anatomy of Abuses, 133
Annals (Stow), 30, 136
Anne, Queen (consort of James I), 58, 60, 95
Arcadia Reformed, see *Queen's Arcadia*
Archer, William, xvii
Arden of Faversham, 136–7
Arden, Thomas, 136
Arenas at theatres (*see also* Standing), 3, 6, 37, 52, 72, 77
Aristotle, 133
Armada, Spanish, 92
Armin, Robert, 96, 165
Armstrong, W. A., 90
Arraignment of Lewd ... Women, 116
Arundel, Countess of, 77
Arundel, Earl of, 66
Astington, John H., 71
Astrologaster, 111

B., T., 172
Backcloth on the stage, 118, 135, 159
Bakeless, John, 111
Baker, Sir Richard, *Chronicle*, 34–5
Balconies, *see* Galleries
Bald, R. C., 125
Ballads, 105, 113, 131, 136, 140, 158, 166, 175
Barnfield, Richard, 131
Bartholomew Fair, 29, 45
Baskervill, C. R., 45

Batman, Stephen, 164
Baugh, A. C., 166
Bear-baiting house (*see also* Beargarden), 3, 4, 19, 30, 37
Beargarden (*see also* Bear-baiting house *and* Hope theatre), 6, 7, 10, 13, 15, 17, 19, 20, 21, 26, 27, 29, 31, 35, 37, 54
Beaumont, Francis (*see also* Fletcher, John), 69, 107, 114, 115, 118–19, 130, 156
Beeston, Christopher, 65, 72, 130; 'Beeston's Boys', 120
Beggar's Bush, 161
Bell Savage, 7
Bentley, G. E., 15, 20, 38, 39, 40, 58, 61, 67, 71, 76, 79, 81, 82, 112, 117, 121, 125, 128, 131, 133, 135, 139, 141, 145, 147, 155, 157, 158, 161, 165, 166, 168, 169, 170, 172, 174, 175
Bernheimer, Richard, 154, 155
Berry, Herbert, xviii, 3, 9
Best, John, 65
Bird, Theophilus, 144
Black Batman of the North, 141
Black Book, 72, 111
Blackfriars theatre, 39–40, 115, 118, 153
van Blyenberch, Abraham, 123
Boase, T. S. R., 136, 137
Boissard, Jean Jaques, 89
Booth, Abram, *View of the Cittye of London*, 8–9, 19, 30
Boswell, Eleanore, 68, 71
Bouncing Knight, 160–1
Bowers, Fredson, 111, 114, 115, 119, 145
Boxes at the theatres, 29, 52, 54, 72, 77
Bradshaw, Charles, 39
Braithwaite, Richard, 102
Braun and Hogenberg map, 2–3, 4, 5, 19
Brakin, Francis, 128
Brazen Age, 134
Britannia Triumphans, 32–3
Brome, Richard, 174
Brooke, C. F. Tucker, 137, 143
Browker, Hugh, 25

Browker, Thomas, 25
Browne, Robert, 62; Touring Company, *see under* Companies of actors
Brownstein, Oscar, 3
van Buchel, Aernout, xiv, 52
Bull-baiting house, 3, 4, 19
Bullen, A. H., 9, 121
Burbage, Cuthbert, 6, 7
Burbage, James, 8, 39, 40
Burbage, Richard, 39

Caesar, John, 172
Camillo, Giulio, 151, 153
Candy Restored, 82–3
Cane, Andrew, 158
Canterbury his Change of Diet, 170–1
Carson, Neil, 47
Cavendish, William, 160
Chamberlain, John, 12, 123, 125, 128
Chamberlain's Men, *see under* Companies of actors
Chambers, E. K., 3, 7, 9, 13, 15, 17, 19, 20, 25, 26, 30, 32, 33, 38, 39, 40, 45, 48, 51, 55, 61, 62, 73, 90, 93, 95, 97, 99, 101, 103, 106, 108, 111, 113, 114, 115, 119, 127, 128, 133, 135, 137, 143, 145, 150, 157, 161, 164, 165, 166
Changeling, 139, 160, 161
Charles I, King, 34–5, 57, 74, 113, 139; (as Prince Charles), 122–3, 124
Charles II, King, 68, 70–1
Charles V, Emperor, 100
Chaste Maid in Cheapside, 54, 55
Chettle, Henry, 45
Children of Paul's, *see under* Companies of actors
Children of the Chapel Royal, *see under* Companies of actors
Children of the King's Revels, *see under* Companies of actors
Chimneys, at theatres, 33, 68, 71
Christ Church Hall, Oxford: plans for conversion into theatre, xvi, xvii, 56–61
Chronicle of the Kings of England, 34–5
Cholmley, John, 6
Cicero, 133

Civitas Londini, 10–11, 12, 19, 26, 27, 32, 37
Clark, A. M., 93, 95, 108, 135, 139
Clark, Hugh, 131
Clifton, Sir Gervase, 140
Clowns, *see* Fools
Cockpit-in-Court theatre (Royal Cockpit), 65–6, 67, 72, 77–9, 81, 82, 157, 159
Cockpit theatre, Drury Lane (or Phoenix), xvi, 60, 65–7, 72, 79, 120, 130, 144, 153, 159, 161
Cockpits converted to theatres, 64–71, 73
Codrington, Robert, 128
Collier, John Payne, 48
Coloma, Don Carlos, 124–5
Columns on the Stage, 29, 47, 52, 54–5
Combat of the Tongues and Five Senses for Superiority, see *Lingua*
Companies of actors: Admiral's Men, 88, 105, 111, 124, 165; 'Beeston's Boys', 120; Chamberlain's Men, 19, 30, 96, 150; Children of Paul's, 60; Children of the Chapel Royal, 60; Children of the King's Revels, 96; King and Queen's Young Company, *see* Beeston's Boys; King's Men, 19, 30, 39, 69, 79, 125, 157; King's Revels company, 80, 140, 158; Prince Charles's Company, 20, 120, 140, 158, 165; Prince Henry's Men, 165; Princess Elizabeth's Company, 20; Queen's Men, 45; Queen Anne's Men, 94, 102, 134; Queen Henrietta's Men, 130, 139, 144, 158; Strange's Men, 47, 107; Worcester's Men, 150
Compleat Gentleman, 50
Constable, Francis, 115
Cooke, John, 102, 160
Cornelianum Dolium, 169
Costumes, 45, 50–1, 62, 68, 72, 80, 88–9, 91–2, 94–5, 96, 99, 102, 104–5, 108, 110, 112, 113, 114, 115, 117, 118–19, 120–1, 123, 125, 128, 131, 133, 134–5, 137, 139, 141, 143, 144–5, 150, 161, 166
Cox, Robert, 159, 160–1
Craik, T. W., 111
Cupolas at theatres, 9, 30, 31, 37, 71
Curtain theatre, 8, 9, 20, 134
Curtains at theatres, xvii–xviii, 54, 72, 80–1, 82, 159, 161

Dalida, La, 72
Daniel, Samuel, 60
Dankerts, Cornelis, 68; Map of London, 26; Painting of Whitehall, 71
D'Avenant, William, 32–3, 82
Davies, John of Hereford, 98–9
Day, John, 8, 9, 98
Dekker, Thomas, 50, 98–9, 142–3, 144–5

Delaram, Francis, View of Bankside, 16–17, 55
Devil Turned Ranter, 174
Dietrich, Margaret, 62
de Dominis, Marco Antonio, 123
Discovery-space, xvii, 69, 72, 82, 161
Doctor Faustus, 109–11, 121, 127, 131
Dodsley, Robert, 103, 164
Drake, Sir Francis, 92
Duchess of Malfi, 69

Edmonds, Sir Thomas, 77
Edwards, P. W., 106, 161
Elizabeth I, Queen, 5, 45, 54, 91, 96, 100, 130, 131, 140, 166
Elson, J. J., 161
Emmet, Alfred, 156, 157
Enchanted Lovers, 146–7
Engelische Comedien und Tragedien, 95
England's Joy, 54
Englishmen for my Money, 166
Entertainment at Althorp, 95
Entrances to the theatre, 52, 66, 71
Epicharmus, 68
Essex, Robert Devereux, Earl of, 130, 133
Evelyn, John, 31
Every Man in his Humour, 69
Exact Copy of a Letter sent to William Laud, 170

Fair Maid of the West, 124–5, 130–1
Fair Quarrel, 98, 112
Famous History of Friar Bacon, The, 120, 126
Fane, Mildmay, Earl of Westmorland, 82–3
Feather, J. P., 97, 165
Fenn, Ezekiel, 144
Ferdinand, Archduke of Austria, 62
Field, Nathan, 98
Fisher, Sidney, 9
Flags at theatres, 9, 10, 13, 15, 17, 20, 21, 31, 32, 32, 33, 35, 37, 52
Flemming, Willi, 62
Fletcher (*see also* Beaumont, Francis), 69, 114, 115, 116, 118–19, 130, 156, 159, 161
Florimène, 77, 82
Fludd, Robert, xvi, 151–5
Foakes, R. A., 3, 7, 9, 13, 47, 90, 106, 108, 111, 141, 150, 166
Fools and Clowns, 44–5, 62, 94, 96, 103, 121, 139, 160
Fool upon Fool, 96
Ford, John (*see also* Dekker, Thomas), 144
Forsett, Edward, 132–3
Fortune theatre, 8, 47, 54, 72, 98, 111, 150, 165
Four Ages, 134
Four Prentices of London, 107–8
Freeman, Arthur, 106, 158
French Dancing-Master, 160

Friar Bacon and Friar Bungay, 126–7, 136, 137
Frith, Mary, 98–9
Frobisher, Martin, 92
Frons Scenae, see Stage-façade

Galleries (in theatres), 3, 6, 47, 52, 54, 66, 68–9, 71, 72, 81, 153, 159, 161
Galloway, David, 67
Game at Chess, 58, 122–5
Gates, W. B., 147
General History of the Turks, 89
George, David, 157
Gleason, John B., 52, 55
Globe theatre: general, xiii, xiv, 19, 20, 21, 26, 27, 28, 72, 118, 134, 142, 143, 153, 157; First Globe, 8, 9, 10, 12, 13, 15, 17, 30, 47; Second Globe, 9, 19, 21, 29, 30, 31, 32, 35, 37, 58, 122
Godfrey of Boulogne, Part 2, 107
Goffe, Thomas, *Careless Shepherdess*, 161
Golden Age, 134
Gomersall, Robert, 167–8
Gomme, Andor, 99
Gondomar, Count, 122–4
Goodman, Nicholas, 25, 29, 32
Gosson, Henry, 106
Granville-Barker, Harley, xvii
Grato, Luigi, 72
Graves, R. B., 37–8, 67
Green, John, portrait of, xvi, xvii, 62–3, 95
Greene, Robert, 126–7, 136, 137
Greene, Thomas, 62, 102–3, 121, 160
Greene's Tu Quoque, 102–3, 121, 160
Greg, W. W., xvi, 47, 93, 95, 97, 99, 101, 103, 106, 108, 111, 112, 113, 114, 115, 117, 119, 121, 125, 127, 128, 131, 133, 135, 137, 139, 141, 143, 145, 147, 161, 164, 165, 166, 168, 169, 170, 172, 174, 175
Grey, Lord, of Wilton, 140
Grosart, A. B., 117
Gurr, Andrew, 7, 38, 45, 51, 54, 55, 71, 115, 119, 155

Habington, William, 70
Hanford, J. H., 175
Hangings, *see* Backcloth
Harbage, Alfred, 147, 161, 172
Harington, Sir John, 133
Harper, J. W., 125
Harris, Anthony, 111, 127, 145
Harris, John, 65, 67, 68, 71, 76
Harrison, G. B., 150
Harvey, Gabriel, 45, 133
Haughton, William, 160, 166
Have with you to Saffron Walden, 133
Hazlitt, W. C., 103, 164
Heads in Taille-Douce (Pepys Library), 45

'Heavens' over the stage, 29–30, 37, 52, 54–5, 68
Hector of Germany, 73
Heinemann, Margot, 125, 170
Henning, Standish, 143
Henrietta Maria, Queen, 74, 76
Henry IV, Part I, 69, 161
Henry IV, Part 2, 156–7
Henry V, xiii, 107
Henry VII, King, 51, 100
Henry VIII, 72
Henry VIII, King, 39
Henry, Prince, 60, 95
Henslowe, Philip, 3, 6, 7, 13, 37, 54, 94; *Diary*, 90, 105, 166; Drawing, possibly of a stage, 46–7
Herbert. *see* Pembroke
Herwologia Anglica, 20
Heywood, Thomas, 50, 91–3, 94, 100, 102, 107–8, 130–1, 134–5, 136, 138–9, 158
Hibbard, G. R., 71, 111
Hide, Francis, 167
Higgenbotham, Richard, 115
Hind, A. M., 7, 9, 15, 17, 19, 20, 35, 125
History of John . . . Faustus, 111
Histriomastix, 74
Hodges, C. Walter, xiii, 9, 11, 13, 19, 30, 37, 38, 40, 51, 55, 71, 73, 81, 155
Holbein, Hans, the younger, 100
Holdsworth, R. V., 112
Holinshed, Raphael, 136, 140
Holland, Henry, 20
Holland's Leaguer, 25, 29, 32
Hollar, Wenceslaus, xiv, xv; Drawing of Bankside, 29–30, 31, 37; 'Long View', 9, 11, 15, 17, 19, 21, 29, 30, 36–8, 40; Sketch for 'Long View', xvii, 31, 37
Holmes, Martin, 90
Holt, Anita, 137
Hondius, Jodocus, View of London, 14–15, 17, 20, 35
Hope theatre (*see also* Beargarden), 3, 17, 20, 21, 26, 29–30, 31, 35, 37, 54–5
Horace, *Ars Poetica*, 68
Hosking, G. L., 90
Hosley, Richard, xiii, xvii, xviii, 3, 4, 9, 11, 13, 15, 19, 25, 28, 30, 32, 33, 37, 38, 39, 40, 55, 161
Hotson, Leslie, 9, 38, 161
Howes, Edmund, 30
Howgego, James, 3, 4, 5, 7, 13, 26
Humour of Simpleton, 160, 161
Humours of Monsieur Galliard, 160
Humphry, Duke of Gloucester, 136
'Hut' over the stage, 9, 10, 13, 17, 20, 21, 32, 37, 52, 55

Idea del Teatro, 151
If You Know not Me, 91, 100
Ignoramus, 128, 133
Ingram, William, 25

'Inner-stage', *see* Discovery-space
Iron Age, 134–5
Ives, E. W., 139

Jack Drum's Entertainment, 113, 123
James I, King, 3, 4, 16–17, 30, 57, 60, 93, 113, 120, 122, 128
Jeffs, Robin, 9
Jerusalem (play-title), 107
Johnson, Lawrence, 89
John Swabber, 159
Jones, Eldred, 51
Jones, Inigo (*see also* Webb, John), xvii, 37, 57, 58, 60–1, 68, 72, 74, 157; Design for unidentified Theatre, 84–5; Drawing for conversion of Tudor Hall Whitehall, 77–9; Drawings for Cockpit, Drury Lane, 64–7, 81; *Salmacida Spolia*, 82; Sketch of a proscenimun, 70; View of London, 33
de Jongh, Claude, xv, 21, 27–8, 37
Jonson, Ben, 29, 45, 57, 69, 82, 95, 98, 105, 159, 165
Jovial Crew, 174
Julius Caesar, 51
Jump, J. D., 90, 111

Katherine of Aragon, 39
Keere, Peter van den, 6
Kemps Nine Daies Wonder, 150
Kemp, William, 96, 150
Kindermann, Heina, 62
Kind-Heart's Dream, 45
King and No King, A, 114, 156
King and Queen's Young Company, *see under* Companies of actors
King Henry IV, Henry V, Henry VIII, see under *Henry*
King, T. J., 161
King's Men, *see under* Companies of actors
King's Revels Company, *see under* Companies of actors
Kirkman, Francis, 159–61
Knave of Clubs, 110
Knight of the Burning Pestle, 107
Knolles, Richard, 90
Kreb, V., 165
Kyd, Thomas, 50, 104–6, 155

Lady Pecunia, 131
Lambard, William, 7
Lame Common-Wealth, 161
Lantern, *see* Cupola
Laud, Archbishop William, 170
Lavin, J. A., 127
Lawrence, R. G., 145
Lawrence, W. J., xvii
Leacroft, Richard, 4, 38, 51, 55, 67, 71, 73, 76, 79, 81
Leech, Clifford, 82
Life and Death of the Merry Devil of Edmonton, 142–3

Lighting at theatres, 58, 60, 69, 159–60, 161
Lipsius, Justus, *De Amphiteatro*, 52–3
Langley, Francis, 25, 54
Leggatt, Alexander, 45, 150
Lily, William, 133
Lingua, 175
Linnell, Rosemary, 9
Linthicum, M. Channing, 45, 93, 108, 113, 115, 166
Lodovick Sforza Duke of Milan, 167–8
Looking Glass for London and England, 105
Lord Admiral's Men, *see under* Companies of actors
Lord Chamberlain's Men, *see under* Companies of actors
Lord Strange's Men, *see under* Companies of actors
Lower, Sir William, 146–7

McKerrow, R. B., 133
Mad World my Masters, 143
Maidenhead Well Lost, 50, 136, 138–9
Maid's Tragedy, 69, 115
di Malfa, Tomaso (Massenello), 172
Markham, Gervase, 140
'Mansions' on stage, 124
Manners, Francis, 67
Maria Magdalena, Archduchess of Austria, 62
Marlowe, Christopher, 7, 88–90, 109–11, 121, 127, 137
Marsh, Henry, 159–61
Marston, John, 113, 123
Mary, Princess Royal (oldest daughter of Charles I), 146
Mary Tudor, 91
Masque of Blackness, 57
Maximilian, Archduke of Graz, 62, 95
Measure for Measure, 138
Melton, John, 111
Merens, A., 9
Merian, Matthias, View of London, 11, 27–8, 32
Merry Devil of Edmonton, 142–3
Merry, Edward, 39
Messalina, 73, 80–1, 153
Metamorphosis of Ajax, 133
Microcosmi Historia, 151–5
Middleton, Thomas, 54, 55, 58, 72, 98–9, 111, 112, 120–1, 122–5, 139, 143, 160, 161
Millar, Oliver, 21, 125
Montagu, Walter, 74
More, Sir William, 39
Morris, Irene, 62
Much Ado About Nothing, 150
Munro, John, 50, 51
Murad, Orlene, 62
Murray, H. J. R., 125
Music and Musicians at the theatres, 54, 68, 74, 77, 159

Nashe, Thomas, 133, 150

Nest of Ninnies, 96
Newington Butts theatre, 6
Nicoll, Allardyce, 82
Nichols, John, 57, 58, 60, 61
Noble Ingratitude, 146
Nobody and Somebody, 62–3, 94–5
Norden, John, 3, 6–7 (*Speculum Britanniae*), 10–13 (*Civitas Londini*), 19, 26, 27, 32, 37
Norland, H. B., 115
Norman, Philip, xvii, 25

'Olde Castle' (?*Henry IV*), 69
Olivier, Laurence, xiii
Orgel, Stephen, xvii, 32, 33, 57, 58, 60, 61, 67, 71, 76, 77, 79, 82, 84, 174
Orlando Furioso, 133
Orrell, John, xvii, 11, 19, 30, 31, 37, 38, 40, 57, 61, 66, 71, 74, 76
Othello, 51
Overton, Richard, 170

Palladio, Andrea, 67, 70
Palma Giovane, 69
Palma Vecchio, 69
Paris Garden Manor, map of, xvi–xvii, 24–5
Parker, Martin, 175
Parker, R. B., 54
Parry, Graham, xvii, 31, 38
Particular Description of England, 5
van de Passe, Crispin, 91
van de Passe, Simon, 123, 125
van de Passe, Willem, 123, 125
Peacham, Henry, xvi, 48–51
Peacock, John, 33
Pearn, B. R., 168
Pedantius, 132–3
Pembroke, William Herbert, third Earl of, 70
Pepys, Samuel, 169
Perambulation of Kent, 7
Periaktoi, 57
Perspective scenery, 57, 60, 70, 74, 77, 82, 84
Philaster, 118–19
Phoenix in her Flames, 197
Phoenix theatre, *see* Cockpit (Drury Lane)
Platter, Thomas, 3
Plautus, 133
'Playhouse', *see* Rose theatre
Playhouses, *see* Theatres
Pleasant Dialogues, 158
Poel, William, xvii
Prince Charles's Company, *see under* Companies of actors
Prince Henry's Men, *see under* Companies of actors
Princess Elizabeth's Company, *see under* Companies of actors
Princess Royal, *see* Mary
Properties, 104–6, 110, 117, 118, 123–5, 126–7, 128, 134–5, 141, 143

Proscenium, 70, 74, 76, 77, 84
Prynne, William, 74
Ptolemy, 110
Purfoot, Thomas, 100

Queen Anne's Men, *see under* Companies of actors
Queen Henrietta's Men, *see under* Companies of actors
Queen of Aragon, 70
Queen's Arcadia, 60
Queen's Men, *see under* Companies of actors
Quinault, Philippe, 146

R., T., 169
Raleigh, Sir Walter, 72
Randolph, Thomas (*see also* R., T.), 169
'Ranters', 174
Rebellion at Naples, 172
Red Bull theatre, xiii, 102, 130, 134, 140, 159
Reed (*or* Read), Timothy, 158, 161
Relieve, *see* Scenes of relieve
Rex Platonicus, 57
Reynolds, George F., xiii, 73, 81, 102, 106, 108, 111, 117, 127, 135, 137
Rhodes, Ernest L., 20, 35, 47, 51, 108, 111, 127, 166
Richards, Nathanial, 73, 80–1, 153
Rickert, R. T., 3, 7, 9, 13, 47, 106, 108, 111, 141, 150, 166
'Roaring boys', 98–9
Roaring Girl, 98–9
Robbers Robbed, see *Bouncing Knight*
Robbins, William, 139
Rogers, William, 91
Rollo Duke of Normandy, 69
Rose theatre, 3, 5, 6–7, 8, 10, 13 (also called the Star), 15, 19, 26, 27, 37, 107, 126
Rowan, D. F., 55, 64, 67, 73
Rowlands, Samuel, 110
Rowley, Samuel, 100
Rowley, William, 8, 112, 120–1, 144, 160
Roxana, 72–3, 80, 161
Royal Cockpit, *see* Cockpit-in-Court
Royal Slave, 57
Ruggle, George, 128–9, 133

S.S., *see* Sheppard, Samuel
Salisbury Court theatre, 65, 79, 80–1, 161
Salmacida Spolia, 82
Sampson, William, 140–1
Sarmiento de Acuna, *see* Gondomar
Saunders, J. W., 73, 81
Sawyer, Elizabeth, 144
Scenery, *see* Backcloth; Perspective scenery; Properties; Scenes of relieve
Scenes of relieve, 70, 74, 77, 82
Schoenbaum, Samuel, 9, 27, 28, 30, 38, 51, 161

School of the Noble and Worthy Science of Defence, 116
Schrickx, Willem, 62
Scott, Thomas, 125
Scottowe, John, drawing of Tarlton, 44–5
Scouloudi, Irene, xviii, 11, 13, 15, 19, 20, 27, 28, 35, 38
Seating at theatres, 58, 60–1, 65–6, 68–9, 77
Second Maiden's Tragedy, 115
Seltzer, Daniel, 127
Serlio, Sebastiano, 67, 70, 84
Seven Deadly Sins, 45
Sforza, Lodovic, 167
Shakespeare, William, xiii, xvi, 12, 19, 48, 51, 69, 72, 107, 113, 128, 137, 138, 150, 154, 156–7, 159, 161
Shapiro, I. A., xv, xvii, xviii, 3, 4, 7, 11, 13, 15, 17, 19, 20, 25, 26, 28, 30, 32, 33, 38, 153, 155
Shapiro, Michael, xviii
Shattuck, Charles, 156, 157
Shepherd, R. H., 92, 108, 135, 139
Shepherd's Paradise, 74
Sheppard, Samuel, 174
Shirley, James, 131, 159
Silver Age, 134
Simpleton the Smith, 160–1
Simpson, R., 95
Sly, Thomas, 150
Smith, G. C. Moore, 133
Smith, Irwin, 3, 4, 7, 11, 13, 15, 17, 19, 20, 26, 28, 30, 32, 33, 39, 40, 51, 55, 73, 81, 161
Smith, Wentworth, 94
Smith, William, 5
Soens, A. L., 112
Southern, R. W., xviii, 76, 79
Spanish Tragedy, 50, 104–6, 161
Speculum Britanniae, 6–7, 10, 26
Speed, John, 14–15
Stage (*see also* Backcloth; Columns; Curtains; Discovery-space; Proscenium; Stage-canopy; Stage-doors; Stage-rail; Stage-wings; Theatres; Tiring-house, Trap doors; Windows), 29, 52, 54–5, 57–8, 66–7, 68–9, 72, 74, 76, 80, 82, 156–7, 159–61; façade, 66, 68, 80, 84; orientation, 37–8; rake, 57, 77; upper stage, 54
Stage-doors, xvii, 54, 66–7, 68, 69, 72, 77, 136–7, 153, 161
Stage-Players Complaint, 158
Stage-rails, 66, 68, 72–3, 74, 80, 81, 159
Stage-wings, 70, 74, 77, 82–3, 84
Stairs at theatres, 9, 25, 29, 30, 31, 37, 64, 65, 69, 71
Standing (for spectators; *see also* Arenas), 3, 6, 37, 58
Star (alternative name for the Rose theatre?), 12–13
Stow, John, 3, 30, 136

Strange's Men, *see under* Companies of actors
Stringer, Philip, 57, 58, 60
Strode, William, 57
Strong, Roy, xvii, 32, 33, 57, 58, 61, 67, 71, 76, 77, 79, 82, 84, 92, 101, 174
Stubbs, Philip, 133
Sturman, Berta, 157
Swan theatre, xiv, xvi, xvii, 3, 8, 9, 10, 12, 13, 17, 19, 20, 24–5, 26, 27, 29, 32, 33, 47, 72; Drawing by Johannes de Witt, 52–5, 67, 73, 153
Swetnam, Joseph, 116
Swetnam the Woman-Hater, 116, 139

Tait, A. A., 67, 71
Tamburlaine, 89–90
Tarlton, Richard, 44–5
Tarlton's Jests, 45
Tarlton's News out of Purgatory, 45
Taylor, John, the Water Poet, 136
Teatro Olimpico, 67–8, 84
Survey of London, 3 (Stow); 25 (Bankside, 1950)
Theatre, *see* Arenas; Backcloth; Boxes; Chimneys; Cockpit; Columns; Costumes; Cupolas; Curtains; Discovery-space; Entrances; Flags; Fools and clowns; Galleries; 'Heavens'; 'Hut'; Lighting; 'Mansion'; Music; Periaktoi; Perspective scenery; Properties; Proscenium; Scenes of relieve; Seating; Stage; Stage-doors; Stage-rails; Stage-wings; Stairs; Standing; Tiring house; Trap-doors; Windows
Theatre of the Empire of Great Britain, 14–15
Theatre, the, xvii, 7, 8, 9
Theatres, *see under* Bear-baiting house; Beargarden; Bell Savage; Blackfriars; Bull-baiting house; Cockpit-at-Court; Cockpit, Drury Lane; Curtain; Fortune; Globe; Hope; Phoenix; Red Bull; Rose; Salisbury Court; Swan; Teatro

Olimpico; Theatre
Theatres, shape and size: as polygonal, xiv, 9, 10, 17, 19, 26, 27, 35, 65, 68, 72, 79; as round, xiv, 3, 7, 8, 13, 15, 17, 20, 25, 26, 29, 30, 31, 33, 35, 36–8; as square, 9, 35, 72, 79; as U-shaped, 65–7, 74, 81
Thespis, 68
Three Lords and Three Ladies of London, 93, 164
Tillotson, Kathleen, 141
Tiring-house, 29, 52, 66, 68–9, 71, 153, 157
Titian, 69
Titus Andronicus, xv, xvi, 48–51
Townshend, Aurelian, 77
Trap-doors in the stage, 69, 81, 110
Travelled Pilgrim, 164
Travels of the Three English Brothers, 8
Troia Britannica, 134, 136
Troilus and Cressida, 134
Troubles of Queen Elizabeth, see *If You Know not Me*
Turner, Olga, 125
Turner, R. K. Jr., 114, 115, 119, 131
Two Maids of Moreclack, 96
Ungerer, Gustav, 51
Utrecht View of London, *see* Booth, Abram

Valiant Welshman, 165
Variety, 160
Venner, Richard, 54
Vertumnus, 57, 60
Visscher, Jan Claes, Panoramic view of London, xiii, xvii, 9, 11, 18–19, 27, 28, 30
Vitae et Icones Sultanorum Turcicorum, 89
Vitruvius, 67
Volpone, 69
Vow-Breaker, 140–1
Vox Populi, 123, 125 (Part 2)

Wake, Isaac, 57
Wallrath, H., 141
Waterhouse, E. K., 101
Webb, John (*see also* Jones, Inigo), 64, 82, 84–5; Drawings for

conversion of Royal Cockpit, 68–71; Plan for conversion at Somerset House, 74–6; Theatre design, 66–7, 84–5; View of London, 32, 33
Webster, John, 69
Wedding, 131
Wedel, Lupold von, 3
When You See Me, You Know Me, 100
Welsford, Enid, 97
Wickham, Glynne, xiii, xiv, xvii, xviii, 3, 4, 5, 7, 9, 13, 20, 25, 30, 32, 33, 38, 39, 40, 55, 64, 69–70, 71, 76, 81, 124, 125, 131, 154, 161
Wilkins, George, 8
Williams, Iolo, 30, 38
Williams, G. Walton, 114
Willoughby, Anne, 140
Willoughby, Sir Henry, 140
Wilson, E. M., 125
Wilson, F. P., 133
Wilson, John Dover, xvi, 48, 50, 51
Wilson, Robert, 94, 164
Windows at theatres, 10, 15, 17, 19, 30, 31, 32, 35, 52, 65, 68, 71, 80, 81, 153
Wine, Beer, Ale and Tobacco, 175
Wine, M. L., 137
Wingfield, Anthony, 133
Witch of Edmonton, 50, 144–5
Wits, xvi, 159–61
de Witt, Johannes, Drawing of the Swan Theatre, xiv, xvi, 8, 9, 25, 29, 52–5, 73
Wolfe, Don M., 170
Woman will have her Will, 166
Women Pleased, 116
Wonderful Discovery of Elizabeth Sawyer, 144
à Wood, Anthony, 57, 167
Wood, Harvey, 113
Worcester's Men, *see under* Companies of actors
Work for Cutlers, 175
World Tossed at Tennis, 120–1
Wyck, Thomas, 28

Yates, Frances, 151, 153, 155
Young, Alan B., 38